IN THE TIME OF GREENBLOOM

GABRIEL FIELDING

In the Time of Greenbloom

THE UNIVERSITY OF CHICAGO PRESS

All characters in this book are wholly fictitious and no reference is intended to any person ever encountered, either
living or dead. Where actual places are named they are not
necessarily correctly spelled nor accurately described in the
topographical sense.

G. F. January 1956.

This edition is reprinted by arrangement with William
Morrow & Co., Inc.

© 1956 by Gabriel Fielding
All rights reserved. Published 1956
Phoenix Fiction edition 1983
Printed in the United States of America

90 89 88 87 86 85 84 83   1 2 3 4 5

Library of Congress Cataloging in Publication Data

Fielding, Gabriel, 1916–
   In the time of Greenbloom.

   (Phoenix fiction series)
   I. Title. II. Series.
PR6003.A7415 1983   823'.914   83–9247
ISBN 0–226–24845–3

To Edwina

My thanks are due and are gratefully given to the following for help or encouragement in the writing of this book: my wife, my brother Godfrey, Miss Erica Marx, Mr. Richard Church whose delightful book *Dog Toby* was especially helpful to me, Miss Muriel Spark, Mr. Derek Stanford, Mr. Edward Juller, Mr. David Nash, Chief-Inspector Drury of the Kent County Constabulary, the De Havilland Aircraft Company, Mr. Hugh Reynolds and Lt-Comdr. J. H. Fordham, R. N. (ret.)

The Sequence

Aspexi terram et ecce vacua erat, et nihil; et coelos, et non erat lux in eis.
—Jeremiah.

1. L'Après-Midi

What can I say that was not sooner said
By poets flowering in the uncut dead?
What say or sing or verbally convey
When in my living I display
A sunken footprint in the earth,
A tongue distorted by its birth?

This one's a rose: it throws a whiter shadow
Than the cloud, and no man knows or sees
The spectre when the eye's unclosed;
The spectre is the rose. . . .

⋖§ *L'APRÈS-MIDI*

The first thing he noticed about her was her whiteness; she was a very white girl, as white in the face as the snowberries which grew under the elms at the foot of the Vicarage drive, and the skin of her delicate arms and legs was so pure in its pallor that it was almost indistinguishable from the tennis frock she was wearing.

Looking at her as she moved, or seemed casually to dance amongst the others in front of the summer house, he was aware of a renewal of the sense of isolation which had held them both, Melanie and himself, when Simpson waved them a jaunty good-bye from the car before dusting away down the Clockwood drive to return to the Vicarage.

It was always like this to begin with; parties filled them both with an angry pride, making them stand away together in place and in mood so that they could touch one another's hands carelessly, whisper small bitter confidences together without being overheard, and jointly challenge any attempts on the part of grownups to make them mix separately with the other guests. Later, if things went well, if they found someone they liked or who liked them, they might disclose a little and let the others come between them for a time; but fundamentally they were united, thinking the same sort of thoughts, feeling at once superior to all the others however rich they might be, and yet distinctly and annoyingly inferior because they were from the Vicarage and the car was only a Ford and Simpson's familiarity was as disgraceful as his second-best uniform.

Today their arrival had been blacker even than usual because it was that sort of a day: still and sticky and with so little air that the birds themselves only moved short distances amongst the bushes, plumping heavily from one perch to another and abandoning their calls when they were halfway through them as though the spit were drying in their beaks. And worst of all it was a tennis tournament, an organized one with lists of names pinned up in the summer house, partners, introductions and prizes at the end.

Clutching their large rackets, patently marked with initials which were not their own (for they used those of their elder brothers and sister), they moved closer together under the hard shadow of the summer house, waiting for the first inevitable moment of challenge from Mrs. Bellingham, from Tim and Carol's governess, or from one of the older Bellingham boys.

And it was now, as Melanie whispered angrily to him, "There aren't even any booby prizes!" that he felt suddenly glad of their close detachment in face of all these little swanks with their shiny new rackets and presses, their unmended clothes and their easy familiarity with one another. Their shared rebellion gave them strength and was delightful; it needed only a motive, a purpose, something around which to cluster and swarm like the stinging bees from a summer hive, and it would become powerful and profitable, would find a way, either overtly or covertly, of making this afternoon truly golden so that they might lay up a sweet honey from its hours and enjoy it long after the holidays were over and the dark winter's term had begun.

The girl, he knew, had noticed them both from the moment of their late arrival. In the narrow white face the great grey eyes sought them constantly as she moved diffidently from one self-contained group to another in the unblinking sunshine of the hard court. Her fine hair, black as a funeral plume, was tossed a little affectedly to one side by occasional quick jerks of her chin as, from her tallness, she glanced over an intervening shoulder or head to steal yet another quick look at them. And then, when she saw that she had his attention, that he was openly, almost greedily, watching her from his high place on the bank, the pendulum swing of her racket ceased instantly, depriving the slow smile she gave him of any place in minutes or seconds, so that as it spread outwards from her lips to her pale cheeks, it gathered an intimacy which seemed timeless and eternal.

Melanie, beside him, saw it too and moved restlessly, watching him a little foxily from beneath the sharp redness of her hair to see if he would smile back; and he did, swiftly and without defiance as he answered her whispered question:

"No, of course I don't know her! But I like her."

He paused, refusing to meet her eyes and then said loudly, "Come on! It's time we got to know people. Let's go and find Tim."

He knew that it was unfair to have spoken so openly but he did not care, and by leaving her there, alone and conspicuous, he forced her to follow him.

He was all arrogance now, was ready to meet any of them on their own terms and beat them too, so long as it did not involve too much tennis; and he would see that it did not. He must find Tim and pair him off with Melanie. He knew these tennis parties; they always started off with a show of organization and enthusiasm; but in an hour or two, when the rabbits began hopelessly to outnumber the hares, a certain laxity always became apparent, drifting into the air as aimlessly as the long sprawl of the late clouds, and bringing with it a mellowness that was at once an opportunity and a delight.

He knew his Melanie too: young as she was, not yet twelve, already she liked an escort, someone in trousers to flutter at, a boy with an address for torchlight letters in the depths of the school dormitory. Tim Bellingham would do, although privately they laughed at him and, on account of his rather sallow face and smallness, had nicknamed him "the lemon pip"; his bounce and importance would please her, and he knew that he himself had only to flatter him a little in order to make him a willing participant in whatever might later develop. So the thing to do was to get hold of him quickly and establish an intimacy and ascendancy over him before the tournament got fairly started.

Looking around, he saw him almost at once, standing beside his elder brother Philip at the net. Carol, too, was with them, and this was a little awkward; he didn't want Carol today.

Somehow, if they were going to the orchard or the hayfield, they would have to give her the slip as unobtrusively and naturally as possible. She was too young, too proprietorial, and would probably give things away afterwards to the governess or Mrs. Bellingham so that later when they reached home, Melanie, if jealous or dissatisfied in any way, might find an opportunity of hinting things to Mother. That was the trouble with Melanie these days: she had lost the spirit of their alliance and seemed increasingly to identify herself with Mary and Mother whenever things had gone slightly wrong.

In the old days, when they were younger, her loyalty had been of a different kind, almost that of an animal; but lately, since they had stopped having baths together and sharing the night nursery, she had become unreliable and increasingly "girlish" as though she had been made party to a secret that was essentially feminine. He would have to see that whatever this afternoon's adventure proved to be she would be as much in it as he was himself and that Carol, by joining them, did not stir up or reinforce any misgivings she might feel.

He glanced behind him. Good! Melanie was following him towards the group by the net. Now was the moment to break in.

He touched Tim lightly on the shoulder.

" 'Lo, Tim! Sorry we were a bit late. Do you know who's playing with who yet?"

Tim turned around, he was obviously a little overawed by the nearness of Philip.

" 'Lo," he said. "Better ask Philip. It's all up on the summer-house door anyway, haven't you looked at the lists?"

From his superior height, across the immense distances separating his public school from their preparatory schools, Philip looked down on them and glancing at his wrist watch drawled, "Ah! Young Blaydon and sister. We'd been waiting for you children to arrive before we could get started because you're both in the first heat. What happened, Blaydon? That old Lizzie of yours break down again?"

"No, it's just that we were a bit late starting. Simpson had to take Father over to see the Bishop," John improvised rapidly; even the Bellinghams might be a little in awe of the Bishop.

"I see! Now where's your partner got to? Tim, go and get hold of Victoria Blount for heaven's sake or we'll never get through the heats. I hope you're in good form, young Blaydon, because your partner's a little inexperienced."

John struck an attitude: he always felt fairly confident before he started.

"I think I am today," he said. "Of course I may be a little erratic, it just depends—"

Beside him Tim sniggered diminutively, hastily muffling his mouth behind his racket as everyone else stopped talking.

"A little erratic!" Philip Bellingham pronounced slowly. "Well! Well! Not quite in your usual centre-court form eh! Blaydon?"

"No," said John, wanting to smash his racket over Tim's yellow ball of a face.

"Blaydon says he's a little erratic—a little erratic—a little erratic!" he chanted to the others, drawing down the corners of his mouth between each repetition of the phrase.

One or two of the younger ones took it up and Melanie came angrily to his defence.

"Well, what is so funny about that?" she asked. "Just because you don't know what it means there's no need to make a fool of yourself, is there, John?"

"Now! Now!" said Philip. "No quarrelling. We want to get started. Tim! Have you found that Victoria girl yet? Ah! *There* she is. Come here, Victoria, I want you to meet your partner; this is John Blaydon and you're going to have to play for all you're worth because, as you've just heard, he says he's a little—"

The white girl, cool and unsmiling, looked into John's face. "Yes," she said. "I heard, he's feeling a little erratic, and I'm *so* glad, because that's how I always feel."

"Splendid!" It was Mrs. Bellingham cooing up behind them. "Well you're going to be *most* suited then. Aren't they, Philip?"

"Undoubtedly! Now then you two, you start at the stable end, versus the Dormains, Pat and Richard. Clear the court please! There are plenty of chairs by the summer house and we must see about getting the grass court into action."

Followed by the others he led the way to the grass bank, leaving them alone in a sudden recession of the noise and the company.

They looked at one another carefully. Close to she had a distinct scent, not sweet or sharp, not really definable, but reassuring and exciting. Boys were like most vegetables, he thought, plain and unwonderful, consisting only of parts; but girls, like flowers, were more than the shapes of which they were composed, and always they had this secret scent. The perception of it, striking him so soon after her defence of him, filled him with a sudden wild gratitude, so that he wanted from that moment more than anything else in the whole afternoon to surprise her and win her interest and admiration.

They turned and began to walk slowly down to the far end of the court where the trees stood darkly over the shadowed fronts of the stables, the golden weathercock on its turret pinned like a brooch against their still green foliage.

There was something a little old-fashioned about her clothes. Was it perhaps that they reminded him of pictures in the encyclopaedia? Girls with long hair standing self-consciously on the tops of horse-drawn buses? Or was it *Alice in Wonderland*? He could not be sure; but he saw that the skirt was heavily pleated and rather long, that the cotton socks were a little thin and that there were carefully stitched darns showing over each heel of her tennis shoes.

There was no time for him to observe more or to think about her more specifically, because the Dormains were obviously anxious to start the game and to win it; but he was glad to discover almost from the first ball that she was if anything even less accomplished than himself, and that their normally aggressive opponents of the summer-house-end became steadily more courteous and sporting as game succeeded game.

"Oh, bad luck!" they called as John or Victoria muffed an easy return; or "Jolly good shot!" on the rare occasions when one of John's rather flamboyant serves landed explosively in the correct court.

But they were not discomfited; after an initial attempt to improve their play with much marshalling of forces and hasty conferences between games, they threw their endeavours to the sun, and without any clowning or self-consciousness proceeded quietly to enjoy their frustration, gradually building up out of the ruin of their ambitions a secret and unspoken pleasure in the magnitude of their defeat. It became almost the thing to lose, so that they were on the verge of apologizing when by some ineptitude on the part of Richard or Pat a straight shot curved serenely and successfully over the net.

And then, at the end of their set, as they made their way to the lemonade table, standing tinkling and frosty under its orange umbrella between the two busy courts, she looked at him delightedly and said, "The trouble is, you know, that you're too like me. You don't *think* about it, do you?"

"About the tennis, you mean?"

"Yes. You think about it for a time; but just when the ball reaches you, when you should be thinking about it hard, you forget about it completely, don't you?"

He wanted to take her hand.

"Of course!" he said, "that's exactly what happens. How on earth did you guess?"

"Oh, it was easy! I was watching the pigeons over the stables, waiting for that white one to tumble again, and then when the others called out 'Service' for the umpteenth time I looked at you and saw that you were watching them too." She touched his hand. "Things like that you know; it was easy."

"Yes, but all the same I don't think anyone else would have known that except possibly Melanie."

"Who's Melanie? Your sister?"

"Yes."

"Oh!"

"Why? Don't you like her?"

"I don't know, but I don't think I've ever been awfully keen on red-haired people, and I noticed that hers is very red; it looks angry. But it's not really that. It's just that I don't think she would have known even though she is your sister." She paused and then added hastily, "Of course I don't really know anything about her, because I haven't got any sisters, or brothers for that matter. I'm an 'only,' but I just don't think she would have known; not like I did anyway."

"Why not?"

"Because she doesn't *look* like you! I look much more like you. You might have been *my* brother: we're both pale and thin and tall, aren't we? And if you let your hair grow, why, some people might even think you were me, mightn't they?"

He looked at her searchingly. It had not occurred to him, but of course she was right; they were alike, dreadfully, excitingly alike.

"Are people always telling you that you look ill?" he asked suddenly.

"Oh isn't it *maddening?*" All at once she was very grown-up; so that momentarily he could feel he was talking to her mother. "Does that happen to you too?"

"Yes."

"But it's so silly, isn't it? We're just pale people, that's all. There are red people, yellow people—"

He laughed, "Like Tim you mean?"

"Yes—and there are pale people, like us. *We* don't go about telling the red people they look ill, do we? They should leave us alone. It's so—*common* to be ill, isn't it?"

"Yes," he said, "I suppose it is." They laughed, and taking her arm he led her over towards the refreshment table.

"Let's have some lemonade and then explode together."

It was lovely lemonade in great sparkling jugs with dew clinging to the sides. A whole bushel of lemons had drowned themselves in it, leaving only a few wisps of rind, a wizened pip or two and a floating debris of particles like transparent grains of corn.

Beside the jug on the limp white cloth there were plates of iced cakes melting in the slow blaze of the sun so that the cherries with which they were studded had slipped out of place and projected like drunken jockeys from their sides.

They drank two or three glasses of the lemonade each and gorged themselves on the cakes. There were pink ones, yellow ones, and white ones, and halfway through his second a sudden idea occurred to him.

"Let's eat only the white ones!" he said, his mouth full. "They're obviously ours and we'll leave the others for the pink pigs and the yellow bellies."

She giggled delightedly. "Aren't they delicious? I always think iced cakes are at their best in summer: sticky and sweet like real Turkish delight. Oooh, this one's loaded with cream! Like a bite?"

He opened his mouth and she popped it in. "There! And now you can lick my fingers for me, they're covered in white icing."

"No. I've got a better idea; come close and I'll tell you."

Tossing her hair away from the whiteness of her ear she leaned towards him.

"There's a lake," he whispered, "a secret one in the depths of the wood. We could slip away and wash our hands in it and see the swans."

"Is it far?"

"No; but what does it matter? No one would mind, and anyway we did so badly against the Dormains that I don't suppose that we'll be playing again for ages."

"What about your sister?"

"Oh, she'll be all right." He searched the courts. "Look! She's playing with Tim and he's pretty good so she'll be pleased with herself. Do let's! If you go first, as though you were going to the house to wash, no one will think anything at all and then I could meet you in the rose garden in five minutes' time."

"All right. But don't be longer or I shall get nervous; I'm a dreadful coward about grownups—other people's I mean."

"No," he said, "only five minutes."

She was drooping over the sundial in the centre of the rose garden when he got there.

"Did it seem very long?" he asked.

"No, as a matter of fact I wouldn't have minded if you'd been even longer." She waved an arm. "All these roses," she said.

He looked around at them as they hung in their fullness dropping slow white petals on to the weedless soil.

"And the scent," she went on. "It must be the heat of the sun—do you know what I was imagining?"

"That you were the Sleeping Beauty?"

"No, not that! You know those little insects you find in roses, the ones with the wavy tails?"

"Yes."

"Well, I was shutting my eyes and breathing in the sweetness deeply and pretending that I was one of those little things sitting quite still in the centre of a huge, an enormous, rose."

"What a lovely idea!"

"Have you ever wanted to be one? A rose insect, I mean?"

"Yes, d'you know, I think I have—when I was younger. It's funny how one forgets, isn't it?"

"It's awful. I keep on saying to myself, 'I must never forget, I must never forget,' about *everything*! I tried to keep a diary once; but it was no good, the words weren't the same, or if they were I couldn't think of them."

"I know! I've tried that too. But I'll tell you what, let's pick a rose and then you can smuggle it home and you'll always have it. You'll never forget what it was like—this afternoon, I mean, *today*."

"Do you think they'd mind?"

"Of course not. They've got hundreds. Look! they're dying all over the place; but I'll pick you a young one that you can keep in your bedroom for a bit and then press and take back to school with you."

"Do you hate school?"

"Yes— Look, here's a beauty." Leaning out awkwardly from the grass verge he snatched it quickly. "Dash, I've scratched myself."

"Let me look," she took his hand. "Oh, your poor thumb." And suddenly she stooped and laid her lips against it nipping at it expertly with her teeth and sucking hard.

"There! It will be all right now, I've got the thorn out for you." She laughed. "I saw a film once—Rudolph Valentino I think it was—and he picked a rose for a girl in a garden, and as they were pinning it to her dress, it scratched him, and do you know what she said?"

"No."

"She said, 'You gave me a rose and you drew my blood.' I think that's rather romantic don't you?"

"What did *he* say?"

"I can't remember that bit very well. I think he didn't say anything, he just folded her in his arms and kissed her passionately. It was in the evening you see and they were in Morocco or somewhere—he was an Arabian sheikh."

"Oh."

"Will you pin on mine for me? My brooch would do."

"All right, but we'll have to be quick you know. I do so want you to see the lake and the swans."

Carefully and with much heavy breathing he impaled the stem of the rose on her brooch and then pinned it to her dress, a little to one side of the neckline, just below her collarbone. He knew that this was the right place because he had seen Robin Clifton, one of his elder sister Mary's young men, do the same thing for her when they were going to a dance.

"Thank you." She sniffed it appreciatively. "Now I feel that you really gave it to me and I'll always keep it, *always*. Which way do we go to get to the lake?"

"There's a gate into the wood at the back of the stables."

"Come on then, I'll race you."

She ran quickly over the grass towards the stable yard, hesitated a moment and then fled straight on through the archway to the wicket gate. She was through it before he himself was halfway across the yard, and he did not catch her up until they were deep under the trees.

"By Jove! You *can* run," he said as they slowed to a walk. She was pleased.

"Yes, not much to carry and long legs to carry it. At school the games mistress calls me Atalanta."

"Who's she?"

"Oh I don't know—some classical person, 'renowned for her fleetness of foot,' I think—I say! Isn't it different in here?"

He nodded and then put his fingers to his lips. "Let's listen; don't make a sound, and then we'll see who can hear the most."

They were silent for a moment.

"It's no good," she said. "I'm puffing so much I can't hear anything but my own noises."

"Well, take a few deep breaths—we both will."

They inhaled conscientiously a few times.

"Now then," he said. "Let's try again with our eyes shut this time."

The silence dropped around them like a curtain, a green curtain; and then, gradually, as their ears became attuned, innumerable little noises became apparent to them weaving themselves into the background like flowers into a tapestry.

From the distance they could hear the sieved laughter and shouts from the tennis courts, and nearer at hand, the rattle of crockery and cutlery, the high backchat of servants from the kitchen of the house; above them, all about them, were the still dry sounds of the woods: the cooing and clapping of grey pigeons, the fall of seed or twigs, and the papery sounds of last year's leaves disturbed by the passing of tiny animals.

His eyes tight shut, he waited; he could picture her standing there in front of him, sharing in her private darkness each identical sound as it came to them through the dim greenness beyond. He wondered how she would look with her eyes closed and tried hard to visualize the sleeping secrecy of her face with the lids drawn down over the large eyes.

Atalanta! Such places as these, he thought, *ought* to have girls in every tree: nymphs and dryads in willows and oaks, and the printless flashing of white feet through sphagnum and fern and the hint of laughter at the stream's edge. Always, on the moors, by rivers, in woodland, in the sudden moments of the inward sun, he had had this feeling that somehow in the corner of the twinkling of an eye the place was feminine; that if only he were quick enough he would catch the bright gleam of a mouth or the whiteness of a hand before they merged tantalizingly into a flower or a stone. And now here she was alone with him sharing it all; he had only to open his eyes and he would see her, not through the slow syntax of his Latin or Greek lessons at the Abbey—though he decided he would take more interest in them next term—but in actuality, and with her eyes closed. He would steal something from her and yet she would never know.

He opened his eyes. At once, mysteriously, even before the light broke in on him afresh, he realized that he was too late; knew that he would see what in fact he was seeing: the grave and unabashed inspection which confronted him in the greyness of her own.

"*Oh!*" he said, "you cheated—you were looking all the time!"

"And how did you know?"

"Well—"

"Yes, 'well,'" she mimicked, "because you were going to cheat yourself; but I knew you would and so I decided to do it first. And besides," she moved on ahead of him looking at her feet, "besides I wanted to see what you looked like with your eyes shut. My mother says that when a person closes their eyes you can tell all about them by looking at their faces. She said my father had a horrid face when he was asleep."

"Did she?"

"Yes, she said that if she'd once seen him asleep before they got married then she'd never have married him in the first place."

"Oh." They moved on down the ride, walking absurdly on tiptoe and swinging their joined hands.

"But how awful!" His expostulation was sudden.

"What?" she asked blithely.

"To be married to someone whose face you hated when they were asleep." He felt her hand, her whole arm, tense against him.

"I mean it must rather spoil things; although I suppose that since they'd mostly be asleep at the same time, it doesn't matter all that much."

"Oh, but it *does*—I mean it *did*," and her hand started to swing again. "But you needn't worry *now*. You see they were divorced ages ago."

"Oh, I see."

"And the funny thing is he's much nicer now; you know, he's polite to Mummy when we meet in hotels and places, helps her off with her coat and things like that. I go and stay with him sometimes and he gives me the most wonderful presents: this butterfly brooch for instance."

"How lovely." He fingered it.

"You see the eyes?" she asked.

"Yes."

"Those are real rubies."

"I say!"

They turned a corner.

"Ooh!" she said. "Look! The lake and the swan, no *two*, just as you said. I do love it when things come true, don't you?"

"Yes."

They quickened their pace so that very soon they were trotting without realizing it.

"When I was young, you know, nearly everything used to come true; but now, even though I'm not awfully old, I'm beginning to be surprised when they do. Enid, that's Mummy, says that when I'm older nothing will ever come true at all, and that when I come out I'm to be sure to have as much fun as—"

"*Please!*" he said.

"What?"

"Please don't talk about that any more."

"Why ever not?"

"I don't know; it just makes me feel uncomfortable. I mean we might as well still be up at the tennis courts, mightn't we?"

She was crestfallen. "I'm sorry! Somehow when I'm with you I can't help saying the things I'm actually thinking about, and I suppose I think an awful lot about Enid and my father, even though I don't really want to think about them."

"*I* know; I do that too. I keep on wanting and not wanting to think about next term, and today, well I jolly well *won't*. You do the same. Just think about today, about the lake and the swans and the cakes we ate—things like that."

"All right." She looked at him carefully. "I'll tell you what! If you promise to be happy about next term, I'll write to you every week and what's more I'll never even mention you-know-what however much I want to."

"Oh no, you mustn't do that; letters are different, and if you are thinking about something you must write it so that I can answer, and then it really will be as though we were talking to each other."

"But it *won't*," she was laughing, "because you won't *let* me talk about it."

He was bewildered for a moment and could think of no reply.

"Don't frown," she said. "It makes you look old. *I* understand; you mean that. because we won't be together we can afford to be nearer, more real to each other."

"Yes that's it. You *are* clever!"

"No I'm not really; it's only that I think I'm a little older than you in some ways—girls are, you know."

They had reached the edge of the lake now; an almost perfect circle with a sagging boathouse on the far side, it lay under the throng of the tall trees in all the stillness and heat of late afternoon. Only a narrow path fringed with rushes and reeds separated its margins from the boles of the trees so that their origins, grey as the legs of elephants, were reflected upon its surface where each vagary of their branches, each fan of their foliage, was darkly contained within its circumference.

Only at the centre where the tops of the trees, blemished with the black nests of the rookery, ended evenly in an enclosed smaller circle, was there a glimpse of the high blue medallion of the sky. The rest, the large periphery, was a closer greener forest strewn over with the white heads of water lilies and swaying slightly from the movements of the two swans by the farther bank.

From the water rose the thin reedy smell of river mud and water plants. Here and there "water boatmen" jerked over the reflections, while every now and again a black bubble rose from the depths and broke softly on the surface.

"Isn't it wonderful?" she breathed.

"I knew you'd like it."

"Oh I do! It's so small—I never thought it would be like this, I imagined it much bigger; but this is like a lake in a story or a peep show, you almost feel you can hold it between your hands as though it were really yours. Almost," she went on, "as though it were enchanted, as though at any moment a hand with Arthur's sword in it might rise out of that blue centre and point at the sky."

"Yes. Come on! Let's go and sit on the boathouse platform;

you can wash your fingers there and we might be able to see some fish."

They walked around the path and climbed carefully on to the lichen-covered planks of the small platform. The swans watched them placidly until they sat down, and then quietly drew away to the farther bank.

"There!" he said. "Now you lie down and dabble your fingers in the water while I hold your ankles."

Obediently, her hair drooping around her white face, she lay down and lowered her hands into the water. She sat up suddenly.

"That settles it!" she said. "I'm going to."

"Going to what?"

"I'm going to bathe of course. It's irresistible, feel it." She patted his cheeks with her dripping fingers. "It's fresh and cool and clean, there must be a stream somewhere. It will be heavenly. Come on! Let's bathe together."

"But can you swim? It's quite deep you know."

"Of course I can—I passed the test last term. Why, can't you?"

"Yes, but—"

"But what?" She was undoing her shoes and peeling off her thin cotton socks.

"Well," he said. "Do you think we ought to—I mean suppose somebody came and saw us?"

"Oh don't be a prude," she said. "You've got a sister, haven't you?"

"Two."

"Well then—"

"But someone might come down from the tennis party looking for us."

"That's just what they will do if you don't hurry up. But if we're quick, we can be in and out in no time and no one will ever know—except us and the swans."

"All right," he said uneasily, "but only on one condition."

"What?" Her question was muffled, coming to him from behind the dress which she was pulling over her head.

"That you undress in there." His hands on her shoulders he swivelled her around away from him. "In the boathouse."

"Why?"

"I don't know, but please!"

Her head emerged from the dress again. "You *are* funny!" she said. "You'll see me when I come out so what's the difference?"

She left him then and disappeared inside, and the moment she was gone he stripped off his flannels, shirt, socks and shoes and tiptoeing to the edge of the platform sat with his feet dipping into the cool water.

A moment later he heard the swift pad of her feet behind him and in a sudden flush of fear pushed himself off into the lake.

Down and down he went, the bubbles of his descent frothing up past his ears as he sank swiftly into the ever colder layers of the water. Although his eyes were open he could see nothing but the clouded green-brownness which surrounded him.

All at once he remembered that other moment when they had stood silent and voluntarily blind beneath the green shade of the wood. He had intended then, by opening his eyes, to see her unobserved, to steal something from her. In another moment the opportunity would be his once again; the round eye of the lake had closed over him shutting her from his sight; but when he rose, when the green eye opened for him again as it must, he would be able to see and steal even more from her than he had at first intended. This time it would not be his fault; it would be nobody's fault.

Then, lunging for the surface, he trod the darkness vigorously with his feet and broke into the air and the light.

Thin as the ivory tusk in the hall, she was standing on the very edge of the platform; on her slender thighs and the naked curve of her stomach, the shaken water threw green and shifting shadows. Something about the narrow sweep of her waist rising to the early fullness of her breasts hurt him like a pain so that he gasped out loud and then raised his eyes to her face as she leaned over him, dipping her lips and eyes into those reflected greens which were playing over the surfaces of her body.

"What's the matter?" she asked. "Is it very cold?"

Through the ringing of the water in his ears her voice came to him indistinctly like chimes in the wind and he could only look up at her, shaking the water from his hair and plucking

at the slippery stem of a water-lily leaf which had twined itself
around his shoulders.

"Here!" she said as, kneeling, she put her hands down to him,
"let me help you."

He grasped them and she pulled him in to the platform so
that he could grip it and heave himself up quickly beside her.

"All right?" she asked.

"Yes." He got to his feet and stood before her. "Why?"

She said, "What happened? Did you get stuck in the mud or
something?"

"No, it wasn't that."

"Well, what was it? You're so pale—you're paler than me now.
What frightened you?"

"I don't know. You wouldn't understand."

"Yes I would."

"No."

"It was *me*, wasn't it? Seeing me when you came up?"

"Yes."

"You *see*!" She danced briefly. "I told you I knew, didn't I?"

"All the same"—and she was suddenly still beneath her frown—
"I don't quite see why—?"

He was shivering and for some reason he felt suddenly angry;
he bit hard on his teeth.

"Well, I'll tell you. It may sound stupid but I was frightened
because when I first saw you I thought for a moment that you
were *me*, and yet I knew you weren't. See if you can understand *that* if you're so clever!"

She looked him up and down intently. "Of course I can; it
was I who told you how alike we were in the first place, and
yet of course we're completely different—we must be, because
I'm a girl and you're—"

"That's just what I mean; we are and we aren't," he said. "And
after being down there where it was dark," he pointed at the
water, "it frightened me, that's all."

"Well I don't see that it's anything to be frightened about."
She was laughing now. "I think it's exciting and lovely to be
the same and yet different." She took his hand. "Help me in

will you? I don't want to get my hair wet because it'll never get dry in time."

With no pause she had dropped quickly to her knees and lowered her legs over the edge of the platform. Stooping down behind her he put his hands under her shoulders, and as she swung away from him he let her slip gently into the water.

She was silent for a moment as she took the sudden shock of the coldness against her sun-warmed skin. A black streamer of her hair snaked across her cheek, its tail clinging to the corner of her mouth as though it had just emerged. Her eyes laughed up at him.

"Ooh, lovely, lovely water," she said as she started rather unsteadily to swim away towards the middle of the lake. He watched her uneasily for a moment.

"Don't go too far," he said. "It's very deep—I never even reached the bottom."

"I'm going to that blue bit," she called. "Right in the very middle where the sun is."

He sat down and started to pick the little tendrils of waterweed from between his toes. She had laughed at him; that was the funny thing. When people laughed it was usually because they didn't understand; but she had understood, and yet she had laughed. He wondered why. Had she understood more than he had himself, in order to be able to laugh, or had she understood less? And who was right? He, to have been serious and frightened, or Victoria to have been excited and laughing? It was like Melanie over again. She always laughed at his secrets, at his more intimate speculations about the nature of girls. But he was sure that really he was right, that there was something that girls wouldn't and couldn't and never would understand even though there were some things they seemed to know naturally which made no sense to him.

One thing he did know. And that was that he loved, yes *loved* Victoria. He would always love her; even when he was old enough to love people he would love her and go on loving her for—

Suddenly, like a knife thrown into his head, he heard her scream; dispassionately, with no engagement of his feelings, he looked across the broken surface of the lake and saw her, noted that her cheeks were round and white as a wind cherub's, that the water was flooding into her open mouth, and that she was riding raggedly up and down in her attempts to swim out of the net of water lilies in which she was caught.

He noted all this, saw it on the instant; but at first it held no fear for him, was no more than an arrested picture at which he through his warm blood and live senses gazed as rapt and objectively as a child at a lantern lecture. Then, as the range of his vision widened to take in the thick tracts of the leaves which surrounded her like the green footprints of some enormous beast, he saw the riding swans, and seeing them, knew at once the full cold measure of his terror.

All that he felt for her, all of pity, guilt and horror, all of the sudden evil risen like a spectre from the lake, became fixed and resident in the swans as they floated in their white indifference a few feet away watching her easily, contentedly, and with no curiosity.

Then as her hands came up and beat the water, as she choked in the sprays and splashes of her own predicament and turned wordlessly towards him in the persistent silence, he found that he himself was at last with her in the lake seeming scarcely to move through its coldness as he writhed his way towards her.

He shouted once, loudly, and up above, the rooks took to the air. High, high above him he was conscious of their dark shapes and rough cries as they swirled in the circle of the sky; and then ahead of him he saw her thin arm rise out of the water, the fingers fluttering like bones against the darkness of the wood, and she was gone.

Measurably, the swans turned; slowly and in unison, with no flicker of their tails nor lingering glance from their painted black eyes, they swept away to the farther side out of his line of vision.

A few more convulsive strokes and he was above her, occupying the very place where a moment ago she had been a reality as, astonishingly diminished, she had coughed and fluttered in the embrace of her panic. He remembered then how far he himself had sunk on that first jump, his passing surprise at the largeness of the waters beneath its bright surface, and at once he dived.

So light she must be, so short the time that had elapsed, that she could not be far beneath him, must surely if her eyes were still alive to it see the green sunlight and the round hearts of the leaves above them both. His feet struck into the air and impatiently he forced himself downwards with swinging strokes of his arms until at last he was deep enough to find full purchase against the water. Two more co-ordinated efforts of all his thin muscles and he was in the sepia-dimness of the middle depths. He turned like an eel, searching all about him with his eyes, every finger and toe alert for the least touch against it; but he saw nothing, felt only the yielding sliminess of the lily stems as they slid past his face and shoulders.

Not yet uncomfortable, bearing no physical burden within his chest or ears, he swam down farther, three full strokes into the darkness where the water was thicker and colder, and turned about him yet again seeking with all his heart and head for some inkling of her presence. But there was nothing. He was in a world of death and emptiness, numbed in all save the urgency and desperation of his wish.

He felt then that he would never, could never, come up without her; that rather he would open his own mouth and draw into himself the coldness and silence so that for that other world, harsh with questions and light, there would never be any necessity for an answer. He saw Melanie, the outraged faces of Mrs. Bellingham and his mother, the emptiness of his bed and the remote dignity of his father; and behind his unshed tears he was happy. There could be no disgrace, no dreadful twisting explanations as to why and whatever-made-you, but only this for ever and ever.

He was on his back now, still and effortless, making no further attempt to seek or to find; and as he lay there he floated a little nearer to the surface counting the thuds of heart and waiting uncritically for the moment when he would know that he must certainly do it and drown. Then above him and a little to one side he saw her; a pale green shape with a drift of black hair swinging against the surface. In a moment, with all his thoughts fled and his arms linked tightly around her chest, he was kicking and pushing beneath her. Still on his back he pumped at the

water with his feet and together, with her hair in his mouth and
eyes, they broke to the surface and the swans.

He swept away her hair and drew in the delight of the air.
They were safe; he had found her. Soon she would breathe
again properly, he would revive her on the bank in the way he
had been taught at school. He would dry her and dress her and
they would run back together. No one would ever know.

Breathlessly, the water sheeting over his face at every progress,
he kicked out with his legs on either side of her narrow hips;
never daring to turn his head in order to see how far they were
from the platform nor even if they were moving in the right
direction. Before him, in the bright sky, mingled with the water,
so that they seemed to be immersed in it like ragged black fish,
the rooks still circled and called over the tops of the trees. Out
of their other world they watched him as the swans had watched
Victoria sink; but not in silence like the swans, for they were
participants in all he did, were excited and involved, keener to
his success or failure and not content to let him have his fight
alone. He did not know what they wished for him: whether they
hoped to see him reach the bank and there build his safety like
a nest, or whether they hoped to see her drop once more from
his arms and fall for ever unattainable into the depths of their
reflected trees; but he knew by their alarms and laughter, by their
shrills and shrieks, that they acknowledged him in a way the
swans had never done.

Suddenly he was aware of a new note in their mockery or
distress, something higher than their threats and more regular
than the gasp of his own breathing. There were voices: his own
name being called over and over again with rising exasperation,
someone else whistling.

"John! *Jooohn!* Where are you?" and then the seesaw of the
whistle, long-drawn and enquiring, again and again.

Nearer and nearer they came, so that he longed suddenly for
the silence of the swans and the clamour of the rooks and would,
had it been possible, have made no sound nor asked for any
interest or help.

But it was too late: a few feet away a head broke through the
ranks of the reeds. It was Wully, the Bellingham cocker spaniel.

For a moment, immobile save for the working of his nostrils and with his long orange ears absurdly cocked, the dog gazed at him; and then he turned his head away to the path and gave tongue. His wild hysterical "*Yollop yollop!*" split the afternoon, quelling even the cawing of the rooks and John heard the drumming of feet breaking into a run as the others made for the periphery of the lake.

"*Here* he is!" It was Melanie alert and angry who was the first to arrive. Typically, she allowed her triumph full play even before she had seen him, her questions and his relayed answers being shouted out over the concealing screen of the rushes and reeds.

"John? Where are you? We've been looking for you all afternoon. You are rude; he is rude, Tim, isn't he? Tim's here and Mrs. Bellingham's coming and Colonel Bellingham has had to go to the ruins. Why ever didn't you tell us—*John*?"

With a last kick he impelled himself and Victoria to the side of the lake just as Melanie reached the platform above it. He heard her, the sudden gasp of her astonishment, but he did not look up. Let her look at him, he thought, take it all in so that she would make no mistakes later when she told Mother and Mary.

"Whatever's the matter with Victoria? Tim, come quickly. John, answer me! What's the matter? What have you been doing?"

"Oh shut up!" he said, "and give me a hand with Victoria; she's fallen in and I had to rescue her."

"But you've got no clothes on! You've *neither* of you got any clothes on."

He spat out some water.

"No, we've got no clothes on," he said nastily. "Tell Tim: '*They've got no clothes on*,' we've got no clothes on, '*they've got no clothes on*.'"

He wanted to go on saying it for ever in a Punch-and-Judy voice like a gramophone record which has got stuck in a groove, but somehow he managed to control himself and wriggled out backwards on to the muddy part of the bank by the boathouse dragging Victoria after him.

"Quick!" he said to Tim who was behind him. "Don't worry about Melanie, we've got to give Victoria artificial respiration; she's swallowed a lot of water and stuff."

Side by side, so that his shoulder felt the warmth of Tim's envied shirt, they squatted on the bank and pulled Victoria out of the water on to the short grass at the top. Their urgency and roughness disturbed her, she half-opened her eyes and closed them again, then gave a feeble cough.

John jumped astride her and kneeling down placed his hands on the chrysalis of her chest where the thin ribs heaved like folded wings against the skin. He leaned forward counting slowly out loud. "One . . . Two . . . Three . . ." and then, still counting, sank back on his haunches: "Four . . . Five . . . Six." He swung forward again: "One . . . Two . . . Three . . ." and heard the bubble of water in her throat as the air was expelled; then back again on to his haunches and the coldness of her thighs. The air entered between her blue lips, beneath his relaxed hands the flat muscles contracted as the tip of her tongue protruded blackly between her teeth and suddenly as he counted again: "One . . . Two . . . Three . . ." she was sick: crystallized half-cherries swallowed entire, a strange debris of cake and white icing streamed out on to the grass from her pale profile like bait disgorged into the bottom of a boat by a hooked whiting.

All three, they watched her fascinated; and then when the spasm was over John leaned forward again keeping up the magical enumeration with a triumphant rise of his voice as the last of the old air rose from the depths of her chest mingled with muddy water.

He was about to ask Tim to run secretly to the house for towels and hot-water bottles when he saw that he was no longer there. Only his ankles and knees were visible and across the whiteness of Victoria's chest there was thrown, like that of a badly taken snapshot, the shadow of a head and shoulders.

Horrified, he looked up: it was Mrs. Bellingham. Against the sun he could not see her face, he could see only the garden-party expanse of the frock over her bosom as it swelled beneath its flare of bougainvillaea and chrysanthemum; but from somewhere above it, between her mauve neck and the shadow cast

by her floppy hat, came the sonorous ominous gong of her voice.
"*Victoria Blount! John Blaydon!* Whatever, yes *whatever* are
you doing?"

The vibrations broke ineffectually against the green doors of
the forest. In the pause he looked up at Melanie, and her sharp
eyes black with excitement looked back into his own for an
instant before she looked away from him to the shadows beneath the picture hat on his other side. This was something like,
he thought bitterly, an enormous woman, a tremendous ally all
flowers and silk and outrage.

The gong struck again. "Get up at once, yes at *once*, John."
Her dress swirled as she turned away from him "Tim!"

"Yes, Mother."

"Run and get Nanny immediately and tell your father where
we are. We shall want some towels and hot-water bottles."

"All right."

"No! Wait a moment—we must cover this child at once, yes
at once. Give me your shirt."

Suddenly, all creaking efficiency, she swooped down upon
him before John was able to move. His nakedness was growing
on him like a mushroom, pushing its way with awful rapidity
through every nook and cranny of his consciousness. From no-
where a parasol flowered over Victoria and beneath it Mrs. Bellingham's white-gloved hands tucked in Tim's shirt so that he
could see only her knees and the upper part of her sweat-dewed
face.

Mrs. Bellingham's head emerged from a scolloped corner of
the silk parasol.

"You had better put *your* clothes on immediately, I think.
Yes, with no delay—and in the boathouse." She looked at Melanie.

"Now then Elizabeth, my dear, run after Tim quickly there's
a good girl and tell him on no account to tell anybody anything.
Do you understand? Not *any*body anything at all!"

"Yes, Mrs. Bellingham—"

"Well run along then, dear."

"All right." Melanie looked at her importantly, "Mrs. Bellingham?"

"Yes dear, what is it?"

"My name's Melanie! I'm John's sister, you know."

"Of course, how foolish of me, Melanie. But never mind that just now, Elizabeth. Run along do and overtake Timothy—oh and you might ask Nanny to telephone the Vicarage for your car. I'm sure that boy—I'm sure that your brother John should get home and into bed as quickly as possible."

From the boathouse John watched Melanie run with never a backward glance until she was deep in the green shadows of the ride where so short a time before he and Victoria had paused in the woodland silence.

He put on his clothes slowly; there was no point in hurrying; the afternoon was over and he could never go back to where he had been before he took them off. They were the same clothes, but *he* was different and once he had resumed them everyone and everything else would be different and go on being different for ever. He was sure of it.

Outside, Mrs. Bellingham was talking to Victoria. She had put away her gong now and the wood pigeons were back: she was cooing.

"Well what's oop this time?" asked Simpson without taking his eyes off the road.

John sat stiffly in his corner in the back seat of the Ford. Let Melanie tell him, he thought. It will be interesting to know what she's thinking.

"It's John," she said. "He left me all alone and went bathing with a girl in the lake. She nearly drowned and Mrs. Bellingham found them there together. They had to get hot-water bottles and blankets to cover her with and send for the doctor. That's why she sent us home, because she was so furious! John's spoiled the whole afternoon for me and disgraced *everyone.*"

Simpson squawked the klaxon as they turned into the Worsley road.

" 'Eavens aboove!" he said. " 'OO fetched t'lass out then?"

"I did."

John edged a little farther away from Melanie and gazed intently at the back of Simpson's yellow head. "I jumped in and swam out to her and I got her back from the bottom of the lake, then I gave her artificial respiration until she was sick." He paused dramatically. "I think I saved her life."

"Tha did?" Simpson turned half around, his hands crossed easily on the high steering wheel. "Tha woont get no disgraëce for that, ya might even get a swimmin'-gala medal. But not from t'mistress."

"Is Mother cross?"

"Ech! She's like a toop'nny cracker on a hot stove," said Simpson. "But tha never knaws. T'mistress mae be thinkin' different when she hears how brave tha were."

Without turning his head John allowed the corner of his brief smile play in the direction of Melanie.

She saw it and responded quickly so that he felt the lurch of the seat as she leaned forward to engage Simpson.

"No she won't! They were *naked*, Simpson! They had no clothes on at all, not even their shoes. Mrs. Bellingham saw them herself without anything on. She was horrified and sent us both home although it was nothing to do with me except that I was the first to find them."

Simpson's whistle was low and frightening and the Ford slowed down.

"Not only that," went on Melanie quickly, "but when Mrs. Bellingham found him he was sitting on her—on her *stomach*— with nothing on."

"I was giving her artificial respiration," said John.

For the first time since they had left Clockwood John and Melanie looked at one another as they waited for Simpson's comment.

"'Ow old is t'little lass?" he asked.

"She's taller than me," said Melanie. "I should say she's at least thirteen. I didn't like her at all. She was very rude to me, from the very moment we arrived she never spoke to me."

"She's *not*, Simpson," said John. "She's only twelve. It's only that she's thinner, that makes her look taller."

"That's not what he means," said Melanie. "Simpson wants to know who is the oldest, don't you Simpson? And even I know that it's wrong to take all your clothes off in front of other people, especially in front of boys."

"*You* were premature," said John. "You jolly nearly died before you were born and sometimes I wish you—"

"Now look 'ere," said Simpson. "What's t'sense in quarrellin' like this before we reach t'Vicarage?"

"It's John. He's always doing these things. At the Drummond's Christmas Party he got drunk on the butler's sherry and set light to the tablecloth with an indoor firework. This time he's done something much worse, something *rude*. And he knew he was doing wrong or he wouldn't have gone off without me." Melanie was not far from tears but his heart did not soften because he knew that she would time her weeping for her appearance in front of Mother. She had said every single thing he hadn't wanted her to say and soon she would be retelling the whole story to all the grownups.

"You did know, didn't you John?"

"Didn't I know what?" he asked.

"Don't be silly, you know what I mean. You knew you were doing wrong at the party and you haven't answered."

"No, and I'm not going to."

"There! You see? He's guilty, isn't he, Simpson? He's *guilty!*"

"Now, now!" said Simpson. "Tha's nearly 'ome now. Joost 'old tha gobs, as they say in Beddin'ton, or t'mistress 'll roast ya both."

They ignored him, glaring at each other over the intervening waste of the shiny black seat. Outside, the elm trees swept past as they turned into the long drive.

John spoke slowly, "Well if I'm guilty, *you're* jealous, and that's how you know."

"I don't know what jealousy means," said Melanie.

"No, and I don't know what guilty means until someone says it; it's a horrid word."

"You'll know what it means when Mother says it, you just wait." She picked up her racket expectantly. "You can let *me* out here, Simpson; I'm not going back with him—I'll walk up the little lane."

"I'm not stoppin' on t'bend," said Simpson. "You can get out at the front door, Miss Melanie, and Master John can go in at the back."

They drew up and she got out quickly without looking at them. She frisked up the front steps and in behind the old glass of the front door while they drove around to the stables. Simpson switched off the engine.

"Ee! Ut looks bad," he said in the sudden silence. "If ya taks my tip ya'll saw nowt. Remember t'mistress is lak a bonfire, more you put on t'more she blaëzes."

"Yes," said John. "Thanks awfully for backing me up, Simpson!" He clambered out of the car.

He couldn't face the kitchen and the maids; the front door was out of the question because Melanie had used it. He would have to go through the French windows into the dining room. That would catch them off their guard, it would surprise everyone including the big square Vicarage. The house would not be expecting him to enter in that way and once he was in he would know what to do next.

He ran through the silence of the beech walk, the shadows roofing him in against the early twilight of the garden. This at least was the same, had changed not at all between the morning and the evening save in its air of expectation of the hours of night. The dews were held here safely from the declining power of the sun and he could smell the greenhouse moistness of the grass and soil; the enclosed air was as cool as a hand against his forehead as he passed down the way; above him on the falling willow a thrush singing carefully.

He looked up at it as he passed. He himself was small, between the hedges no one could see him even though they might be looking. He was smaller than the thrush and no guiltier. One day, he decided, he would *be* a bird living in green places, seeing everything, knowing nothing save how to fly, to sing and to hide. This very night when it was all over he would come out here again for a little time and forget all but the secrecy and the silence. He would close his eyes and out of the air and the night scents fashion words without meaning and notes more remote than flowers. There in his bird-brain he would recapture the loveliness of Victoria as he had seen her by the lake, and no one would ever know of it or praise or blame him for it or alter it in any way.

He ran down the broad steps by the yellow broom bushes and across the flagged garden by the French windows. As he approached he saw at first only the unreal reflection of the garden in the dark panes of the glass; a drowned garden with all its shadows emphasized and its colours muted, against which his distorted countenance moved like some pale fish a little way under the water. He stopped then, his gaze fixed on the glass, trying to recognize the trees and the flowers behind him, to fasten this other face into the unreality of its other world. He tilted his head a little so that his image-face leaned and swam against the fall of the glass willow; and then as he moved nearer, as the reflection of the screened room solidified and its interior absorbed his vision, he saw the others, all of them.

Mrs. Mudd's jet-black coat and Sunday hat with its shining crow's feathers trembling over the daze of her expression as she stared blankly back at him; beside her, Emma Huggins, her busy wig making up for her lack of eyebrows and eyelashes; Grace Boult in her usual pale blue and rouge with a golden bun on the back of her neck. All of them, faces and hats, bosom on bosom, stretching down either side of the long oak table like the opposing ranks of some terrible female army; and at their head, small against the blue-white array of the Crown Derby on the sideboard, Mother, a tiny, fiery general in conference at an armistice.

How could he have forgotten? It was Friday, the first Friday of the month and the day for the Meeting of the Mothers. He had heard them planning it at lunch: the maypole cake, the Indian tea, rock buns and Yorkshire tea cakes. The events of the afternoon had driven it out of his head and apparently out of Simpson's and Melanie's too. Well, that was one good thing anyway: whatever Mother had heard of the telephone message, Melanie would not have had time to fill in all the awful details, and if things fell out well for him he would get his story in first.

He smiled brightly in through the glass at Mrs. Mudd, put his finger to his lips and started to tiptoe elaborately away over the flagstones. If he didn't look back, if he kept to the middle of each of the stones, all would be well. The great thing was to

forget them all in there, to pretend that this was a normal afternoon drawing to a nonchalant close. Mrs. Mudd, Emma Huggins,
Grace Boult were none of them there and therefore could not
possibly have seen him, and that being so, it would be quite
natural to break into a run at any moment, to race for the summer house and see if there were any cigarette ends between the
cracks in the floor boards.

He broke into a run. Behind him he almost thought he heard
the door open and the chilling egress of high and confused talk,
but it was probably only imagination and to look back was forbidden. He went on up the stone steps. If only he could reach
the beech walk everything would be all right. The beech walk
was Sanctuary and no one could touch him once he was within
it. He slowed down to a walk. Had someone called? Impossible!
A hen squawking or a cock in the paddock signalling the dusk
as they sometimes did. It was safe to look now because he was
hidden by the shrubbery and would see nothing, so he halted
and looked into the leaves and branches by his shoulder.

Nothing, nothing at all, only footsteps. Quick footsteps clip-
ping across the flags like a rain of nails. His whole face tingled
suddenly as though the blood were being sucked out of it by a
whirlpool in his chest. It was Mother. Through a gap in the
branches he could see the bobbing black and white of her
Mother's Union dress, and she was not speaking or calling, she
was simply chasing him in silence.

Unable, like Herod, to summon him again for the sake of
them that sat with her, and yet furiously angry, she was pursuing
him with all the impersonality of a nightmare. In his mind he
could see her intimately: her fists tight by her side, the whites
of her pale eyes netted with full vessels, her tiny chin clenched
against her upper teeth like it had been the time Bessie bolted with
them in the phaeton when she had been at the reins.

His heart smithied inside him, the blows reverberating up into
his throat and head. Swiftly he slipped into the gap between
the beech hedge and the shrubbery and crouched there with his
eyes tightly shut. Up the steps she came; in the half of a second
she would be level with him and he would not see her. He was

cheating by keeping his eyes closed and vengeance would befall him if he did not look. So he looked.

She was standing there waiting for him in the bright green light and he felt as though she really had caught him, as though he had been doing something wicked and dreadful in the darkness under the tree.

"Come here," she said softly.

He slunk out of his hiding, looking into her face to see it as it really was; and it was the same as he had imagined it only much more terrible.

Without a word she took his wrist tightly in her own small, dry hand and led him under the archway into the beech walk where a few moments earlier the thrush had sung. They went along it in silence, faster and faster, so that if she had been bigger and he smaller, by the time they had reached the summer house after crossing the tennis court, she would have been dragging him as she dragged the dog at the end of its lead when it had offended her.

She shut the door behind them and in the smell of the tennis net and distemper confronted him in the wooden silence. There were laden spider's webs in the corners of the windows, and the closed croquet box spoke of the holiday that was so nearly over.

"Well!" she asked. "What have you to say for yourself?"

"What about?" The hand holding his own shook and suddenly she began to twist his arm.

"You're a coward," she said, "a dirty little coward. Don't be a liar as well."

"I'm not—I'm not—I'm *not* dirty."

"Oh, yes you are." She gave his arm another twist. "You have disgraced me, haven't you?"

"No."

"Yes you have." She drew in a deep breath. "You saw all those people in the dining room, didn't you? My Mothers?"

He made no answer.

"Didn't you?"

"Yes."

"Tomorrow or the next day they may all know what I know;

they may know more, they may know both the things you *did* do as well as the things you didn't do; and I want to know them first so that I shall know what to do with *you* and what to say to *them*. Do you understand me?"

"Yes, Mother."

"Don't call me 'Mother,' answer me. What did you do?"

Still he said nothing and suddenly she dropped his arm; it throbbed by his side far more grievously than if it had suffered at the hands of anyone else.

"Look at me," she said. "No, look into my eyes, John. Let *me* look into yours."

He met her newly hateful eyes; nothing but her eyes mattered to him now. While it was still not too late he would look into them and hold them before the truth was lost, before it sank into the roots and mud over which they were both sustained, before it merged into something which he now knew would always be there and always be terrible. He remembered the lake and the terror which he had thought past, and he remembered Victoria as she had stood there in the sunlight. He had done nothing but love her, nothing but want her to keep for himself, to wait for as he waited for the happiness which though he always expected it always eluded him.

Her eyes slipped away from his own.

"Very well then," she said coldly. "You will stay here until you are prepared to tell me—*all night*—if necessary, with only yourself and your nasty impurity for company. While you are waiting I shall go and telephone Mrs. Bellingham and apologize to her for my son's behaviour. I shall explain that I can do nothing with him and that I shall quite understand if he's never invited anywhere again. I shall also write to this girl's mother and make our apologies—mine and Daddy's—to her as soon as I know her name." She paused. "What was her name?"

"Victoria Blount."

"And how old was she?"

"Simpson asked me that—and I don't see that it matters."

"Of course it matters, you young fool!" she blazed at him, and he remembered the bonfire. "That's why Simpson asked you; it's what they'll all be asking tomorrow."

"I don't see why," he muttered, bewildered by the new access of her anger.

"How old was she? Was she older than you or younger?"

"Older—a little; I think she was twelve and a bit."

"Why did you make her take her clothes off?"

"I *didn't*! I tried to stop her."

"*What?*"

"I tried to stop her," he spoke rapidly. "I only took her to see the swans, Mother. I only wanted to be alone with her and the swans, and when we got there she wanted to bathe. She—"

"Yes?"

"Nothing." It was dreadful to have to talk about her at all; like saying a prayer backwards.

"What did you say her name was?"

"Victoria, Victoria Blount."

"From Newcastle?"

"I think so."

"And were her parents there, both of them?"

"No."

"Why not?"

"Because she hasn't got two parents. She told me that they were divorced or something."

"Ah." Her mouth relaxed. She looked at him again almost kindly for a moment as though he had stopped a pain for her, a headache.

"Of course," she said. "I remember now," and she sighed again.

They stood there together. For the first time since they entered they heard small sounds from the garden outside. His body seemed to be working again; he was aware of his knees, his ears, the curl of his fingers by his side. In some indefinable way he knew that it was nearly over now, that soon he would be able to go on with things again where he had left them so long ago by the edge of the lake.

Opposite him, against the flaking distemper, she was watching him once more.

"One thing more I want to know," she said, "to feel *quite* happy about you."

"Yes, Mother"

"When she was—after she had taken all her clothes off did you do anything to her? Did you touch her in any way?"

"No."

For one last moment her eyes looked into his again and this time he looked away.

"You're sure?"

"Yes."

Her face was utterly relaxed for a moment; then when she spoke he saw the first flicker of personal interest she had betrayed that afternoon.

"Did you look at her, John?"

Yes, he thought, I did, I looked at her and I saw her as I see her now, as I'll always be able to see her even without closing my eyes, whether I'm asleep or awake. I saw her, all of her that was to be seen, and that no one else will ever be able to see again no matter how long they may look or live.

In this moment there was no one there but himself; they were all gone under the clock and did not matter at all. They were fixed for ever in the dining room, in front of their empty cups, under their absurd hats, and he would tell them nothing.

"*Did* you?"

Her insistence roused him from the secrecy of his thoughts; he recalled the question and considered it afresh: *her* question, what *she* wanted to know.

"Yes," he said boldly. "Yes I did—in a way."

She drew breath to reply. He saw her lips dilate to shape words, but before she had time to utter even the first syllable of the expletive which he knew must follow, he spoke again.

"But *that* wasn't wrong, not to *see*. I didn't *look*, I *saw*! If other people want to turn seeing into looking it's they who are wrong, not me, isn't it? So we needn't ever tell them, need we?" He felt his hands clasp convulsively together in front of him. "Oh please don't tell them, will you, Mother?"

He saw her eyes, pale as ever, falter; and her neck, braceleted with creases, flushed with quick pink as she replied, "No! But—"

She never finished; her voice was far, far away; it was more a memory even than the song of the thrush, and he smiled to himself as she turned away from him and opened the door that gave on to the garden.

He watched her hurry across the dimming lawn into the dusk, saw her black dress, her eager, thrusting little body become one with the darkness under the beech hedge, and turning, caught sight of himself in the long cracked summer-house mirror. Tall and thin, pale as Victoria, the shadows clung like fine dark hair to the temples of his forehead.

2. The First Wedding

Do you love me? Yes I love thee
Though I do not know what Love can be
If Love be separate from me
Or you be other than my love.

ᴥ THE FIRST WEDDING

She had seemed until this morning far away from him; Victoria had seemed so impossibly far away that from the very beginning of the term, he had refused to allow himself to think of her.

He was good at this "not thinking" now. It had taken him a few terms at the Abbey to learn the trick of it; but once mastered it had stood him in good stead, particularly at nighttime; for with the night, with lights out in the Browns at nine o'clock, the sharpest and the most lovely of his memories would seek admission (like visitors from home), through the still blue curtain of his cubicle, their aspects profoundly dear yet terribly changed.

The cubicle, with his name and school number printed clearly on the pasteboard slip:

BLAYDON J. 55

was their meeting place, their certain rendezvous, where, assisted by touches from Northumberland—a sprig of bell heather, a cushion cover from the old nursery, some letters and a photograph or two—they could be strongest and most importunate.

But this morning, with the arrival of Victoria's letter postmarked Richmond, the swift reply to his own hastily scribbled note of Sunday last, the rule had been waived; he could think of her again freely, for David had kept his promise and had invited her to his wedding.

True, she had to be back at her own school by 5:00 P.M., but that could easily be managed; John himself could take her back to Richmond on the Underground. They would roar along in one of those fiery red trains eating sweets and talking about the wedding; and perhaps at the end of it all, when the time came for him to make his own lonely way back to London and then four more confusing weeks at the Abbey, he would be clearer in his mind about Marston and know which of the two he loved the most and why.

Slyly, at his desk in the middle row of the classroom, he patted the crinkled envelope of Victoria's letter as it lay in his pocket, and then turned his head slightly so that he could see Marston's fair hair and dusky Madeira-sunned cheek as he leaned down over his desk and gazed intently at his *Chardinal.*

At that moment, Monsieur Camambert, totally forgotten until now, raised his grey head against the blackboard and addressed him.

"Blaydonne, you will now commence by translating from where Fleming 'as left off."

Remembering by some trick of the attention the last words Fleming had uttered, John found his place with a trembling finger and began to flute out the words. He felt suddenly triumphant, like a tightrope walker who has succeeded in doing a difficult pirouette and then swayed surely back on to his wire. Everything was going right for him today; nothing, he was sure, could go wrong; and, to crown it all, he would give the rest of them a lesson in French.

"*Dans notre jardin*," he began. "In our garden, *nous avons des fleurs rouges et blancs*, we have flowers both pink and white . . ."

Monsieur Camambert looked up, and a head or two swivelled.

"*Rouge?*" he demanded.

"Red."

"Not peenk, *mais* 'red'?"

"*Oui*—I mean, yes, sir."

Monsieur Camambert frowned; he never smiled; he was either very, very depressed or very, very irritable, and whichever he was, he was equally dangerous.

"Also," he went on, "I do not see zer word 'both' in my *Chardinal.* Perhaps you 'ave it in yours?"

"No, sir."

If only the old fool would let him get started, he thought; already the others were beginning to take the wrong sort of notice. He had intended to have their admiration this morning, especially Marston's; but if this went on they would soon, from mere force of habit, begin to laugh at him and by so doing would bring out the wasp in Monsieur Camambert.

"Very well, do not translate words satt are not there, Blaydonne. Proceed!"

"We have roses, I mean flowers, red and white," John said flatly. "*Nous avons aussi, des arbres et des petits oiseaux,* we have also trees and little birds, *qui chantent, tous les soirs,* which sing every evening."

He paused; did they never have big birds in France? Why were *les oiseaux* always *petits,* and he pictured to himself a swarm of minute birds whistling and creakling every evening in the delicate land of France.

"Well Blaydonne, why 'ave you discontinued? What is the difficulty?"

"No difficulty, sir—"

"Proceed."

"*Et dans l'Eté, nous avons des petits hirondelles—*"

Little what? Obviously some sort of a bird. He had looked it up last night with Marston. They had shared sugar cane from Marston's home in Madeira and he had told him all about his eldest brother's, David's, wedding on Saturday. He hadn't told him about Victoria though; he had wanted to, had longed in fact to tell him all about their bathing incident at the tennis tournament, the row with his mother and David's cleverness in smoothing her down by explaining that it was only their innocence which had made it seem so dreadful. But somehow he had been unable to mention Victoria at all last night; she had seemed out of place, "a home person" and therefore untouchable and unmentionable. Or at least so he had persuaded himself *then* though underneath he had had a feeling, scarcely acknowledged, that there had been another reason for his reserve, something very, very uncomfortable and wrong, if not actually wicked. But perhaps tonight, if Marston gave him the swimming lesson in the indoor bath and then came into his cubicle as he had promised, he would be able to tell him everything.

Under the swiftness of his thoughts, he had still sought the missing word and still automatically measured the pause which his delay had necessitated. "And in the summer," he repeated, "we have little—little—*cheeses*." The word projected itself into the silence before he even knew that it was there. Desperately he plucked at its tail, trying to crumple it down unnoticed by correcting himself loudly. "I mean sparrows, sir, Monsieur Camambert."

But already the expectancy, even the titters of the others, were filling the room. On the dais Monsieur Camambert was reaching for his red-ink pen. The fatal word, transmitted down the school year after year, never forgotten, never forgiven, was the centre of a joke almost as stored and yellow as the French master's goatee beard, and for him, still as prickly and as proud; the very last insult which he would receive or which John had intended.

Watching him search the pockets of his grey alpaca jacket for the tissue paper on which he wiped the nibs of his many pens, John saw the wedding and all that it meant receding like the train, the wonderful train to London which whistled and plumed over the marshes he could see from his cubicle window in the Browns.

His pen poised like a tiny arrow in his left hand, Monsieur Camambert looked up.

"One hour drill," he whispered.

"But sir—" John's ears were glowing, his eyes floating in the superfluity of unshed tears. If only he could explain; the pen was moving now, delicately and remorselessly over the slip of paper on the desk.

"For impertinence," said Monsieur Camambert with satisfaction, "it is *always* One Hour Drill."

"But sir, excuse me sir, couldn't you this once—I mean tomorrow is my brother's wedding day, and if the Badger—I mean Mr. Bedgebury—"

There was a roar of laughter from the others. Behind him Fleming put on his stage heroine voice.

"Tomorrow ith my wedding day," he squeaked in an absurd falsetto.

Someone let out a peal of contralto laughter, and at the back Beckett Major, the dullest and most unenterprising of them all, unleashed the only turn in his repertoire: a long low infinitely lewd and mournful passage of wind.

The sound of it, long continued, ending in a semitone that contrived to be at once a commentary and enquiry, so shocked them all that instantly there was silence.

Monsieur Camambert trembled. His usually pale yellow face took on momentarily the glow of health as his anger flushed up from his wing collar.

"*Two* hours drill. And leave the class," he pronounced in a whisper that sawed through the silence.

John gathered together his books and stumbled out between the hard corners of the desks and past the intimately known faces to the red-tiled passage.

He caught Marston when the class came out at twelve o'clock, managed to edge in behind him and follow him down to the locker room in the basement where one or two of the others were collecting their swimming kit. Seizing his chance, he stooped down beside him as he kneeled to open his locker.

"I say, you haven't forgotten about my swimming lesson, have you?" Marston's smooth cheek remained in profile; he did not even turn to look at him.

"What swimming lesson?"

"You know, you were going to teach me the crawl."

"Well, don't whisper about it," said Marston loudly as he closed his locker with a bang. "Fleming! I say Fleming! Shall we teach Blaydon how to do the crawl?"

Fleming came waltzing in from the dark passage, his swimming trunks in his hand and his towel around his neck. He looked at John sharply for a moment, as though he were unused to giving him his serious consideration; then his eyes turned up and his mouth opened slowly like a clown's showing his wet tongue and large white teeth.

"Oh, no," he sang, "we never teach worms how to do the crawl, do we?"

"Oh, no," said Marston.

Fleming seized him around the waist and together they executed the dance they were rehearsing for the end-of-term concert: a high kick to the left, a high kick to the right, and then a pause on tiptoes.

"Not even when tomorrow *is* their wedding day!"

"Not even then," shrieked Marston.

"Oh, no," said Fleming. "And anyway he likes *girls*, doesn't he?"

"Does he?"

"Yes," cooed Fleming. "He writes letters to them and dreams about them in the si-hilence of his cu-hubicle."

"Fishy! Fishy! Fishy!" said Marston. "In Madeira we call them—"

"And he's a holy holy Roman," said Fleming.

"I'm not!"

"Yes you are! You were confirmed by His Warship the Boss-shot of Lourdes last term, wasn't he?"

"Yes he was," said Marston.

"So if he wants to learn the crawl," said Fleming, "he should get the Holy Father to let him practise in the font."

"He should," said Marston, "in Madeira he'd be in the choir with all the dagos, and everyone knows what *that* means."

"In Madeira they're even queerer," shrieked Fleming, who had spent part of the summer holiday with Marston in Funchal. "Come on, let's get up to the baths and turf some other worm out of a cubicle."

They smiled at each other then as John had seen them smile after the summer sports, when they went up to get their prizes for three out of every five of the events. Then side by side, they rushed up the staircase leaving him in the dimness of the locker room heavy with its scent of old home-made cakes and incarcerated fruit.

He was still standing there trying to collect the absurd hurts of his grief into one recognizable whole so that he could deal with it adequately and make some plan for the remainder of the day when Spot Fisher came in and found him.

John looked with distaste at the small circular blemish on the tip of his nose. He hated Fisher both because he was a vicarage boy like himself and because he was a prowler and snooper who had never been found out by the masters. He was a Bishop's son and clever too, head of the school and by dint of his large pear-shaped head and summer tuition from his father had managed to get a scholarship to Eton. Next term, like John himself, he would be leaving; and already an ever more unsmiling air of responsibility was accompanying his every action and gesture.

"Ah there you are, Blaydon," he said. "I've been searching the school for you. Mr. Bedgebury wants to see you in his study."

"You mean the Badger."

"I meant what I said—Mr. Bedgebury."

"Suck-up," said John. "We can always *spot* a suck-up especially when he's got one on his nose."

It was weak and crude, unsatisfying, not nearly so good as the retort he would think of later; but it annoyed Fisher. His round mouth closed and he blinked as he leaned odiously forward.

"That's guff," he said. "I've half a mind to take you along to the Badger myself—to Mr. Bedgebury—to make sure you don't sneak out of it."

"Try it," said John. "I'll kick and scream all the way."

"You'll be doing that this afternoon; you've got two hours drill and the sergeant will be swiping your bottom every ten minutes."

"One of these days when I'm grown up I'll come back to this filthy school and I'll swipe the Sar'nt's behind every *five* minutes; and if you're anywhere about, I'll squash your nose so flat that no one will be able to see the spot any more."

"You're a nasty little squirt," said Fisher, "just what one would expect from a High Church vicarage, but I've no time to argue with you now. You'd better watch out for the rest of the term though, because I shall be on the lookout for you."

"Well mind you don't get spots in front of your eyes," said John edging quickly past the flying kick Fisher sent after him.

He made his way slowly up the stairs, whistling purposely out of tune and rasping his hand along the worn rail of the banisters. Reaching the corridor he straightened his tie and pulled out the flaps of his grey flannel pockets. The door to the gymnasium was open and the wide brown space empty. At the far end he could see the rack in which the wands were kept when not in use for punishment drill. Two hours, he thought, with the Sar'nt smoking that disgusting tobacco and strolling around flicking the tight little seats with his cane. Up and down, round and round, in and out, then places again, then up and down with that tense feeling at the back of the knees as the muscles stretched: the tickle of sweat and wool around the neck, the slow, sickly thumping in the head keeping time like a metronome with the tick of the unmoving clock on the far wall.

Next door there was water, cool and blue in the indoor baths; but there would be no swimming for the drill class. At the half-hour some would go; at the hour, he would be left alone with only the Sar'nt behind him.

Mother had never met the Sar'nt, neither had Father nor David nor any of them. Yet they had sent *him* here and given the Sar'nt complete control of him for two hours this afternoon. The Sar'nt, the Badger and the Toad, all of them or any of them could do what they liked to John here in the far south while they, the family and the home people, carried on their normal lives in the north where everything was perfect.

He could not even write to them about this afternoon, about Marston, about the interview with the Badger. By the time he wrote, it would be all over; it would be back in time, nothing could be done about it; and anyway, if he were to put it all in a letter, *everything*, it would take him weeks to write it, to make it sound real.

Outside the Badger's door he paused. Suddenly he was totally unconcerned with whatever might await him on the far side. He no longer even minded about the wedding tomorrow. If the Badger stopped him going it could make no real difference, might in fact be better in the end. What was the good of getting out of this world for a day when you knew you had to come back to it at night? It only meant more difficulty in stifling thoughts and longings afterwards, more difficulty in getting to sleep at night, in keeping alive and alert to it during the day.

They were none of them real: not the cricket matches, nor the Toad's Latin prose classes when he slung you about in your desk by your collar, nor the Sussex hens with their huge green turds and suspicious glances, nor the polite Church services, nor the giant matron, nor Spot Fisher, nor any of them. They were all just a punishment which everyone had to undergo, a taste of unhappiness to make home all the more real and desirable; all except Marston of course. Marston was real, because you loved him. He was beautiful like a girl and strong like a man. Only Marston could really hurt or harm you in this place because he was the only one you loved, and that meant that only the things you loved could be real; what you hated was always unreal. In future he would think only of the things he loved; he would no longer discourage them when they tried to sneak into his cubicle at night; he would welcome them and discover them afresh.

With one last tug at his tie he knocked on the door and the Badger's voice said, "Come in."

Above him, as he sat at his desk, there hung the portrait painted by the Old Boy who had worked in the gym last year putting the finishing touches to the picture which the school was presenting in commemoration of the Badger's fifty years at the Abbey. Beneath it, in unreal and somehow lifeless replica of the wizened face which looked out of the canvas, the Badger sat at the bottom of his glasses gazing through their bone-rimmed tunnels from the shadows which surrounded him.

The Badger rarely spoke; he was an old man of the night. Meticulously clean in his morning coat, gold-linked cuffs and high wing collar, he waited. A watch chain straddled the concavity of his sunken waistcoat and around his face the white hair stood out like a ruff.

The Badger waited as he had always waited, as thirty years ago he must have waited for Fleming's or for Fisher's father to commit himself and walk unwarily over one of the many deep caverns he had dug on the outskirts of his lair.

Behind his glasses the milky eyes blinked once and then resumed their distant vigil over John's forehead while he too waited obstinately knowing that there was plenty he could think about.

There were the Doctor's boxing gloves, for instance, there on the window sill behind him with the dust a little thicker than this time last year.

Who had the Doctor really been? And what had he really done? They said that he had loaded one of the gloves with a shoe of his sister's Shetland pony and that the Sar'nt had found him out. There were slits in the gloves all right, and they looked understuffed as though some of the horsehair had been removed. But there had been more than that about the Doctor. Perhaps, after an interview like the one John was just beginning, he had been expelled for something; for something worse than cheating and more serious even than fouling at boxing. But no one really remembered the Doctor; he was just a name perpetuated by the older boys who remembered having heard about him when they first came to the school. There were stories about his nickname; that it had been given him because he had been so good at biology. It was said that he had performed brilliant but terrible operations on the guinea pigs, toads and white mice which then, as now, the boys were allowed to keep in the school stable.

He might even be dead. He might have been the Doctor in the time of Fleming's father; a legend going back beyond Disraeli and Gladstone to the very founding of the school by Badger the First, or further than that. But even if he had never really been at the Abbey he was still inordinately there, a more powerful and frightening personality than any of the boys who had succeeded him.

In the outside lavs where the striped caterpillars could be picked off the surrounding bushes in the summer, they still pointed out the "Doctor's mark" high on the wall of the standups just beneath the never-silent cistern; and whether or not its significance was what they implied, no one, even after three glasses of lemonade, had ever been able to reach it.

But the Doctor had never been solely funny. One version of his story was that he had circumvented his expulsion by committing suicide in the indoor baths. He had come down the Browns' stairs early in the morning, they said, stolen the keys from the Badger's study and entered the swimming bath while it was in process of being cleaned. Only two or three feet of water and sediment covered its glazed white tiles, and the Doctor had climbed up on to the high board and then dived.

They even said that the little mound in the Toad's rose garden, carefully tended by his wife Kay, the Badger's daughter, was not the grave of a dog at all.

Thinking of it John shuddered; no matter what they did to him they should not do that. He would leave instructions as Shakespeare had, putting a curse on anyone who prevented his body from being put on a train for burial in Northumberland on the wide curlew-called moors. To be buried at the Abbey! To spend the rest of one's life, or rather one's death, at the school under the shadow of their lovelessness—

"Well?" The Badger had spoken at last; John, or rather the Doctor had won.

"Yes, sir?"

"I asked you what you wanted, Blaydon?"

"Did you sir? I'm sorry; I didn't hear you. I was told that you wanted me?"

"And you do not know why I should want you?"

"Yes, sir, I think so."

"Well?"

"About the drill sir, this afternoon."

"You mean tomorrow afternoon, Blaydon."

"*Tomorrow*, sir? I thought it would be this afternoon as usual."

The Badger blinked. His heart beginning to thump, John realized that beneath him the thin surface soil was already subsiding; in a moment it would give way and he would be deep in the rooty darkness of the trap.

"You are quite right, Blaydon. Drill will be this afternoon as usual for *those* who have the usual amendment to make. For others, and I believe you are the only one this year to have transgressed so far as to have been awarded the very unusual punishment of *two* hours drill, it will be tomorrow, Saturday; and Saturday, as you know, is a half-holiday, and will therefore permit of the school sergeant taking so long a period of detention without dereliction of his many other duties about the grounds."

"But sir—"

Now that it had happened he realized how false had been his nonchalance of a few minutes before; how loud and unavailing his whistling at the wedding in London where they would all most magically be: Mother, Father, Melanie, his brothers—and Victoria. And the train, the wild train hurtling over the marshes towards the tawny smokiness of London, he would not be on it; he would be here stooped under the shadows like the Doctor in the rose garden.

The horror was deeper than tears. He did not want to cry; he wanted to call out loud to whatever gods there were, powerful listening gods who would hear and understand and explain to the Badger and to them all that this was wrong; that no one had any right to behave like this, that the knots in the net spreading out from that one word in Monsieur Camambert's class, were knots tied by blind men in nothing more binding than cotton, and that they should be instantly broken.

But none of this could be said; it went on somewhere behind his eyes as a series of unfinished scarcely visualized pictures, and he realized that just as the Badger seemed to him to be so infinitely old that he was far away on a high hill, he himself must seem just like any ordinary boy to the Badger.

"Yes, Blaydon?"

"Nothing, sir. It was only that you gave me your permission to go to my brother's wedding tomorrow."

Could it be that he had forgotten, that it was not a trap after all? The Badger never forgot anything; his memory was as clean as his small cold-bathed body, as crisp as his white cuffs; but perhaps, this once, just this once, he had forgotten.

"You said you'd written to my people, sir."

"So I had." The words were really sad as though the Badger were more disappointed than was John himself. "But now I shall not have time to write to them again. I shall have to telegraph them at their London hotel."

"Yes, sir."

"Perhaps before you go, Blaydon, you could give me the address; your father omitted to mention it in his letter to me."

The Russell Hotel, Russell Square; but if he said he did not know it the Badger would not be able to tell them and they themselves might ring up.

"I'm afraid I don't know it, sir."

"Really?" He leaned slowly back in his chair so that it creaked. "Perhaps then it is just as well that this has happened, Blaydon; because you would have found it a little difficult, in your ignorance, to meet your parents for the luncheon they had arranged, would you not?"

"Yes, sir."

As clearly as John himself had seen it, the Badger had seen the lie; and he knew that for the Badger it had blotted out the last little chink of light at the bottom of his lair, had confirmed him of the rightness of the latest of his fifty years of actions as a headmaster. They looked at each other dully.

"Very well Blaydon, you may go."

"Thank you, sir."

He ran to the door as he had remembered running to doors all his life, quickly so that he might reach them before his sobs could be heard or the contortions of his face be apparent. In the passage, he closed it behind him and walked, holding his breath, back to the day room.

In the darkness, above the whispers and smuggled laughter of the others, he could hear, in the eaves, the hooing of the wind: wind, which, like thunder travelling down the sky over strange downs and distant towns, might only a few minutes before have resounded over the very roof of the Russell Hotel where the family were staying, where soon they would all themselves be going to sleep.

Even in the midst of their preoccupation, their gaiety and excitement over the family's first wedding, they must surely have thought of him and missed him a little. Nearer home, he was sure, Mother would never have permitted this awful thing to happen; she would personally have "tackled" the Badger and wanted to know exactly why John was being prevented from coming; and when she had heard the Badger's reasons she would either have overridden him by a storm of vehemence, or undercut him by a sudden display of extraordinary sweetness. She must have been too busy, too concerned with trying to appear smart and happy in front of Prudence's very London family; otherwise she would certainly have done something, for whenever she could find the time she loved him. She probably loved him as much as Nanny did and a great deal more than Melanie who, of late, had become much too full of herself to love anyone other than Mary, who was just an older and more powerful replica of Melanie herself.

Michael and Geoffrey of course would have accepted John's situation; they knew what schools were; and as for David, he could scarcely have been expected to remark his absence more than casually. But of course they none of them knew yet that he wasn't coming. To him his absence from something that had not yet taken place had already begun; for them it would not be apparent until tomorrow, and this time tomorrow night David would be on his way to Madeira with Prudence, to the island where sugar cane and custard apples grew by the warm sea in which Marston had learned to swim beautifully, powerfully, like a golden fish.

He thought of Marston, remembered his rebuffs of the morning, and in his heart, thudding there behind the fullness of his chest, he felt a sudden warmth, a glow which mounted like a blush through the column of his neck to the still thinking centre of his head. Behind his eyelids he felt this warmth initiating the tiny prickling movements which presaged tears. He was going to cry because tomorrow no one would miss him, neither those who were there nor those who were not; whereas he himself was already missing them.

If the Doctor really had crept down those stairs in the morning and gone into the swimming bath while it was yet scarcely day, then he must have done it after just such a night as this. How did they know, how did anyone know what the Doctor had suffered first? For anyone to understand why he, John, wept like this, they would have to know everything: all about Victoria and what it had meant to dream in the daylight of seeing her again, all about the wedding, all about the showing off in the French lesson, the lie to the Badger, the anticipation of two hours under the Sar'nt, the wind that blew from London and the ship that would be sailing for Madeira. They would have to know all this and a lot more he scarcely knew himself; they would have to be God, and even God didn't care.

The Doctor might, if he knew; if he were still alive somewhere, either in this world or another. Yes, the Doctor might care.

Still weeping quietly, he got out of bed and climbed out on to the half window sill he shared with Figgis in the next cubicle. Under the moon beside the ilexes he could see the rose garden where the Doctor must lie. If anyone came, if a shadow formed out there where the shadows were and then moved across the playing field to stand with its grey face smiling up at him, he would not be afraid; he would throw up the window and shout to him eagerly and dive as *he* had dived, down and down on to the hard asphalt.

He shuddered. Behind him, the rings of the curtain were shaken softly. Someone was there. Not daring to look behind him, scarcely breathing, he waited; and again he heard it, the whisper of metal being drawn over metal; then silence, until someone touched him on his heel. He turned then, his whole skin creeping, his tears trickling unheeded down his face.

"Who is it?" he whispered.

"Shut up! It's me of course, get into bed you ass; we can talk there."

Marston's breath hissed against his ear, and obediently he got down from the sill and scrambled into his bed. Marston got in beside him, and having lifted the pillows on to their faces, pulled up the clothes high against the head of the bed.

"What were you doing?" he whispered, "peeing out of the window?"

"No."

"Well, what were you doing?"

"I don't know—I was just—"

"Good Lord! Are you blubbing?"

"Yes."

"Why? Because you're afraid you won't be allowed to go to your brother's wedding?"

"Yes, partly."

"You *are* a kid, aren't you?"

"No, not really; only you see I had been looking forward to it. I was going to meet—" John hesitated; it was no good, he just could not mention Victoria's name to Marston.

"Who were you going to meet? Your people?"

"Yes."

"Well you'll be seeing them in four weeks' time, so why blub about it?"

"Don't you ever want to see your people before the end of term?" John asked.

"Of course I do, but I don't blub about it. I've got my friends."

"You mean Fleming?"

"Yes—and someone else."

"Who else?"

"You, of course."

"*Me?* Do you think I'm your friend?"

"Of course I do." One of Marston's arms came swiftly around his shoulders. "You're a funny devil, still an awful kid considering that this is your last term, but I like you. I nearly asked you home to Madeira with me last vac, you know."

"*Did* you?"

"Yes. If only you weren't such a wet at games I would have asked you with Fleming."

"I see."

Marston's body was warm against his own, the intimacy of his breathing filled and made wonderful the blackness within the bed. It was unbelievable that everything could have changed so much in so short a time. Gratitude leapt up in him as though a prayer had been answered. A few minutes ago he had been alone, had wickedly longed to die by throwing himself out of the window; and now, in a matter of minutes, he had found a friend, someone whispering to him and understanding him, confessing to liking him and holding him in his arms.

"What are you thinking about?" asked Marston.

"I was thinking about the Doctor."

"The Doctor? What on earth for?"

"I was wondering whether that *was* his grave in the rose garden."

Marston laughed. "You ass! Of course it isn't. The Doctor was expelled years ago."

"What for?"

"Can't you guess?"

"Was it for—for—?"

"Yes," breathed Marston, "for this" and suddenly he kissed him softly on the cheek.

John lay still; his delight stealing over him as swiftly as his tears had done, and like them leaving him suddenly cold and shrunken in its wake. But he remembered them and all of the confusion that had accompanied them. If this were wrong then so were they.

"Were you really going to invite me to Madeira last hols?"

"Yes."

"Well then I love you, Marston, I love you."

Marston said nothing, but his arm about John's neck tensed and for a moment they lay in silence under the pillows. John thought suddenly of Victoria, of the whiteness of her body as she had stood above the lake, and of the softness of her skin against his own as he swam with her to the bank. Girls always wanted to be loved; they were always wondering about it. Men were supposed to love them. But he wanted to be loved as much as he wanted to love. Who was Victoria and who was he? This, he realized suddenly, was what he had wanted all the time; this which was happening now was the measure of his greed for her and its only true expression; and the wedding, the marriage of their two selves, of the self that wanted only to be loved and the self that wanted only to love must end like this. In some mysterious way the self that was him and the self that was Victoria could only finally unite into a self that was them both, in a darkness, a secrecy, and a delight that was like this.

Marston's hand stole over his chest, stroked the skin over the muscles gently and hesitated. Like a bell alarming a sleeping household, something quivered in the rapture of John's thoughts. At a touch the whole dream of Victoria vanished and the intimation of that other world of weddings and blossom and ships rocking over foreign seas was dissolved like sugar disappearing in vinegar.

He hurled the pillows from him and sat up.

"What's the matter?"

Beside him Marston also sat up.

"What were you doing?"

"I wasn't doing anything."

"Yes you were." The words spoken aloud echoed from the wooden walls of the cubicle.

"Shut up you fool," hissed Marston. "Lie down and keep quiet or you'll get us both sacked."

He put his arm around John's neck and attempted to force him back against the pillow. John thrust himself violently away from the strong grasp and with his free hand punched out hard into the shadows beside him; he felt his fist jab and slip on the wet mouth, and, as Marston's grip slackened, leapt sideways out of the bed. Beside him, as he sought to regain his balance in the darkness, the iron washstand with its contained jug and basin teetered on its three legs, paused, and then crashed to the bare floor. They heard the jug fracture like a giant egg and the immediate wash of water under the bed followed by the steady drip drip from the larger sections of the basin. Horrified and unmoving they kept their positions in the silence, and John counted the seconds waiting for the passing of time to make them safe. If no one spoke, if no one moved, if no lights went on, or if someone laughed or called out idly for whoever it was to "shut up!" everything would be all right.

"You little turd," whispered Marston. "You've made my nose bleed. In the morning I'll—"

He was interrupted by the screech of the curtain rings as they were drawn swiftly over the metal bar above the doorway. A torch blazed upon them from the passage between the opposing rows of cubicles and someone stepped on to the wet floor. It was Fisher.

"What's going on in here, Blaydon?"

"Nothing," said John.

"Don't lie, what's Marston doing in your bed?"

"He was blubbing," said Marston, "and I came in to see what

was the matter and he said he wouldn't tell me unless I got into his bed with him."

"I didn't," said John. "I tried to kick him out because he was kissing me. I *was* blubbing, but it wasn't anything to do with anyone—I was quite happy really."

Fisher smiled slowly. "So you were quite happy really, and yet you were blubbing? And nothing was going on in here, and yet you've broken a jug and had another chap in your bed. One of you is obviously lying, and I think I know which I prefer to believe. Marston, get back to your own cubicle. I shall report this in the morning."

Marston got out of the bed and stood beside him.

"Now look here Fish, don't go and make a stink," he whispered urgently. "Remember what we arranged at the beginning of term. This little turd simply isn't worth a chaos with the Badger. I can explain everything to you if you'll only give me the chance. Fleming knows about it; we could neither of us get to sleep because of the noise Blaydon was making snivelling around his cubicle."

Fisher looked at him quickly.

"I don't think you need say any more, Marston," he said. "If Blaydon got you in here by pretending to be ill and then forced you to get into his bed, there's nothing more to be said." He smiled. "Your nose is bleeding; how did that happen?"

"He hit out at me when I wasn't expecting it," said Marston. "He said he was lonely and scared of the Doctor. I think he's barmy."

"No, not barmy," said Fisher, "just a nasty little squirt with nasty ideas like the Doctor." He sniggered, "And he'll probably end up like him too—by being expelled."

John sat down on the bed. Expelled from what? he thought; you can't be expelled from nothing. Adam and Eve were expelled from Paradise; the world from which they were driven had been beautiful. Everything in it, trees, flowers, birds and beasts were doing and being what they were meant to do or to be. When they went out, when they passed the angel with the flaming sword, they did not walk into a wilderness but into a jungle where nothing did what it was meant to do. But if he were to be expelled from the Abbey he would be going out of, not into, a jungle, and nothing beyond its bounds could be more confusing or twisted than the things which lay within it. He should never have been sent there, they should never have sent him there. He got up.

"Get out of my cubicle," he shouted. "Get out, you liars! Beastly liars both of you—get out or I'll *kill* you." He stooped suddenly and picked up a piece of the broken basin. They backed away from him as he crouched forward towards them. Above them, in the next cubicle, Figgis' head appeared; below the crumpled ruff of hair the face gazed down upon them mutely, the mouth loosely opened. Above it, against the rafters of the Browns' ceiling, the electric light flicked to life.

They heard the measured thuds of the Toad's tread, and in a moment, square, warty and malarial, he filled the doorway of the cubicle.

The eyes with the yellowed whites moved speculatively from one to the other of them, the square, perpetually sulky face hung above them with dreadful displeasure as they stood there on the wet floor by the bed.

The Toad spoke: "Fighting eh? Cut along to my study."

He stepped back into the passageway and they sidled out and made their way over the cold linoleum to the corridor. Behind them the Toad summoned Fisher.

"I want you, Fisher."

"Yes, sir."

John and Marston slowed down like dogs hearing the call of their master and the Toad's Sandhurst bellow rolled down the corridor.

"*Not* you two. Move on there! Wait for me in the study. *Double* up!"

They ran: straight past the entrance to the Greens, the door to Matron's rooms, the bathrooms and the new bug's dormitory and fumbled windily at the green baize which separated the school from the schoolhouse. John opened it and they found themselves in the Badger's warm world, a world of red Turkey carpets, oak chests and Church-of-England chairs.

Down the stairs they padded over the shining stair rails to the hall and then past the chair with its yellowing notice, DON'T WORRY, SMILE into the Toad's study next to the dining room.

"Shut the door," said Marston.

"No, he'll think we've been talking."

"Well half-shut it then."

John closed it as far as he dared and Marston moved over to him.

"You know what he'll do tomorrow, don't you?" he whispered.

"Make us box."

"Yes, and if you say anything about loving-up, I'll beat you up so badly your mater'll want to bury you."

"Spot will have told him anyway, so I don't see the point," said John.

"No he won't."

"How do you know?"

"He thinks I'm gone on *him*, that's why."

"That won't stop him; he hates me more than he likes you." Marston smiled.

"Well that's just too bad for *you*, Blaydon."

"I know it is; but I don't care. You're stronger than me and a better boxer, but you won't be able to hurt me—or if you do you'll only make me blub."

"You wait and see—"

"I *am* waiting."

"When I've finished with you, you'll wish you *were* the Doctor."

"I do already."

Marston's lips pursed and he spat out a little puff of breath.

"You're barmy, Blaydon, barmy."

"I know," said John.

"Barmy Blaydon!" Marston looked suddenly satisfied with himself as though he had made a happy decision. "I'll tell you what, you don't really think I was going to invite you to Madeira, do you? Not really?"

"You said so."

Marston put back his head in the way Fleming had and tittered up at the ceiling.

"Invite *you*? To *Madeira*? It was just a cod, that's all. I'd sooner invite a dago to England."

"Well, why did you say so then?"

"Mind your own business."

"Yah yah! Feeble," said John. "You're a coward like me really, and *you've* got nothing to be cowardly about."

"No I haven't, but I hate this stinking place just as much as you do and that's why I'm going to bloody you up in the morning when the Sar'nt puts us in the ring."

"I know something about you," John said. "I've just discovered it. I wonder whether I'll tell you."

Marston looked unconcerned. "Nothing *you* could tell me would worry me."

"This will!" said John.

"Well, what is it?"

"You hate dagos, don't you? You're always talking about them, aren't you? And I've just realized why. It's because you're half a dago yourself. You look like a dago, look at your skin; you're fat and smooth and you live in Madeira. One of your people must be a dago and that's why you hate them. You hate yourself and whatever you do to me you'll go on hating yourself afterwards."

He stopped, appalled at the change in Marston. His face had turned grey; he seemed to be standing in a different way, limply like a scarecrow; he looked small and weedy. Then, as John watched him, he saw a flush bright as a scarlet rag appear on either cheek; he saw the lower lip drawn in between the white teeth and bitten so that the blood from it began to mingle with that which had flowed from his nose. Marston's eyes were bright with a hatred which he had never seen before, a hatred that seemed to gather up and contain within it all the hatred he had himself felt throughout that day, and he was terrified by its intensity. He cringed:

"I'm sorry, Marston, I'm terribly sorry. I don't know what made me think of it and if you hate me, then you are right to hate me. Let me off, please let me off. If you'll let me off I'll do anything you say, anything at all."

But for a few moments Marston seemed not to be there; it

was as though the measure of his anger had swept him to a different place, separating him from John, making them invisible to
one another.

"All right," he said at last. "Do you know what I want you
to do, Blaydon?"

"No, but I'll do it. I promise."

"I want you never to speak to me or look at me again for the
rest of the time you're here."

"Well I won't then." He was chilled. "Is that a bargain?"

"No," said Marston, "it's not, because I'm going to make such
a mess of you that you won't want to anyway." And he laughed
again for the last time, jubilantly, his brown eyes glinting out
from between his screwed-up eyelids.

Behind him the door opened and the Toad came in. They
looked at his face and saw at once that Fisher had told him
everything. His thick lips drooped at the corners and between
his eyebrows was the single crease-mark of the active frown he
so seldom wore. His head was carried a little higher than usual
so that they immediately stood to attention. They thought of
the Great War, of pictures they had seen in the war diaries in
Kay's drawing room: generals and grim colonels talking to politicians in the trenches, or putteed ranks of men standing stiffly
on parade grounds.

He glanced at them and then looked over their heads to the
wall on which the regimental photographs were symmetrically
arranged.

"We don't discuss things like this—filth of this sort," he said.
"You'll find the head boy in the gymnasium. Put your running
kit on—and your boxing gloves."

At the door John hesitated.

"Sir?"

The Toad turned swiftly.

"Unless you are ready in three minutes, Blaydon, I will myself
cane you before you fight."

In the gymnasium Fisher had marked out in chalk a square of
the correct measurements and they took up their positions in
opposite corners. The Toad walked in and leaned against the
wall bars. He looked brown, a brown and yellow man fully

grown in the way that an animal is fully grown; he did not look happy or unhappy; he crossed his feet and took a silver stop watch out of his pocket. He looked up.

"Would you say they were evenly matched, Fisher?"

"Yes, sir."

"What age are you Blaydon?"

"Twelve and a bit sir."

"Marston?"

"Twelve."

"Good. You will box three two-minute rounds and you will box hard. If I suspect either of you of pulling his punches that boy will forfeit all half-holidays for the remainder of the term. And now—first round. Time!"

They came out into the middle of the square, touched gloves and hit out. Marston's left glove jarred hard and hateful on to John's nose and before he could see where he had moved to he felt the immediate violence of a bruising blow on his upper lip. He had been hit twice almost before they had started and all he could see was the brave shine of Marston's hair standing up from his head in the falling light. He looked awfully beautiful. His face was flushed, his cheeks smooth and furry as those of an apricot, and he was smiling. He circled expertly around John and came in again. He kept his shoulder full in front of his chin, and in front of that his right glove hovered like a dark brown balloon. He came even closer and John started to weave his left hand from side to side wondering where he was going to be hit next. If Marston came very close he might be able to hurt him, he decided; he remembered something the Sar'nt had said about an uppercut in close fighting. If he could only land an uppercut, one that came from the floor with all his back muscles behind it and his long wiry arm like a thin hammer to carry his hatred into that lovely face.

"Barmy!" whispered Marston. "Barmy Blaydon."

And then his fists in their smooth tight gloves started to streak and thud out under the light; one skidded off John's cheek from under his right eye and another, agonizing as freezing water, crashed on to the root of his nose. Briny blood trickled between his lips and Marston's hammering body jerked against him. He could smell the leather and the sweat as he bent his knees and let his right hand drop down towards his stomach allowing his heels to rest on the floor. And then suddenly he straightened himself to all of his gristly height and simultaneously drove his right glove up into the air below Marston's chin. It travelled up like the shot that rang the bell at the fair in Beddington, it travelled to almost the full extent of his reach and hit nothing. Marston laughed and came in again; he had time to hit John twice, once on the Adam's apple, before the Toad called out, "Time."

They separated and sat down in their corners.

Fisher came over with the bucket and a towel and dabbed cold water on John's lip and nose. The Toad looked up. "You are not fighting, Blaydon!" he said. "If you don't fight in the second round you will fight a fourth round—if necessary, a fifth round. This is the last warning I shall give you."

John said nothing. The blow on his throat had made it painful even to breathe; it seemed to be clinging there like a crab. He was thinking of Marston's face. It must be possible to hit it; if he could only hit it once it would be enough, for he would know then that it was real, that unlike everything else, the lies, and the truth he had never found, the fear and the hope, it was something immediately solid on which he could be revenged.

Next time he would watch it not only with his eyes but with his mind as well, and wherever it moved, wherever Marston's will might take it, he would follow it, reach out to it and smash it. He would smash everything; all the misery of the night, the empty day that was to come, the Toad's disbelief and Fisher's complicity. He would load his glove as the Doctor had done, not with a horseshoe, but with the steel of hatred that should be drawn to Marston's face as though to a magnet.

He pushed Fisher to one side and got to his feet. The Toad called out, "Box" and he ran in to meet Marston for the second time. His gloves slid past the touch and straight on towards the blushing face; but they met only the leather of the countering fists as Marston, dodging neatly to one side, buckled John's ear with his left hand and swayed away like a Jack on a spring.

John turned then and ran at him, remembering only his face,

his sweet confident face; it was distinct again, the hair looser than ever under the light and suddenly it was easy to realize and reach it. If he hit straight out at him, Marston would move to the right as he had done before; but if he *aimed* to the right, it would be there waiting for him. He pretended to hit with his left and then quick as thought sent out his right glove to the empty space beside Marston's head; and it landed. The head jerked backwards and John hit it again right and left with all his force.

Marston took in a breath and jabbed John on the chest. He shook his golden head and then came at him with blood dripping from his nose and making rouge marks on his cotton zephyr; a blow landed in the V of John's chest and remained there, blocking his windpipe so that he could take in no air and fought on a string suspended from some point high above him. He tried the uppercut again, and this time it came right up under Marston's chin, but it was weak and made no difference. Marston seemed to be propping him up; if he had not been there John would have fallen, but they were fighting very close now and Marston's body supported him like a galloping horse; he was hit in half a dozen places and he could do nothing. He prayed for the Toad to call out, "Time," and when the voice came he wobbled across to his corner and sat down on the boards within the chalked right angle.

Fisher stayed with Marston for a few minutes and then came over to him.

"You've cut his eye, Blaydon," he said.

"Go away!" said John. He felt noble. He was enjoying the blood and the pain. If this were the worst that anybody could do to him he despised them all. If Fisher loathed Marston, if Marston loathed himself, and if the Toad loathed all three of them and wanted them to suffer, then, once they had suffered they were beyond him and there was no longer any need to be afraid of anything.

"You've got a better reach," Fisher whispered urgently. "Use it, Blaydon, and you'll beat him; you'll spoil his beauty like Jack Dempsey in America."

"Fizz off!" said John. "You stink like a fish."

In the third round they fought all the time. What Fisher had advised was sound: John never allowed Marston to remain close to him. He darted in, hit or was hit by him, and then backed away; the blows no longer hurt either of them; they were like drunken supermen, out of breath, their gloves as heavy as Sussex flints and their legs and feet clumsy and unimportant. They both bled freely, and in the engagement of their eyes there was no longer any hatred, only a dull hostility, an unspoken agreement that they could no longer harm one another and that they had lost all interest in what they were supposed to be doing, only waiting without even impatience to return to their beds.

At the end of the round, the Toad sent Fisher upstairs and, still leaning against the bars, addressed them. "As I said before, there is to be no discussion of this either now or at any time in the future. As far as the rest of the school is concerned you were caught fighting in the Browns and then given the usual opportunity of settling your differences in the gym. Do you understand?"

"Yes, sir."

"Very well then, see that you obey me."

"Yes, sir."

"You both fought reasonably well, but I think I should tell you that if anything of this sort occurs again, you will both leave the school immediately."

"Yes, sir."

"Marston, you may go. Wash and return to your cubicle. Blaydon, come here. I think you should know that your mother telephoned the school this evening and that Mr. Bedgebury has consented to your attending your brother's wedding in London tomorrow. In view of the fact that you did your rather poor best tonight I shall recommend that your punishment drill be deferred until Tuesday of next week."

"Oh, thank you, sir."

"You had better see Matron first thing in the morning about that eye of yours."

"All right sir."

"Cut along now." Remaining as he was the Toad reached out and switched off all the lights.

John left him there filling his pipe in the darkened gymnasium and followed Marston up the wooden stairs to the Browns.

Binns, the Badger's chauffeur, took him down to the station in the morning and saw him on to the train.

It had been arranged by Mother on the telephone that he should take a taxi straight to St. Juliana's and meet the family there at eleven o'clock. He was sorry in a way that the wedding was so early because it meant that he could not have lunch on the train and he loved lunch on the train. He had the change from two pound notes in his pocket, enough to have lunch *and* a bottle of cider; enough to sit in the Pullman with the frosty fields streaming past the window, with the wires sagging down the glass and being punched rhythmically upwards again silently and inevitably by each telegraph pole all the way to London.

He knew that this morning he was looking white and queer, and therefore most especially he would have liked cider today; it would have restored his self-confidence and made him feel splendidly noticeable. When they went through a tunnel he could see his reflection in the window: the ugly girth of the upper lip, his left eye smaller than his right owing to the swelling of the lid where Marston had hit him in the second round.

He wondered what they would all think when they saw him; probably it wouldn't even be worth making out that it had been an heroic fight, a question of honour, because they wouldn't be interested. Mostly they would all be looking at David and Prudence in the way people did at weddings, greedily, as though there were something special about them that might never show or be seen again. But Victoria would notice; she would wonder what had happened to him. She might not like him because of it, it might embarrass her and make her decide to ignore him and pay attention to someone else. But he didn't think so; she wasn't like that, and as soon as he could explain in a roundabout way that but for her it would never have happened, she might even be pleased that he'd fought for her. Yes, she might; and if she were pleased it would have been worth it.

He sat farther back in his corner and looked at the other people in the carriage. They were all very correct and old; nobody young except himself. They seemed to be annoyed at having to travel together, sat very carefully in their own places with their own things above them on the rack and their own papers, hand-bags, pipes and magazines in their hands. They would obviously have liked it better if the seats had been subdivided by glass partitions with little blinds that could be drawn down so that they would not have to know whether or not anyone was next to them; and yet, if the train crashed, if there were lurches and shrieks from the wheels on the rails, thumping rendings and tearings from the front or the rear and a few people killed, they would probably be very kind and very friendly, sharing their thermos flasks and biscuits with the dying and with one another, and tearing up their shirts and pyjamas to make bandages. People always were kind when things were bad enough. However silent and separate they might have been when things were going well and they were moving safely from one place to another, they would link arms and sing when ships foundered. Perhaps Mother had been right when she had said that disaster was necessary. He was sure that when she got to Heaven she would occasionally prod God if she felt that things were going too smoothly down below.

After the Lewes stop he went into the corridor and walked down into the guard's van. It was full of the usual leathery smell as though it had been carrying a cargo of sheepskins overnight. There were a number of packing cases, three milk churns and a sad-looking dog in a box with a barred door. The guard was absent and John sat down in his seat and looked out through the window directly along the sides of the leading carriages. From this position it was possible to see that they were not travelling in a straight line as he had imagined but in a series of beautiful curves, winding along between hills, villages and towns, gliding over embankments and slicking through sinuous cuttings. They could not go wrong; the driver had only to watch the signals and keep his hands on the right levers, and, provided the signal-men were awake, by twenty to eleven the train would inevitably have reached Victoria Station however many curves and digres-sions it might have made on the way. Were he in charge of it he would make it go even faster; he wanted to get there; he wanted to see them all; and then, afterwards, if he could, slip away somewhere with Victoria, take her a long way back to school and tell her very nearly everything.

He had hardly slept at all during the night. In his imagination he had travelled the railway to London over and over again, had been through the wedding and the reception twenty or thirty times working out ways of fitting everything into them: Victoria, the family, the talk with David and Prudence, and then Victoria again. And now as the train clicked and swayed on the shining rails, as the tunnels and telegraph poles flicked past, as the churns rattled and the dog whimpered in its locked box, he dozed contentedly against the red plush cushion and waited for the terminus to arrive.

As soon as they crossed the Thames and began to slow down at the approach to the station, he went back to his carriage, collected his boater and camera, and was first out on to the platform. He found a taxi quite easily, jumped into it, and was swirled swiftly around Buckingham Palace and deposited a few minutes later outside the sooty porch of St. Juliana's.

Just as he had imagined it, there was the red-and-white striped awning jutting out over the pavement, the red carpet, and the rows of patent leather limousines. The organ was playing and an usher, after looking at his card, led him into the nave and down the wide centre aisle.

At first he could not see the family at all; the pews were full of half-familiar backs and shoulders, shiny straw hats concealing profiles he only vaguely remembered. At last, however, he recognized Mrs. Walton and two of the Walton girls looking as though they had been taken out of a cupboard, dusted and polished and put on show on some proud chimney piece; and when someone else turned as he passed and flashed him a familiar wink from beneath hair as compact and yellow as brass, his heart hesitated with immediate grievous delight as he recognized Simpson with Lizzie beside him, and next to her, Cissie Booth, the housemaid.

But the others! He could not think how they had all come, nor why they had set out. There were people like the Hadleys whom he had only seen once at a point-to-point race meeting, and who always said that everything was "bleak"; there was

Fischmann, David's Oxford friend who wrote books about foreign poets, and with him an ex-grammar-school boy who made a living by selling tinted antique maps to his friends; there was Emma Huggins, Grace Boult and her husband, the auctioneer, who could talk faster than any grownup he knew and who had a whole collection of jew's-harps in his sitting room in Beddington, while in a sombre little group halfway down the aisle there were two moth-bally pews full of more humble parishioners: Lizzie's father whom Mother had forced to sign the pledge, Mrs. Mudd with her crow feather hat, Ernie Smelt, and Gladys, the girl who always fainted at the Eucharist. It would not have surprised him to see Fish Harry there in his white apron with his basket and spring scale beside him on the seat of the pew. And seeing all these people, so much a part of his own peculiar and individual home life, he began to feel very important and to wish more than ever that he had been looking his best.

Mother must have hired a charabanc to fetch everyone down here all the way from Beddington, and he realized that there was something extraordinarily grand and *Blaydonish* about the mixture of them. If only Father had been a bishop, a gentleman bishop, or better still a lord, then this would have been like one of those *Tatler* weddings where the tenants were given beer outside the stables while their wives curtsied to the Rolls-Royces sweeping past the second lodge.

But still, he thought, it was a pretty good effort and he bet that Victoria was very much impressed. Thinking of her, he immediately stopped in the middle of the aisle. The usher beckoned him but he took no notice; and then he saw her—the swift white smile from beside Mother's shoulder, the creamy schoolgirl-hat with the brim flattened against the nape of her neck. He had just time to feel his face spreading delightedly outwards into the flush and expansion of his own answering smile, before he was shown into his pew, the second from the front and immediately behind hers as she sat beside Mother and Father. He himself, he found, was sitting between Michael and Nanny. He squeezed Nanny's nervous hand, leaned over and kissed Mother, smiled at Father, wonderfully tall and parsonic in a morning coat, and then kneeled down on the blue hassock and said his prayers.

She was here, they were all here; the whole of Home, the whole of Northumberland; and she was with them. Wonderful David to have kept his promise and won Mother around about Victoria and Mrs. Blount. Afterwards, he would thank him; he would even try to like Prudence and hope that she too would be happy even though she was taking him away from them all. For there would never be anyone like David again; Geoffrey was in Canada, farming and going bankrupt, Michael was an owl-face and would probably become a solicitor, while Melanie and Mary didn't count, they were just two halves of one person, replicas of one another, both red-haired and as boringly predictable as marmalade cats. He crossed himself and eased himself back on to the pew, edging up as close as possible to Nanny. On her opposite side Melanie leaned over to him.

"Whatever's happened to your face, John? You look awful."

"I don't feel it, I feel wonderful," he whispered back.

"It's all swollen."

"I know," he lied scornfully, "I had eight teeth out yesterday."

He was longing to attract Victoria's attention but was intimidated by her nearness to Mother; he also wanted to see what was going on up at the altar and make sure that David was there with the best man, Alexander Flood.

Alexander was very aristocratic and drank whisky. He was a school friend of Michael's and John remembered the discussion about his suitability during the summer holidays. Mother had said that she didn't want David going out on a lot of "daft stag parties" the night before, and Michael had said that he was Lord Remove's nephew and would therefore be bound to meet with the approval of Prudence's side; and this, though it had not stopped her writing warning letters to David, had finally decided her in Alexander's favour.

Suddenly the organ paused and everyone stood up. There was a rustle all the way down from the back of the church, the organ started to play again and everyone turned around. Prudence, with her uncle beside her and followed by twelve bridesmaids, including Mary and the third Walton girl, came slowly down the aisle and passed through the arch of the rood screen to the chancel. The tremors of the organ died away and there was a silence into which the voice of the priest rose indistinctly.

Now that they had all gone beyond the rood screen the remainder of the church seemed darker even than before. The congregation picked up the cards on which the order of service was printed and waited eagerly for the first hymn. In front of him, John saw Mother tweak Father's sleeve impatiently; Father leaned over her reassuringly and patted her shoulder very quickly and gently as he always did when he suspected that she might be going to be upset. But he had misunderstood her, and lowering her lorgnette, she looked up at him fiercely and whispered, "Change places with me, Teddy. I can't see anything."

"What's that, dear?"

"Oh," she breathed, "don't be so tiresome! I'm stuck down here and I can't see over that great screen." And she started to burrow angrily behind him until she forced him to step out into the aisle and was thus enabled to take his place.

Once there she craned out over the upright of the tall pew, gazing through her lorgnette and through the archway of the rood screen, as still as a small statue. From where he stood John could see the side of her cheek and just the translucent segment of one pale eye to whose lid clung a half-formed tear which she brushed impatiently away. The hand holding the printed card was trembling and when the first hymn began she was so rigidly preoccupied in trying to see what was going on up at the altar that she quite forgot to join in the first verse; and this, as Nanny would have said, was "very surprisin," because usually Mother sang very loudly and eagerly and always at first a little faster than anyone else. She prided herself on not stopping at the end of a line unless there were a comma, and those of the family who were sitting near her took their time from her, so that by the middle of the hymn at the latest, most, if not all, of the congregation, like herself, would be just half a bar in front of the organ.

But today she did not seem to be at all interested in the singing and even her amens were quieter than usual. When they knelt she no longer sank her face into her hands, but at every possible opportunity raised her lorgnette in an attempt to see the kneeling figures just visible between the opposing lighted rows of the bridesmaids as they stood in the chancel.

Her attention, so desperate, as intense as though everything— the course of the service, David's happiness, and even the future of all the bridesmaids gathered up there before the altar—depended upon it, was very distracting. It was like being near someone in great pain, someone whom agony had deprived of speech so that she was no more than a mute and dreadful presence claiming all of one's sympathy and allowing no thought which was not directed towards herself.

In front of him, only a few feet away, he could see Victoria as she stood and kneeled in unison with him. Her ears, he knew, heard the same swells and chords of the music from the great grey pipes of the organ; her eyes sought the chancel and the bride and he was sure that she longed to turn and smile at him intimately just as he himself longed to acknowledge the secret which they shared and which the smile would express. But neither of them could do so because they were both involved in and fascinated by Mother; and he knew that they were not the only ones. Beside him, the others were all watching her. Glancing down his pew he could see that although they were pretending to sing and pray, their eyes continually strayed to all that they could see of her from their different positions; and he was sure they were afraid that at any moment one or other of them would have to go to her and be near her; and what was more, they were watching jealously; he was sure of it; anxious to be the first to stand by her side if she should start openly to weep or to demand a change in the order of the service, the positions of the bridesmaids, or even a postponement of the whole ceremony.

He tried hard to switch his mind away from her, away from them all, to think only of Victoria standing in front of him, to remember the things they had written, said and promised in the long days of the old summer and in their constant secret letters to one another.

But it was very nearly impossible. Even in the opposing pews he noticed that heads were turning and taking swift looks at Mother. She must have attracted their attention when she and

Father stepped out into the aisle at the beginning of the service; and now everyone sensed the uneasiness of the family, the anxiety which had spread back down the "home" side of the church to the very last row of pews.

Mrs. Cable, and Josephine, Prudence's sister, and their immediate relatives and friends were beginning to look silently disapproving. They were all very smart people and even before the service began he had known that they were different in every way from his own people. The men stood more casually and the women looked more used to their clothes; it was obvious that they had worn fine and expensive things before and had not just borrowed or bought them especially for the occasion. There were fewer of them too; the pews were less liberally filled and there were no common people at all. There were one or two stuck-up looking boys, some girls with plaits and several pink-faced men with big stomachs, carnations and proud white hair; and all of them, he was sure, had their weather eye on the Blaydon front pews and on Mother.

He began to pray earnestly that nothing would go wrong. He apostrophized God and said, "I will not think even of Victoria, O God, if you will only promise that Mother will not *do* anything, that she will just keep quiet until the end of the service." And then he began to think of David and thanked God hurriedly for having put him on the far side of the rood screen where he could not see Mother and where she could only see his back.

He prayed so hard that he forgot to listen out for the promises of David and Prudence, and this was a leaden disappointment. He had longed to hear them saying, "I do" and, "I will"; to mark David's voice saying, "For richer for poorer, for better for worse, in sickness and in health," but he was so concentrated on his own intercessions for quietness from Mother, for no alarms, no dreadful unexpected action or interruption from her, that the spoken words were passed before he was alert for them, and when they rose to their feet again he was ready to weep for having missed them.

But so far everything was all right, and with warm relief he saw that Mother was beginning to sing in her old style now that the last hymn had been reached, while simultaneously he sensed a relaxation in the attention of Michael, Melanie, and Nanny. He could feel the whole congregation warming to the task it had so nearly completed and saw that small smiles of satisfaction were being exchanged between adjacent pews; and then, when the organ paused for the blessing before sounding out into the triumphant melody of Mendelssohn, when David and Prudence came down the aisle from the vestry and went lightly past them to the western end and the waiting car, he was able at last to greet Victoria, to stretch out his hand to her and stammer his delight. She said nothing; but her hand, softer than anything he had ever held, lay passively in his own, and she smiled with such beauty and gaiety that he could not long meet her eyes and, instead, kneeled hurriedly to say a last prayer before leaving the church. But he caught her again in the porch whither she had been swept by the tumble of people on their way out.

He could not be sure, he never could be sure of these things, was forever uncertain as to whether or not he had imagined them out of the stress of his fears or desires; but she seemed to be awaiting him with a diffidence which was almost indifference, as though already she were regretting the openness of the delight she had shown him only a few moments before. And he for his part, conscious of Melanie and Michael's observation of him and the closeness of the family, was stiff and awkward in his manner.

He heard her "Hello" and his own restrained somehow silly echo of it with dismay and anger, wanted to take her hand again but could not; and instead, jostled by the others on their way out into the gaping street, said firmly, "You're coming with us, aren't you? I mean there's nobody with you, is there?"

"No," she said.

"Come on then, stick close to me and we'll follow the others."

Obediently, she edged up behind him and they joined the rest of the family on the pavement. A number of passers-by had stopped on either side of the red carpet: strange London women with big fronts and faces, one or two thin business men and some children. The little rectangle before which the cars and taxis drew up was very public and in the middle of it Mother was showing off. She had collected Mrs. Mudd, Lizzie, Lizzie's father and Gladys and was insisting that they should all travel in the family taxi.

"But there won't be room, pet!" Father remonstrated awkwardly.

She smiled him a fierce smile. "Nonsense, Teddy! Of course there'll be room, or if there isn't—" and she gave Lizzie's father a harvest festival grin—"then som'on us'll 'ave to walk, won't we Mr. Smith?"

Mr. Smith took her mood at once.

"They 'ull that, Mrs. Blaydon, an' 'twouldn't do no 'arm for some on 'em fat folk to stretch their legs a little, would it?"

"If they wants their 'am and salad," said Mother, more North country than ever, "then let'm splodge for it same at t'Bondagers."

At this several of the onlookers tittered, Simpson whispered something to Lizzie, and Michael looked pained. When Mother was in this mood there was no knowing how far she might go; but fortunately, at this moment, Alexander Flood appeared. His hair, very Harrovian, his sparkling white carnation, something expert and habitual about the fall of his morning coat over his well-bred behind, discomforted them all even more; and Michael stepped forward eagerly.

"Really, Mother dear, I think it'd be simplest if we took a couple of taxis, don't you? I say, Alexander! You're so good with these fellows, do you think you could get someone to flag another taxi?"

"Nothing simpler, my dear fellow," said Alexander drawing himself up and stepping to the curb. He raised a long hand, tilted his topper a little further forward over the high bridge of his nose and in a moment two more taxis drew up in front of the awning. Then, with exquisite courtesy and leisure, as though his very facility bored him, he ushered Mother, Father, Michael, John and Victoria into the first, Nanny, Simpson, Melanie and the Smiths into the second.

They drew away into the flux of traffic and Mother leaned forward to Father who was perched beside John on a folding seat. She was angry at the curtailment of her turn by the intervention of Alexander.

"Teddy, look out of the window and see if Mrs. Mudd and the Boults are all right."

"John," said Father, "do what your mother tells you."

John got up and put his head out of the window. He could see nothing but red buses and the receding spire of the church. London was a thousand cities and already they had moved into a new one. He sat down again and lied brightly, "Yes, they're just behind us and Mrs. Boult is sitting in the front with the driver."

Mother sat back. "We mustn't just think of ourselves," she said more quietly, "they're our people and they've come all this way to horrible old London for our sake. Just because this is a so-called fashionable wedding we mustn't forget our responsibility to them; although they may not say much, they know what I'm going through. There were tears in old Smith's eyes when he was speaking to me just now—"

"Probably," interrupted Father drily, "at the thought of all the drink he'll have to forgo." He gave Michael one of his most cumbersome winks.

Mother's mouth closed tightly and there was a slow silence.

Father pretended to be unconcerned. He looked at John, then at Victoria, his gaze brushed past Mother and came to rest again on Michael.

"Surely we must be nearly there, Mick? Hadn't you better ask this fellow where he's taking us? When they think they've got a greenhorn in the back they're just like the old cabmen, they'll take you all over town to get a bigger fare out of you."

Nobody answered him; they were all looking at Mother, whose mouth was still a thin pink line and whose eyes were looking straight ahead of her. Outside the windows, the traffic moved faster and faster; everyone seemed to be overtaking them, and in front of them the taxi driver sat grimly, as though he were following some slow tortuous procession of his own and was determined to be at the end of it.

Michael spoke. "Go on with what you were saying, Mother, about old Smith. *I* noticed that he was looking a little upset."

"So did I!" said John, taking Michael's cue. "He was, wasn't he, Victoria?"

"Who? That old man with the cap and the moustache?"

"What's the use," said Mother in her removed voice. "I shall say no more! What we've just seen was enough; that dreadful service, all those worldly people and *her* rudeness to me in the vestry when they were signing the register. I don't know how I stood it; it was all I could do to sing. Everybody felt it, I know they did. They're taking David away from us! They want to turn him into one of those fashionable effeminate clergy like Willie Wilson, and it's not what God intended. He always wanted to be a missionary and instead she's going to suffocate him with wealth and drink." She looked at Father. "Yes *drink!* Laugh at that if you can, and then when you've finished laughing at me, ask David what Gertie's wedding present is to be. *Ask him!*"

"I'm sorry pet. It was only a little joke."

"Of course it wasn't a little joke. You know what Lizzie's gone through with her father—night after night in the Cross Keys until I got him to sign the pledge. You were deliberately trying to hurt me simply because you were annoyed at not being able to officiate at the wedding of your eldest son. Well, it's not *my* fault. *She* arranged it all, she's got a Bishop in every pocket. It's true, isn't it? You can't deny it."

"I was a little vexed, Kitty, and I'm sorry if I hurt you." He patted her knee.

"You had every right to be—the whole thing taken out of your hands, out of *our* hands. We wanted them to be married in our own parish amongst our own people in Beddington. The Bishop would have come, he never refuses me anything, and you could have assisted and everyone could have been there, the Bellinghams, the Bolshotts and Lady Blake. It would have been wonderful, and what is more, it would have been *right*; it would have pleased everybody. But no! That didn't suit her at all. Having done the impossible and found someone willing to marry her flat-chested daughter, she has to proclaim it to her world and subject us all to this silly flunkeyism. We have come all this way, put on these ridiculous town clothes, and brought half the parish with us, solely in order to eat humble pie at Gertie's expense. And *her* people, who are they? Only business, *trade!*"

David was at Oxford, you were at Oxford, your grandfather and your father were at Oxford, whereas old Cable was only a board-school boy, I'm sure of it; but no one will ever know! That's where she's so clever—because he's been dead so long; he had nothing but money and she uses it to influence the Bishops. It's what I've wanted to say all along at every Church Assembly—they'll never get real Christianity in England till the Church is disestablished—and this year I *shall* say it and I'll get York to back me up."

At the mention of the Archbishop there was silence and Michael looked out of the window. "We're nearly there. Cheer up, Mother pet, we're all with you and we'll back you up."

Suddenly gallant, she smiled at him and, getting out her handkerchief, dabbed at her nose. Then, opening her compact, she smeared the tiniest trace of lipstick on to her lips and fluffed a little of her fair powder on to her cheeks.

"Now you see what they've done," she said suddenly to Victoria, "they've upset me and spoiled this absurd make-up."

"I think you look very sweet, Mrs. Blaydon, younger even than Mummy!"

"No I don't," said Mother. "I'm just a tired old woman. I'm nearly fifty and I look like seventy. I've had seven children—"

"Six dear," said Father.

"What do you mean six? If you'd had them you wouldn't have forgotten the first one—my little dark-haired daughter." She resumed her smile and looked at Victoria. "Yes, I've been married over thirty years and now I'm losing my David; and though that's bad enough I wouldn't mind if I didn't feel that God was losing him too. But don't worry, I shall accept it as I've accepted everything else. Just remember, though, all of you, that this is *our* wedding as much as theirs. I want you to see that our parishioners are looked after, each of them's worth half a dozen of these Londoners with their proud faces—now where's my bag, Victoria? We'll wait for the others and then we'll all go in together."

"I don't see how we can, Mother," said Michael. "For one thing we'll have to go to different cloakrooms. And for another, I'm sure that Mrs. Cable will expect you and Father to stand with her behind the bride and groom."

"Oh no!" said Mother. "If she's going to take him over, and I know she is, then she can do it without my help. I have the rest of the family to think of. David will understand." The taxi drew up and the driver opened the door.

"Victoria! You come with me you poor little thing. It's a dreadful thing to be born a woman. If I only had my Mary with me it wouldn't be so bad; but even she is denied me until this horrible day is over. We'll find Melanie and we'll have our refreshments together in our own corner."

Holding Victoria's arm she joined the stream of people moving through the glass-fronted entrance and disappeared into the hotel.

Michael paid the taxi and then, having collected old Smith, the four of them made their way to the downstairs cloakroom.

"I'm very worried about her," said Father very contentedly, "and now I've put my foot in it. Silly of me, of course, but I didn't think she'd take it like that."

"I shouldn't let it spoil things," said John. "See if you can make her drink a glass of champagne. That will cheer her up."

"Never touches it, says that if she once started she'd never know when to stop—like old Pall."

"Poor old grandfather!" said John. "I wish he were here now, he'd have known how to manage her."

Father turned to Michael. "I say, Mick, what did your mother mean about the wedding present? What *did* she give David?"

"Who? Mrs. Cable?"

"Yes, but not so loud, the walls have ears in these places; whisper it!"

"A cellar allowance," said Michael.

"A *cellar* allowance! Is that all? Good Heavens! I couldn't think what it must have been, but she's funny about wine, always has been. It's old Pall, of course, he led 'em an awful dance."

In the reception room, brightly lighted by the frozen inverted fountains of the chandeliers, Mother had taken up her position in the corner farthest away from the bridal group. Throughout the rest of the room, flanked by two gleaming tables on which a buffet luncheon was spread, people stood in twos and threes making an aimless pattern between whose motifs pale waiters moved with trays of half-full glasses. Somewhere, lost behind the murmurs and cascades of sudden laughter, a quartet played chamber music. The long room, warm and scented, was strung with polite hostilities, and late arrivals stood hesitantly in the doorway searching uneasily for a route or direction which would lead them safely past the bride and groom to their own particular friends.

Mother's party consisted principally of backs; for all the people she had gathered around her in a green corner of palms on pedestal tables, springing ferns and hydrangeas, were evidently facing her where she stood concealed as she talked eagerly to Alexander Flood, with Victoria still by her side.

Following the others, John saw the back of Mr. Boult with Grace Boult by his side, Lizzie and Mrs. Mudd, the Hadleys and Mr. Scrutton-Thompson, one of Father's church wardens. Simpson, with two of the prettiest bridesmaids smiling up at him as he drank gingerly from a champagne glass, was standing next to Melanie and Nanny; while Mary, he noticed, was on Alexander's other side listening to his exchanges with Mother and wearing what he privately called her sweet-intelligent-look-at-me-looking-at-you expression.

Father and Michael took their places on the outskirts of this large group, forming a tall black outpost against all comers as they plied Mr. Smith with glasses of lemonade and asparagus rolls. Occasionally, blundering strangers, remote members of Mrs. Cable's entourage, would wander up to the corner and try to get into conversation with Mrs. Mudd or Emma Huggins, and finding that they were apparently not understood, would drift away again, carelessly as though they had never really intended to say anything in the first place.

At last, however, David and Prudence accompanied by Mrs. Cable and her brother, Major Albright, came slowly up from the far end of the room and paused on the outskirts of the corner.

"Where is my little mother?" David asked. "Has anyone seen the Bridegroom's Mother?" He stood on tiptoe and caught sight of Father. "Oh hello, Father dear! What have you done with my mother?"

Near him there was a swift lull in the talking as everyone turned to look openly into the corner they had hitherto so scrupulously ignored.

"I am sure," said Mrs. Cable loudly, "that Mrs. Edward Blaydon must be holding court in there somewhere." And she waved her ringed hand vaguely at the palms. "But then, David dear, your mother *is* so small that no one could be quite sure."

David, dropping Prudence's hand, leaving her brown and smiling by her uncle's side, dived dramatically into the group and shouldering everyone aside picked Mother cleanly up in his arms.

"*Here* she is! We've found the Bridegroom's Mother. We've rescued her from the dragon of obscurity and exposed her to the serpent of publicity."

Mother, bright as quicksilver, her tiny feet thrashing the air, her pale blue eyes smiling delightedly up into David's face as she lay in his arms, called out, "Put me down at once, David, you naughty boy! You must have had far too much champagne."

David took no notice of her. Gleeful and shining, his brown eyes looking straight into Prudence's, he deposited Mother neatly beside Mrs. Cable and said, "Photographs, Mother! in the next room; and after that, speeches toasts and telegrams—and then we're off, off your hands for ever and a day."

"Not for *ever*, David!" she said seriously.

"Of course not, darling; you'll *never* be rid of your eldest. He'll always need you." He kissed her swiftly. "Come on, Father; you're wanted too."

Mother smoothed down her blue silk dress and took Father's hand. She looked minutely pretty, suddenly, and secretly radiant like a person who has received a promise.

"Really," she said to no one in particular. "It's a good thing we're getting rid of him at last, he always was expensive and difficult; but now he's getting *quite* out of hand."

"Ah!" sighed Mrs. Cable, "*we* haven't found that! David is quite easy to manage if one has the hands, isn't he Prudence?"

"I'm sure he is," said Prudence fondly. "I've had no trouble with him so far."

"You just wait," said Mother, "both of you! In twenty-five years *I* never succeeded in breaking him in—"

"No," David interrupted, "but then you see I'm not a harness horse, Mother darling, I'm not even much good on the flat— I'm a 'chaser by nature."

"*That*," said Mother quickly, "is exactly what I meant." And she smiled triumphantly at Mrs. Cable who turned down her mouth like an elderly débutante and said, "Well, we shall see! But in the meantime I do think that we ought to get these tiresome photographs taken."

Somebody laughed, little conversations were resumed and the musicians who had been silent for some minutes, struck up surprisingly into "Jeanie with the Light Brown Hair." The bridesmaids followed the others out into the foyer, and John, ignoring Melanie's questions, made his way over to Victoria who was standing a little forlornly where Mother had left her.

"Have you had any champagne?" he asked.

"No I haven't had anything yet—but I don't mind."

"Neither have I, but I *do* mind! To me, everything seems to be going wrong! This isn't at all the sort of wedding I imagined it would be."

"Isn't it?"

"No it isn't. I thought everything would be gay and friendly. This is worse than a railway train. And another thing, I've hardly seen you and you've hardly seen me."

"I know. I've been talking to your mother."

"So I saw. Didn't you want to talk to me?"

"I think your mother's wonderful! She's the most wonderful woman I ever met. I'd no idea she was like this."

"Like what?"

"Oh *different*—so exciting! She seems to understand everybody the moment she meets them."

He groaned. "Oh Lor'! Has she been understanding *you*?"

"Don't be silly, I didn't say that."

"I know you didn't, but it's what you meant."

"It isn't at all." She looked at him speculatively. "You don't understand your mother, that's the trouble. You're too young. Your mother's sweet. She was telling some of the bridesmaids that men never do understand women and that that's why they often marry the wrong people. I think she's right."

"You don't mean to say she's been telling everyone that David oughtn't to have married Prudence? She can't possibly know yet, they've only been married for an hour."

"There you are!" she interrupted. "I never said anything about your brother and his wife, and neither did she. As it happens, she was talking about *my* mother and father; she understands how—uncomfortable it is to have only half a home as I have; she was awfully kind, and *clever*!"

"I'm sorry," said John. "I admit I was wrong, but I've been worrying all through the service about Mother. I thought she was going to do something dreadful. Did you notice how she changed places at the beginning of the wedding? It was terribly embarrassing."

"Don't be silly! It was only because she couldn't see anything; she's so short, smaller even than you or me. What was embarrassing about it?"

"Oh nothing."

He looked around him miserably. Everyone was talking and laughing, the music was still underlying the lights and the movement; but he felt suddenly alone and tragic, lonelier than if he had remained at the Abbey, lonelier even than he always felt on the second day of the holidays when the greetings had worn thin and the excitement briefly flagged after weeks of anticipation.

"If you're going to sulk—"

"I'm not sulking, Victoria; really, I'm not. It's only that you don't seem the same."

"You don't even *look* the same! Whatever's happened to your face?"

"Oh that! I was going to tell you, but somehow it doesn't seem interesting any more."

"What was it? A fight?"

"Yes."

"How silly! *We* never fight, but I suppose boys are different."

He took a deep breath and looked at his feet. "As a matter of fact, if you want to know, it was for *you*! Someone was beastly about you, and I went into the ring with him and beat him up."

She was silent, and after a moment or two he looked up just in time to catch her eyes breaking away from their regard of him. Moving closer to her he took her hand impulsively and shook the slender fingers hard.

"Please! Do let's start again. Let's be different so that we shall end up by being the same. I didn't mean to quarrel with you and all this could be so wonderful."

"All right," she said, "but you mustn't criticize your mother any more or it will spoil everything."

He smiled. "I promise," he said. "Let's have some champagne like we said we would in our letters. Let's drink to our First Wedding before *she*—" he corrected himself hastily—"before they all come back."

"Be quick then," she said. "It was very sweet of you to fight someone for me. What was his name? What did he say? How old was he?"

"I'll tell you later." He was filled with returning gaiety. "But will you tell me something first? Just this once and I won't mention it again?"

"Yes."

"Where did you have all this talk with my mother?"

"Some of it in the Russell Hotel before you came, and some of it in the cloakroom just now. She'd had a long letter from Enid, thanking her for inviting me to the wedding, and in it I think Mummy must have been rather sad about her own wedding."

"Oh."

"That's really what upset me. I kept thinking about them, Enid and my father starting off like this in a church years and years ago and then ending by getting divorced."

He thought hard, trying to imagine her life with Enid who was her mother, so smooth-faced and arranged, a very careful woman. like a program. He imagined the hotel holidays, the occasional breakfast-table letters from her father and the annual visit to the rich farmer who lived in the moors and was always wanting to marry Enid and be Victoria's step-father. It had never worried him before; but now that Mother had somehow unexpectedly got mixed up in it, it was important that he should understand it. If he didn't, Victoria might begin to feel differently about him, she might think that he was in an outside world and turn against him and then he would have no one to dream about or write to, no one to love as gloriously and secretly as he had loved Victoria and the very idea of her ever since the lake.

"I'll get the champagne," he said, "and something for you to eat. Would you like a meringue if I can find one, if all these people haven't scoffed the lot?"

"Your mother said I wasn't to worry—she said that some marriages weren't made in *Heaven* at all—"

"Don't let's talk about it any more. Oh dear, they're coming back! It's too late for our feast now."

"Never mind, I'm quite happy. I had coffee and sandwiches with your mother at the hotel. Have you had anything to eat?"

"No, nothing." He was emphatic. "But I'm jolly well going to. Don't move away from here, will you?"

"No, but you'll have to hurry because I've got to leave at two-thirty. Miss Empson made it a condition that I was to be back at Hill Cote by four at the latest and it takes a good hour to get out to Richmond."

His heart put in an extra beat. "But you can't be," he said. "I'm going to take you on the river, we're going to find an island and eat fruit and sweets. Don't you remember?"

"Oh I know, it was a lovely idea and things *are* rather horrid today. I tried terribly hard, honestly I did; but she wouldn't budge. She kept on saying, 'Now remember, you're only thirteen, Victoria, and it's a very great concession that you are being allowed to go at all.' So there wasn't anything I could do. I just had to promise."

"I see."

"Now go and get us some meringues," she said, "and don't be miserable. I've got some wonderful news for you. Something that will cheer you up no end."

"Nothing could."

"I bet you this will."

"What is it?"

"I'll tell you just before I go—it's about the holidays."

At the far end of the room Major Albright called loudly for silence and everyone stopped talking.

Carefully and quickly John made his way to one of the tables and helped himself to an asparagus roll. It tasted of nothing, but he ate it dully and with a certain satisfaction, following it up with several more while the cake was being cut and the telegrams read. He didn't want to hear anything or to look at anyone; the strangers filled him with a cold hostility, and the family he had loved and so desperately imagined both in the absence that lay behind him as well as in that which lay ahead, were the centre of a sorrow and a pain that was colder even than hostility.

He wished he had never come. It didn't do to see people in the wrong places, in the wrong settings. They should all have stayed in Northumberland; Mother was quite right and should have insisted on having the wedding there.

Even Victoria was changed by all this. London and school had done something to her so that she seemed older and more remote. She too was unhappy; she had said so. Everyone was unhappy, and so was Mother; Mother most of all.

He gulped at a half-empty glass of champagne and then slid it quickly back on to the tablecloth. The wine fizzed down inside him like Eno's fruit salts and left an exciting taste on his tongue. Mother! Mother! Mother! Always Mother. She had bewitched the wedding, she had bewitched Victoria; Mother had bewitched London. It wasn't London that was wrong and it wasn't Mother. It was the two together.

In front of him a fat man with a round back and purple cheeks suddenly called out, "Speech!" and then turned and gave a gobbling smile to a bridesmaid by his side. Several other people took up the cry. From different parts of the room, the word, short and raucous as the squawk of a hen, was echoed by the standing figures; and as each one pronounced it he looked immediately pleased with himself, as though in uttering it he had made some important discovery or had in some way finally established himself in the sight of everyone else. After a few seconds the cries reached such a crescendo that the noise became embarrassing and made a short silence which was ended when the fat man started to clap. Soon everybody was clapping, and then there was another pause in which Alexander Flood could be heard clearing his throat.

John edged past the fat man so that he could see the group in front of the wedding cake. Prudence and David were standing together, and next to David, Mother, Alexander Flood, and the officiating clergyman, the Reverend the Hon. Stephen Counter. On Prudence's other side Father stood between Mrs. Cable and Major Albright. With the exception of Alexander Flood who was smoothing his already smooth hair and evidently trying to look at something just above the heads of his audience, they were all looking at the carpet. Mother and David especially, he noticed, looked isolated; they were standing very close together like the middle and ring fingers of a hand, and he saw in fact that David did give her hand a little squeeze just before Alexander Flood started to speak.

It was a silly speech scattered with pauses and throat noises. He told everybody how often he had contrived to be a best man before—and how much he always enjoyed being a best man—even though it entailed making speeches *ha! ha!* which he always believed in keeping very short *ha! ha!*; and then he proposed a toast which everyone, even including Mother, drank very quickly. Then David, who was looking very flushed, made a speech begging that Prudence be excused from making a speech, because, as everyone knew, or should know, Prudence Blaydon was almost as shy as Prudence Cable had been, and had taken a lot of catching (at this Mrs. Cable looked extremely pleased), so much so in fact that he had been forced to go into the cage to get her (at this Mother looked very pleased), but that now he had got in he had no wish to get out again because it was a most delightful cage.

At this point people began to change legs or brush ash off their coat sleeves, and there was an unpleasant pause which was ended by Major Albright clapping loudly and someone else proposing a second toast which was drunk busily. Then, from the back of the room someone, either Simpson or Lizzie, called out, "The mistress!" and the rest of the parishioners immediately took up the cry.

Mr. Boult, the auctioneer, nudged by his wife Grace, increased

the noise so effectively by bellowing out the words "Mrs. Blaydon! We want Mrs. Blaydon!" that everyone else was deafened;
and Mother, exactly as if she had heard her cue when taking the
lead in one of her own plays, stepped forward and waited.

She looked excited, for she loved speaking and never pretended otherwise. She would speak on any possible occasions:
at meetings, open-air festivals, bazaars, fêtes and pageants and,
of course, at the annual Church Assembly in London. She had
only to confront an audience from a sufficient height in order
to hold its instant attention and to set its members trembling
inside themselves with bright expectations.

Now as she stepped forward John could see that her little fists
were white, her eyes hazy and misty, pale blue and disembodied
as though they floated in some other world whose visions sad-
dened her with the enormity of her desire to express them. He
felt his heart sink and rise again in a vertigo of fear and exultation.
He wished he was back at the Abbey, under the sea, or safely in
bed in a foreign country miles and miles away; and yet he longed
to hear what she had to say and would have sprung at anyone
who tried to stop her.

Everyone else, he knew, felt the same; this time no one was
looking at their feet, even unruffled strangers were looking rigidly
and directly at the tiny pale blue red-headed figure as though
it embodied an imminent threat; a threat so loud and bright, so
inevitably near, that, like a thunderstorm, there was no point in
trying to cover it up or ignore it, or even in attempting to flee
out of its path; and strangely, he knew that everyone was glad.
All morning, from the very first, there had been mutterings,
sudden silences, flights of dark fancies, the accumulation of
omens, followed by welcome but fleeting clearances; now the
tempest was here; it had gathered and would burst. They were
glad to stand their ground. They clapped impatiently and Mother
started to speak.

"I suppose it's not very usual for the bridegroom's mother
to speak at her son's wedding," she said, "but then I am not
very used to having my children marry. In *that* sense, this is
my first wedding, the wedding of the first of my four sons, and
I've come a long way to know it, a very long way."

She paused and looked from one face to another, and John trembled at the gentleness of her start.

"Such a long way, in fact," she went on, "that my husband and I had to pass our own *silver* wedding on the journey. So you'll see that for me it was not a very usual wedding. But that doesn't really matter and it's not what I wanted to say. What does matter is that for you too it is a most unusual wedding because it is the wedding of a priest, and that is always an event—quite different from the weddings of doctors or solicitors or anyone else. As my husband would tell you, a priest is more than a man and therefore a priest's wedding is different. In a sense, when a priest gets married it is always a case of *bigamy*! That sounds shocking, I know, and as an admission I'm sure it would make our friends in Rome laugh at us—but I'll deal with that in a minute. What I want to make clear now is that every priest, whether he's a bachelor or not, is married at his ordination; he is married to the Church and the Church is his first wife, as she will be his last wife whether he dies a widower or not."

People rustled and made small movements; one or two of them looked at Mrs. Cable.

"The Church may not be a wealthy wife," Mother went on, "and she may have very little to offer him in the way of worldly comforts, and that is as it should be. Another thing, she may not be very young; some of us claim that she is nearly two thousand years old! But even so she is a rival to be reckoned with and any priest will tell you which of his two wives keeps her looks the longest."

With perfect composure she stopped and smiled at Father, and this time John looked at Mrs. Cable as she stood beside Prudence. They looked amazingly alike, almost as though they were one young-old person; their expressions were so similar, the very way they stood with their hands frozen in front of them. It embarrassed him to look at them and he began to have misgivings about the meaning of Mother's words. She was talking much faster he noticed, and an anger of which he had at first been unsure was becoming more and more frighteningly obvious.

"Some Christians, not of our persuasion, think it wrong for a priest to get married in this *wordly* sense at all. There are a good many references which they will quote in support of it. I can only remember two of them, one from an epistle of St. Paul where he says that for a priest to be unmarried is 'the more excellent way' and another, I think, from St. Matthew, which quotes Our Lord as saying that there are some who are eunuchs for His sake. I must admit that there have been times when I have wondered just how much of an asset I have been to my husband in his work as a priest, and other times when I found it in my heart to hope that any son of mine who took Holy Orders might find his vocation a sufficient consort."

So intense now was the attention of the crowded room that the people in it might have been figures in a shop window.

"But that is all over now and it's a consolation to me that my son David has been blessed with such a happy choice. Prudence, my new daughter, I know will bring with her those qualities which he is going to need in the arduous years that lie ahead of them both. She need bring nothing else, *nothing at all*," she repeated with a quick glance at Mrs. Cable, "neither scrip nor purse—and I hope she won't; these things are only an encumbrance to the cure of souls. For my part, I care for nothing but their happiness in their *work*; and if that happiness is to be sure they must have it in the sight of that rock on which all true marriages are founded, the rock upon which God struck the Ten Commandments, the rock which Moses smote for water in the wilderness, and the Rock upon which Christ built His Gracious Church. And that, if you wish nothing else, is what I would like you to wish for them today, that nothing, no man *or* woman should come unscathed between them and their Witness, so that not only this marriage which you have seen today but that other more important marriage to which I referred earlier should continue strongly in the sight of God." She touched her eyes with a tiny handkerchief. "And there is no more to be said."

From the back of the long room came a gathering movement, a disturbance which became a murmur and a murmur which became a sound in the determined clapping of hard hands, in cries and even shouts. Someone started to cheer, others took it up. A wind seemed to be sweeping the taller trees at the back and John felt tears as sharp as blown sand behind his eyelids. She had done it; Mother had done it again and momentarily he was proud of her: all his animosity was swallowed up and lost, completely dissolved in the strong solvent of his affection and pride. But beside him, the clapping was soft and short-lived. He looked about him and saw wooden faces, tall dresses, and necks stiffening under the draught; sensed an anger blind and hunted, which, although it knew no sure direction, was as real as a boar driven between the standing trunks by unseen hunters.

Mother saw it too; she quivered and retreated a pace; she held up a small peremptory hand. There was silence.

"I thought I'd said enough. I may have said more than enough; I don't know," she said, "but then I'm not very used to London and London may not be very used to me. In the north it's different; they know me up there"—"We do that!" shouted someone—"and I know them, and I'm no more afraid of them than I'm afraid of London."

There were laughs now, proud laughs from the back; but John did not contribute to them, he was dumbly terrified that she would go too far as once she had gone too far in an election speech; but he feared even more that she might drift into what he privately called her Gracie-Fields-ending.

"And the reason I'm not afraid is because I know there are only two people here who could object or have any right to object to anything I have intentionally said: my son David and his wife Prudence! And *they* won't. So now, *I'm* going to propose a toast! It's the first one I've ever proposed and I hope it'll be the last." She turned to Alexander Flood, who although he had not moved for quite ten minutes, contrived, like a man suddenly awakened from a strange dream, to hand her a full glass of champagne which she held up before them.

"And the toast I propose is, The Church!"

"The Church," they echoed, and they drank.

At the back they drank deeply and with audible satisfaction; at the front they tilted their glasses with a dreadful reluctance. Mrs. Cable sipped as hurriedly and abstemiously as if her glass had held poison, and even the Reverend the Hon. Stephen Counter looked as though he were being forced by his enormous wife to swallow a disagreeable medicine.

There was a last burst of clapping and then people started to move. Major Albright, brighter, more red, more apoplectic than his name, seemed to feel that some sort of a precision and a direction ought to be given to the trancelike movements by which he was confronted. He announced in a loud uncertain voice, "Well–ah–I think now that aftah all that–ah–the bride and groom will have to–ah–change and–ah–be on their way."

Alexander Flood rocketed forward into the crowd as though he had been fired by Major Albright from an invisible gun, Prudence kissed Mrs. Cable desperately, David hugged Mother like a wrestler and taking Prudence's arm swept her down the length of the room through the aisle cleared by the best man, and disappeared with her through the glass-fronted doors.

When they had gone the waiters, summoned by Alexander Flood, reappeared. He drove them before him anxiously like a collie mustering sheep, and people began to snatch glasses from their full trays and drink with the abandon of passengers rescued from a sinking ship. The group in front of the wedding cake broke up. Mrs. Cable, Major Albright and the Reverend the Hon. Stephen Counter and his wife made four backs with a talking centre from which the words "Madeirah" and "weddin's" echoed out into the room. Father, finding himself alone, walked around to Mother and began to lead her slowly down towards the corner.

In the front ranks nobody seemed to see them. The red-and-white men, the tall women with the lacy hats and pigtailed daughters, were all apparently having difficulties with their digestion or else trying to remember some newly forgotten fact which had now become extremely important. But halfway down the room the atmosphere changed: people swept forward, loud Northumbrian voices boomed out greetings and Mother was seized by the hand and drawn into their midst. Mr. Smith lighted his pipe and adjusted the gold watchchain which spanned his waistcoat, while Lizzie could be heard ordering a cup of tea from one of the waiters:

"And be sure it's none on your Indian; it moost be China, the mistress doesn't like t'other sort."

In a few minutes the room was as noisy as ever. There was much laughter from the wedding-cake end, sudden sharp society

shrieks, and a steady boom of conversation, even of thigh-slap-
ping altercation from the Boult end.

Moving from his vantage point in search of Victoria, John
passed Mrs. Cable's group. She was looking very dashed, not
really cold or alarming at all; Major Albright was being brotherly
to her, like John himself sometimes felt towards Melanie, talking
loudly and fast to the others but watching her drawn face with
his eyes all the time and trying to persuade her to eat or drink
something more.

The other clusters of people he passed were the same, speaking in high jerks, embarrassed by silences which befell them
with no warning, like those which afflict people who have been
given bad news. One or two of them, but not many, were safely
angry; he heard remarks like, "I'm told she writes," and, "Ap-
pallin' bad taste." These he was not sorry for; but his journey
past the others confused him, bleeding him of his earlier elation
and making him feel increasingly old; old, because their silences
and embarrassment made them seem young.

He thought of the boxing match with Marston and realized
with dismay that what he had witnessed had been only a repetition of it in the world of the grownups. Mother and Mrs. Cable
had fought in public just as he and Marston had fought in private,
and there had been no older proportionate Toad to oversee the
fight. They had mauled and hurt each other over their love for
David and Prudence with no one to see fair play or establish a
reason for their fight.

The comparison sickened him; he did not want to feel sorry
for anyone; he wanted to be a Fisher, happily taking sides, *changing* sides if necessary, sure of his sympathies and ready to cham-
pion Mother or Mrs. Cable to the death; but he could not. He
lacked both the self-confidence of the Toad, who had been sure
of his reasons for calling the fight, and the partisanship of Fisher,
who had revealed himself as loathing Marston because he had
loved him.

This realization weighted his step as, passing through the ruck
of Mrs. Cable's supporters and beyond them into the silly and
noisy elation of Mother's Northumbrians, he reached the fern

corner where Melanie and Victoria were talking jubilantly to each other.

"Wasn't Mother wonderful?" said Melanie.

"You see?" said Victoria. "You see?"

They were standing close together like Marston and Fleming in the locker room; he expected them to dance and taunt him.

"Yes," he said, "at least, I don't know—"

"It's the north against the south, the north against the south," chanted Victoria, "like the American Civil War; and your Mother's quite right, people shouldn't get married until they're sure, should they, Melanie?"

"Mrs. Cable's been horrid to Mother all the time," replied Melanie, "telling her that she's going to get *her* Bishop to make them live in the south so that she'll hardly ever be able to see David."

"Horrible old south," said Victoria. "They'll never be happy if they live down here; after a few years they'll start quarrelling over money and get divorced."

"They can't do that because David's a clergyman," said Melanie. "And anyway God'll beat Mrs. Cable; He's always on Mother's side. She'll pray about it and David will get a living in the north from Mother's Bishop, won't he, John?"

It sounded perhaps more like a game of chess, he thought; if it was, it was the same thing, a fight just the same.

"I don't know," he said. "I don't know whose side God's on. Toad was on no one's side—"

"*Toad!*" Melanie looked scandalized. "Who's Toad?"

"Oh, no one! *You* wouldn't understand."

"*I* would," said Victoria. "Tell *me*."

"Well," he said, "it was the fight I was talking to you about, at the Abbey. The master who made us fight was called Toad and he stood by while we were in the boxing ring. If you can understand I think he was like God—"

Melanie interrupted. "Don't listen to him, he's being blasphemous, calling God 'Toad'!"

"Oh *shut up*, Melanie," he said wearily. "You don't understand; you haven't seen Mrs. Cable, she's looking miserable and ill. Mother's ruined everything for everybody—"

"She hasn't! It's just you, you always go against everybody. Mother was wonderful and brave, and you're just being wicked. Come away from him, Victoria, he's only trying to get you on his side."

"I haven't *got* a side," said John. "I'm like Toad, or God, I just watch and feel sorry for everyone."

"*There!* He's said it again: Goad—I mean, Toad and God; *I'm* not going to stay with him and I'm surprised at you, Victoria. I suppose you like it because you believe in divorce, but *we* don't."

This time they both turned on her.

"Oh go away!" they said; and she went, flouncing off angrily in her party dress, her red hair glowing like hot coals.

"Was Mrs. Cable really looking sad?" asked Victoria, "or did you just say that to beat Melanie?"

Delighted by her intuition he smiled at her. "She really was," he said. "I wish you could understand, Victoria. I felt sorry for her. She looked so lonely, with only her brother, that Major Albright man, to cheer her up; her husband is dead and she's only got Prudence and her sister and now she's lost—"

"Like Mummy! Like Enid!" said Victoria. "Poor Mrs. Cable." She craned on tiptoe to try and see her, but she could not sustain the pose long enough. "Perhaps you're right," she went on, "and even if you're not, I think Melanie's a beast."

"She's always like that," he said. "She and Mary and Mother always stick together, that's why Mother was being so nice to you—trying to get you on her side."

"Well, I won't be; don't worry about that. *You're* my friend; you understand me and I'll always stick up for you." She paused. "And now," she said, "I'll tell you the good news."

"Oh, please do!" All his gaiety returned in a blaze. "You are wonderful, Victoria, to go on being the same. At first I thought—"

"*Never!* It's like we said; we're the beginning of each other and we'll go on and on, and nothing will ever separate us for long. I'll tell you; it's about the holidays."

"What?"

"Well you know I was talking to your mother at the Russell Hotel?"

"Yes."

"Well, since she was in such a good mood—towards *me*, I mean—although she did rather go on about that old bathing thing, I thought I'd ask her if you could have some of your holiday with us on the moors. We're going to George Harkess, his farm in Danbey Dale; *you* know, I've often told you about it."

He drew in his breath. "What did she say?"

"She said that you *could*!"

"No!"

"As it happens she said it was a very good thing because it turns out we shall be at Nettlebed, that's the farm, just when your family are making the move to go and live in Anglesey."

They looked at one another delightedly. For John, confusion receded, speculation was replaced by shining fact; but before he could speak again they felt the renewal of bustle behind them and they both turned around.

David and Prudence had come in to say good-bye. Outside, through the wide glass door, the brightly labelled cases, the great bouquets of flowers and the hat boxes could all be glimpsed standing in the hall. Two pages and a porter were beside them, waiting expectantly; and inside there were swift greetings, kisses, the whiteness of handkerchiefs and the rustle of rose-leaf confetti. Alexander Flood threw wide the door; there was a surge and its silence, a pause and the scattering of the sad syllables of the last good-byes, and the wedding was over.

Back at the Abbey, Saturday evening was nearly at an end. Very soon now, Kay, with her large face and golden centre-parted hair, would replace her *Tatler* on the occasional table and show them all out of the drawing room.

These Saturday evenings, of course, were meant to give them the illusion of home. John remembered the kindly, sensible way in which Kay explained to the parents of the new boys that, once a week, twenty or thirty of "the school" were her guests in this drawing room. He could imagine how pleased the parents must be at the thought of this one cosy evening marking the start of the week end for the little new boy so far away from the familiar faces and comforts of his own home.

But it was not *like* home, he thought angrily as he pedalled away at "Tit Willow" on the pianola; it was worse than the Russell Hotel, which even Mother hadn't managed to make cosy. Everyone in it was too quiet and formal; the boys were miniatures of the smart buttoned-up people at the reception. The furniture was wrong, and the papers. In the Vicarage, nobody took the *Tatler*, and if a *Sphere* or an *Illustrated London News* found its way there it was only because somebody had been on a long journey like this wedding week end. And anyway, Kay herself was all wrong, like a magazine picture, like the Virgin Mary if she had taken up hunting as a girl, with a face like a great pink-nosed, blue-eyed horse. How he wished that he had Victoria with him standing behind the pianola and agreeing with everything he was thinking. No one like Kay would ever get into his home; they simply would not *be* there unless they were someone like Mrs. Cable whom Mother had been forced to invite because she was David's mother-in-law.

His legs aching after the long stand during the service and the reception, his face tense with the fury of his determination to finish "Tit Willow" before Kay dismissed them, he peered round the rosewood corner of the pianola and stole another glance at her as she sat there as stately and upright as she would have been in the hunting field, as though at any moment she might be going to take a five-barred gate on her low blue chair.

Toad's wife, he thought; that meant they must have been married. A wedding years and years ago like the one he had attended that morning. He was sick of weddings; they weren't true. They were as unreal as people fighting. People fighting did not hate one another, they only loved themselves and it was because they loved themselves so truly that they fought so bitterly. People at weddings did not love one another, they only loved themselves and what they thought represented themselves. The friends of the bride thought they loved the bride and they were suspicious of her husband, but the groom's people thought they loved him and distrusted the bride. But then, of course, it had been a priest's wedding, and perhaps Mother had been right when she had insisted that the marriage of a priest was different. How could a priest have two wives? She had made it sound as though he only really had one. She had made the first wife and the first wedding sound beautiful, as though it were something that no one could ever get at because it was above them all; she had made the love sound real. Victoria's mother and father were divorced, neither the Toad nor Kay ever looked particularly happy; perhaps one day David and Prudence would end their marriage as he and Marston had ended their fight, with only themselves at the end of it. But that other wife, the one you could never reach—

In front of him the pianola trilled. The willow wren sat forlornly on its branch and called out of its agonizing loneliness from the depths of the rosewood.

He was back! But only for four more weeks, and *then*, Northumberland! Danbey Dale, Victoria, and one day the new home in Anglesey. He must get into the habit of not thinking again. From somewhere far behind his immediate consciousness he heard the scratchy gramophone on the kitchen table in the Vicarage as the voice of some elderly light-opera singer sang out the words of the tune the pianola played:

"Is it weakness of intellect, birdie?" I cried,
"Or a rather tough worm in your little inside?"
With a shake of his poor little head he replied,
"Oh, Willow, titwillow, titwillow!"

3. In Danbey Dale

In what pale pastures leaning up to mountains
Browsed her flock of sheep
Whilst she the blue girl deep past counting
Drowsy ewes slipped further into sleep?

Why call them back who wandered from her
  dream
To some white watershed of earth and sky
Whence she herself streamed down in ringlets
Like a lamb with Heaven in her eye?

❧ *IN DANBEY DALE*

Scuffing along the dusty white road that led from the village out towards the farm, he refused to allow himself to think of the school. His luggage, neatly labelled, JOHN BLAYDON, RUDMOSE'S HOUSE, BEOWULF'S SCHOOL, OXFORD, had been sent on well in advance and by now it would be awaiting him and the start of his first term, in some basement or day room he had never yet seen. In five days, at the end of this strange holiday with Victoria, when the time came for him to follow it south and eventually claim it from amongst the piles of the other new boys' possessions, it would have a profound significance for him, even a sort of sanctity; for not only would it preserve beneath its labels and rope tangible and absurdly hurtful evidence of Nanny's love for him—the boxes of chocolates and slabs of toffee smuggled in between the layers of folded pyjamas and shirts—but also, like some kingly sarcophagus, it would contain the very last of the air of the Vicarage and of his childhood that he was ever likely to breathe again.

He paused in his rather hurried walk from the village shop and, placing the haversack on the grass, leaned against the moorland wall by a holly tree. Never to see the Vicarage again! It seemed impossible, like never seeing one's parents again or even oneself; for it had reared him, had mirrored him in its wide windows and gleaming corridors. He had grown under its elms, sat in the sun astride the huge V-shaped tiles which crowned its roof and explored, on winter afternoons, every cobwebbed cranny of its attics. It was his home: unchanging, receptive, even

103

merciful; it was his abiding safety at the end of every term, the sure star of his ultimate direction during his every absence; and at present he could not conceive of his life going on without it. Yet the rest of them seemed to have left it without any regrets, had set off on that memorable Wednesday last week for the new life in Anglesey with never a regretful glance nor even the semblance of a dropped tear.

No longer swinging his legs, no longer worrying about the time, he allowed the insistent memory of that last morning at Beddington to rise unrestricted in his mind.

He had watched them from the nursery window: Simpson piling the last of the cases into the trailer; Melanie suddenly appearing with a minute fir tree from the garden and insisting on having a place found for it; Mother here there and everywhere, telling Father that he must sit in the back, asking Nanny if she were sure she had brought the china tea and chivvying the maids about the tongue sandwiches.

Something had been forgotten and Simpson had been sent to find it. He had come clumping up the bare stairs and discovered John as he stood there by the uncurtained window trying to look unconcerned.

"Hello, what are tha doin' here? Aren't ya coomin' down to see 'em off?"

"No, I said good-bye after breakfast."

"Tha looks proper down, lad. Coom on with me and kiss'm all good-bye."

"No thanks, Simpson, I'd rather not."

"Well, cheer up anyway. Holy Moses! you'll be going off to your little lass's in half an hour, you know—what'sa name, the little gal at the wedding in Loondon?"

"You mean Victoria."

"Ay, ut's the one. Ya wouldn't catch me lewking lak a Christmas dewk if I was laiking for a week in t'moors with t'little lass whose nobbut me own, I can tell thee."

John had smiled. He liked Simpson and was glad he'd be coming down to see him off at the station.

"It's only that I don't like leaving the Vicarage," he had confided. "I don't *want* to live in Anglesey. I want to live here where I always have lived, where they have red tiles on the roofs and red cows in the fields. According to Melanie all the cows in Anglesey are black or black and white, and there are no tiles, only Welsh slates, and I think it sounds stinking."

Simpson patted his back.

"It's a graët place—fishing, swimming and climbing. Tha wait till end of next term, Master John, and tha won't want ever to coom back to old Beddington again, I can tell thee. When ya see Anglesey ya'll—"

But he had never finished, for the angry braying of the horn had cut him short.

"Ech! listen to 'er. Ut's Miss Mary again; fair time she got married to some big fella ut'll wallop her three times a day and teach her the meaning of patience. 'Ave ya seen ya mother's spectacles? She swears blind she left 'em oop in t'bathroom."

"No, but I bet she's found them by this time or Mary wouldn't be blowing the horn like that."

Simpson had left him at that and rushed down the stairs. Out on the drive Mary had given the horn one last triumphant opportunity and then as the waving arms came out of the windows in response to the farewells of Lizzie, Susan and Simpson, the car and trailer had swept off around the barberry hedge on its long journey across the Pennines. Only Father, at the very last minute, had seen John. Something had made him glance out through the black rectangle of the rear window and for a moment John had caught his eye, the somehow comical sympathy of his smile as the three women drove him away, before Melanie's absurd horsetail of a tree swayed between them and hid him from sight.

Ah well! he thought, you could only leave a place once, and it was all over now; that is to say, as much over as anything that affected you deeply was *ever* over.

He sighed and getting down from the wall picked up the haversack and started to run along the gritty road. This afternoon there was the expedition to the caves; he would think about that. After all, there were still five days left with Victoria and if he concentrated on those, on every live minute of every brilliant hour, they would lengthen and enchant him even longer.

Had he remembered everything they had decided to buy? Yes, he thought so. Mentally he ran through the list: six candles, a loaf of brown bread, a pot of heather honey, four boxes of Bryant and May's matches in case they lost any, a new penknife for digging up the truffles when they found them, a new battery for Victoria's flashlight, first-aid tin with bandages, iodine and plaster and two reels of white cotton to spread out behind them in case they lost their way in the galleries.

He rounded the last bend and saw Victoria at once. She was standing on the open gate swinging herself backwards and forwards under the shadows of the oak tree.

"You *have* been a time," she called as she saw him. "I've been waiting here for ages and ages. Annie Moses is furious with you."

"I'm sorry, it was farther than I thought."

"Whatever kept you? Did you go into one of your dream sessions?"

"No, not exactly. At least—"

She jumped off the gate. "You *did*!" she said. "It was about going to your school, to Beowulf's, wasn't it?"

"No it wasn't." He was definite about this; for once she was wrong.

"Then it was about leaving the Vicarage?"

He said nothing.

"Yes?" she said, turning around as she danced ahead of him. "Yes?"

"Yes," he said.

"There, I told you I knew, didn't I?"

"Yes, you always do—very nearly always."

"Of course I do! I get it from Mummy, she's got psychic powers too. She *could* have been a clairvoyante, and I take after her. When I grow up I might be a clairvoyante."

"What exactly is a clairvoyante?"

"You know, it means clear-seeing; they're people who see things clearly before they happen and I think they can somehow feel other people's thoughts."

"You mean anybody's thoughts?"

"Oh no, not anybody's; there has to be a special bond between them, they have to have been born under sympathetic stars."

"It sounds awful rot to me."

"That's because you're jealous! But you oughtn't to be really, because it means that we're fated. I mean I find you the easiest of anyone, so there must be a very strong bond between us, the same destiny." She jumped at an overhanging acorn. "Did you remember all our things for the expedition?"

"Yes, everything."

"I bet you forgot one thing."

"What?"

"The revolver!" She was laughing at his frown. "You know, I told you, in case one of us gets pinned under a fallen rock and the other one has to put him out of his agony."

He shuddered. "Horrible!" he said.

"But it was cruel of you, especially after I'd reminded you and reminded you; and it's not horrible at all really! *I* wouldn't mind dying a bit as long as I'd been loved—I mean, as long as I'd *known* I'd been loved—" She stopped suddenly and confronted him. "Now *think*!" she said. "Think very hard, as darkly as though you were in your bed at night when thoughts become so real that you live in them and they are your life; and just suppose that it was me and that with my last breath I was begging you to finish me off with the blood coming out of my mouth. Wouldn't you feel awful if you couldn't? If there was nothing to do it with?"

"Don't!" he said. "Not even as a joke. It makes me feel ill."

"But I'm not joking," she said. "We were reading *Romeo and Juliet* last term and it was wonderful. In the tomb scene I felt much happier at them dying than I would have done if they'd gone on living and got old and out of love. I know Romeo's last speech by heart:

> "Eyes, look your last!
> Arms, take your last embrace! and, lips, O you
> The doors of breath, seal with a righteous kiss
> A dateless bargain to engrossing death!
> Come, bitter conduct, come, unsavoury guide!

> Thou desperate pilot, now at once run on
> The dashing rocks thy sea-sick weary bark!
> Here's to my love! O true apothecary!
> Thy drugs are quick. Thus with a kiss I die."

She swallowed and looked at him, her eyes suddenly uncertain. "There, don't you think that is beautiful? I think it's the most beautiful thing that was ever written."

He was discomforted by the brightness of her eyes, the tiny involuntary tremor of her lip. "It's only a story," he said. "It never really happened."

"What difference does that make?" she said so sharply that he did not know whether she were angry or amused. "Things that never happened are often more important, more beautiful, or sadder than things that did. If Shakespeare made her die like that in Italy four hundred years ago, it's much more terrible than if a girl was *really* knocked over by a bus only yesterday. And anyway, it's different! You think I'm crying and I'm not, I'm happy."

"Well it's a funny way of showing it," he said awkwardly. "As Simpson would say, 'you look like a dying dook.'" He laughed loudly and alone. "Oh, come on! Cheer up. We're going to have such fun."

"I'm not sure that we are; and what's more, I don't think you care at all. Mummy says men are different, that they don't really mind about things—don't feel them like we do."

"That's not true; it's *because* we feel them so much more that we don't show it."

"Well you *ought* to show it. How's anyone to know if people never show what they feel?"

He abandoned his attempt to be reserved and ran up to her.

"I do mind, really I do! I mind so much that I don't even like to *think* about you dying let alone talk about it."

"*How* do you mind about my dying? Tell me."

"So much that if you died I should want to die myself."

"Oh, but that's not enough."

"Why not?"

"Well, anyone could say that. It's not wonderful; it's not like

Romeo. You must say more than that, or I'll know you're not my true love. You must make a speech and tell me beautifully how much you would mind. Look! I'll show you." She flopped down on the grass by the hawthorn hedge. "Now! You imagine that I'm dying in the darkness by the light of one of our candles and then tell me what you feel."

"I can't," he said. It was getting late. They ought to be at the house, they ought to be having lunch; if it wasn't late, it ought to be late.

"Please get up, Victoria! We'll be late for lunch and Mr. Harkess and your mother will be disapproving."

"No," she said. "Not till you tell me."

"Oh all right." He kneeled down beside her and leant over her white unlaughing face. It was not because it was difficult that he had fought against it, but because it was so easy; it was so much what he had most naturally wanted to do, what in some foreign country perhaps he would have done beautifully like Romeo with music and singing; it was easy, so much wanted, and so uncovering, that it must be wrong. Extraordinary, that beyond letting him, she should actually have invited him to find words for all the miseries and delights which like ravens and doves encircled her image in his mind.

"If you died," he said slowly, "it would be like—being blinded." Searching for words he looked down at her as she lay there with her eyes closed, her lashes resting like crescents of dark pollen on her cheeks, so still and so silent.

" 'Else a great prince in prison lies,' " he quoted softly. "My brother David once told me that if you took one flower to a man who had been locked up in prison for a long time and let him look at it he might go mad or die. Well, that's how I used to feel whenever things were beautiful and I was alone. But now I dare to look at them because they can answer me with your voice, look back at me with your eyes and touch me with your hands. I'm not in prison any more." He leaned and whispered into her ear, "I'm a great prince and I'm free. But if you died, if you were to die, there'd be just nothing for ever and ever."

She opened her eyes.

"That was beautiful," she said. "You *must* love me if you can talk like that. If you like you can kiss me."

"Not here," he said.

She got up quickly and, picking up the haversack, ran on ahead of him towards the rickyard.

"I know someone who would like to kiss me," she called out, "even if you wouldn't."

He caught her up by the haystack and held her against its sweet-smelling side.

"Who?" he asked.

"A hiker."

"A hiker? Where did you see him? What hiker?"

"By the gate when I was waiting for you. He had crinkly golden hair and very smart khaki trousers and a haversack like Daddy's old army one. He said he'd got a big car too up by the Stump Cross. Didn't he pass you on your way back? He was going towards Corby."

"No, no one passed me that I remember." He frowned as he recalled the ghost of a noise, the essence of a shadow between himself and the sunlight as he had sat by the holly tree a few minutes earlier. "Unless someone went past without me knowing while I was sitting on the wall."

"That's it," she said. "Whatever were you doing sitting on a wall? Oh I know, thinking of your home; and you've got nothing to be sorry about really, because by this time you'll have another home; and from what your sister Melanie said to me at the wedding it'll be much more exciting and unusual than the Vicarage ever was—come on, let me go now," she tried to duck beneath his arms but he was too quick for her and held her shoulders firmly. "We must get this soup back to the house."

"No. I want to know why you said that this hiker man wanted to kiss you."

"Well he *did*."

"How do you know?"

"By the way he looked at me."

"What way?"

"Oh! Just the way people look at something they like or want. Greedy old women in cafés look at buns in that way sometimes—or the way George Harkess looks at Mummy in the evenings, *that's* really what it's like. Anyway, I always know."

"Do you?"

"Yes, all women do. Mummy says so." His fists slackened on her shoulders as he laughed. Swinging the haversack between them they walked across the cobbles towards the kitchen door.

"You're not a woman. You're only a girl."

"I'll be fourteen on my next birthday, and besides—"

"Besides what?"

"Nothing," she said.

They pushed open the kitchen door and Victoria dumped the tins of soup on to the table. "It's quite all right," she told Annie Moses. "It's still five minutes to lunchtime and you've only got to heat it up in a pan."

"That bloomin' clock's ten minutes slow Miss Victoria, and Mr. Harkess has been in and out like t'bell ringer at Ripon this last quarter of an hour. Whatever have the two of you been up to?"

"I got off with a young man at the gate, a golden hiker."

Annie Moses clucked her lips, "These blessed visitors," she said. "Danbey'll be as thick with 'em as Scarborough uff ut goes on like this with all these motorcars and by-cycles. I can't think what they cooms for. Thur's nobbut t'old church and t'Shep-wash Cairn an' t'Stump Cross fur 'em ter look at when they does get here."

They laughed at her and left her there, stooping over her scrubbed white table, as they closed the door behind them and made their way through the hall to the study.

George Harkess was standing by the mantelpiece staring moodily at the aneroid barometer in its glass box. He looked up as they came in, frowned afresh, and then, catching Mrs. Blount's appraising, rather small grey eyes, smiled with his eyebrows and moustache.

"Well! Well! He's back," he said glancing at his watch. "I'd begun to think I'd put my shirt on a wrong 'un or that the handicap had been too heavy—and after all of the thirty furlongs, John, did you get the soup?"

"Yes, sir, two tins of oxtail."

"Bless my soul, he's not only a stayer, he knows the course as well—he's got a memory! I was afraid by this time you might have forgotten what you went for. Still, I'm in your debt Blaydon, my dear boy; thanks to your delay, I still have time for a third pink gin whereas usually I can only fit in two before me lunch."

Mrs. Blount smiled carefully at him. "George dear! Do you really think you ought to?"

"Certainly *not* Enid! That is to say not when I'm alone, a lonely old bachelor-farmer! But with *you* here, it's a different matter. What do you think, young lady?" he asked, turning heavily towards Victoria who was perching on the arm of Mrs. Blount's chair. "Don't you think I should be allowed to celebrate just once a year when your charming mother condescends to visit Nettlebed."

"*Uncle* George," she retorted, "I won't answer you."

"Tut tut!" His frown, though momentary, was disconcertingly real. "Getting into my sere and yellow, always forgetting that you will *not* be called 'young lady,' whereas you, my girl, never forget the '*Uncle* George' when you want to use your whip. But for all that you know you *are* a young lady, and a very lovely young lady, as lovely as—"

"As lovely as Mummy," she slanted at him.

The frown this time was directed a little greedily at his half-empty glass as though he were vexed by his thirst. Then he straightened his tweed-clad body and stroked the heavy hair at the back of his head. For all his size, the deliberately great scale of his clothing, there was an air of uncertainty about him, a hesitancy which, as John had earlier observed, quite evidently irritated Mrs. Blount. As it was, on this occasion too she was quick to resent his attempt to placate Victoria, and intervened quickly.

"Victoria dear! Don't you think you and John ought to go and get washed while there is still time?" With her usual exquisite care she rose from the chair on which she had been sitting as Annie Moses sounded the gong for luncheon. "There now! You see?" she went on, her hand placed lightly on George

Harkess's arm, "Now you *are* going to be late, you naughty children."

"Shoo!" said George Harkess. "Shoo! Off with you, the pair of you," and he herded them through the doorway into the hall.

They raced up the stairs together and into the bathroom.

"Do they know about our truffle hunt?" John asked as they shared the basin.

"Yes, I told them while you were in Corby."

"What did they say?"

"Not much, they didn't seem very interested." She looked at herself in the glass over the washbasin. She tilted her chin up towards the ceiling and through half-closed eyes looked along her horizontal cheeks like a ballet dancer on a bright stage. Then suddenly she dropped the pose and said casually, "I think they're going to get married this time."

"*Do* you?" He was amazed by the calmness of her tone.

"Yes. Mummy seems much fonder of him than before and they've been talking a lot about money—at least *he* has."

"What's that got to do with them getting married?"

"Oh," she said, throwing him the towel. "You are *young*! People always talk about money when they're thinking of getting married."

"They *don't*!"

"Of course they do."

"You're thinking of funerals," he said, "people making wills and so on."

"No I'm not."

"Well it's not what David and Prudence talked about before they got married. I don't think they ever mentioned it once."

"Well, what did they talk about?"

"The sort of things we talked about by the hedge this morning."

"What things?"

"Oh, about how much we loved each other and what we'd do if the other one died."

"Silly!" she retorted. "That's only young people like you and me! If we were older you'd soon find that you'd have to talk about money as well as love; in fact, one day if Enid and

George really did get married and you still wanted to marry me, you might find you'd have to talk about money to George."

"I *won't*! I wouldn't! I'd never discuss *you* with him at all. You're nothing to do with him even if he does marry your mother."

"You don't like George, do you?"

"No."

"That's because you're jealous." She faced him from the doorway. "But you needn't worry, because I don't like him either."

"Don't you?"

"No. I don't like the way he eats and I don't like his moustache or his hair and I don't like his eyes."

"Neither do I."

"It's as though he was wearing one of those masks the street boys wear at the fair when they want to do things they wouldn't dare to do without it. You know, hiding behind it and making the eyes move and the moustache waggle and smile, when all the time their real faces are doing something quite different. That's why I hate George calling me 'young lady'; I know that it's only the mask saying it, and that the other face means something quite different."

"Yes, that's it," he said. "I wonder what it is he really means and why he doesn't say it?"

"Oh grownups!" she said. "That's just what I was telling you, they never say what they really mean. When they talk about love they have to talk about it with money. There's something they're ashamed of somewhere, but no one's ever ashamed of money unless they haven't got it, and so they use it as a cover for everything they do; they make out they're doing it for money, or that they're *not* doing it for money; but, except as a joke, they never like to say they're doing anything for love."

"Do you think it's something in love that makes them feel guilty?"

"It must be, musn't it?" she said. "I'm sure it is with George. He's always either all grinning and awful about it, or else he's like a cat walking on eggs. But he'll talk about money without using his mask."

"Down with George!" he said.

"Down with George!" she echoed. "If it wasn't for the farm, for Nettlebed, I wouldn't let Mummy see him at all. But I love this place because it's in the moors and because you're here to share it with me. After this holiday I may even *let* her marry him so that we can keep on coming here if we don't go to Anglesey."

"Could you stop her?"

"Easily." She took his hand. "Come on, let's go down very quietly. I'll bet you they're talking about money again."

"How could you stop her?" he whispered as they tiptoed down the thick stair carpet.

"By giving her looks at the right time when she's with him."

"*Looks?*"

"Yes, nasty ones, amused ones, as though I thought she was looking silly or stagy. And not only that, but I could make little jokes about him when Enid and I are alone. It's the easiest thing in the world to make her feel old and ridiculous about men."

They walked quietly over the hall rugs and as they neared the dining-room door heard the clatter of George's knife and fork punctuating the murmur of his conversation.

"Settlement," they heard. "*Mumble* . . . Transfer my Canadian holdings . . . *Clop* . . . Dollars."

Victoria glanced brightly at John and then flounced ahead of him into the room. They sat down at the foot of the long refectory table.

Mrs. Blount smiled at them briefly and then turned her attention again eagerly, almost deferentially, to George Harkess on whom the gesture was as lost as were all gestures when he was at table. His face remained directed downwards, so that from where John and Victoria sat the full length of his yellow parting was visible between its banks of iron-grey hair; only his moustache and his hands moved as he ravaged busily beneath a chicken bone on his untidy plate. John found himself watching his manœuvres with a fascination which made him momentarily oblivious of his own appetite. Some people were not safe to watch under such circumstances; but there were others, and

George Harkess was one of them, whose senses extended no farther than their skins; and so it was not until Victoria's knee nudged him beneath the table that he was able to take his eyes from the grownups at the far end and give her all his attention.

"We'll go up past the Stump Cross," she was saying quietly, "and then cut directly across to the dingle. I've got the kettle ready-filled for our tea, in case there's no water in the cave, and Annie Moses has been a brick, she's done us a hard-boiled egg each." And then, as she noticed his attention straying once more to the other conversation at the darker end of the room, "*John!* You're not listening."

"Yes, I am," he said. "You said a hard-boiled egg each, and with all the things I bought we'll be able to have the most super meal. Do you know what I vote?"

"No."

"I vote we actually picnic *in* the cave."

"All right. But only if it's perfect and I think it will be. In fact I know it will be."

"I thought you said you'd never been in it before."

"I haven't, but my hiker has, and he said that if you once get through the narrow bit beyond the entrance, it opens out into a great chamber hung with those icicle things."

"Oh, how exciting!" he said flatly.

He felt a sudden distaste for the whole afternoon; it was disappointing to know that they were not going to be the first to discover the depths of the cave. If only they were at *his* home away from all these strangers: George Harkess, the village people, Annie Moses and the hiker. The hiker was a stranger himself, a stranger to the dales, a motorcar man who had no business to pretend that he was a hiker. The thought that *he* knew the very cave to which they were going and claimed to have been in it more than once, made it seem depressingly public. Nothing was so easily made public as a wild place, he thought angrily. Corners of the parks in Eastbourne were quite wild simply because they were surrounded by so much "publicness"; but one charabanc or a small group of hikers could spoil a whole mountainside.

He wished again that they were at the Vicarage together where he could have her safely to himself. He imagined the days they would have shared in the absence of all the others: meals in the kitchen with Lizzie, dreamy afternoons in the haystack, whole mornings in the orchards adjoining the strawberry beds. But, of course, he had forgotten, that could never be again. The Vicarage had gone; without moving a brick or tile it had gone for ever. By now it would be empty! Just the same, but empty and vanished.

With little appetite he continued to chew the same mouthful of tasteless chicken, was half-aware of a resumption of conversation at the far end of the table. Grownups, he thought, seem to have the trick of almost inaudible conversation without ever having to resort to whispering. What *were* they saying?

"A short trip only, Enid! Say a month at the most . . . *Mumble slop* . . ." Annie Moses must have left the pudding on the sideboard. The first-course plates had disappeared and George Harkess was now shovelling large spoonfuls of sponge roll and custard beneath his incessantly moving moustache. Mrs. Blount's head was turned half away from John, as she continued to give all her attention to whatever it was he was telling her. He glanced at her plate, at the spoon and fork which never seemed to move in the useless little hands and noticed that a small section of the sponge *had* disappeared; yet there was nothing in her cheek and no movement of her smooth boneless chin, not even any audible betrayal of the presence of food in her mouth as she murmured some question to her companion. He hoped Victoria would never grow like that: so frightened for herself, so careful of her getting up, her sitting down, walking and eating, even of her smiling. Victoria was so different; she—

"*What's the matter?*" Her whisper penetrated his preoccupation like a sudden breeze through woodland. "Are you cross again?"

What *was* he saying? What *was* George Harkess going on about?

"Lawyers, my dear . . . *Mumble mutter* . . . Settlement . . . *Clop* . . . Never lack for anything again." His enormous hand momentarily abandoned its spoon and briefly overlaid that of Mrs. Blount, who smiled up at him resignedly.

"John! I asked you if you were cross," said Victoria.

"No, not exactly," he whispered back. "Things just seemed flat suddenly, that's all. But I'm not cross."

"Please don't be," she implored. "If it was the hiker, I promise I won't mention him again."

He smiled across at her. "It's all right," he whispered. "I don't think it was that exactly; I just didn't like the thought that he'd been there before us—"

From the other end of the table George Harkess's ordinary voice boomed down at them.

"What's all this?" he enquired. "All this whispering and tragedy? Have you two been quarrelling?" He turned to Mrs. Blount and put on his quizzical face by raising one eyebrow and narrowing his normally wide nostrils. "Little birds in their nests should agree, shouldn't they, Enid? It's no good leaving these young people to themselves for the afternoon if they're going to spend their time in bickerment and disorder."

They smiled apprehensively up the length of the table towards the two attentive faces.

"Victoria dear!" Mrs. Blount's cheeks were smooth with concern. "Don't you think it *is* all rather silly? I'm sure you'd be much better to come to the races with us instead of spending your time in a dreary old cave—and I'm quite sure you won't find a single truffle for your trouble."

"Oh but we will, darling—I know we will. Someone told me only this morning—"

"Who, dear?"

Victoria glanced swiftly at John: a signal.

"Annie Moses," he said quickly. "She told us that the villagers often find truffles at the mouth of the Stump Cross cave."

"Oh, *Annie Moses!*" George Harkess's laugh frothed out over his raised tankard. "You don't want to listen to Annie Moses. She's lived here all her life, but she could give you a better description of the Scarborough cinema than the Stump Cross caves. I'd lay a pony to a pound note she doesn't even know where they are," and he sank his face into the tankard for a moment and then brought it up again with froth clinging to his moustache and the small whiskers which grew on the tip of his nose.

"Well, my dear," he went on. "We haven't time to argue

with these young scallywags! We've got a twenty-mile drive
ahead of us to Redcar."

Mrs. Blount teetered down the length of the table and kissed
Victoria.

"Very well, my darling, if you must go to your nasty cave,
you shall go; but will you be sure to remember to post this letter
for me on your way through Corby? I do so want it to catch
the early post in the morning, and George is going to be so
horribly impatient once he gets me into the car that it will be
quite impossible to persuade him to stop at the post office."

"*Going* to be!" roared George Harkess from the doorway.
"It's not a question of going to be, I *am* impatient already. I give
you just five minutes to take off your theses and put on your
thoses, and then we're off." He marched like a drum major into
the hall. Mrs. Blount smiled after him and then looked waver-
ingly at John; her eyes surveyed him like prisoners over the
barbed wire of her mascaraed lashes. "You'll take care of her,
won't you John? She's all I've got, you know, everything in
the world."

"Yes, Mrs. Blount, I'll look after her."

She moved delicately over to the door. "Good-bye, my dears."

"Good-bye!" they said. She waved a hand, the door received
her, closed behind her, and they were alone.

"Phew!" said Victoria. "Thank Heaven for Annie Moses.
Mummy hates me talking to strange men."

"So do I," said John.

"I know you do and I love you for it! I love you both
terribly."

She got up and coming around to where he sat, hugged him
impulsively. He responded eagerly. In her cotton frock she was
as sweet as the haystack. She moved away over to the window
and facing him put her hands behind her on to its white paint
and leapt easily on to the sill.

"I expect it's because she's frightened of them," she said
swinging her legs, "and the funny thing is that I could swear
that George Harkess is much more terrified of Enid than she is
of him."

"What are you talking about?" he interrupted.

"About Mummy, about her being afraid of me talking to strange men."

"Oh, I see, well, I think she's quite right."

"If men are so dangerous why is it that George Harkess is so frightened of Mummy? I'm sure all that shouting and banging and pretending to bully her is just a game. And if that's so why does he pretend? Why is he so nervous of her?"

"I don't really know," said John. "I think it's something like that money-idea of yours. It's not that people despise love or that men are afraid of women or that women are afraid of men, but they're all afraid of something to do with love. I often think of love as a tiger; you know, Blake's tiger 'burning bright in the forests of the night.'"

"What a lovely idea," she said jumping down from the window sill.

"I think it's rather a frightening one," he said.

"Oh, no," she said, "the tiger of love. Beautiful—"

He opened the door and she ran out ahead of him through the shadowy hall to the kitchen chanting at the top of her voice:

"What the hammer? What the chain?
In what furnace was thy brain?
What the anvil? What dread grasp
Dare its deadly terrors clasp?"

Later, they climbed eagerly out of the dale, following the farm-track between its black lichen-clad walls until finally it petered out altogether on the high periphery of the moorland. From there onwards heather grew on either side of the close-cropped grass which ultimately led them to the flint road encircling the southern side of the dale.

Below them they could see the whole of Danbey, an ovoid, green saucer over which the cloud-shadows sailed like dark birds from end to end, covering in their flight the little villages, the fleecy woods and the steeples of the three churches. The wind brought them the rumble of carts, the thin paeans of laying hens and, occasionally, the sound of a motor horn. They could watch the total life of the dale going on in miniature beneath them: a group of cyclists hump-backed on tiny flashing circles making their way between one village and another, the cottage women stringing up their flags of washing in the green fields, and the windmilling of the harvesters cutting the last of the summer's wheat.

Sharing their baskets they were content to say nothing under the merry wind, to watch the blown saunterings of butterflies and grasshoppers disturbed by their passing, and to tread the dusty road easily to the crown of the moor where the Stump Cross, lacking half an arm, stood like a grey priest in sorrowful benediction over all that lay beneath them. Reaching it, they sat down for a moment on the crumbling hexagon of steps which encircled its base. Victoria gave him a peppermint and waved down at the vale.

"As long as they stay down there, I don't mind them so much; they can have the old dale, but they're not to come up here."

"Who, the cyclists?"

"Yes, all of them, 'trippers and soochlike,' as Annie calls them." She chewed her mint happily. "Anyway, there *is* one good thing."

"What?"

"Charabancs! They can't even get them into Corby, let alone up this far, can they?"

"No, but they can get motorcars up here." He shaded his eyes and pointed. "Look! There's one just starting on its way up now."

"So there is."

They watched it as, far below them, gleaming and minute, it began the long hairpin-weave to the top.

Victoria got up hurriedly. "Curses! I wanted to climb the Stump Cross and balance on the top, and now I shan't be able to. Come on, let's run and get into the dingle before they get here. Give me the basket and you keep the haversack; we'll be quicker like that."

He followed her as she fled like a pale butterfly over the heather and the smooth pathways, never pausing until they were safely below the steep lip of the dingle.

"Don't stop," he said. "Let's get right to the bottom where

the stream is, and then actually into the cave itself. We'll be safe there."

She looked at him for a moment and then ran on ahead weaving her way between the larches and mountain ash which grew amongst the fallen boulders on the floor of the dingle. Suddenly she disappeared from his view behind an enormous grey cube of rock on the top of which heather-green plants and even small trees were growing. It thrust through the standing bracken like the stern of a great grey ship moored to the wall of the dingle, and for some minutes he was quite unable to discover where Victoria was hidden. At length, however, he found her waiting for him on its shadowed side behind the standing curtain of the bracken. Behind her, too, hidden until now by the bulk of the rocks, he saw the mouth of the cave, a small dark triangle with stone lips and a green earthen tongue in which small ferns were growing. Between the lips above and the tumble of mossy boulders beneath was total blackness; but even from where he stood he could hear the glassy music of the unseen water which must be feeding the ferns and moss as it passed underground to join the stream in the floor of the dingle.

"Why were you hiding?" he asked as he came up to her.

"I wasn't hiding," she said, "at least not from you. I was just escaping because I was being chased."

"Only by me."

"No," she said, "it's never *only* by anyone. If anyone ever chases me, I always feel there's a tiger after me. Don't you get that feeling if someone's chasing you?"

"But nobody *was* chasing you," he protested.

"No, I suppose not, but what does it matter if I felt that they were?"

"But who Victoria, *who?*"

"Oh, I don't know, how should I know? I'm only telling you that if I run and someone else runs after me I always get in a panic." She frowned at him. "I've *told* you, it's the tiger-feeling; we're always ready to run and *he's* always ready to chase. I thought you'd understand like you usually do when I tell you anything secret about myself."

He dropped the haversack and approached her, stepping out

of the bracken into the steep circle before the mouth of the cave. "I do understand," he said. "I've had the same feeling myself; the person behind you seems to be growing larger and larger, and you seem to be getting smaller and smaller, until at last you have to stop and turn around and break the spell."

"Oh, yes, that's it. I'm so glad you did know what I meant; I hate to be alone inside myself all the time."

With great certainty he put his arm around her shoulders. He wanted to kiss her but he didn't; it would be silly to kiss flowers, young rabbits, kittens, all small delicate living lovely things, at his age; it would be silly. Instead he comforted her; he said, "Anyway, you're quite safe now, Victoria, there's nothing to worry about now."

"No, there isn't, is there? I was just being stupid, I suppose. Nothing could happen to me when I'm with you, could it?"

"Nothing," he said, and he meant it.

She *was* being silly; she had frightened him, standing there like that, large-eyed and white in the shadow of the rock. How could anything happen to her when he was with her? She was what he saw; and because he loved her, because he loved what he saw, the love must have been present within him and awaiting *her*, before ever her image came to claim it. People didn't carry love with them like they carried shining hair or hurtful smiles; they simply found and assumed what was already there like a garment, gathering it from the person who loved them and then walking away in it looking newly beautiful.

No harm could ever come to her through him, because there was no harm against himself in what he felt for her; alone of all his hidden feelings in the wildest places of his heart, this one which lived for her was sound, safe and forever bright.

Still with his arm about her shoulders, he moved around to face her and leaned his forehead against hers as she stood there forlornly, still trembling in the aftermath of her fear. Her eyes opened widely; he saw the black pupils so closely that she appeared to have only one eye, grey and startled, pausing like a deer disturbed at its grazing before taking instantly to the horizon and the wind.

Frightened himself, he drew away and fumbled for the haversack with a blind hand. Backing away from her down the slope towards the tall bracken, his eyes watched her still: a white figure suddenly sprung from the living ground. How came she there in that empty place? he wondered. And what was it that forced him to see her again as though for the first time? A loveliness as external and disturbing as that he had glimpsed by the lake more than a year ago.

For now, as then, he realized, she was still entirely her own. The moment of fear, of sympathy, of most intense *caring*, while seeming to end their isolation, had in reality thrust them further than ever apart, estranging them, building up in their silence an embarrassment as discrete as some third person whose presence made it impossible for them to go on behaving as they had behaved even though they most deeply wished to do so.

He found the haversack at last and at once became very busy with it, getting out the candles and matchbox with the strange new hand that still looked as though it belonged to someone else; and when at last he spoke he noticed that his voice was no longer careless and ordinary.

"You *are* game to have tea inside, aren't you?" he asked.

She moved suddenly, breaking down the planes of her immobility with an almost visible effort.

"I don't know."

"Perhaps it would be best if I saw what it's like first; I mean, whether we'll be able to carry the things or not. Give me your flashlight and I'll make a reconnaissance."

She laughed. "What a silly word."

"It's not, it's a perfectly good word. My brother David often uses it."

"I *thought* it wasn't yours."

"Of course it's mine; don't be so superior. If I use it, then it's mine, isn't it?"

She handed him the flashlight. "It doesn't sound like you," she said. "It's not your sort of word, it's a *David* sort of word, and I think it's you who's trying to be superior, not me."

He was on his hands and knees now at the entrance to the cave; he wanted both to get out of the light, the strange dusky circle, green grey and white, which lay before the cave and to move into the darkness beyond. He did not look back as he called out to her, "If you're going to be like this, I'll stay inside! I just won't come back, that's all."

She made a run at him, he could hear her feet slip on the shale as she rushed up the slope and grasped him desperately by the heels.

"I'm sorry, John, I'm awfully sorry. I didn't mean it. It was just that I thought we *should* quarrel because everything felt so difficult."

"I know," he said. He wriggled in a bit farther until he was right out of the sunlight and then he turned and looked back at her—still standing out there in the open. "But it's all right now," he said. "You wait there for me, I shan't be long."

He shone the light ahead of him and saw that the roof of the cave rose steadily from the entrance and swept away from him over the jumbled stone-clad floor to another, farther constriction about thirty yards ahead. Holding the flashlight in his mouth to give him greater freedom with his arms, he made his way rapidly to this distant orifice.

As he drew nearer he saw that it shone, and for the first time glimpsed the water whose music he had heard earlier; high above him, as he stood there shining his light upwards, he saw it trickling over the stone threshold of another higher gallery; and for some moments he watched it as it fell in a clear fan-shaped pendulant before losing itself in a mound of wet rocks piled beneath its jaw. He climbed these rocks, and on his haunches began to crawl awkwardly along the new higher level of the cave. Small stalactites scraped against his blazer, his gym shoes and socks soaked up the water from the stream; but the beam of his light enabled him to see that once again the roof was ascending, and that a few more feet of progress would allow him to stand almost upright. Ahead of him, the gallery in which he was moving turned sharply; from where he crouched its two shining, rifled walls merged so closely together that it was only by shaking his light and making their shadows dance that he was able to see that they were separate at all.

He determined that before he made his way back to Victoria he would reach this bend and discover what lay beyond it. So far, he was sure, he had been only about five minutes; but he must allow for the return journey and not forget that if she once became really frightened it would spoil everything: they would have to have tea in the open air, and there would be no shared memory of this new darkness and danger, the magic that he was sure lay beyond the present discomfort.

Bent like an ape, the flashlight still in his mouth, he began to run clumsily over the wet, uneven floor, balancing himself by stretching his hands against the walls, and watching the leapings and posturings of the shadows which moved with him. Then at last he was there, safely around the corner and able to stand quite upright and flash his light ahead of him. Ten feet from him, the narrow tunnel by which he had entered ended abruptly in a coffin-shaped arch, and beyond it he could see nothing. The pale beam of his light passed through it into the remote darkness of a vast space. Heedless of his torn shirt, wet head and chilled feet, he stepped forward breathlessly; this must be the place, it *must* be.

As far as the flashlight could reach and beyond, it stretched ahead of him: a wide, high, windless cavern colonnaded by stalactites whose gleaming surfaces took the light and tossed it in bright sequestrations to the roof. There was every sort of formation, from graduated pipes like those of an organ, to hanging curtains, sculptured chalices and shrouded monklike figures. On the sloping floor, the limestone, tunnelled and gouged by centuries of water, was eroded into a thousand shapes and runnels, while in the darkness beyond, water drops fell incessantly and musically from the roof on to rocks and the surfaces of pools.

He waited no longer; he had seen enough to know that whatever the more remote particulars of his discovery, they must be found and shared with Victoria; so he splashed his way back to the dry deceptive entrance and crawled out once more into the open air.

It was greyer than he had expected; the prolonged rush of the wind had at last summoned up more clouds than it could disperse, and over by the Pennines there were swathes and banks of a stony-blueness which had no kinship with that of the pure sky. Though as yet there was no rain, they knew that it was on its way, that soon the first premonitory drops would begin to stir the heather and confuse the butterflies, driving them to shelter beneath leaves and bracken.

Victoria had gathered two neat bundles of sticks and was rolling them up into her mackintosh as he emerged. The wind, strong enough now to descend into the dingle, blew her dark hair about her head, alternately hiding and revealing her face and neck so that she seemed as inconstant as a shaken flower.

He leaned on her shoulder and shouted into her ear.

"You do look strange, were you frightened?"

"No, I was far too busy. Look! I've got some lovely dry sticks for our fire. It's going to rain, and whether we want to or not we shall have to picnic in the cave. What's it like? Any good?"

"You wait till you see it; it's—breathtaking! A little bit wet perhaps, but by the look of things it couldn't be wetter than it's going to be out here. If you can manage the sticks, I'll take the basket and haversack. We'll have to go slowly; but then, we're not in any hurry, are we?"

"None at all!" Her smile was swift. "We needn't be back till nearly seven, and they're sure to be in a good mood after the races because George will have had plenty to drink."

"Surely he won't be in a good mood if he's lost money?"

"It doesn't make any difference either way, because George always drinks to success if he wins and to failure if he doesn't; so you see, he's bound to be nice to us!"

They wriggled their way into the entrance, passing their things to one another at the difficult places, and then by the light of the flashlight stumbled along to the high, wet throat of the first cavern.

"If it's very wet where we're going," she said doubtfully, "I suppose we could always come back and have tea in this part— it's so nice and dry here."

"Never! This is the most wonderful cave I've ever seen, and it'll be worth it even if we get soaked."

"Is it really? What a swindle for George! He thought we'd never find it."

"That's why I was so determined that we *should*," he said emphatically.

"It wouldn't have mattered if we hadn't. We could have invented a beauty between us—I've been practising already. What do you call those things that hang from the roof?"

"Stalactites."

"And the other ones? The ones that stick up to meet them? Are they stalagmites?"

"Yes. But you needn't worry about inventing *those* because we'll be able to bring some real ones back as proof of the fact that we did find the cave, even though there don't seem to be many truffles here."

"Oh bother the truffles," she said, "they were only an excuse really, weren't they?"

"Exactly!"

"Like the races are an excuse for hundreds of men like George to go and get drunk."

They paused for a moment below the waterfall.

"It's not very big, is it?" she said.

"No, and a good thing, too, because we've got to crawl through it for several yards."

"You know, I'm beginning to wish we'd brought towels with us," she said, as he helped her into the higher gallery. "Enid gets into such a fuss when I get my hair wet."

"I *did* bring towels," he said proudly, "there's one in the bottom of the haversack. You seem to forget that I've been in caves before, with my brother David. I'm quite a spelaeologist."

"What's that? A cave-man?"

"Yes." He passed the basket up to her.

"Well, what's a cave-woman?"

"I don't know—yes I do! A cave-woman is a troglodyte; you're a troglodyte."

"No I'm not, it's a horrid word."

"But you are," he said, as they crouched beneath the oppressive roof, "it only means that you love the darkness. We're both troglodytes for today, anyway."

"I'm not sure that I do love the darkness," she said. "Promise me you won't go on too far ahead."

"I promise. Now have you got your share of the things?"

"I think so."

"All right then, I'll lead the way, and you're not to say another word until we reach the real cave. The password is 'silence.' "

" '*Silence*,' " she repeated.

"That's right."

They made their way awkwardly along the narrow tunnel, turned the corner and reached the last coffin-shaped orifice.

"There!" he said. "Now let's light our candles and you'll see why I was so excited."

They held them up before them, and immediately the nearest stones and their shadows, rock formations and stalactites, leapt out of the far darkness as though an empty space had been newly filled by the utterance of some powerful and forgotten word. For a moment they stood there, instinctively clutching one another's hands. Beyond them, the ceaseless falling of the water, the lisps and chords of notes sounded by water moving and falling from high places to low, the whisper of water through darkness and against limestone, these and the sense of an ancient wind moving in hidden fastnesses, chilled and awed them as they waited.

"I don't think we should have come," she whispered. "Let's go back, John; let's go back! We've seen it now."

"Nonsense," he said loudly, the cave echoing him. "We'll build our fire and have tea here, just as we said we would. We can't possibly go back now; we would be ashamed of it for the rest of our lives."

". . . *rest of our lives*," echoed the cave.

Victoria dropped the mackintosh; the hand holding her candle shook as she plucked at his blazer.

"Don't go in any farther," she said. "*Please* don't. This is a horrible place—even this bit where we're standing! I don't like it; I feel that we're waiting to hear something terrible."

"Don't be silly!" he said. "It's only a matter of getting used to it. It's an echo, that's all."

"But I *hate* echoes! I don't like them; I've always been frightened of them; and besides, this one's not like an ordinary echo—"

"Yes it is, except that it's an underground one."

"No it's not; it's different."

"How is it different?"

"Well, it wasn't like your voice; it answered with another voice, a cruel one like George uses when he's ticking off the mastiffs."

"*You* try then. I'll listen and see if it sounds like you."

"No."

He glanced at her by the light of the candles. Her face swam with shadows and colour, he had never seen it so soft and bright before; but glimpsed in profile at this moment, it was flat and two-dimensional as though suspended on some transparent surface beside him in the darkness.

"I promise," he said, and it was because he was so abject before this sudden beauty that he was so insistent. "I promise that if it doesn't sound like you, we'll go straight back. I won't argue any more. Please just try once."

"What shall I say?" she whispered, and her generosity in acceding to him made him reckless.

"Oh, anything, anything at all! Only shout it loudly, Victoria, that's always a good way of getting yourself unfrightened."

She tensed:

"The rest of my life!" she shouted.

". . . *rest of my life . . . of my life!*" came the wavering retort.

Beside him she took in another breath:

"I hate you!" she shouted. "I don't know who you are, but I hate you!"

". . . *hate you . . . hate you . . .*" the echo repeated.

He felt her move; she stood on tiptoe, trying to reach high up into the darkness that lay ahead, and he put out a hand to restrain her.

"Stop!" he said, "that's enough, don't go on!"

She turned on him. "Well, *was* it the same? Was it?"

"Yes," he said, "I think so; yes, it was, of course it was." He picked up the mackintosh. "Follow me. We'll get the fire going; that will make all the difference. It will be cosy and all the stalactites will glitter."

With the flashlight he started to pick his way across the sharp, wet floor towards what he guessed must be the nearest wall.

"Look! The very place." He pointed towards a great buttress of limestone with a flattened top which jutted out into the body of the cavern. "We'll make our fire on that—it's almost dry because the water is trickling down the wall at the back instead of falling direct."

She handed him the mackintosh and he unfolded it and placed the sticks and paper on the rock.

"Now give me the haversack," he said.

"I haven't got it, I was so frightened I wanted to hold on to you instead."

He took off his damp blazer and spread it over the mackintosh. "You'd better sit on that while I go back and get all the other things."

Nursing her candle in both hands she sat down fearfully and he hurried back to the archway. He was frightened himself, but he wasn't going to show it; if she once knew there was anything he dared not face she would never forget it; and then one day she would love someone older and braver than him and he would lose her. She had been right though; the echo had not been the same; it had been higher and more remote, quite different.

Up above him he could visualize layer upon layer of rock, the great weight reaching up and up to the surface soil on which the heather grew, and here below, where they were, bearing down upon them and upon the darkness like a hammer on an anvil. The more he thought about it the more frightened he became; why had he ever left the fair light of day, the fresh wind and the hurrying clouds, when ordinary night and the countless fears to which it gave rise were both inevitable enough? He knew now that he could very easily allow himself to become frightened right to the sharp edge of panic; and he knew that if he once did so, a chance of being trusted and of showing that he could endure would be lost for ever. Therefore he resolutely banished from the outskirts of his mind all these images which sought from its dim horizons to wing their way inwards. The thing to do, he resolved, was to go eagerly through all the motions of taking pleasure and seeming busy, but to get it over as quickly as he decently could and then return with her proudly to the farm.

He almost ran back with the haversack, and a few minutes later with the aid of a melting candle he had the fire kindled and the small picnic kettle sitting unsteadily on its mound of sticks.

Victoria peeled the eggs as they squatted together on the mackintosh. "Well, anyway," she said, "I bet we're the first people ever to picnic in here."

"Yes." He took a bite of the rather damp bread and butter. "Except possibly prehistoric men thousands and thousands of years ago."

"Do you really think so?"

"I can imagine them," he said, "grunting and quarrelling; hairy babies wrapped in skins in the driest corners."

"And the funny thing is, that they would feel safe in here; for *them* all the danger would be outside: wolves and mammoths —the tiger-feeling."

"Yes," he said, "the tiger-feeling."

"Do you know something?" she whispered. "I've been wondering if this cave is haunted."

"Of course not."

"After all, if they did live in here years and years ago there's no reason it shouldn't be haunted."

He got up and put some more sticks on the fire. "It's getting very smoky in here—rather airless; I hope the fire's not using up all the oxygen."

"But why shouldn't they have ghosts?" she persisted. "They were men weren't they, not animals?"

"I wish you wouldn't whisper."

"I didn't know I was whispering. I'm very sorry."

He squeezed her hand. "Good! The kettle's nearly boiling, can you hear it?"

She listened. "It's not singing, it's whistling."

"No," he said, "it's singing."

"SSh—!"

"What is it?"

"Listen very carefully," she said. "There *is* someone whistling!"

He leaned forward towards the bright flames, staring over them towards the entrance. He heard three high careless notes far away as though someone were indeed whistling, but before he could be sure, it had ceased and he could discern only the constant music of the water underscored by the minute melody of the kettle.

"No," he said, "it was only the kettle; it was the steam lifting the lid."

She shivered. "Well, I wish it would hurry up. I'm longing to have my tea and get out of here."

In the darkness a stone fell with a splash into a pool; the noise was deliberate and dreadful. In the silence they squatted there not daring at first even to look at one another. Throughout the unseen reaches of the cave water continued to drip far and near, a relentless pattering like a thousand clocks. Not very far away, in the tunnel perhaps, perhaps behind them in some other part of the gallery, somebody swore pleasurably, an obscene, lingered-over word.

John jumped to his feet; his back to Victoria, his trembling shadow tapering off over the floor, he shouted out into the darkness, "Who's there?"

Oblivious of the echo, his voice interrupting its own reverberations, he yelled again, "We can see you. Who are you?"

In the throat of the tunnel a match was struck and they saw the pink sheltering hands, the laughing face with the shadow of the nose thrown broadly up between the eyes.

"But for that bloody stone," said the man, "if you will forgive my French, you would not have heard me until much later." He started to stumble towards them. "Can't see a foot ahead of me. Show us a light, will you? I'm getting too old for this sort of game."

The match went out and he disappeared again, but they could hear him: his rapid breathing, the ugly noises of his feet in the water and the secret chuckles of his amusement.

"A pity!" he went on, "a great pity! I had an idea I should find you here; but then one never knows, one never does know."

John stepped forward a pace.

"Who are you?" he asked. "What do you want?"

"All in good time," said the man. "One of you knows me, or she should do; and if there's a cup of tea going, well, like the song 'I'm young and healthy.' " He struck another match. "And now," he asked, "does my young lady of this morning recognize me now?" He thrust his face forward into its light. "Nothing to be so very frightened about surely? Speaking the truth, my friends tell me I'm quite good-looking."

Victoria got up. "It's my hiker," she said rather flatly. "However did you find us?"

"Well isn't that just typical of a woman?" said the man. "She tells you where she'll be at a certain time and then when you arrive she makes out that she's surprised." Kneeling down on the wet rock, he suddenly grasped her hand and kissed it. "Your servant, young madam—more than that, your willing slave."

Victoria laughed. "You are funny, I'm not a woman, I'm only a girl. Do get up—you make me feel stupid."

The man got up. "There now," he said. "I've creased my trousers for you; but never mind, it's all in a good cause." He turned to John, "Now then, introductions please, this is—?"

"This is my friend. I told you about him. His name is John Blaydon and I am Victoria."

He bowed. "And my name is Jack—Jack Noone," he announced.

"Is that your real name?" asked John.

The man turned to Victoria. "Suspicious, isn't he?" he said. "Doesn't seem to trust us, does he? Let's say that it's good enough for me, shall we, and get on with the tea-making? From what you were saying a few minutes ago I gather that the kettle's just on the boil, so who's going to be mother?" He sat down on the mackintosh and started to prod at the fire, and Victoria, with a little shrug of her shoulders, sat down too. John remained standing.

"How did you know the kettle was boiling?" he asked.

"Because, young feller, I was listening to you—I was *eavesdropping!*" Abruptly he laughed out loud and then, with a discomforting effect, equally suddenly cut his laugh short. "A terrible crime, isn't it, listening to sweethearts—in the dark?"

He looked swiftly from one to the other of them, his face

briefly two-headed in the flicker of the firelight. They said nothing and their silence seemed to spur him on to further speech. "But you needn't worry, I didn't hear much, and I saw nothing because it was too dark. To tell you the truth, whatever you were up to in here, I wouldn't tell; I'm not so old myself yet, and I don't suppose kids have changed much since my day—I'll bet there are still some things we don't tell our parents or our teachers—eh?" He laughed incompletely, and in the sinking firelight they were again silent, not even looking at one another.

"But I see I embarrass you," the man said. "Heavy-footed, that's me. Forget it! We'll talk about something else—sweethearts must have their little secrets to themselves, mustn't they? Who's going to 'mash t'tay,' as they say up this way? I think the lady should."

"As a matter of fact," said John coldly, "we weren't going to have any tea after all. We were just thinking of going when you arrived—it's so wet in here."

"It's not so wet as it is outside," said the man. "Cats, dogs and puppy dog's tails! All the things that little boys are made of. So I think you'd be very much better to have your tea in here, don't you, Victoria?"

Victoria looked at John, but he would not meet her eyes, and as he looked away he heard her voice change; it became suddenly defiant, it was her daring voice, "Yes, let's!" she said. "We said we would, and we *will!*"

"That's the stuff!" said the man, smiling at her. "I like a girl who knows her own mind, and I don't mind betting you'd take a bit of moving once you'd made up *your* mind; you'd be more than a match for the pair of us, I'm sure, eh?"

Victoria looked pleased. She filled the teapot with a flourish.

"*You* don't deserve any tea," she said, with a pretty sideways smile. "We were petrified, weren't we John? We kept hearing noises, didn't we? By the way, was it *you* whistling just before that stone fell?"

"Me?" he said. "I never whistle. You must have been hearing things." He picked up a cup, "Only two cups? Tk, tk! One of us'll have to share then! Fancy inviting a man to tea with you and then expecting him to share."

"I *didn't* invite you; I just told you we were going to picnic in the cave. I had no idea you were even thinking of coming."

"Now! Now! Don't deny that you didn't sell me on the cave and the tea party. It'll do *him* no harm to be a little bit jealous; he's got all his life ahead of him yet and he's starting young enough."

John got up. "What do you do for a living?" he asked suddenly.

"What do I do?" asked the man. "I do everybody," and he laughed for the third time.

"I don't understand," said John obstinately. "My father's a clergyman, and Victoria's father a gentleman. Well, what are you?"

The man looked suddenly serious, "He's trying to frighten me," he said, and then he smiled in a very friendly fashion. "Well, to tell you the truth I'm a C.T."

"What's that?" they both asked.

"A traveller—commercial."

"Oh, then you're not a hiker at all?" said Victoria.

"Far from it, I'm what the hikers look for when they're tired of hiking—the gent with the car."

He put down his empty cup and John rinsed it out before filling it with fresh tea.

"Particular isn't he?" said the man. "Anyone would think I'd got foot and mouth, wouldn't they? What's the matter, don't I look clean?"

John looked down at him. "I can't see your face very distinctly in this light," he said politely.

The man turned eagerly to Victoria, "Well what do you think? You saw me in the daylight, didn't you? I'm not so bad am I?"

"I didn't notice," she said shortly. "I think we ought to be going, it must be getting very late. Do you know what the time is?" She got up and he looked at his watch.

"It's just after six," he said. "Why, what time have you to be back—wherever you're going?"

Victoria ignored the question. "Heavens!" she said to John. "Mummy'll be back at seven and I promised we'd help Annie with the supper."

"No hurry," said the man. "Once we get out of this hole I'll have you back in ten minutes."

"You needn't worry," said John. "We'll walk. It doesn't matter if we *are* a bit late, does it, Victoria? And we don't mind the rain, do we? We're wet enough as it is."

"No," she said doubtfully. "It's Annie's evening out though, and she may miss her date if we aren't there to help her. Then Enid will be upset."

Stumbling around the uneven floor of the cave John and Victoria collected the things and packed the haversack.

"I'll lead the way," said John.

From behind him the man lifted the haversack and the mackintosh from his arms and thrust the flashlight into his hand.

"Now," he said, "no arguments; I'll be the porter and the lady can come in the middle—"

"I can manage thank you," said John. "I got them in all right—"

"I told you," said the man, "if you want to argue you'd better pick someone your own size. And now, lead on, Macduff!"

With tight-lipped obedience John took the lead, and in single file they negotiated the uneven tunnel, clambered down the entrance chamber, and came out into the dark green daylight beyond.

It was still raining heavily as they made their way back to the road, and in the middle of the dripping bracken which flanked the entrance to the cave their companion made Victoria put on her mackintosh.

"We've got to look after you," he said as he turned up the collar for her and fastened it swiftly beneath her chin. "Can't have your mother thinking we didn't know how to look after her daughter. I expect she'll be back by now and worrying herself cold wondering what's happened to you."

"No she won't," said John. "I told her we'd be back before they were, and they said we were not to expect them before seven."

"Oh, your father's expecting you too is he, Victoria?"

"No not my father, my mother's friend Mr. Harkess who owns the farm where we're staying."

"And they're both out? Well, well, that takes a bit of beating."

"What does?" asked Victoria.

"Leaving the two of you alone in the evening in a place like this. Where have your mother and her friend gone to?"

"The races at Redcar—and anyway we're not alone; there's the maid and the two dogs," John said with relish. "I'd like to see anyone try and break in, I can tell you! The mastiffs would tear lumps out of him."

The man picked up the haversack and started off along the wet, rabbit-nibbled pathway.

"Blood-thirsty, isn't he?" he said to Victoria. "All the same, you wouldn't catch me leaving a couple of teen-agers alone at night in this part of the world, even if I trusted *them*. Why, your folk might have a breakdown or a puncture or something and not get home till all hours. That would be nice for you, wouldn't it?" He stopped so suddenly that Victoria bumped into him. "I'll tell you something," he went on.

"What?"

"I'll bet your mother wouldn't carry on like this if your father was here."

They looked at each other briefly and then started to trudge on through the rain and the greyness of the moorland dusk, while for a moment he stood where they had left him, a tall laden figure from whom they longed to escape and from whom, for that very reason, they did not hurry but walked perhaps a little more slowly than the rain and the hour warranted. It was only a moment before they heard the squelch of his footsteps as he ran to catch them up. "Where is your father then?" he asked as he drew level with them.

"She hasn't *got* one," said John, "and if you don't mind she'd rather not talk about it."

Because he so sharply expected the laugh, it was a shock when he heard it. "My mistake, apologies all around," said the man, "but how was I to know? You said he was a gentleman; you never said he was a *dead* gentleman!"

"He's *not* dead!" said John. "He's very much alive but he's— abroad, isn't he, Victoria?"

"Yes," she improvised. "He's in New York, but he writes to me every week and soon he'll be coming home on the *Majestic*."

"Well, well! That's what I call nice," said the man. "Every girl needs a father these days."

They breasted the upper limit of the dingle and came out into the full aggression of the wind hurling its rains against their faces. It was a relief to be on a high level place once more. John felt that the most unpleasant part of the afternoon was behind them, that it lay somewhere in the dark hollow of the dell, and that out here in the open they could be no more than they were: three ordinary people who had picnicked on the moors. The rain was like a wet sheaf of chrysanthemums in the light of his torch, the separate drops swirled into the centre of the light like the loose ragged petals of the flower, and from it came the mingled scent of earth, grass and heath.

Ahead of them they saw the low shape of the motorcar as it crouched beside the road, and at the sight of it their companion became suddenly gayer and more confident.

"*There* she is!" he said. "That's one thing about a car, if you put her in gear and leave the brake on she'll be there when you come back; you can trust a car. Between us we'll have you home in two shakes and then yours truly will have to be on his way back to—Huddersfield."

They did not argue about this, they wanted only to get home; so they quickened their pace eagerly and were soon sitting together on the back seat. Their companion fumbled at the dashboard; they saw him searching for the ignition switch with a bunch of keys, and after a short delay he switched on the sidelights and started the engine. "It gets dark quickly this time of the year," he said, "and though I should know 'er like the back of my hand, she's got so many little gadgets that I make mistakes sometimes. Pity about the short evenings; I like a country drive myself, looking at things you know and just easing along through the country lanes."

"You do a lot of driving then?" Victoria asked politely.

"Nothing but," he said. "I'm a devil for it! That's why I took this job—mostly. You get your car, you get your petrol, you get your expenses, and then you get your area *and* you get paid for covering it. Suits me."

"What do you sell?"

He laughed loudly above the noise of the engine. This time his laugh was prolonged; they thought he might never stop; but he did, suddenly, slowing down the car as they descended the narrow road into the floor of the dale.

"To be honest," he said, "that's something I'm not prepared to answer," and he turned half around so that they saw the stubby outline of his profile against the running windscreen.

John spoke: "Why do you always say 'to be honest'?" he asked. "You keep on saying it; you keep on saying, 'to be truthful,' 'to be honest,' and things like that. Why do you say them?"

"If you had to do what I have to do, you'd know there's a lot of liars about, and you've got to know who to trust. Now when you're selling things sometimes, you have to tell a bigger one than the chap you're selling to; it's part of the job. But among friends there's no necessity for that, so just to let them know that it's not business, you tell 'em that you're on the level. Satisfied?"

"No," said John. "I could understand it if you said something, and then the other person wanted to know if you were telling the truth; but if you *are* telling the truth and yet you keep on saying 'to be truthful,' it sounds as though the other person who doesn't believe you is *yourself*."

"Oh forget it!" said the man. "To get back to the question of my commodities, the product of the old firm, I can tell you it is a garment your girl friend would have no use for yet— I'm sure of that," and he started to laugh again.

John leaned forward, "We're nearly there now," he said. "The entrance is by that clump of trees on the left. You needn't take us in. It'll only upset the dogs and frighten Annie."

"Sure?" he asked. "It's no trouble."

"It's very kind of you and thank you very much for the lift, but we'll be quite all right now. We're in splendid time, aren't we Victoria?"

"Yes, we are, but we must hurry if we're to be in time to help Annie with the supper. It must be nearly half-past six."

"Half-past six! It's ten to *seven*," said the man as they drew up by the gate. "Like me to come in and peel the potatoes for you? I'm quite handy in the kitchen, well-trained, and one good turn deserves another."

"No thank you," said Victoria. "It's very thoughtful of you but—" Her hands thrust deep into the pockets of her mackintosh, she stopped. "Heavens!" she said bringing out a crumpled envelope. "How awful! I'd forgotten all about Mummy's letter. Just look at it, it's in an awful mess and it's terribly important."

In the diffused light from the side lamps her mouth tightened and her eyes grew large. "Oh dear! I *promised* it would catch the last post, and now if it's ten to seven I can't possibly do it."

The man moved across the seat and stretched his hand out through the open window; he lifted her chin and when he spoke his voice was thick with sympathy. "The end of the World," he said. "Darkness and Death! Give it me. *I'll* pop it in the box for you."

"Oh *thank* you! You're sure you don't mind?"

"Not me, just tell me where the post office is, give me my directions, and Bob's your uncle."

She could hardly speak fast enough.

"Well it's past the grocer's shop on the right; you have to turn down towards the church and then cross over the bridge and the post office is down a little side street; it doesn't look like a post office, it's—"

"Here hang on! Give us a chance. I'm not a geography teacher and time's getting short."

"Oh dear, do *you* know where it is, John? I'm sure you could explain better than me; I get so excited, I hate catching trains and posts—" In her agitation she was dancing about in the road.

"I'll find it," said John. "Let me go with him and then I could run back."

"No!" she said with decision. "You're such an old muddler, you'll go into a dream and forget it or drop it and Mummy'll never trust me again. *I'd* better go, and you go in and get on with the supper and tell Annie."

He drew in his breath to reply but found that he was unable to speak the words.

Beside him, with a greater reality and solidity even than the shape of the car, he saw and sensed that the man was waiting for them to finish. He was waiting dreadfully, with a dry patience for whatever they were to decide; he was like people he had seen at race meetings, completely still and finally committed to such an extent that they no longer cared in the very least about the result. Something of his deliberation affected John himself so that although his alarm was supreme, he was momentarily immobilized and watched Victoria open the door and jump into the front seat with all the remoteness of someone performing this action behind a plate-glass window. Then, when it was too late, words and action returned to him and he sprang forward.

"But Victoria! *Victoria!*" She blew him a kiss and must have seen some enormous comedy of dismay in his face, for she laughed before she spoke.

"Don't *gloom!*" she said, "I'll be all right, I'll be back in ten minutes."

Through the window he clutched at the letter in her wet hands.

"Please," he said. "Please, Victoria! Let *me.*"

The car started to move forward.

"Now then," said the man. "Watch yourself laddie, she's made up our minds for us and I told you we were neither of us a match for her."

John jumped back as the car gathered speed. He saw the dark lips of Victoria's smile through the window, the movement of her hair in the wind, even the last white flutter of her hand as she was carried past him; then he was alone on the wet road. He looked up at the uniform blackness of the raining sky, at the almost indistinguishable oak trees, and picking up the haversack and the mackintosh he walked slowly down the drive to the farm.

Making his way through the yard, he entered the kitchen and found it in darkness. Tim, the farm cat, was sitting on the rag mat in front of the open range, and in the firelight he could see that over the dresser the hands of the pendulum clock stood at five minutes past seven. Annie must have given them up and gone to keep her date, he decided. He switched on the light and looked around to see if she had left any messages for them about the vegetables or the oven; but there was no scrap of paper to be seen, so, leaving the haversack on the kitchen table, he walked out through the wide hall and into the dining room. The table was set for four and on the sideboard was a cold ham freshly crumbed and the half-carcass of the roast chicken they had eaten for lunch. With memories of the Vicarage fresh in his mind, he looked around for a bowl of salad and a tureen of baked potatoes; but there were no signs of them, so he returned to the kitchen and opened the oven door. The potatoes were sitting there just as he had visualized them, and in the larder he found the salad in its glass bowl.

There was nothing for him to do then except wait. Victoria would be upset of course; she hated breaking promises and would be hurt by the silent reproach of the cosily prepared meal; but she would soon get over it. She would be so glad to be back in the farmhouse after the ordeal of the darkness and the rain that she would not allow the prospect of Annie's teasing or Enid's unspoken displeasure to weigh heavily against the immediate delight of her return. She should not be long either; that fellow was very obliging, he would almost certainly insist on running her back to the farm. In ten minutes at the very most she would be—

His thought shifted, in fact he was *too* obliging; the way he had fastened her mackintosh and patted her chest, the fuss he had made about the letter, his irritating interest and sympathy about—and then offering to come in and help with the potatoes like that. Couldn't he see that they hadn't wanted him? That they were longing to be rid of him? It should have been obvious from the moment he first appeared. Or did he perhaps think that Victoria liked him, that she had been bored by being with him alone, with himself, with John Blaydon? She had been eager enough to go off with him in the car; her anxiety about the letter might just have been an excuse. Girls always liked someone older, he knew that; his brothers, Michael and Geoffrey, were always drumming it into him. For all *he* knew, she might really have invited the man to join them at the cave; he hadn't been there to hear her conversation by the gate, and her coldness when the man had actually arrived might have been due less to distaste than to guiltiness at not having told John the truth. If only he were older himself!

Taking off his mackintosh he hung it in the hall and went into the sitting room. A log fire smouldered in the hearth and the room was faintly scented with the smoke from it. He lay down on the hearth rug and stared at the patterns of the glowing logs. Their surfaces all divided up into separate rectangles with black centres and grey edges, they looked like crocodile skin. Gusts of wind down the wide chimney played upon their surfaces, firing them to redness so that the charcoal whitened and flaked off into the mound of ashes on which they rested. Different from the picnic fire, different he was sure, from the fire in the boiler house at Beowulf's; schools never had fires, only semi-hot-water pipes in the day rooms and classrooms; so this would be one of the last real fires he would see for nearly fourteen weeks.

In the hall a clock struck. A quarter-past seven. He sat up suddenly in the unlighted room; twenty-five minutes and no sign of her. What could she be doing? Walking slowly back down the drive? Sitting in the car talking to the man? Or trying to get rid of him, tactfully preventing him from coming in to help?

He ran out through the front door. It had stopped raining and the wind had dropped a little. In the darkness he could smell the hay piled high in the dutch barn and hear the gusty fall of water through the wet leaves of the trees. The dogs in their enclosure behind the cowshed were silent. Annie must have fed them before she left or they would have barked at his coming. They were not yet quite sure of him, and for his part, though he had not shown it in front of Victoria or George Harkess, he was terrified of them.

There were dogs and dogs, he thought, and the nature of them depended more upon their owner than upon the dog. Some people shaped their dogs out of an absurd and boisterous affection and these dogs leapt out of their owners on a lead, rolling and grovelling on the carpet at one's feet. They were lovable, rather comical projections of some aspect of their owners which lay hidden in the absence of the dog. But there were other owners who bared their dog's teeth and reddened his eye with an aggression and hostility which was carefully concealed when they were dogless, and these dogs of George Harkess's were like that. They had their uses though; they did not like strangers, and even in play they were immediately dangerous, jumping up suddenly in a half-fierce way, as though unsure of the mood they must reflect, and proud and heavy enough to knock even their owner flat on his back if he were unprepared for a sudden display of their affection.

He made his way through the yard, past the cowshed and around to the converted pigsty in which they were housed. Tiptoeing through the mud and over the cobbles in the darkness, he approached the tall wire-netting fearfully and fumbled for the latch of the enclosure. On the other side, through the door of the sty itself, he heard the straw rustle and a wet rumble of sound from the throats of the mastiffs; then there was silence.

"Good lads," he called out harshly. "Jenkins boy! Maxim! Good dogs," but there was no response; they were waiting. Six feet away from him on the other side of the wire-netting he could almost feel the cock of their ears and the tension of their gleaming black bodies. Swiftly he sought for the latch again, found it, and wrenching the gate open, turned and ran back around the corner of the cowshed, across the yard, and in at the back door.

Behind him, the dogs were after him soundlessly; he heard no bay or bell note as they ran, but only the fall of their pads through water and mud as they tore across the yard in his wake. They sensed his fear and they would have had him down if they could for his very cowardice; but he was too quick for them and slammed the door on their muzzles when they were still nearly six feet away from it. Outside, he heard the thud of a heavy body against its lower panel as one of them tried, too late, to check his speed over the wet cobblestones. He smiled and wiped his feet carefully before returning to the sitting room. Well! That was something done anyway. If Victoria came alone she would be all right; but if anyone came with her, anyone unknown to the dogs, he would not get very far.

He put another log on to the fire, switched on the light and was suddenly still in the middle of the room. Up above, on the other side of the ceiling, someone had moved. He listened; the springs of the bed in Mrs. Blount's room relaxed; he heard their brief rusty sigh as they returned to their normal position, and then the diminished thud of stockinged feet crossing the carpet.

He felt like a dog himself then, a dog that was a black-pointed ear, all its other senses resting and subdued to this one over-riding interest, the discernment of the prickle of sound or silence in a place adjacent. Someone else in the house, some moving thing, some sweating, odorous animal trespassing upon the selected domain. He knew now how a dog felt; it was an invasion of the dry form, a threat to the water trough and the carrion, and it made him bristle with fear and indignation. Someone else up above, someone stealthy who did not wish to be heard; and now that the dogs were loose he was on his own, a house-prisoner responsible for his own imprisonment.

He took off his shoes, switched off the light he had just switched on and tiptoed out into the hall cocking his ears to the fall of the staircase. There was no sound; only the hollow rapping of the clock from its place by the panelled wall in the well of the staircase. He leaned over the banisters so that the stairs should not creak under his weight and drew himself slowly up hand over hand to the landing and there lay down on the carpet. There was no light coming from under the door of Mrs. Blount's room and the silence was absolute. Down below him, from the front door, he heard the growl of one of the dogs, the snuffing of its nose against the threshold as it drew in and questioned the dark air of the house. Quickly he got to his feet, slid down the length of the banisters, and running to the front door, threw it open wide so that he was penned safely behind its thickness.

Slipping and skidding over the polished tiles of the vestibule, the dogs hurtled into the hall; without pausing to investigate his own presence they galloped up the staircase to the landing. The house and the hall resounded to their barking as he switched on all the lights he could find and raced up after them. They were standing outside Mrs. Blount's door, their tails thrashing as they whimpered and called and leaped against its shining panels.

With no pause, he strode over to them and pushed open the door which let them onwards into the darkened bedroom.

Dimly, he saw them hurl themselves on to the great double bed, the eruption of bodies, bedclothes, and eiderdown against the pale rectangle of the window; then he himself stepped into the room.

"Got you!" he shouted. "Got you, you swine! Stay where you are or the mastiffs will tear you to pieces."

He switched on the light.

George Harkess and Mrs. Blount stared back at him from the chaos of the bed. The dogs, their tails wagging, their great mouths drooping with saliva and affection, bestrode their half-clothed bodies, and Mrs. Blount struggled feebly to cover herself with the corner of an eiderdown which still remained on the bed. Her face white and old, ridged and bare as unglazed china, she regarded him with blurred, horror-stricken eyes. She screamed loudly, the sound tearing out under the white ceiling, scream after scream, each one higher than the last, as though she were building a castle of agony beneath the electric light. Then she turned suddenly over on to her stomach and started to bite and tear at one of the pillows, her veined legs kicking in the air.

George Harkess, in his shirt-tails, leapt out of the bed and sprang across the room. John saw only his wet moustache, the dogs around his thin old-man's legs, the mat of his thick grey hair against his forehead before he switched off the light and, taking him by the shoulders, threw him with all his force across the landing. He felt the hammer of the standing wall against his shoulder, the numbness and sense-loss of the whole limb which precedes pain, as he slid peacefully and gratefully down on to the floor.

He remembered only the smell of the whisky and the brightness of the light.

Under his eyes the basin was very white, the water clear and cold, rocking backwards and forwards as it was agitated by the hands. It reminded him of having his hair cut: the clumsy, comforting, haste of the hairdresser finishing a shampoo; had it not been for the pain somewhere to the right of him, he would have enjoyed it; it was soothing.

"Whisky," he said aloud, "whisky!"

Beside him a soft voice spoke in reply. He couldn't place it, though he knew he had heard it before. He sat up; he was in the bathroom and Mrs. Blount's arm was around his back. He looked up into her pale, tortured face; it filled his gaze, blotting out all the ceiling, and rocking gently like the water.

"He had been drinking whisky," he said with another voice that was quite effortless. "Have *you* been drinking whisky?"

"There, there!" she said, "you'll soon be all right."

"Where are the dogs?"

"I don't know! I don't know! You mustn't worry, John— we want to—you must be quick."

He smiled at her; she was a very kind woman. Then he drooped down over the basin again, and with his left arm began to splash the water over his neck.

Behind him, someone else came into the bathroom.

"The young fool—I told you it was a mistake." It was George Harkess's voice, thick and angry.

"*Ssh—*"

He could almost see the finger to her lips.

A hand, coarse, with black whiskers and nails, came under his chin and lifted his face upright.

"Better? Are you better? Sit up, man! *Sit up!*"

John sat up.

"There's no time to be wasted. What have you done with Victoria?"

"Victoria?"

"Pull yourself together! This is no time for acting and the vapours."

He was shaken gently and he felt his head wobbling backwards and forwards like a doll's. He stood up unsteadily; he was dizzy with the onset and fluctuation of his anger. It was warm, as satisfying as milk, and he loved it; he felt his face twisting under the grip of it.

"She hates you," he said, "hates you! She doesn't know who

you are, but she thinks you're a fat pig with filthy ideas, and so do I."

The tweed waistcoat swayed towards him and he backed away; beside him, on the white-tiled shelf, there was a tumbler of water. He seized and brandished it.

Mrs. Blount stepped quickly in front of him.

"George!" she wailed, "for pity's sake—he's ill."

John jumped in front of her and faced George Harkess.

"I'm not," he said. "She'll never let you marry Enid—*never*. She said so before she went off with the hiker and left me. You're too old and too—" he swallowed his thin saliva—"people of *your* age—"

George Harkess's hand closed on the tumbler; he inverted it slowly and removed it from John's hand.

"Sit down," he said, "there! On the chair."

John sagged on to the chair.

"Now, what's this about a hiker? When did she go off with him, *when*?"

"I don't know; ages ago. What's the time? I don't know how long anything is. It was before I found you in the bedroom."

"*Think*, man!"

"I *am* thinking."

Mrs. Blount kneeled in front of him on the squared linoleum. Her eyes floating in their moisture above the tired cheeks, she took his hand and looked up at him.

"Please, John," she said, "for my sake, try and remember. It's only a few minutes ago—where did you leave Victoria?"

"I can't remember. I am trying but I can't. All I can remember is seeing you in the bedroom—your legs—the eiderdown—Mr. Harkess—"

"Yes, yes," she said, and a tear trickled over her left eyelid. "But before that, John? Before?"

"I heard noises upstairs—the bed squeaking. I thought the hiker, the man with the motorcar—it was a Sunbeam—I thought *he* might try and come back with her, so I let the dogs out; and then when I heard the noises upstairs in the bedroom—"

Beside him George Harkess grunted furiously.

"For God's sake, boy! You're like an infernal gramophone! What man and what motorcar?"

"The hiker—he wasn't a hiker at all, he was a commercial traveller. He was selling something, he wouldn't tell us what it was, so I don't know; but he took her into Corby to post the letter. I didn't want him to, I tried to stop her going with him; but she was worried—the car nearly knocked me into the drive. Then I came back here and I let the dogs out because when I was downstairs I heard the bed—"

"But *when*?"

"What time was it?"

They had both spoken together.

"To catch the last post," he said with triumphant remembrance, "*that* was it. That was why she went with him. She would never have gone with him otherwise; I know she wouldn't. She didn't like him, he hinted at things all the time. We couldn't get rid of him."

George Harkess straightened himself.

"Three-quarters of an hour ago," he said, "say an hour ago at the outside. Don't worry! I'll have her back inside ten minutes *and* this fellow, whoever he is."

"Oh George! Please be quick. It's not like her; she *never* speaks to strangers. Don't waste a moment. Go straight to the police station. If—if she's not in the village, they'll put out a message; they'll stop all cars."

He frowned.

"For Heaven's sake don't panic, Enid! There's no need to call in the police at this stage. Think, girl! Have some sense! We don't want them up here at Nettlebed questioning this blasted— asking the boy questions. She'll be in the village, you'll see. I can't think what came over the young monkey." He paused, chewing his moustache. "How old is she?"

"Oh George, whatever does that matter?" From her place on the linoleum she gazed at him tearfully.

"It matters a great deal. Come on now, what is she? Fourteen? Fifteen? I've never been able to make up my mind."

"She's *thirteen*, only thirteen; but please don't waste any more time—"

"*Is* she, by God! Well that's too young by half—or too old, whichever way you look at it. You give her too much rope Enid, running around the moors, having her boy friends to stay with her in the holidays. For thirteen, she's too well on, too provocative; she—"

Her face grey with hostility, Mrs. Blount rose stiffly. Beneath her eyes there were tender blue marks like new bruises.

"You know nothing about my—Victoria," she said, "and this is hardly the time to start criticizing the poor little thing. If you won't call in the police, I shall do so myself at once; and if they must question us, then they must. For my part I shall withhold nothing, nothing at all. I shall tell them everything they want to know."

George Harkess's moustache lowered itself suddenly over his long teeth.

"Now look here! There's no point in crossing our bridges— Good Lord! This is the twentieth century and I've got to think of my standing in the neighbourhood. A little thing like this—"

"Look after John," she said, "while I go to the telephone." And she began to cross the linoleum towards the bathroom door. She was as wooden as the White Queen in Alice's game of chess; she still walked carefully, her narrow skirt gleaming and stiff in the bright light. She had reached the door before he caught up with her.

"My dear, you don't know what you're doing; you're behaving like a mad woman. What on earth's the matter with you? Now just consider the facts afresh: barely an hour ago, Victoria took a lift from a fellow with a motorcar to post a letter in a lively little village."

He was blocking the doorway and she was too cold and upright to struggle with him or to try to pass him; but the pace she took backwards, as though she had stepped further into her most private self, dismayed him more than any battle would have done.

"I don't *want* to examine the facts," she said coldly. "Not those facts. There are others which I as a woman can see at once." She turned to John, looking at him as though something significant towered above his chair. "You heard what John said about him? That should be enough for anyone. It is certainly enough for me, after—after—"

In the doorway George Harkess felt for the thick hair at the back of his neck. He smiled kindly.

"All right, my dear, let us waste no more time in arguing. I know when I'm beaten and when a woman's in this state a man has to present her with a fact; *after* that, he will exact his apology!" He looked at his watch. "I'll be back in a quarter of an hour. In the meantime, pull yourself together! You might pass the time, or some of it, in getting yourself and that boy a cup of tea in the kitchen."

They heard his hasty descent of the stairs, the closure of the front door, and the excited salutations of the dogs as he stepped out into the night.

Mrs. Blount shivered. "I'm sorry, John, that you should have—" She broke off. "He's quite right; I should never have let you go off like that. I felt uneasy about it from the very first. All the time at Redcar I was worrying. That's why I took something to drink. This isn't my normal self, John; you know that, don't you? You know that Victoria's mother—usually I'm very careful; I have to be; but today—"

"That's all right, Mrs. Blount."

She didn't hear him, or if she did her eyes gave him only a fleeting acknowledgement. "I allowed myself to be persuaded against my better judgement. I knew this was going to be a difficult week. I warned Victoria; in a way, I tried to tell George; but, of course, you wouldn't understand how difficult it is to tell him things. *Really!* I very nearly put off the whole idea of the holiday because of something that happened one Sunday. And now, how I wish I had. Oh! How I wish—"

John stood up unsteadily.

"I'd love a cup of tea," he said. "It will be warm in the kitchen. Let's go and sit in the kitchen and make some tea—my shoulder's hurting."

"You poor boy! Of course it is. How selfish I am. Let me dry your neck for you."

She took the towel from him and with rapid abstracted movements dabbed it around his ears and neck.

"Are you sure you can walk down the stairs?"

"Yes, thank you. It's just that I can't feel my arm properly. Do you think I might have broken something? Melanie fell off a Shetland pony once, and her arm went dead and they took an X-ray photograph of it and found that it *was* broken. It was in plaster for weeks and my brothers used to strike matches on it."

"Oh dear, I don't know! We'll have to see about it in the morning. I know nothing about nursing, I'm afraid; I'm useless, quite useless. I can't even look after myself let alone after anyone else. If I'd done what my instincts had told me, and not *only* my instincts, none of this would ever have happened, simply because we would none of us ever have come here. On that Sunday I mentioned, there was a distinct warning; but I chose to ignore it."

She took his arm and side by side they made their way slowly down the stairs through the empty creaking hall to the kitchen.

Mrs. Blount filled the kettle and searched the dresser cupboard for the tea things. All her movements were ineffectual as she prepared the tray and put the kettle on the hob. She seemed to be unused to anything ever exactly fulfilling its function. Her hands themselves, as though they were unaccustomed to her control of them, fluttered and hesitated as they performed their duties; even the kettle lid was awry, and the kettle itself, when she transferred it from the hob to the black range, was not in the centre of the opening over the grate. She was quite unable to find the tea caddy, and ultimately, she sat down in Annie's rocking chair and started to rock herself backwards and forwards rhythmically. But she did not weep, and though she did not weep it would have been much more comfortable if she had. John had seen people rocking themselves in the Vicarage hammock, and other children seesawing under the trees in summer, strangely abstracted from the world in which they rocked or swayed. But this rocking of Mrs. Blount's, though it implied a detachment as complete as that of the people he remembered, was a movement which came out of a dreadful dry-eyed grief, as if she rocked in the dark.

He went into the larder, found the milk, tea caddy, and sugar and made the tea. Then, glad of the opportunity of disturbing the cycle of her sorrow, he handed her a cup which she took gratefully, starting immediately to sip from its hot rim.

"He knows I don't mean it of course," she said. "If only I did, if only I *could* mean it and go on meaning it, not just now but in the future too; then, I suppose, things would be different for us both. Oh! If only we could change things without changing ourselves, but we can't and he knows it. Men are all the same." She looked up at him. "How old are you?" she asked. "I always forget, John, whether you are older or younger than— Oh, my darling, *darling* little Victoria. Whatever came over me? How could I have let you go off like that in a lonely, horrible place like this? He was right, I must have been mad."

"I'm younger," said John, "but only a little. I'm twelve-and-a-half and she's just over thirteen; but please Mrs. Blount, don't go on worrying like this. Mr. Harkess will bring her back—he'd bring *anyone* back! In the morning everything will be all right, you'll see; it always is."

She smiled at him wanly, and for a moment he saw Victoria staring out of her tired face. Before he could stop himself, he sobbed once, loudly. Mrs. Blount stopped rocking.

"I'm sorry," he said, improvising swiftly, "it was only my shoulder—I think it's coming back to life and it's jolly unpleasant."

"John?"

"Yes."

"There's something I want to ask you, but it's very difficult for me." The difficulty took shape under the hand of her silence. "You remember what I said in the bathroom to George—to Mr. Harkess?"

"Not very well. I don't remember much at all, I'm afraid."

"It was about the police," she said.

"Oh, yes! You mean about not telling them everything?"

"Yes, you see, John, I've been thinking—and I think, yes I'm sure, that if it should be necessary to call them in, we must help them, we must do everything in our power to help them; but on the other hand—" Her lips ceased to move, but her eyelids opened and closed eloquently.

"You mean about my shoulder?" he said brightly. "Please

don't worry about that! I've thought of it already and I've decided I'll just say that one of the dogs knocked me over in the drive. Don't you think that's good?"

"Yes, dear, I do. You're a brave boy, very brave!" She put her cup on the table as though it had never contained anything and smiled at him painfully. "But it wasn't only that. You see, they might want to know how it was we were so long in notifying them; they might ask us why it was that when you returned alone— What time was it by the way when you did return?"

"Five past seven by the kitchen clock."

"Well they might want to know, they might wonder what Mr. Harkess and I were doing at that time not to have—telephoned them or something."

"Oh, I see! You mean about being in bed together?" He looked directly into her face and she looked down at her dainty bedroom slipper.

"Yes. You see, John, Mr. Harkess and I were, that is to say we *are* thinking of getting married and—I'm sure you understand what I mean, don't you? Because I haven't any sons of my own, and it's very difficult for me to know exactly how to say what I feel I *ought* to say before the police come."

"Yes," he said. "I understand, you just don't want me to tell them that bit, that's all; and I *won't*. We can easily think of something else between us, if it's necessary; but I don't think it will be, I'm sure they'll be back any minute, Mr. Harkess and Victoria, I mean." He looked up at the clock, but her eyes did not follow his.

"It's not that there's anything for us to be ashamed of, or anything like that, John," she said, "though I expect at your age, with the sort of ideas you've been brought up on—your mother, Mrs. Blaydon—"

"No," he said, "of course not! Everybody does it. I mean grownups; they always make love in bed, don't they? I know all about it. In the parish we have terrible things happening, even brothers and sisters; there was a girl called—"

Mrs. Blount sighed uncomfortably and John hurried on, "But yours wasn't like that. After all, you're going to marry Mr. Harkess, aren't you? And Victoria said that after the races he'd almost certainly be drunk. My grandfather drank sometimes, and Mother says that when he was like that he wasn't responsible for his actions, he didn't know what he was doing; and I'm sure Mr. Harkess was too, or he'd probably never have—"

"No dear! He wasn't *drunk*." She seemed to be very alive again and sat upright on the rocking chair. "Mr. Harkess is very lonely, and when men are lonely— Good Heavens! If I thought that he *drank*! You see he has no faith, John, nothing to live by and that is what makes him so terribly lonely in a way which we might find it difficult to understand. You and I—"

"Do you go to church?" he asked. "I never knew that. Victoria never told me."

"Not your sort of church, dear, and not services like your father's. But I have my religion, I could never have lived without it, and I worship the same God, but in a different way."

She was very calm, almost happy, and even began to rock herself again peacefully, as though she were nursing a pleasant secret.

"Oh," he said. "Well, what is your religion?"

"I'm a Christian Scientist, John."

"I see. Yes, I think I've heard of them; but it's awfully funny that Victoria never talks about it. Is she one too?"

"No dear, not yet. I've always tried to let her make her own mind up about everything; and for the most important thing, I think it's most important of all to let one's children decide for themselves."

"You *are* different from my mother. She says that it is the one thing that parents *must* decide for their children; she—"

The kitchen door opened and they both turned towards it

Annie Moses, her red cheeks shining, her dark hair and navy mackintosh black with rain, bustled into the light and warmth. She blinked at them and blew out her cheeks. Mrs. Blount stood up.

"Oh, it's you mum," said Annie. "Eeh! what a night, and all that way for nowt, not so much as a tizzy in a beggar's 'at, for 'e turned me up at t'end of it."

"Have you seen Miss Victoria, Annie?"

"Why naw Mrs. Bloont, not sin' she passed us in t'car when

I was waiting to meet him off t'Scarboro' bus. Isn't she coom back yet?"

"You saw her? In the car?" Mrs. Blount stumbled forwards. "Which way were they going? When was it?"

"This way, mum, towards t'farm, 'bout five or ten past seven. Looked as though they was in a tearin' hurry too. Miss Victoria waved at us as they passed."

"But that's over an hour ago!" Mrs. Blount's voice soughed under the low ceiling. "And she waved at you, she *waved*! (Oh, my brave little darling. Where *was* he taking her?)"

Annie took off her mackintosh slowly and hung it on the back of the kitchen door. She shook her wet hair with deliberate movements and circled the kitchen table to the range.

"Did she look happy?" asked John suddenly. "Did she wave as though she was happy?"

"Happy? I never thought. She joost waved to us, that wer all." She closed her eyes. "Coom to think of it, Miss Victoria did look kind of fretted—white-like, as I said. 'Ees going too faist for Miss Victoria, I thought to myself, and then I thought it weren't that at all but 'er broken promise about helping me mak t'supper! But bless 'er, she needn't have frettted, I'd finished t'salad and spuds even before you and t'master coom in at quarter to six."

"Who else was with her?" asked Mrs. Blount.

"Only t' driver; saw'm quite sharp, I did, under the light by t'bus stop. Never see *him* before. There weren't no one in t'back of car, it was black empty. But what's oop, Master John?"

She gazed at him placidly a moment and then, taking a large black comb from her handbag, started to rake through her wet hair.

"We think Victoria's been kidnapped by that man she met this morning. He said he'd give her a lift into the village to post a letter, but they've never come back and now it's over an hour and a half since they left."

Annie put her comb on the mantelpiece and went over to the kitchen door. She shook her mackintosh loudly like a carpet and then put it on.

"Then it's police we want," she said, looking at the clock. "I've got me bike in t'stable and I'll go and get Sergeant Sanders before *that* wastes any more time."

"No Annie," said Mrs. Blount, "it's very good of you, but you needn't trouble. Mr. Harkess has gone into the village already and he'll be back any minute, so I think we'd better wait for him."

"Is he fetchin' police?" asked Annie squarely by the door.

"No. Well, yes—at least I'm sure he will when he realizes—"

"He's not," said John.

"Reet!" said Annie. "Well if he ain't, then I am. I know them tourists in their motorcars. He weren't up to no good the way he went rummagin' through Corby and Miss Victoria as white as—"

She broke off at the sound of George Harkess's car passing the kitchen door on its way to the stables, and without looking at one another or making the smallest movement, they waited in the silence which succeeded his passing. Before the fire, crouching behind its black bars, the cat sat safely in its warm world, the tip of its tongue protruding beneath its nose. In the hall the clock struck and their eyes went up to the white face over the kitchen dresser: the minute hand stood at twenty-five minutes to eight.

"Grandfaither's slow," said Annie flatly and Mrs. Blount looked at her wrist watch. Behind them the door opened and George Harkess came storming in and went straight over to Mrs. Blount. His large cheeks were mottled by the cold and he rubbed his hands with unnecessary vigour. They knew at once that he had accomplished nothing.

"The police'll be up here in a few minutes, Enid," he said. "They were seen all right at the post office. Victoria posted the letter while the fellow turned around the car by church—told Mrs. Lawler that she was getting a lift back to Nettlebed and seemed perfectly happy, and—" he blew out his cheeks—"there's nothing more to tell you."

They could think of no questions to frame and he must have sensed the deadness of their disappointment and the vitality of their fear, for he went back to the doormat and started to wipe his shoes thoroughly on its wet surface.

"Thought it would be as well," he went on, "to check with the police, so I ran down to the station and had a word with Sanders; he was most helpful and by this time he'll have telephoned his headquarters at Scarborough and within half an hour some sort of a description of the car and its occupants will have been circulated throughout the whole of the North Riding. In addition, of course, they'll put out every available man in this area, even those who are off duty, and patrol all main roads. All we've got to do is to keep calm and behave as normally as possible."

Still they did not speak. Mrs. Blount in her grey dress watched him hungrily from the other side of the table; only her ineffectual hands with their jewelled rings moved against the stillness of her hips. John watched them writhing like the white fingers of a squid in a fisherman's net. Her lips were slightly parted and as pale as Victoria's. She seemed to have forgotten herself entirely in the desperation of her desire to hear him say something more; for the first time since he had known her she was quite careless of how she might be looking. The remains of tears and mascara sullied her pale cheeks, her carefully tended hair had fallen into disorder on her temples; there were one or two drops of milky tea on the bodice of her dress and in her eyes was the same cold hostility which had first appeared in the bathroom half an hour earlier.

George Harkess himself must have observed these things too. Rubbing his feet on the mat he glanced across at her twice, the first time warily, the second time with hot anger.

"Well, for God's sake don't stand there like that. I can't tell you more than there is to tell, can I? It's not the end of the world. They'll be somewhere in this area and with all the resources of the police force, the *modern* police force, they're bound to be found within a short time."

Mrs. Blount watched him coldly for a moment; her eyebrows manifested surprise that he should dare to speak to her like that in front of Annie. When she spoke it was with an icy care that atoned for all the imperfections of her appearance.

"It is just as well you waited, Annie," she said. "I was quite sure Mr. Harkess would be back in a few moments, and I'm glad that you've been saved that long trip on your bicycle in the rain."

"Ah, Annie," said George Harkess walking over to her with great joviality. "Didn't notice you, me dear! You're back very early aren't you? Didn't expect to see you this side of tomorrow morning. What happened? Did your boy friend give you the slip again?"

Annie looked quickly at Mrs. Blount and then raised her eyes boldly. "He did, Mr. Harkess, but I'm not wurried now about that with all this here that's happened sin' I got out."

"No, no, of course not. But bless you, things aren't that bad; there's no need for *you* to lose your head, your good North Country common sense, over it. Bit different for Mrs. Blount, we can all see that, but it won't help anyone if you're going to start having the vapours as well."

"I know that, Mr. Harkess, but it would tak' a cool yed not to be bothered by a thing like this. You see—"

"Annie *saw* them," said John.

George Harkess frowned at him and then turned to Annie again quickly.

"You did? When? Where were they?"

"She saw them at ten past seven going very fast up the Stump Cross road towards the farm where she was waiting for the bus— for her friend to get off the bus."

"Shut up, boy! Don't speak until you're spoken to." His light brown eyes transfixed Annie again. "Well?"

"It was joost as Maister John said. I didn't know anything was oop until I got back, Mr. Harkess."

From the other side of the kitchen table Mrs. Blount interrupted them. She drew in a long breath so audibly that even the cat abandoned his immobility and glanced up at her with wide yellow eyes.

"She *waved*! She waved to her, George; the poor little thing waved at her as they passed. Annie saw her, she told us when she first came in that Victoria was frightened to death and that she'd waved to her through the window as she was driven past." She sat down suddenly on the rocking chair and covered her face with her hands. George Harkess hurried over to her, the anger left his face, his mouth sagged into its usual planes; he patted her back and then, with his arm around her, lifted her to her feet.

"I think we must have a discussion in the dining room," he said. "There's not much time left, my dear; I expect the sergeant here at any moment. Did you do what I told you and have a cup of tea in my absence?"

Mrs. Blount walked easily out of his embrace and took a handkerchief from the cuff of her long sleeve; she wiped her nose daintily. "I think so," she said.

George Harkess turned to John. "Did you have a cup of tea?" he asked.

"Yes, sir, yes, Mr. Harkess, but I don't think Mrs. Blount drank all hers."

They watched her as she walked out into the hall.

"Well, this time she's going to have a strong one, *and* something in it."

He turned to Annie. "Make a fresh pot of tea, Annie, and fetch the decanters from my study. Don't bother with the syphon." He followed Mrs. Blount to the dining room, and in a few moments John joined them as they sat there at the supper table.

Annie brought in the tea and the whisky and George Harkess helped himself to a half-tumblerful and then stocked up his plate at the sideboard.

Returning to the table he pushed the potatoes off his plate on to the white cloth. "These potatoes are overcooked," he said, and raising his glass, he looked over its rim at Mrs. Blount and then, distastefully, at John before draining it. He filled his mouth with a large slice of ham and chicken and began to chew automatically, his eyes directed at a space somewhere just in front of John.

"You there," he said. "When the police come, you're to say nothing about the—trouble upstairs. Have you got that quite clear?"

"Yes, sir."

"Good! We shan't want you here much longer tonight. I don't

imagine there's much more you can usefully contribute at this stage, though you'll almost certainly be wanted in the morning." He chewed for a moment longer. "I only want to be quite certain before you leave this room that you understand what questions it will be necessary for you to answer, and to be sure that you will not start volunteering useless information as you did in the kitchen a few minutes ago."

At the far end of the table his moustache twitched and he darted a glance at Mrs. Blount, grey and silent as a cloud as she sat beside him. His hand slid across the table to the decanter as his eyes resumed their duty at the empty space before him. "You're to say, *if* you are asked, that Mrs. Blount and I were talking business in the study and that being possessed of *some* manners, you didn't like to—that on your return from this damned outing you decided not to interrupt us, but to wait until we had done."

John said nothing. He picked a piece of egg out of his salad with the sharp prongs of his fork and studied it carefully. Another Toad, he thought; it would make no difference even to Mrs. Blount or to Kay still at the Abbey, so many miles away, if they were changed around. Neither of them would ever know the difference as long as you remembered to change their clothes as well.

"D'you *see? Answer me, boy!*"

Mrs. Blount stirred, she plucked at her cup of tea. "George! I don't think I can stand it if you are going to go on shouting at him. My nerves simply will not stand the strain."

"I'm not shouting at him," he roared. "I'm simply demanding an answer to my question."

Mrs. Blount's cup clattered into its saucer; with her hand to her ear she leaned away from him like a tree in the wind and he lowered his voice.

"I'm only thinking of you, Enid. I simply cannot understand your behaviour over this wretched business. You seem to have thrown all your normal horse sense to the winds. Don't you realize that if this young fool starts behaving as hysterically as he did in the bathroom before I went out, we're going to have a first-rate scandal in the village? It doesn't matter to me, but there are certain things that are sacrosanct, and I'm damned if at this stage in my life I'm going to be the means of ruining a woman's reputation. We've got to make sure that this boy doesn't refer to the—situation upstairs. It's of no possible connection with the object of Sergeant Sanders's visit this evening, and it's just the sort of thing that will spread like wildfire through the county if it once gets out."

Mrs. Blount pushed her chair back from the table. "You may find *my* behaviour difficult to understand," she said, "but yours, your utter selfishness, your brutality and cowardice— Good Heavens! Do you really think that any mother could care about her reputation at a moment like this. If it was only your behaviour that bewildered me I should not feel as I do; but it's this new *you*, this complete change in someone I had wanted to respect and of whom I hoped I was beginning to be fond, it's *this* that I don't understand. You're not interested in me or my reputation; you're not even interested in Victoria, she doesn't enter into your considerations at all. You're only interested in yourself and the opinion of the village, and I was utterly foolish ever to think that at your age and in your circumstances you could possibly care for me in my own right." She stood up. "But it doesn't matter any longer; if Victoria isn't found tonight, if I don't see her again soon and take her in my arms and kiss her sweet forehead, nothing that you or anyone else can do to me will ever matter again. You can do what you like, George! Bully the boy, lie to the police, make love to the maid. Whatever happens, whatever this terrible night may bring, you have ended something for me which had never really begun."

With dreadful care, with no sob or sigh, she walked over the thick carpet to the door, opened it and went out into the hall. They heard the sound of the clock from its place by the stairs before the door closed; they heard no other sound as she passed from them and went silently up to her bedroom.

George Harkess put down his knife and fork. "You can forget all that," he said. "You can place it with certain other incidents which have happened this evening and which you should never have witnessed."

"You can't forget things that have happened," said John, "not things like this, and nobody can make you. If you can't make *yourself* forget them, how can you expect anyone else to stop you remembering them?"

"I'm warning you that on this occasion you *will* forget certain things."

He got up, towering darkly over the carved back of his chair. "I think it's about time you realized, Blaydon, young as you are, that but for your presence here this situation would never have arisen. In the first place, you were not wanted at Nettlebed. I have no connection with either you or your family, and had it not been for the respect and affection I owe to Victoria's mother, you would never have been invited. As it is, by your influence over the girl and your persistence in making your own arrangements, you are directly responsible for the inconvenience to which my entire household has been subjected. Therefore, you had better give me your assurance, and give it quickly, that you will say nothing to the police about my personal relationship with Mrs. Blount."

John looked up. "What do you want me to say, sir?"

"I've already told you that you are to tell them, *if* you are asked, that on your return to the house you were under the impression that Mrs. Blount and I were talking business in the study and that consequently you thought it would be impolite to disturb us."

"Don't you think, sir, that they might decide that it was rather careless of me to waste half an hour when I was so worried, just because I thought that you and Mrs. Blount were talking?"

"It's not your business to speculate about the probable or improbable decisions of the police. It's your business to do what you're told, by *whom* you're told, like any other decent schoolboy."

The voice stopped speaking, and in the quietness of his own mind John sensed the creation of a decision which he was powerless to alter. He had been uncertain of what he would do or say many times during that day, had been foolhardy when he decided to insist on having tea in the cave, timid when the hiker arrived for tea, and too slow to take and post the letter; but now, only a few feet away from the anger and insistence that reached him from the body of George Harkess, he was quite certain that he would give himself his own time and his own right to act as he wished over the question of the police.

"I'm not going to have them thinking I'm a fool, sir," he said quietly, "not for anyone. If I'm going to be a fool now, and be laughed at and lied about, I'll be a fool for ever. I'll still be a fool when I'm as old as you are, so I won't tell them a story that only a fool would tell and only a fool would believe."

George Harkess watched him ruminatively for a moment.

"Very well then, just what *do* you propose to tell them?"

"I'm not sure. How can I be sure until I see what happens? This afternoon I was quite sure what was going to happen when we went out to the caves, and it all did happen; but other things happened as well that I had never expected, so how can I be sure what's going to happen when the police come? When I went upstairs to the bedroom with the dogs I thought I'd find a thief or a burglar up there and that I'd been very clever to do what I did do; but when I opened the door and put on the light there was no thief and no burglar; and I wish there had been, because then whatever the dogs had done and whatever the man had done, it would have been right, and *I* would have been right. But you showed me that I was wrong; although you're a man and I'm only a boy, you smashed my shoulder in and lost your temper in the bathroom; and all because I thought, *before* I found you, that you were a criminal doing something wrong in somebody else's house. So you see I'm not going to decide for certain what I'm going to say to the police until I know what they're going to say to *me*."

George Harkess left his chair. He strode over to him and took him by his bruised shoulder. "I think you had better realize that you are not going to leave this room until you have told me what you are going to tell them," he said.

"If you'll take your hand off my shoulder I'll tell you what I *might* say, but that's all."

George Harkess grunted behind him, the hand was removed and John stood up.

"I might say that when I got in I found the house empty,

that there was no sign of anybody, and that I was alone for nearly half an hour because you and Mrs. Blount were out giving the dogs a run in the home field."

"I see. Yes, that is fairly sensible, and in any case there's no time for further discussion now. Mind you stick to it."

He stood there for a few moments longer biting his upper lip with his teeth, and then he turned and walked out into the hall. Two minutes later John heard him knocking at the door of Mrs. Blount's bedroom. He knocked three times and again three times, but no voice answered him and at last he came heavily downstairs and going into the study closed the door behind him.

The house did not sleep that night; all the night long throughout the throng of the dark minutes and their hours it remained as restless as he was himself, the very fabric of its walls and floors creaking and stirring minutely like the joints and tissues of a person who wills sleep so intensively that in the very smallness of his movements he refuses to acknowledge his wakefulness and attention. Twice he heard footsteps on the landing outside his door, the sound of water running in the bathroom and the groaning of concealed pipes in the wall; and once, the high, despairing sobs of Mrs. Blount as they reached across the landing when she opened her door to move out upon some errand of her sleeplessness.

He thought of Sergeant Sanders, of his quick questions and air of knowing just what he, John, had been going to say before he had actually said it. He had liked him; his clean blueness, the fresh blood in his cheeks and the easy regard of his grey eyes. He wished that he was out there now standing somewhere sentinel in the hall or on the landing, keeping everything in order, commanding silence and sleep from the house, inspiring the running rats and mice with so much terror that they would obediently slink back to their holes in walls and wainscots.

Sergeant Sanders had been confident; and in the short time he had stayed talking to them all, his confidence had so fortified them that their suggestions of search parties by torchlight and vague journeyings by car had begun to seem not only impracticable, but unnecessary too. Standing at his ease in front of the study mantelpiece, his shoulders braced and square against the looking glass, he had explained to them that the police were even then converging on the area from all sides and that if Victoria and her companion were anywhere within it they would certainly be picked up by the early morning at the very latest. Then after closing his notebook and drinking a very small glass of whisky with George Harkess, he had left as suddenly and briskly as he had come.

No one, thought John, could say that Sergeant Sanders had seemed to be enjoying his enquiry. He had not smiled once with his eyes in the half-hour he had stayed, or shown any other sign of pleasure, but he had seemed to be impersonally "busy" about it in a manner that suggested it was not at all real to him in the sense that it was real to John. He had even felt that the very act of describing the hiker to Sergeant Sanders had made him sound progressively less real despite the fact that every particular he had given had been true. Somehow it had not been enough to say that the man had fair hair, a fresh complexion and a Sunbeam car, that he had smiled often, talked with a slightly "brown cow" accent and worn a wrist watch with a white strap. These insufficient words with which he had attempted to clothe and make real the man he had seen, in order that the sergeant might himself see him through the borrowed senses, had seemed to stylize him into a totally different, less solid and therefore less ominous, person; so that by the time he had finished answering the questions he had been asked, he had begun to feel that in some extraordinary way he had cheated the sergeant of the truth; even that he had confused him by equipping the man he was describing with some secret part of himself.

He remembered that immediately after he had finished his own interview and moved away to a more shadowy part of the study, he had tried to evade his discomfort by persuading himself that he might perhaps have imagined the whole incident, that it might like some dream by daylight have accrued from the putting together of a whole series of unrelated trifles: his jealousy over Victoria's talk with a stranger, the conversation they had shared about Blake's tiger, the lonely motorcar ascending the steep of the dale and the sense of some third, invisible personage attending them during the moment outside the cave.

His confusion of mind had continued for several minutes; and it was only when Mrs. Blount had been committed by the sergeant's questions to a description of Victoria in similar terms, that he had realized with the most acute relief that the unreality had no part in the person questioned, but was something to do with Sergeant Sanders himself; for he had noticed that the moment the sergeant was told anything, it at once became wrong in some way, not fully accurate, not enough, scarcely true. Even the words, "Victoria Blount," though they undoubtedly made up her name, sounded different after the sergeant had repeated them, and it was perhaps for this very reason that his visit had temporarily cheered them all to such an extent that after his departure they had for a little time been able to talk normally and optimistically and had even managed to say good night quite cheerfully before making their way upstairs to bed.

But, for John, the sense of a lightening in his thoughts had been very short-lived. Like the house itself, every part of his body was restless and ill-at-ease, seeming to be possessed of a separate interest and intention, refusing to remain subservient to the singleness of his being. He could feel very soon after he had switched off the light the singularity of his heart, the creeping mobility of his muscles and the living pain in his injured shoulder. In the infinite darkness of his head, thoughts rolled and heaved like an ocean under the night sky; and soon pictures began to spring unbidden to his mind, causing him to mutter words aloud in the darkness. Insistently, again and again, as clearly as though he were experiencing it truly for the first time, he saw Victoria's last sombre smile through the window of the car before she had been driven off into the village. The image was so real that he began to feel she was herself vitally in the room with him, even that she lay beside him in his bed trying to awaken him not from his sleep but to some dark nightmare of her own.

The conviction of her presence was so intense that he uttered hoarse and strident words which resounded coldly and continuously in the blackness about him and wrung the fingers of his clasped hands as he reproached himself for not having realized

what her smile had conveyed at the moment she had given it to
him. He writhed beneath the cold sheets when he remembered
that there had been a moment when he might have flung open
the door of the car and seized her in his arms to pull her out on
to the wet road. If it were true that thoughts were swifter even
than lightning, there might have been an instant between the
show of her self-confidence and her passing down the village
road when in some way, at the very last, even as she was smiling
through the closed window, she might have anticipated these
present moments of the night: her own absence from the house,
the flat emptiness of the bed in the next room, the comings and
goings of the others on the landing, and the movements of unseen policemen on the moorlands surrounding the house.

He longed for light, for the sounds of the morning. Nothing,
he felt, could happen during the night; there could be no good
news of any sort before dawn. But then, when dogs barked,
when cocks crowed, and the men came into the yard, there
would be something healthful to do. They would find Victoria
by daylight; it was the friend of them all and would not permit
her to be hidden from them any longer.

Wherever the man had taken her, whether to Scarborough, or
to York, as Sergeant Sanders had seemed to think, he would stand
no chance of concealing her when the bright world awoke and
the people moved out into the roads and streets with their eyes
seeing and their ears hearing. Then, after they had brought her
safely home, then would be the time to deal with the man for
the terror he had caused her and the fear he had visited upon
them.

Sergeant Sanders had suggested that even the car might not
have been his own, that in all likelihood it would have been one
which he had stolen during the morning; and for that offence
alone the man could be sent to prison for many months. He had
also said that the police had a strong suspicion that he had a
record and that as soon as they were able to identify him they
would be able to charge him with a number of other crimes,
not so serious as the present one but quite serious enough to
ensure that he would be grievously punished. The sergeant had
explained to George Harkess that criminals grew in crime and

that it was the tragedy of detection that although the development of a particular tendency in one man might clearly have
been foreseen, they were powerless to punish or prevent it until
it was too late.

Too late, he thought aloud. Could it be true if Sergeant Sanders had been with Victoria in the cave and had heard everything
the man had said as he, John, had heard it, that he would have
known that at some further point in time he would suddenly
decide to run away with her? How could the sergeant have
known something that the man had not appeared to know himself? At the very last minute when she had snatched the letter
and decided to post it herself, the man had almost shouted at him
"It's too late, she has made up our minds for us," or if he had not
said "too late" in those words, he had *meant* that it was too late.
This, the very last thing he had said, suggested that until that
moment he had taken no final decision about stealing Victoria.
If that were so, if his decision to kidnap her had appeared to *him*
to come from somewhere outside himself, although to the sergeant, knowing everything, it might have seemed inevitable, then
perhaps everything that had happened since, everything that was
happening at this moment in the moonless hours of the night,
might be combining to make the man commit some further un-
foreseen and yet inevitable act. To the sergeant, knowing what
he did know, it would seem that there was time to prevent this
act, but to the man who would not know what he was about to
do until he did it, it would seem that there was no time in which
to change his mind. And therefore it was not altogether true to
say that anything was too late.

Too late, too late! The words rang in his mind as he lay there
in the darkness, their meaning becoming ever more obscure and
confused with each repetition of the formulated but unspoken
syllables behind his eyes. Three *times*, he thought: the sergeant's
time, measured by the watch he carried in his breast pocket; the
man—Mr. Noone's—time, measured by something other than the
wrist watch on the white strap, and John's time, recorded by
the grandfather clock in the hall, moving somewhere between
them both in the misery of the night. He wondered if there
might not be a further "all-inclusive" time which took account

of these separate slow and remorseless tickings, a time which would have room in it for whatever Victoria was experiencing out there on the moors, and Mrs. Blount in her bedroom. What sort of a time, he asked himself, was God's time?

He turned over on to his stomach, pulled the bedclothes above his head, and waited.

Perhaps because he had ceased ever to expect it and perhaps because the pain in his shoulder had become so constant that it no longer emphasized even the passing of his own time, the morning came quite suddenly with a small wind which blew in through the window, cool and milky, seeming visibly to thin the darkness of the room. He saw the shape of his clothes on the chair by the wall, the hollow reality of the wardrobe, and the gleam of the jug and basin on the washstand. The room began to fill with the scents of the farm, thin and fresh, the delicate scents of the early morning: hay and the bitter smell of straw, early chimney smoke and the scent of bruised bracken. These things were so familiar, so heart-warmingly comfortable that quite effortlessly at the height of his distress he fell immediately asleep and awoke only when Annie knocked on his door and called him down to a late breakfast.

Dressing and washing quickly, he ran downstairs and found Sergeant Sanders and George Harkess awaiting him in the hall. They followed him into the dining room and George Harkess sat down at the table with him while the sergeant stood facing him with his back to the window.

George Harkess made the first remark. He gave him one of his large moustache-lifting smiles. "Well, my boy, thought we'd let you sleep it out. How's that shoulder of yours this morning?"

"I can move my arm now, thank you," said John, "but I don't think I want any breakfast—at least not much. Does it matter, sir?"

"Of course not, old chap, but I think you'd be in much better shape if you tried to stuff down a little toast and marmalade. Don't you agree, Sergeant?"

"I do indeed, sir," replied the sergeant without moving. John looked up at him; his navy-blue blotted out nearly all of the light from the rather small window and he was discomfited by the fact that it was impossible to see his face beneath the shadows which underlay his peaked cap.

"Do you always wear your hat in the house?" he asked suddenly.

The sergeant laughed. "Only when I'm on duty," he replied. "Why, don't you like it?"

"No," said John. "It makes me feel uncomfortable."

"Well, that's easily settled," said the sergeant. He took it off and tucked it under his left arm. "Is that better?"

"Yes, thank you."

"Anything we can do," said George Harkess, "just let us know, young man, and we'll do it. Have you any further complaints?"

"No, sir—well only one; I'd like to know when Mrs. Blount's coming down."

"She's in the study," said George Harkess, "and you'll be seeing her in a few minutes. But first of all, we wanted to ask you a few questions, didn't we, Sergeant?"

"We did, sir." Suddenly, unblocking the light from the window, the sergeant moved over to the fireplace. "How do you feel about it, son?"

"All right, Sergeant. I'll answer anything you ask me if I possibly can."

"Good! Well here's the first one: Mrs. Blount mentioned that you had said you did not like this man you met in the cave yesterday?"

"That's right. I didn't, I hated him."

"Why was that?"

John put down his toast and looked up.

"I don't really know, Sergeant, I just didn't."

"Come, come!" The back of the sergeant's neck made a steep angle with his blue collar. "You must have some reason for a statement like that, mustn't you?"

"Yes, I suppose I must."

"Well?"

"It's hard to think of it, that's all. It's hard to know why you don't like a person you've just met."

"Well, let's see if we can help you." He paused. "Now you like Mr. Harkess here, I'm sure, even though you've only known

him the inside of a week; and if I were to ask you *why* you
liked him, I imagine you'd very soon be able to give me a few
reasons, wouldn't you?"

In the opposite chair George Harkess coughed; as a preliminary to something he was about to say, his moustache moved
quickly upwards. John glanced brightly at the sergeant.

"No, that's just it," he said. "I wouldn't be able to give you
the reasons, because you see I *don't* like Mr. Harkess very much,
and it's always so much easier to know why you like a person
than why you don't, isn't it?"

Neither of them moved. John did not look at them; he did
not want to look at them; but their sudden stillness was as audible
as any movement would have been. He felt he had been rude and
said, "I mean, you do want me to tell the truth, don't you, Sergeant Sanders? It's no good my telling you any lies, is it?"

The sergeant said nothing for a moment; he looked as though
his body were uncomfortable, as though his uniform were
prickling him. In front of him, George Harkess leaned back in
his chair and let out a bellow of laughter.

"We've hooked a tartar, Sar'nt!" he said. "Do you think it
might be better if I joined Mrs. Blount for a few minutes while
you and the boy sort this out between you?"

"I don't think so, sir." Sergeant Sanders took his watch out
of his breast pocket and glanced at it. "There's little time for
private interviews and we must keep to the subject in hand. Now
look here, son, what I'm getting at is this. Was there any particular reason why you should have taken such a dislike to this
fellow with the motorcar? Did he say anything you didn't like,
or *do* anything?"

"Yes, he did. He made a great fuss of Victoria and kissed her
hand and said he'd been eavesdropping on us."

At this George Harkess's heavy head swivelled around to the
sergeant, but the sergeant ignored him; he looked only at John.
"I see," he said. "Did he say anything else?"

"Yes, he made out that Victoria and I were hiding in the cave
because we wanted to—"

"Go on," said the sergeant.

"He thought we were in there to make love."

The sergeant stood as still as the grandfather clock.

"And were you?"

"No. At least I might have kissed her later—I sometimes do feel like kissing her—if *he* hadn't come; but I never really thought of it because he stayed and stayed; we couldn't get rid of him."

"Couldn't you have pretended that you were going to leave yourselves, anyway, that you had to be getting back home?"

"That's just what we did pretend. I said that we'd decided not to have tea there after all, but he said it was raining very hard and that we ought to wait until it was over."

"He was set on it, was he?"

"Yes. We didn't want to be rude to him. In a way he seemed lonely and to begin with I think we both felt a bit sorry for him."

"Good enough," said the sergeant. "Can you remember anything else now? Any other suggestions he made, or anything else that he did and which you didn't like?"

"There was one other thing," said John; "it may not seem much to you, but even if I think of it now it annoys me, although it was only a little thing."

"And what was that?"

"He put on her mackintosh for her and I didn't like the way he did it."

They said nothing. The sergeant was very still again and George Harkess was just breathing heavily like an animal in a shed. John waited for them to say something, and because they said nothing he felt that their silence was a loud question which must be answered.

"He did it as though he knew her awfully well," he blurted out, "as though she was his—daughter or something."

"I don't understand," said the sergeant.

"Explain yourself," said George Harkess.

"I can't, but if you'd seen him do it you'd know what I meant. It was the way he did up the buttons and patted her chest afterwards, like someone touching something they'd like to buy and have for themselves. Can't you understand? It was just as I said the first time; it was as though he owned her."

This time they looked at each other and then away again rather quickly.

"Yes son, I think we understand. You've made a very good point there and I think that'll have to do. I think we know all we need to know for the present, and there's not a lot of time left for any more questions at this stage." His square fingers tapped on the mantelpiece and George Harkess stood up.

"Mrs. Blount?" he asked.

"No," said the sergeant, his eyes brooding over John. "I don't think so, sir. Not yet anyway."

"Sergeant! May I ask you something?" asked John.

"You may."

"Have you found Victoria? Any sign of her, anything at all?"

"No, we haven't found her, son, not yet; but we've found the motorcar all right—sixty miles away in *York* of all places and only a hundred yards away from the car park from which it was stolen the day before yesterday."

John swallowed. "Is that a good sign?" he asked.

"In some ways yes and in other ways no. Between midnight and one o'clock this morning there was heavy rain in York, but the roadway under the car was dry, which means that by this time he has had nine hours' start on the police, and in a case of this sort the time-factor is really all that matters."

"Are they watching the stations?" asked John.

"They are *now* and so far no two people answering the descriptions have been seen, though there were a number of single passengers on the milk train this morning whose movements and identities we're checking."

"But no one with a girl like Victoria?"

"No," said the sergeant, "and that's why I'm here and why I wanted to talk to you."

"Oh," said John. It was strange that when people were lost they had to be sought for behind many questions and answers. It seemed to be a waste of time to be talking and making these noises in the throat, moving one's lips and looking at another person while questions were asked about time and place. If a needle were lost in a haystack and it was really wanted, the only thing to do would be to take the haystack to pieces a little at a time and search every hollow stalk; but when a person was lost the place in which he might be found was hidden behind a haystack of words.

"If he's gone to London why are you bothering about Corby? Why don't you make all the police in London look for him there?" He checked himself. "Oh, of course—I'd forgotten. You said that she wasn't with him."

"We feel he may have—gone on without her," said the sergeant very slowly. "We found a handkerchief in the van and a quantity of yellow clay. We have some dogs outside in the police van, and in addition, some photographic equipment of my own. I managed to borrow two dogs from a keen sportsman"—he paused —"a poacher, I should say, in the village. We thought it might be as well to have a run around the moors with them in the immediate neighbourhood of the house."

Trembling, John got up.

"But that's ridiculous," he said. "It's a waste of time, isn't it Mr. Harkess? She would never have stayed out all night, she would have walked miles, she would have run like," he choked, "like the wind, to get here to us. She's very fond of us, sergeant, she loves us, she would have hated us all to be worried like this. She would rather have died than—"

In the enormity of their silence, he stopped. The sergeant stooped over him and patted his forehead; his hand was cold and he smelt of blue-suits.

"I'm sorry, son," he said, "but we need your help you see."

Over the wastes between them John looked up at him.

"We thought for a start we ought to have just a little look around that cave of yours. Criminals are queer fish; if they've taken a fancy to a place, they often like to visit it again. You needn't come in yourself, of course, but you could take us up there and give us an idea of where you actually had your picnic; we thought it would be a good idea to get that done before we went any farther afield. If she's on her way back, if he dropped her in the dales between here and York and she put up somewhere for the night—and she might have done you know—then of course she won't have spent the night in the cave; but we

can't just stand about waiting for her to arrive or telephone, can
we?"

"No," said John.

"You'll come then?"

"Yes. I'll come."

"Good lad."

George Harkess opened the door. "You'd better put on your
mackintosh," he said, "it's raining."

He was tempted to wait in the hall a moment and hear what
they said to each other; he knew they were going to talk about
him, but he was afraid that they might say something about
Victoria too and so he ran straight through to the cloakroom
and waited for them there.

They left George Harkess's car and the police van by the
Stump Cross and then walked back along the road to the place
where the hiker had left the Sunbeam the day before. Without
stepping off the road Sergeant Sanders examined the tire tracks
in the grass and told the two constables from the van to put ropes
and posts around them. The other man, in ordinary clothes, the
man with the dogs, remained sitting in the back of the van with
the dogs lying at his feet. He was smoking a cigarette. Sergeant
Sanders told him they would let him know later if there was
"anything for him" after they had had a look at the cave. Then,
with John and the sergeant in the lead, the five of them followed
the path to the dingle with George Harkess lagging behind and
carrying on his shoulder the scaffolding of the sergeant's big
camera which the two constables shared.

When they had reached the entrance of the cave the sergeant
told his men to put all his apparatus inside and use their flashlights; then he turned to John.

"Now," he said. "Just you lead on and show us where you
went yesterday. Here's my light, it's a fine big one, and you
should find it easy to follow in your own path."

"Thank you, Sergeant."

"And listen! We know you're not enjoying this and that you
may be a little frightened when you get farther in. If that should

happen and you decide you've had enough, just sing out and we'll hand you back to the entrance."

"All right, Sergeant."

John stooped into the entrance and made his way quickly towards the pile of stones which mounted to the throat of the first gallery. Behind him, he heard the grunts of George Harkess as he moved and slithered over the uneven floor, and he thought of Mrs. Blount and Annie Moses waiting together at the farm wondering where they had all gone and why they themselves had been told so little. He wished desperately that he too might have stayed with them, that he too had been born a woman, so that he might only wait for news instead of having always, for all the rest of his life, to go out to meet it.

Although there were so many of them, the increasing darkness within the body of the cave separated them all from one another. Outside, it had been possible for them to consider themselves as a friendly, talkative, almost noisy group. George Harkess had blustered through the rain and made jokes about the police force. One of the policemen had whistled a little tune over and over again and the other had talked about grouse shooting; but now they were strung out like beads in the darkness, each one thinking his own thoughts as they grunted and swore and struggled between the surfaces of the rock.

After a few minutes the two policemen began to talk quietly. A long way behind him from the tail of the procession, he heard the muddle of their conversation: brief words of one or two syllables, elongated and multiplied by the echoes which they roused; a strange language in which the cave participated, as yesterday it had taken part in the words he and Victoria had shouted into its emptiness.

He tried to make out what they were saying as he crawled along on his hands and knees to the true cavern. They were joking, he decided; there was a flat and chilling joviality in their tones as they called to one another through their discomfort:

"Yo'rl right?"

"Steady!"

"Gie 't me then."

"Mud?"

"Naw, 'ts cläe—yaller cläe."

"Yaller fer jalousy!"

"Go on! oo's jalous?"

"Oop an' over!"

" 'Ang on!"

"Bloody wet!"

"Brought y'r g'loshes?"

These words were interspersed with the groans of George Harkess, with an occasional snort of laughter from one or other of the speakers, and the loud noises of their boots against water and boulders.

John had never heard a human conversation that was so discomforting, or one that had so great a capacity for making even the most deadly silence seem warm and cheerful by comparison. Above all he wished that they would not laugh; their forced cheerfulness filled him with surprising anger, making him long to turn around and tell them to "shut up!" Every foolish, meaningless ejaculation of laughter was a confession of the fear they would not acknowledge and seemed to stir up and make more actively venomous the personal fear which lay coiled within him like a serpent. If he had been Sergeant Sanders, he decided, he would have turned around and told them that if they were frightened they could give up and return to the open air; but Sergeant Sanders was the most silent of them all. He made no sound as he followed John and George Harkess through the gallery.

At last they reached the wider entrance to the cave itself, and John stopped and waited for the others to gather together beneath its dripping roof. Sergeant Sanders straightened himself and stepped up beside him.

"All right?" he asked.

"Yes, thank you, Sergeant."

He waved the beam of his light into the darkness ahead, watching it taper off into a grey ghost of light as it reached out into the vastness of the cavern.

"We were in there," he said. "Not very far, about fifty yards, I think. You'll see the remains of our fire."

"Which side was that?"

"That side," he pointed, "the right-hand side; but if you don't mind, Sergeant, I'd rather not go any farther just now. I'll just wait here and let you see if you can find—any clues."

"What's he stopping for?" George Harkess and the constables had at last joined them. "For God's sake get a move on, boy! We don't want to spend the whole morning down here."

"He's doing very well, Mr. Harkess," said the sergeant, "and I don't think he's wasted any time."

"No, no. He's done very well, but you must admit this isn't the most comfortable way of spending a morning."

"It's got to be done, sir."

George Harkess rubbed his hands. "Of course," he said. "Well, what do we do now? Get busy on the search? It looks a pretty large area from what one can see of it."

"I think it would be better if I went on alone, Mr. Harkess, and searched the floor. It's quite possible that something might have been dropped, a cigarette packet or a matchbox or a bus ticket."

"I'll come with you if you like, Sar'nt?"

"Better not. We don't want it to be a case of too many cooks. My inspector has a rule about not fouling the ground; he's a great one for following up when a case goes badly."

"Very well, Sergeant! We'll wait here and show you a light."

"Thank you, sir."

He stepped down on to the floor of the cave, and shining his torch a little way ahead of him, started to move slowly away from them over towards the right-hand wall. The two policemen moved up and stood behind John, one on either side of him, directing their lights on to the sergeant's back. He turned around angrily, screwing up his eyes in the double glare of the beams. Under the peak of his hat his face looked curiously white and dead like a mask in Madame Tussaud's.

"Not on my *back*! You damn fools," he shouted. "How do you expect me to see anything but my own shadow if you're going to direct your lights on *me* rather than on the floor? Have some sense, Haykin!"

They changed the direction of the beams and he moved a few paces forward. Then he stopped again. The beam of his own light crept ahead of him inch by inch over the clear pools and the smoothed coruscations of the limestone, against its brightness his shoulders and back were silhouetted clearly. At the distance of some sixty yards he looked quite small and very still, like the toy soldier who had fallen down the drain in Hans Andersen's story. Suddenly he began to run, he came to life like a soldier in face of the beautiful doll he loved, he ran about five paces and then stopped again. They heard his exclamation, a sharp indrawn cry, ugly and short, which echoed about them for a moment before it was drawn into the silence.

John winced as the heavy hand of George Harkess came down upon his bruised shoulder. The great body of the man leaned over him and he could see and smell his condensed, unsweet breath as he peered out ahead towards the sergeant. Nobody moved, they were as still and absorbed as Victoria and John had been the afternoon before when they had stood in this same place and called out into the cave; and as their own candles had done, the flashlights of the two constables began to shake, making the shadows created by their beams rock and sway against the uneven surfaces. In the silence they all four heard clearly for the first time the falling of the water from the high places beyond them; and then, with the sergeant still far ahead of them, still immobile and quiet, George Harkess suddenly leaned further over John and bellowed out into the darkness.

"What *is* it, Sergeant? What have you found?"

The sergeant turned around deliberately, the white face of his flashlight winking back at them as though it were conveying a message in Morse.

"We'll want the camera," he called. "Tell Haykin to get the camera!"

"I will, Sergeant! But tell us, what have you found? Have you found—?"

"Yes," shouted the sergeant. "Yes, she's here."

"Is she—?"

Above John, weighing over him more heavily than all the weight of the rock between the darkness and the daylight, the body of George Harkess shuddered in its heavy tweed. He cleared his throat.

"Is she all right?" he asked quickly.

The sergeant turned around once again.

"No," he called. "No." And capriciously the cave echoed his terrible negative. He raised his voice.

"I *told* you! Send Haykin for my camera and take the boy out. *It is murder!*"

4. In the Time of Greenbloom

No Angel knows
No fire-hung Seraph knows or could
What I, the fallen son of fallen fathers
Now and then within the cirrus understood.

❧ IN THE TIME OF GREENBLOOM

He had stolen the asparagus after chapel on Friday evening and sent it via the waiter to be boiled for supper five minutes later. He had enjoyed it too, even despite the glances and nudges which ensued throughout the meal at the upper end of the table. Fortunately the label had come off the tin in the process of the boiling in the school kitchen, with the result that on its return it had been, if not unrecognizable, at any rate unidentifiable. He had no idea to whom it belonged, though in his mind he had narrowed down the possible owners to three: Hopper, whose father kept a hotel in Worthing; Liverman, who had asthma and used green ink, or Coke, who said his prayers and was a promising Rugby football player on the second team.

John had snatched it from the cloisters in the dark when the rest of the house was fumbling about trying to find the sardines, baked beans, and tuck-shop eggs which they had placed there before chapel started. It had been a fairly easy theft, scarcely deserving of the pleasure its contents had later given him. No one was to know that he had sunk the whole of his weekly two shillings on doughnuts and coffee in the shop within half an hour of Rudmose doling it out to him; no one was to know that he felt quite clearly that he was owed considerably more than the odd tin of asparagus by the whole school for his unpopularity, his increasing solitude, and "the moors."

No one else had had the moors; no one else could ever have the moors; it or they had been reserved for him alone and now that it was half-term for the rest of them, now that they could

see their parents at Commemoration and talk to them or go out
with them or even go up to London with them for the night,
they owed something to him: a minute interlude of greed, of
cosiness such as he had experienced while eating the asparagus,
or the odd sixpence or shilling he was able to filch from the hanging trousers in the changing room during afternoon games; they
owed him more, they owed him the passing or forgiveness of
any suspicion or certainty they might have that he was the thief.

Last term he had been in the papers for weeks: his name, his
photograph, all the details of his past, of his last days with Victoria in the moors. He had been and still was "The Boy in the
Danbey Dale Tragedy," "Young John Blaydon, the sweetheart
of Victoria Blount so hideously murdered by Person or Persons
Unknown" nearly five months ago. Everything, his evidence
at the inquest, the coroner's sympathy, the background stories
of his home, flashlight photographs of the Stump Cross caverns,
even extracts from the letters he had written to Victoria had
been printed in the newspapers for weeks which had mounted
into months before Father's Bishop had at last persuaded the
editors to leave him out of it.

But by then of course it had been too late; the whole of his
relationship with Victoria had become a lurid and vulgar adver-
tisement splashed on every hoarding and concealed behind everyone's gaze. The end of that winter term and whole of the
Christmas holidays which followed it had been lived through
the daily and recurring horror of the black and white publicity.
Each night he had gone to bed attempting to absorb whatever
fresh pain the day's print had inflicted; each morning he had
awakened pale and taut to the threat of whatever might await
him at the breakfast table.

One paper, he remembered, a Sunday one, had likened Victoria
to Juliet and himself to Romeo, an excruciating piece of intuition
on the part of some reporter who had known nothing of the
secret part of that dead, and to him, most dear conversation. It
had compared the cave to the tomb of the Capulets and gone on
to suggest that the two of them had hidden themselves there in
order to do their "innocent courting" and so "outwit strong
parental opposition to their friendship." Another had implied

that he himself had clues which might help to identify the "Commercial Hiker" of the evidence and was withholding them from the police out of shyness or because he had been threatened with blackmail; a third when the publicity had been at its height had put in a strong plea for an end to that part of it which was focused on the "Blaydon Boy," and on the next day had given an account of a long and entirely fictitious interview in which he was supposed to have opened his heart to "our Lady Correspondent."

All of them, of course, had been sympathetic in so far as his own evidence was concerned, though they had hinted that it had been unwise of the parents to allow two young people "such freedom of opportunity," whatever that might imply; and poor old Father in view of his priesthood had come in for particularly odious reproof in the editorials.

At Beowulf's during the latter part of that first term there had been some attempt on the part of his housemaster, The Rev. Robert Rudmose, to organize an ineffectual censorship of the dayroom papers; and initially everyone had been kinder to him during that term than during the present one. They had even allowed him to be beaten as usual for such minor offences as "cutting detention" or crossing the playing fields on a Saturday afternoon, and wryly, he had appreciated the tact of the staff and prefects in reporting him on these occasions and carrying out the brisk punishment as thoroughly as they would have done if no unusual event had ever involved him.

But no amount of kindness, of unaccustomed grins from shining prefects, of gentleness from the blues and half-blues who taught Greek and Latin, could conceal the fact that by the others, his contemporaries, he had gradually become less liked and more suspected than ever. For he did not fool himself; he knew with certainty that he was not the sort of person who would ever have been popular even in the absence of the publicity which had attended his late arrival during that snowy first term. Even with no murder, no public, precocious and un-English love affair to his name, he would still have been a singular and awkward epitome of the heroes of modern school stories. Unknown, ingenuous, given to hopeless sentimentality, with no athletic prowess with which to sugar the pill, he would, with the long line of contemporary and unheroic school heroes, have been out of step; and the other fellows would not for long have liked him.

As it was, on the house runs, on the long walk by the canal to the boathouse, he now travelled increasingly alone. Even square, kindly old Bass, whose father owned a coal mine in Sheffield and who had initially been dumbly pleasant, preferred not to be seen with him; and consequently he had come to rely more and more upon himself and upon his own imaginings for an escape from Beowulf's and the all too real world of the school.

That was how he came to take the asparagus and why he was quite determined to go on taking anything that might come his way during the remainder of the term. He was not quite sure why he had begun stealing; until "the moors" it had not been one of his particular temptations; but latterly he had experienced an increasing and consuming greed for "things" of all sorts: food, sweets, penknives and pens, anything old or new, useful or serviceable, and of course for money too!

In his uneasy nights he reasoned that if you climbed a tree and took an apple that did not belong to you, you were risking a dog, a shouting farmer, or a slip in haste. Nobody, he felt, really owned anything except themselves; the body they stood up in, the voice they shouted with, the thoughts and words they made. In the beginning man had lived in caves and went out from them and took what he could at the risk of his life. He took fish from infested rivers, fruit from snake-hung trees and flesh from animals armoured with fangs and claws. If he got what he took, well and good, he had made something real to himself which before had been unreal in that it was merely a desirable part of a shadowy and hostile environment. If, on the other hand, man did not get what he wanted then he himself became unreal, he died—and became a part of the vacancy in which he lived.

Stretching out of himself to appropriate the asparagus in the darkness of the cloisters yesterday evening, he had been fishing naked in the silence. He had succeeded; and if now the waters were disturbed, if faces mouthed or looked things or threatened or hated, it did not in the least matter; it was only to be expected and was, when you understood it fully, quite without significance.

If after what had happened Mother and Father had wanted him to behave differently, to respond differently, then they should never have sent him on to Beowulf's in the first place. Perhaps all things considered it had not been entirely their fault, it had probably been more the fault of that fool of a doctor with his talk of "normality," of "not making a case of the boy," of "letting him face up to things and resume the ordinary progress of his education." But they should not have listened to him; they should have consulted David or old Father O'Brien in Newcastle.

As he himself saw it, the one good thing which might have come from so much blackness and horror would have been an escape from the Beowulf's process, the evasion of the public school days about which he had heard and read so much in contemporary novels. He had always hated the idea of those four years which, like Michael, Geoffrey and David before him, he would be expected to endure; and though he had said nothing to either Mother or Father, he had longed from the time he had reached the end of his years at the Abbey, to dodge them if possible; but neither Mother nor Father had apparently had the time or the wit to see it, and humbly and dumbly he had acquiesced in their expectation of his starting at the school as soon as the inquest was over.

And now, he thought, as he looked at the calendar beside him on his desk, here he was on the morning of half-term, and with forty-two more days to get through before he returned home for the Easter holidays. For the others, half-term was something of an event, and half-term Saturday a date marked on their calendars with gay scarlet ink; but for him it was no more than the top of a hill from which he was able to see, if he cared to look, only the farther hills and valleys of the school year stretching ahead into the remote distance. Only one consideration afforded him any comfort as he sat there at the prebreakfast prep: the thought that for the next forty-eight hours, everyone would be too busy to think about or notice him, and that consequently the asparagus might be forgotten at least until Monday. Before banishing the remembrance of the theft from his mind, he accepted with painless despair the certainty that by this time next week they would all be interested in more recent thefts.

No one would be coming down to see *him* during the next forty-eight hours; he would have to take what slight pleasure he could in the infinitesimal slackening of school discipline, in his secret and malicious speculations about the parents and relatives of the more fortunate majority, and in the slightly more enjoyable meals. For breakfast this morning, he was sure, it would be sausages in the plural instead of in the singular; this afternoon there would be a school match followed by a fairly festive tea, and this evening a long, coldly sentimental sermon from the prebendary, Oily Albert. There might, he supposed, be a letter from Mother or Father later in the day, though he very much doubted it, as, unlike other parents, they seemed to have no cognizance whatsoever of school dates and were as uninterested as he was himself in all the feast days and fast days by means of which successive boards had tried to give Beowulf's an Etonian flavour in the space of only sixty years.

There might possibly be a message or a card from Michael at St. John's to say that he would take him out for tea tomorrow; but that too was unlikely if only because Michael had promised it. Like John himself, Michael resented obligations most particularly when they were self-imposed, and would have been far keener to give his young brother a treat were he not committed to it by an earlier promise.

He opened a book hurriedly and reached for his pencil as someone walked over to his desk; it was "Myrtle" Franks, one of the house prefects.

"Blaydon?"

"Yes?"

"Mr. Rudmose would like to see you in his study after breakfast."

"Thank you."

Desks opened and closed and Myrtle, both hands in both pockets, the permitted swagger of the house prefect, strode magnificently down the length of the dayroom and out through the door at its far end. Good Lord! Prep was over and he had done nothing, nothing but think; and now Rudmose wanted him.

Could it be the asparagus, he wondered, already? Could it be the asparagus? Had they discovered him so soon?

He put away his books and slamming the lid of his desk made his way alone across the quadrangle to breakfast. How easily they fell into twos and threes. How well they knew their places, sizes, each other's faces. How faultlessly organized it was; as neatly disposed as an ant's nest; little tiny maggots in one room, slightly bigger and more adolescent maggots in another, and smooth, prefectorial cocoons in a third. But who was *he*? And what did he represent in the total activity of the nest? He did not know. But he longed for one of them, or two of them, to drop easily into step beside him and begin one of those wholesome, deadly conversations of which they never grew tired. He wondered if there were nothing he could do to take them in, to make them see him as he wished to be seen; unexceptionable, fresh faced and normal. Somewhere there must be something wrong, something not altogether connected with the moors. Johnson's father, he remembered, had exhibited himself in a barrel at Blackpool the year before he himself had arrived at Beowulf's; and Johnson was still one of the most popular prefects in the school. Onions's mother had jumped from the fourth-floor window of an unsavoury hotel half a mile from the Marble Arch; yet Onions had dozens of friends. What was it then which made them all hurry past him, talk back carefully and briefly when he spoke to them, or become absent-mindedly engrossed in whatever they were doing or not doing when he approached? And how long would it last?

In the roar and clatter of the dining hall he ate the sausages with relish, eking them out with six slices of margarine and bread and afterwards legged it back to the dayroom, collected his books for the morning's work and knocked on the door of Mr. Rudmose's study.

The housemaster opened it almost immediately.

"Good morning, B-Blaydon," he said with his quick stammer.

"Good morning, sir."

"Come in."

He followed him across the carpet to the wide fireplace gaping beneath its cluttered mantel: photographs of Old Boys, not so old boys, and young boys, the multitudinous accessories of the Georgian pipe-smoker, three spill-stocked Worcester vases and an empty crucifix; and waited despondently while Mr. Rudmose took up his position in front of his past. In a moment he had to meet the grey unsated eyes piercing out across the ruin of the cheeks and the pursed lips. The face, it occurred to him again, looked as though it had been sucked in the mouth of some young and dreadful experience, sucked and rejected before its lineament had quite dissolved. He had disliked it from the moment of their first interview six months ago, and looking into it now, he realized that the most painful distortion of which it was capable was that of the smile, the smile of a quite unutterable despair pathetically sweetened by a desire to please and to be loved.

"Well, J-Joseph?" The pet name hung on the air.

With an effort he smiled back, and it was as though he had blown into a dying bonfire, a wisp of smoke wrinkled the nostrils and spread in a little blaze to the eyes. Inside himself, horrified by the swiftness of the response, he shrank back from its warmth.

"I've been wondering how you've been getting on this term, Joseph?"

"Have you, sir?"

"Still the dreamer, Joseph?"

"Yes sir, rather bad dreams I'm afraid."

"Poor Joseph!" Once again the smile bared the teeth. "Remember the d-dream of the sheaves, and take heart!"

"Yes, sir, I will," he replied hopelessly, wondering who was ever going to bow down to *him*. "Did you want me, sir?"

"I did, Joseph, I did! I have some g-gnews, a letter from your brother Michael reached my breakfast table this morning asking my permission to take you out this afternoon and requesting a late pass for the evening."

"Oh." He eyed the card which Rudmose had extracted from the envelope on the mantelpiece. He was quite unexcited; it was better than nothing, but there was never anything comfortable or cosy about afternoons with Mick, he lacked something that the rest of the family had in superabundance, a quality of reassurance, of a warm vitality that could shut the door on the

world and make one glow intimately and safely within its ambience.

Pretending to a livelier pleasure than he felt, he managed an
eager smile. "Will I be able to go, sir?"

"My d-dear Joseph! Of course you will." He slithered about
on the greasy pole of his impediment, speaking in little rushes,
hesitating, swaying, all but losing his balance and then with astonishing agility recovering himself and rushing on again.

"But you know, Joseph, I don't think, my dear friend, that *you*
think, and I m-must say I entirely ag-gree with you, that *one*
afternoon, one s-small break in the c-louds will quite solve our
problem for us."

"No, sir." He was right; but how strange and terrible that
understanding and the love it must presuppose should come from
this quarter.

"No-no indeed! You have wisdom, Joseph, you realize that a
change portends, do you not?" He paused, smiling horribly,
and then without waiting for an answer patted him tenderly on
the back, allowing his cold hand to rest on the nape of his neck.

"To pursue the metaphor, Biblical and appropriate from myself to your father's son, it is time you got out of your dry
w-well, abandoned your coat of m-many colours, and left your
brethren to their fate. If the dream of the sheaves is to come
true, Joseph, I think you would be better served elsewhere, and
from his letter, I think that opinion seems already to be shared
by your elder brother M-Michael too."

How cold is his hand, he thought; cold and heavy, clutching
at warmth. The weight of it seemed to smother his thoughts and
he was quite unable to reply. People should never touch one
another without warning, it was very dangerous. He imagined
himself a piece of seaweed in the grip of some cold and hungry
crustacean, a lobster or a crab.

"Well, Joseph?"

"Do you mean that you think I ought to leave Beowulf's, sir?"

"My d-dear boy, did I say *that*? Did I even m-minimally imply
such a thing? You must not be so impetuous."

"I'm sorry, sir, I thought that was what you meant. What
did you mean, sir?"

"I m-meant, Joseph, that at a later date it might be as well to consider going elsewhere. B-but that is not at all the same thing as l-leaving the school, in the middle of the term, I mean."

"But that's just what I thought you meant, sir."

"But we must be circumspect, we must become accustomed to the idea and discuss it b-before we even think of making it a fact."

"Yes, sir." What did he mean? Next year? At the end of this term, sometime or never? "When did you think I ought to leave, sir?"

"Certainly not before the end of term, Joseph. That might look as though you were fleeing or *we* were pushing; remember that it is only the wicked who 'flee when no man pursueth but the righteous' and that I am your friend, Joseph; you may not have admitted it to yourself yet, though I think you welcome it, but I do want to do what is best for you."

"Yes, sir." If only he would remove his hand. "Would you mind telling me why you think I ought to leave, sir?"

The hand gave a little wriggle, a dying convulsion.

"Why, for your own s-sake, Joseph, of course! Not for ours, you must *never* imagine even in your deepest dreams that we would wish you to go er—into Egypt!" He paused, the hand was removed and all at once with a lightning change its owner be-came the Reverend Rudmose again, the housemaster who did not like the headmaster and who was therefore determined to be faultless in the discharge of a difficult commission. "I want you to know, Joseph, that I have already written to your parents and told them that we think it would be better for you if you were to start your schooling anew in some other and m-more fortu-nate establishment; and I think, though even the wisest of us may be mistaken, that they too feel *n-now* that it was perhaps a mistake to let you return here, to *start* here, so soon after— after—"

"After the moors, sir?"

"Yes, Joseph, after the m-moors."

"All right, sir."

For the first time he was able to smile brightly and sincerely into the haggard face so near his own. In his imagination his trunk and tuckbox were already packed and he was on the train for home; the horror was over. Inside him, gaiety limbered up like an athlete on a frosty field.

"And can I got out with my brother this afternoon, sir?"

"After the necessary formalities, the usual interview with the p-p-p—"

"The prebendary, sir?" He knew that Rudmose loathed the headmaster and that there must be a long delay in the pronunciation of the bizarre and hated title.

"Yes, the p-p—, the headmaster! You could talk all this over with your brother Michael, could you not? And then perhaps when I have had your father's reply I could tell you about my g-good friend Mr. Victor of Worthing."

"Mr. Victor?"

"Yes, Joseph; an euphonious name! A name instinct with g-good omens for the future. He is a c-coach, a crammer, an am-am-m-m-anuensis, and a very able one who would, were he given the chance, soon make the d-dream of the sheaves a reality. I have already mentioned him to your father and advised him how greatly you might profit from his tutelage. He has served Beowulf's very well in the past, and more than that, he is a p-personal and unusual friend of my own." He hesitated and his face assumed the unmistakable air of greed which precedes a confidence. "I wonder if your father or mother have ever told you about the R-Remnant, Joseph?"

"The Remnant, sir? I don't think so. What is it?"

"I must refer you to your Bible! Like m-most things of real importance you will find it there. The L-Latter Days, Joseph! the Return of the decimated portion of the Chosen Race to the fold! Wars and r-rumours of wars, signs in the Heavens and, I might add, s-signs in Worthing!" He grinned delightedly, and waited.

John tried to look intelligent. "It sounds like Revelations, sir, and I've never been able to understand them."

"Revelation in the singular perhaps, Joseph. But you must search the pages of the *Old* Testament if you are to d-discover my reference."

"Yes, sir." He longed to escape to the celebration of his

thoughts but felt that a little more kindness and politeness was demanded of him.

"What has it got to do with Mr. Victor, sir?" he asked eagerly.

"A strange man, Joseph, an unusual man in whom East and West have found their c-consummation! Mr. Victor is a Jew, but a Jew with a d-difference. He is a Christian Jew, a keen churchman and a friend of Canterbury. It is rare indeed for one of these to re-enter his religion by way of the Reform. Today, Joseph, all roads do *not* lead to R-Rome!" he ended triumphantly.

"No, sir."

"It is my hope that in the not-too-distant future you will make more than the acquaintance of this very dear friend, that he will be able to take over the guardianship of those r-rich dreams in which I know you indulge."

"Thank you, sir." He moved and by his movement succeeded in changing the direction of the conversation. "He sounds very interesting, sir. By the way, what time have I to be back tonight?"

"T-ten o'clock. The porter closes the gate at that hour and we do not want our young friend to have to k-knock like Macduff at the door of the castle—and, J-Joseph!"

"Yes, sir?"

"Remember, no c-colleges!"

"No, sir."

"B-boys are not allowed in the colleges!" He smiled again for the last time, a slow strangled smile.

"R-remember P-Potiphar's wife and do not go into a college, Joseph."

"No, sir."

He closed the door briskly behind him.

Michael took him to the Carpenter's Arms, a small pub somewhere behind Carfax where he said he was occasionally in the habit of having a game of darts or shove-ha'penny with the "real Oxfordians." "One should get everything out of one's time at a university," he said, "and learn to be a good mixer. You'll like the Carpenter's, John, it's an *honest* little place! Although I rarely go there, I like to feel it's there in an emergency, if you know what I mean; and of course the beer's very *sound*. Just the place for a family talk."

"We won't get caught, will we? I mean it's absolutely dead against the rules, even more sinful than going into a college."

"Good Lord no! That's exactly why I'm taking you there instead of the Mitre, the Ploughman, the Tenth Folly or the—" Michael checked himself. "In the Carpenter's one never meets anyone who is in the least likely to know one in the social sense; and in any case, John, I shouldn't worry too much about the school rules if I were you; from what you tell me of your little *causerie* with Rudmose you won't be there very much longer, and frankly I think it's a good thing."

"Do you really think so?"

Perhaps he had been unjust in his attitude to Mick, perhaps he was not after all so undiscerning as he had thought. He warmed to him. "It's awfully decent of you to be so sympathetic."

"Think nothing of it!"

"I've never said much about it at home, perhaps because of Mother's rule that once it was all over any discussion of the moors thing was forbidden. But honestly, Mick, I've loathed the place from the very beginning—" His voice trailed off, he swallowed and resumed. "*She* discusses it of course; *you* know, in her bedroom at night when she thinks I'm moodier than usual, 'haunted,' as she calls it. I think it's very sweet of her to go on trying to help me, but with the rest of the family the rule is still in force; even though we're all supposed to be praying for— Victoria and Mrs. Blount. I'm pretty sure she discusses it with everyone including Betty *Cae Ficer*, but for some reason, *I'm* not supposed to talk about it to anyone except her." They walked on a few paces. "When you were up with us last vac did she say anything about it to you?"

Beside him Michael's face lengthened. "Look here, old chap! I really think it would be better if we buried the bone. I think Mother does know best about this. Myself, I always found her advice very reliable when I was in my teens, though of course when one begins life at Oxford or Cambridge one has to give a little credence to one's *amour propre*."

When Michael resorted to French, as he did increasingly these days, and when in addition his features assumed the old and familiar lugubriousness for which he had always been marked, it was useless to argue or wheedle. John changed his approach.

"You're probably right," he said, "but if you really see how I feel, *you* know—worse even than your Lancing days, perhaps you'll back me up with Mother and Father over the Rudmose idea of starting afresh with this tutor friend of his in Worthing or wherever it is?"

A little impatiently Michael changed his black floppy umbrella from one hand to the other.

"Of course I shall." His spectacles were directed at the pavement. "It would be far the best thing. In my opinion it was madness, a sort of 'insanity *à deux*' on their part, ever to send you to Oxford in the first place; so embarrassing for—everyone, myself included! Of course, I told them both that I was quite prepared to do my bit and shepherd you through the first rather unpleasant months, and I think that on the whole we have managed to keep in touch and that I may have succeeded in tempering the wind a little. Even so, I don't honestly think I've been able to do enough for you to make it really worth while from either of our points of view; I mean, one does get a little sick of people muttering in pubs and in the societies and pointing one out as the brother of the Blaydon Boy. *Il faut souffrir*, one realizes that; but nobody likes to suffer unfruitfully and from your point of view, quite obviously, you ought to be given the chance of escaping the effects of that frightful tabloid publicity." He quickened his pace as they approached an inn sign on the opposite side of the road. "To summarize, it's really a question of *sauve qui peut*, and since for better or worse, *I* am committed to finishing my course here, I think that *your* removal, your escape and opportunity, is what we should aim at."

Well in step they crossed the road and halted on the pavement beneath the inn sign. Michael flashed him a hot smile through his horn-rimmed spectacles. "Let's leave it at that, John," he said, in a brighter, somehow moister, voice. "You just wait here for a moment while I see if it's all clear inside. It may take me a few minutes, and to fill in the time, you might just scan the pavements and see if you recognize anyone from the school. Better take your hat off too, those large straw things are so conspicuous."

John took it off and fumbled with it. "What shall I do with it?" he asked, feeling suddenly chilled at the thought of Rudmose and Potiphar's wife.

Michael snatched it hurriedly.

"Here, give it to me," he said. "I'll deal with it."

He turned around, and the next moment he was gone; the little doorway with its frosted glass seemed to have sucked him in like a vacuum cleaner, leaving in his place only the faint farm smell of hops and sawdust. John waited dutifully for about three minutes, and then, beginning to feel obtrusive, walked purposefully across the empty street.

It was all indefinably and yet typically depressing; just the sort of place Michael would choose, he thought bitterly. Upright little Victorian houses with bulges all over their pillars and bow windows pushing out into minute squares of tiles and grass surrounded by chains, railings and brick walls.

People, he thought, always gravitated naturally to their proper surroundings. This was quite obviously Michael's world; heavily respectable and rectangular outside, hinting at security and a rather frowsty cosiness within, but in reality full of seedy, unsympathetic people with long serious faces and a fluent excuse for everything they did. He *betted* that Michael came here often, very often. It was his area, his wall, his tree, a sort of camouflage that blended perfectly with his most prevalent mood. He saw him suddenly as a solemn spectacled caterpillar like the one in *Alice*, moving carefully on to the shadowed side of his toadstool well away from the bright sunlight.

The image made him smile, and momentarily he felt more at ease; but a little later it occurred to him sharply that to criticize his own brother like this, even though it were to himself alone, was merely to increase his isolation. Whatever happened he must not cut himself off from the family; if a time came when he could no longer attempt to tell them the things he suffered or enjoyed, if they could not hear, there would be nothing left for him. In addition, he felt sure that there was another factor in his increasing solitariness, that somewhere there was a defect in himself. It was all very well to sneer one's way through life as he was doing, to have scoffed at the Abbey, to continue to praise Father and condemn Mother, and go on to become an evil judge of persons and start off in the same old way at Beowulf's; but if it went on, if everyone else were to be measured by the faulty eye and weighed in the biased balance all through the days of his growing-up, there would come a time when there would be no one left but himself, the same crooked and unpleasant self with which he had evidently started. He must love Michael and forgive him seventy times and seven like the man in the Bible, and at last reach the point at which he would understand that there was really nothing to forgive which did not lie within himself.

He turned and started to walk back towards the Carpenter's Arms. Yes, he must cling on to Michael at all costs, and then Michael would become fonder of him and as he became fonder would become more discerning and more of a help.

He crossed the road; and as if to reward him for his moment of generosity, Michael's face, redder, rounder and more affectionate, suddenly appeared in the brown doorway of the Carpenter's Arms. He beckoned, and John trotted over to him and into the L-shaped saloon bar. There were only five or six people in there, all of them men, and all of them wearing serge suits of a colour peculiar to the working class, something between bluebell blue and mauve. They all wore white long-pointed collars and striped ties with the exception of the landlord who had a highly polished face and wore nothing save a woolen shirt and a brass front stud in place of collar and tie. They all seemed to know Michael very well indeed; and Michael himself, once he and John were standing comfortably in front of the bar, assumed a quite different manner towards John. He became more openly brotherly and behaved as though he were very much older and John very much younger than was the fact.

"My young brother, Mr. Cudlopp!" he said to the landlord with a loudness that contrived to make the others party to the announcement. "He's at Beowulf's and between ourselves it's just as well that no one at the school—"

"I know! I know!" Mr. Cudlopp shook with the laughter which, as John later discovered, accompanied even his most prosaic remarks. "Again' the rules, eh? Don't you worry, Mr. Blaydon! What's said in the Carpenter's doesn't ever go out into the street, especially in a case like this where it could cause a young man more than a red *face!*" He beamed at John. "If you know what I mean?"

Playing up, John cringed appropriately. "It certainly could," he said. "I've had two beatings this term already."

"Well, what's it to be?" went on Mr. Cudlopp. "Another of the same, Mr. Blaydon? And a nice glass of cider for your brother?"

"That would be splendid, and you must join us, Mr. Cudlopp."

"Thank you, sir, thank you."

They took their glasses over to a small table beside the screen adjoining the entrance. Michael fumbled comfortably in the pockets of his tweed jacket and produced the pipe Mother had given him for Christmas. He stuffed the bowl carefully with John Cotton's tobacco and after a certain amount of grunting and patting eventually puffed out a sigh of smoke. "Had a little one while you were keeping *cave*," he said quietly, "just to establish the atmosphere and so on. The host here's a good fellow—great bowls player, but inclined like most of them to be a little hail-fellow-well-met on the slightest provocation. Just as well to have him on our side though; so although I could ill afford it, I thought it would be as well to stand him one, but no doubt you'll be able to pay me back sometime?" He paused. "I'm not worried about breaking the school rules but I think we should keep on the right side of the licensing laws; when's your birthday?"

"March the twenty-fifth."

"Sixteenth?"

"No, fourteenth."

"Confound it! I told him you were sixteen. Still, never mind! Just remember though, won't you?"

"Yes, Mick."

"How's the cider?"

"Lovely, thanks; but I do hope you've got some peppermints.

I don't want anyone to smell my breath when I get back to Beowulf's."

"What time have you to be back?"

"Not till ten; they've given me a late pass."

"It will have worn off by then—takes about two hours and thirty-five minutes without screening, one hour and fifteen with. Whisky of course is different, that's why I rarely touch it; it doesn't do to go in to lectures reeking of whisky."

"No."

They sat on in silence for a time and John noticed that Michael's attention was tending to stray increasingly in the direction of the shove ha'penny board where two of the purple-suited men were enjoying what was evidently a keen game. He lifted his glass and took a second long pull at his cider and then waited for its effect. It was not long delayed; the feeling of warmth and lightness began to seep into him from some central point within himself. The air of the bar became sweeter, the bar itself more spacious and better proportioned, and he realized with increasing delight that all the people in it were fundamentally rather pathetic and very lovable. He drained his glass.

"I think I'll have another."

"What's that?" Michael jerked his face away from the shove ha'penny battle.

"Another cider," John repeated a little thickly.

Regarding him sadly, Michael engulfed the remainder of his pint.

"I wouldn't just yet, old chap. At your age one wants to start the way one means to go on; and it's a bad thing to get into the habit of taking one's beer too fast." He glanced at his watch and got up. "I'll get you another one in—half an hour. Cider's potent stuff, and it's a pity really that you don't care for beer because the alcohol content is about half that of these fermented fruit juices, and incidentally you can't beat malt and hops as a thirst-quencher; that's why, on the whole, I've made a sort of local rule always to stick to it myself, unless of course I'm in a hurry. By the way, I suppose you have brought a little money with you?"

John smiled; all at once his thefts seemed extraordinarily, almost painfully, funny. "I haven't got a penny," he said. "Not today."

Michael frowned. "I thought you were given your pocket money on Saturdays?"

"No, on Fridays."

"But surely, that was yesterday, wasn't it?"

"Yes." How amusing that he should be angry with him for not having stolen anything lately in the way of money. The money *he* was spending belonged to Father, who'd been left it by his father, who'd made it out of cotton before the Great War. Money was very amusing, particularly in relation to Michael, who was looking more solemn than ever as he absorbed the broad smile on John's face.

"Do you mean to say you've spent the whole lot in twenty-four hours?"

"You mean the whole two bob? Yes I have, in the tuck shop yesterday."

"Good Lord! What on earth did you spend it on?"

"Doughnuts and jam puffs—I was hungry. Anyway I don't think it's an awful lot when it's supposed to last a week."

"From my point of view I admit that it wouldn't be a lot. This morning's already cost me about double that, and by the time I get you back tonight it'll probably be considerably more! The point is that one's income is in scale with one's position, and you have spent in a single day the equivalent of my weekly allowance, part of which I'm having to spend on you."

Within the irrational gaiety which had seized him ever since he had finished his cider, John tried to feel responsible and penitent.

"I'm awfully sorry, Mick! If I'd known you were going to take me out I'd have kept some of it so's I could stand you a drink."

"It's not that, old chap. It's just that I feel I ought to remember Mother's commission and give you a little advice on things of this sort." Smiling briefly he turned and went over to the bar. "That bitter's uncommonly sound this morning, Mr. Cudlopp. I think I'll try another glass before you change barrels."

Mr. Cudlopp frothed with laughter as he drew the glass. "Shall I repeat the young gentleman's too, Mr. Blaydon?"

"Not yet— Oh well, I suppose you might, but I don't think I'm going to let him drink it just yet. He put down that first one in five minutes flat."

"Then sir, if you'll forgive me, he must be a chip off the same block," said Mr. Cudlopp as Michael brought the drinks over to the table.

"About lunch," he said, "I don't suppose you're very hungry yet, are you? Half-terms, as far as I remember, were usually marked by fairly substantial meals and it's only two or three hours since your breakfast. In about half an hour, that's to say at closing time, we'll be going around to Horab's rooms. Can you hold out till then?"

"Who's Horab?"

"That Jewish friend of mine at Balliol—you must have heard me mention him. As a matter of fact he'd have been with us now but for the fact that today is Shabbath."

"Shabbath?"

"The Jewish sabbath; starts on Friday, ends with the evening star on Saturday night. Horab has to stay indoors until it's over; but he always has plenty of food in his rooms. It's kosher stuff of course but I think you'll enjoy it just the same; it's supposed to be very much more wholesome than our own food. Do you think you can manage to wait until then?"

"When is closing time?"

Michael looked tired. "I told you, about half an hour, say an hour at the outside."

"Oh." John's stomach rumbled beneath his grey waistcoat. "Yes, I think so. I don't suppose they'd have a sandwich here, would they?"

"They could probably *make* you one; but they're not very easy on the pocket you know, John. In fact, they cost almost twice as much as a pint of their best bitter."

"Oh, all right. I'll hang on then."

"Good laddie." Michael flexed his knees like a policeman. "In that case there's just time for me to have a game of shove ha'-penny with my friend Albert over there. I occasionally give him quite a good run for his money and I think I may be in form this morning. It's a very skilled game, teaches one to be deliberate and to think ahead. I always call it the 'working man's chess,' and if you can acquit yourself well on the shove ha'penny board you'll find that you'll always enjoy the confidence of even the poorest clients later in life. If you like you can come and watch the game."

"No thanks! I think I'll sit here for a bit, but I can't guarantee not to touch my cider for another half-hour."

"Oh don't worry about that, one mustn't become a slave to one's own rules. If you drink it reasonably slowly you'll find it will sustain you until it's time for us to go and meet Horab. Cider's a very healthy drink you know; apart from a little fruit-sugar and water there's nothing much in it really."

Pint in hand he moved over eagerly to the far end of the room.

John drank his cider very slowly, trying to make it last out against the clock behind the bar. In the long intervals between the sips he watched Mr. Cudlopp drawing beer and accepting drinks from new customers, and became more and more interested in his manner of drinking. The high polish of his face, he noticed, was particularly marked over the upper lip where the surface of the beer rested when his glass was raised to his mouth. He wondered if perhaps the beer, in the course of the years, might not have had some subtle effect on the skin, and began to calculate how many pints, quarts and gallons must have lain against that particular area of skin prior to its transit through his body. The trouble was that he did not know Mr. Cudlopp's age, nor how long he had been drinking at his present smooth pace; but the picture of an amber waterfall of beer at the rate of, say, four gallons a week impinging almost ceaselessly on this human basin year in and year out, quite fascinated him and made him wonder why Mr. Cudlopp allowed it to happen.

He certainly did not look as though he were enjoying it; the torrents of his laughter, the ponderosity of his winks, the chuckles which underbubbled his remarks, were all belied by the dead and desperate look in his eyes. When he actually drank he looked suddenly vacant as though he were steeling himself against some private and painful ordeal. More puzzling still, he did not seem to acknowledge even to himself that he was drinking at all. There was no perceptible movement of the submerged upper lip or the

pouting lower one, no filling of the cheeks or of the throat itself; the glass was raised, tilted against the teeth, and then replaced nearly empty on the counter. It looked as though time
really did stand still for him when he was drinking, so that since
there was no before or after for Mr. Cudlopp, he was allowed
to remain precisely the same for several hours in every week.
It was a strangely depressing thought.

For John himself the hour dragged on to its close; and at last
Michael, having been "stood" another pint for his victory over
Albert, suggested it was time they made their way to his friend
Horab Greenbloom's rooms in Balliol College.

It was only as they were climbing the dark staircase to the
first floor that John remembered he had left his boater at the
Carpenter's Arms. Michael said they could get it later when "they
opened again" and that in the meantime they were better off
without it in view of the fact that by going into a college they
would be breaking another school rule. John found himself
quite satisfied with this argument. The day seemed to be taking
a particular and predestined shape of its own; and perhaps as a
result of the cider or perhaps because of a hollowness which he
had sensed somewhere inside him ever since the moors, he was
able to assume a new courage and nonchalance about everything
that was happening.

Of late he had been worried by an increasing tendency to
discount all the appearances of the world through which he
moved. The spaces about him seemed to be filled with persons
and things as remote and insignificant as the stars of the night
sky. He found it difficult to believe in all the sounds sights and
movements which betokened the living world, and if he had
been blind, dumb and deaf and so inhabited a dark consciousness
of his own, he would have felt no more divorced from the appearances which his senses continually forced him to accept; he
might even have accepted them more readily. Within his mind
there were unused dimensions which were quite different from
those his senses offered him; dimensions of light and shade, of
nobility and degradation, better fitted than those the world had
used to clothe the passions and aspirations which walked its sur-

faces. Opening his eyes to people and things, seeing their faces
and façades, listening with his ears to the sounds they made, he
was often tempted to rock with a dreadful laughter at their demand for serious acceptance, and at such times knew himself to
be poised on the edge of a void filled with conceptions more
awful even than those which he sensibly encountered.

Now, as he walked with Michael past the black gates of St.
John's College, he looked about him greedily, willing himself
to accept the trees in the walled sanctuary, the embellishments of
the Martyr's Memorial and the wide-windowed front of the
Randolph Hotel. These things, he told himself, were all that
there was, he must walk beneath them, around them and through
them as other people walked on their two legs, seriously giving
them their due.

At the head of the stairs in Balliol College, Michael knocked
on the outer door and a muffled though somewhat raucous voice
called out, "Come in!"

Michael shouted that since the door was locked, they could
not *get* in, whereat on the other side of the door they heard the
utterance of a tired blasphemy followed by a long pause. They
heard the springs of a chair squeaking, the sound of something
being knocked over and a few moments later the thud-pad of an
uneven and impatient walking; then a hand scrabbled at the yale
lock and at last the door before them was opened.

The room beyond it was in semidarkness, all the curtains being
drawn and only one low-calibre bulb shining out from a standard
lamp beside an armchair. Against this background the small face
of their host shone out with palest green clarity. It was an almost Egyptian face with pitch-black hair and beautifully painted
little eyes enclosed between smooth lids, eyes like nothing so
much as those depicted on the faces of attendants around the
burial chambers of dead Pharaohs. The cheekbones and their
overlying cheeks, as rich as cold cream, were high, the lips thick
and gelatinous as Turkish delight, and the nostrils of the neat
little nose exquisitely curved and petulant.

Petulance, in fact, was the prevailing mark and mood of the
whole person; the little head jutted forward over the narrow
shoulders with so great an impatience that it seemed about to

disown the remainder of the body and fly off into space upon some urgent purpose of its own. Beside the tiny hips in their expensive, sagging "Oxford bags" the white hands hung limply like those of a skeleton, and when their owner on what was obviously an artificial leg led Michael and himself into the darkened room, his whole gait and movement were themselves expressive of that devouring and vexatious haste which was so much a part of his expression.

"Whass the time? Switsh off that damn' light for me would you, Mick, an' draw half a curtain? Oh! an' one of you might pick up that table I knocked over. You woke me up."

Michael moved over to the window and very gingerly pulled aside one of the dark green velvet curtains.

"Not too much, Mick! Not too much." Turning half around in his chair Greenbloom glared at the grey incoming light. "What the Hell's time? Any stars out yet? Can you see any stars?"

"I'm just looking."

Greenbloom drew himself down deeper into his chair and then glared sickly at John. "Who's this you've brought with you?" he asked.

"Who's what?" asked Michael from his position by the window.

"*This*," gestured Greenbloom. "There's two of you, there's someone standing in front of my chair here. Who is it? It's not Fritters, it's no one I know, who is it?"

"I told you," said Michael. "It's John, my brother. If you remember you invited him to tea when I mentioned him to you yesterday."

"When?"

"Yesterday."

"Oh *yesterday*! Why didn't you say so, you know what my memory is." He sat up a little higher in his chair and craned forward towards John. "Who are you? Let's have a look at you. Wass your name? An' if you don't mind, for God's sake pick up that table! And if there's anything broken chuck it in the basket."

John stooped down by the small occasional table which lay

on the carpet. There was a decanter of whisky lying beside it unbroken but the stopper had come out and the whisky had run into the thick pile like a puppy-patch and wetted a number of five-pound notes and some loose silver nearby. He picked the notes up first, shook them quickly and then handed them to Greenbloom who waved them away distastefully.

"Put 'em on mantelpiece," he said, "or give 'em to Mick— *Shabbath!*"

"Here you are," said Michael moving over to him, "you'd better let me have them. Horab's not allowed to touch money today because it's the Jewish sabbath."

"What is your name?" croaked Greenbloom again. "No one will tell me who you are. I've asked three times already and neither you yourself nor Mick will answer me."

"Blaydon," said John. "John Blaydon—I'm Mick's brother."

Greenbloom sat up suddenly like a puppet being inexpertly manipulated.

"Not the *Blaydon boy?* You *John* Blaydon?"

"Yes." John mopped at the whisky with his handkerchief.

"Christ! Whyn't you tell me Mick? I'd no idea."

"My dear Horab, I told you twice yesterday; I mentioned it again this morning when I came in to ask you if there was anything you wanted, and I've just refreshed your memory again. What on earth's the matter with you?"

Greenbloom frowned. "Yes, all right, all right! Don't embarrass everyone."

He turned to John. "Look here, has he given you anything to eat? I mean have you had luncheon somewhere?"

"Well actually no—not yet—"

"Some food in the scout's hole, or there should be." With surprising agility he got to his feet and, lurching across the room to a large table covered with bottles, seized a plate of cakes and limped back with them.

"Kosher," he said. "Like kosher?"

John took one of the little iced squares and put it whole into his mouth. It did not seem necessary to answer the question; he just ate the cake and then took another one.

"Tea!" said Greenbloom. "Make Yerba Maté! Or 'd you rather have a drink?"

"No, tea," said John, slipping easily into the monosyllabic pattern of the conversation.

"Make tea, scout's hole, Mick," he ordered without looking around. Behind them Michael promptly disappeared through a door in the wall opposite the windows.

"Egg?" asked Greenbloom.

"Love it!"

"*Egg!*" shouted Greenbloom in his strange sandpaper voice.

There was no audible answer from Michael in the adjacent kitchenette and in the silence John stole another glance at the face so near his own. It was watching him greedily, almost affectionately, hungry with interest; and it returned his glance without any embarrassment. There was no shyness or self-consciousness in the long eyes confronting his own, they were as certain and demanding as those of a child who sees something that is urgently desired.

"Better?"

"Much, thanks."

"Mick's a selfish devil. Shove ha'penny?"

"Yes, he did have a game."

"Win?"

"Yes."

"Beer all the time?"

"Yes."

"*Muck!* Whisky?"

"No, he only drank beer."

"Not him. You! Would *you* like a whisky?"

"Oh, no thanks."

"Hock? Burgundy? Schnapps? Vodka? Pimms?"

"I'd love to try some vodka."

Greenbloom yawned again. "S'on the table—help yourself. No that white bottle, half full. Sorry I can't stock your glass but can't do any manner of work until Shabbath is over."

"I see. It's quite all right, I love pouring out drinks. You've got a colossal selection over here."

"Got to. Essential. Not always, you understand, but most

of the time. What *is* the time? Will no one tell me? Clock's stopped and I can't wind it or use the telephone until those damn stars make their appearance."

"Well we left the Carpenter's at closing time and then we went to Mick's room for a bit and then went for a walk along the river. Michael gave me some biscuits, he thought we ought to have some exercise. I suppose it must be getting on for five."

"Good. Hop over to the window, will you, and see if there's any sign of a star yet?"

John scanned the sky above the college square. It was pale grey-blue and above the buildings he could just see the thin uppermost limit of the mists which were descending on Port Meadow and the Whitham Woods.

"*Any* star?" he asked.

"Yes. Try over in the direction of the Radcliffe. Usually shines out there this time of the year."

Until it grew darker no star would penetrate that white and tenuous vapour.

"I can't see one—I'm awfully sorry, Mr. Greenbloom."

"Never mind! It'll give us time for tea before we start. Call me Horab if you don't mind."

John turned away from the window and sipped his vodka. He was feeling happy, peaceful; he liked this dark room, the richness hidden in the shadows and resident in the pale grandeur of his host. Feeling immediately mature he walked easily over to the marble chimney piece and, leaning his elbow on it, gazed into the surface of the antique mirror which surmounted it. Greenbloom obviously accepted him as a person of significance, an equal. He wished that Michael would fail to return, he would be an unnecessary interruption coming between them and the unspoken fellowship which he was sure they both sensed. Emptying the little glass, he put it down in front of him and spoke into the mirror towards the tall shape of Greenbloom hovering against the light of the dusk.

"Are you going out?" he asked.

"We're *all* going out! *London!*"

The figure in the glass turned into sharp profile against the windowpane. "Mick, hurry up with that egg will you? Got to get shaved."

"There's something the matter with this gas!" shouted Michael. "The water won't boil. You'll have to have an underdone egg John or else come and cook it yourself."

"I'd rather you cooked it," said John, "and personally I don't mind if it's raw."

There was no reply and in a few minutes Michael appeared with an egg balanced on a napkin ring, a flat loaf of unleavened bread and a little packet of butter. He placed these on a small table, lighted a cigarette and then somewhat irritably told John to go and make the tea.

"What's this about London, Horab?" he asked.

"Shave first," said Greenbloom, "razor's in bedroom."

Michael called to John, "Is the kettle boiling yet?"

"Yes, I'm just filling the pot."

"Splendid. When you've done that I shall want your help. Do you know how to use an electric razor?"

"No, I don't think so, but I can try. Why?"

"Horab needs shaving."

"Oh."

Well why should *he* have to do it? he thought angrily as he put the tea things on the tray and carried it through into the sitting room.

Michael took it from him. "Would you mind getting Horab's razor from his bedroom and giving him a quick shave while I pour out the tea."

John went into the bedroom. It looked as though it had been inexpertly burgled the night before. In the middle of the floor there was a pile of evening clothes surrounded by a gleaming chaos of silk sheets; against the wall on a black leather nail-studded chest there was an open dispatch case containing a litter of foreign paper currency from which he selected three thousand-franc notes and five hundred Reichmarks. From the washhand-stand he took a packet of bath salts wrapped in mauve cellophane and one of two dozen bottles of exciting-looking brilliantines. The dressing table shone redly with an assortment of gold, silver and tortoise-shell hairbrushes, hand glasses and combs. Beside the black bed which was surmounted by a silver reading light and three black ostrich feathers, there was a revolving bookcase filled with new paper-covered books. He saw French titles, German titles and copies of English books printed in foreign countries; open, on the top of the case, was a book called *Là-Bas*, by someone named J. K. Huysmans. He would have liked to have spent at least ten minutes or a quarter of an hour in looking at the pictures on the walls, intent-looking relatives, and religious paintings from India with elephants and Buddhas, in ruffling through the half-open drawers from which hung enormous subfusc ties and black silk socks, but realized that a too long delay might arouse suspicions, and so although his fingers were itching for fresh plunder, he called out, "I can't find it. Where is it?"

"Try the dressing-table drawer," shouted Greenbloom, "that's where my scout usually puts it and I told him I didn't want disturbing this morning so it should be there."

Eagerly John pulled open the top drawer. It contained an unlocked pigskin box in which there were small trays divided into separate compartments each of them filled with cufflinks, dress-shirt studs and jewelled tiepins. They looked extremely valuable, far too tempting to take. Behind the box was the electric razor made of grey plastic and shaped like a tiny racing car.

"I've got it," he said as Michael entered.

"Good."

"How does it work?"

"Plug it into the light, Mick," said Greenbloom. "I think you'd better do it, I don't want him electrocuting me."

"No," said Michael in a flat voice. "I'm tired." He yawned. "John's been sitting down all morning while I kept the flag flying at the Carpenter's. He's all right, Horab, really he is. He's going to reach Medicine later and you'll find he's got a much surer touch than I have myself."

"Well, for God's sake get a move on one of you." He stretched his long legs out over the carpet so that his small head lay just above the level of the arms of the chair.

John removed the bulb from the standard lamp and plugged the end of the flex into the socket. When it started to whirr he handed it to Greenbloom, who waved it away wearily.

"Fire!" he said. "Blue sparks, can't touch fire during Shabbath. Go on Mick, take it from him and shave me." He turned his small white face up towards the ceiling.

"Look," said Michael to John. "Perfectly simple, use it like a curry comb on a horse. It's just the sort of thing you're so good at, you've got that wonderful sympathy for anyone in trouble."

John glanced up at him but there was no shadow of a smile on Michael's sombre face. Very gingerly he started to run the razor over Greenbloom's chin which he now saw was covered with fat black hairs like the legs of tiny insects protruding through the skin.

Greenbloom closed his eyes and lay so completely inert and silent that for a moment John had the unhappy feeling he was shaving a corpse, a royal corpse from some remote oriental kingdom. It struck him that this was a unique response, as individual to Greenbloom as his limp. He had seen other men reclining in hairdresser's chairs or in Turkish baths but they had always appeared either sensual and full-blooded or else tired and ill, like children in the arms of their attendants; but about Greenbloom there was an air of mortality. He consented to this physical experience as actively as a corpse consents to death. It was implicit in his passivity, his bloodlessness, the dimness of the room, even in the bierlike design of his bed next door and made this a moment which he welcomed coldly as something essential to his being. John was sure that, unlike Mr. Cudlopp when he was drinking, there was for Greenbloom a real sense of time only when under such circumstances as these he was able to abandon all active participation in his day and drift into some twilit neutrality of his own.

The conviction, immediately intuitive and barely visualized, distressed John; he lifted the razor from the cold cheek and asked nervously, "Is that all right?"

His eyes still closed Greenbloom raised a hand and ran the fingers critically over the shaved area.

" 'll do," he said; "closer if possible though and a little more casually if you don't mind."

"Casually?"

"Yes, don't be so intense about it."

"Horab's very sensitive to anxiety," said Michael, moving over to the other side of the chair and inspecting the operation. "He's very sensitive to what he calls 'personae.' "

"What on earth are personae?" asked John.

"No time to tell you now."

"No not now," grated Greenbloom, "please not now."

"And don't forget his neck," went on Michael. "You're doing splendidly, old chap, but he likes his neck shaved right down to the line of the collar, don't you Horab?"

There was no reply and John resumed the shaving. Greenbloom made no attempt to raise his chin so that the skin over his thin neck muscles and Adam's apple could be reached by the razor, and therefore, somewhat reluctantly, John had to push down the pillow to the level of his shoulders and with his left hand tilt the waxen jaw higher towards the ceiling. In a few minutes he had completed his task and stepped eagerly away from the chair.

"Give him his tea," said Michael.

"What, now? I think he's gone to sleep."

"No, he's always like that." Michael raised his voice. "Wake up, Horab! There's a cup of tea for you."

"I *am* awake," whispered Greenbloom. "Has he finished?"

"Of course he has."

"Good! Got a drink?"

"No," said Michael.

"Get one! Not for me though." With his eyes still closed he sent out his hand in quest of a teacup and John placed one between the long thumb and the fingers.

"Thanks," said Michael. "I think I will. I don't usually like anything at this time of the day but I've been feeling a little shagged lately and something short and astringent would probably improve my reactions." Walking over to the table he poured himself a stiff whisky-and-soda and slumped down in the chair with his back to the window. John saw him feeling comfortably for his pipe and tobacco pouch as he invariably did when he was preparing to enjoy himself.

The increasing darkness of the room, and the fact that the

effects of the vodka he had drunk were beginning to subside, depressed him. Unplugging the razor from the lamp he re-inserted and switched on the bulb. The fall of the light on Greenbloom's closed lids disturbed him and sitting up he began to drink his tea hurriedly, spilling little drops of it down the front of his dressing gown. Having emptied the cup he limped across to his bedroom. They heard the water running in the basin and through the open door saw him patting his livid face with a hand towel. In a few minutes he re-emerged with one of the bottles of French brilliantine, two gold-plated hair brushes and a tortoise-shell comb. They continued to watch him as once again he inspected his face in the blued venetian glass above the mantel and then deftly oiled and parted his black hair.

"Any stars, Mick?" he asked.

Michael craned over the back of his chair for a moment.

"Yes," he said deliberately. "I think I can see one over in the direction of the Observatory."

"Sure?"

"Yes, just about."

"Quite sure, Mick?"

Michael took off his spectacles, polished and resumed them, and then gazed out even more intently through the window.

"It's quite distinct," he said. "A little misty perhaps but there's no mistaking it."

"Get binoculars," said Greenbloom.

"Fetch the binoculars, John!"

"Where are they, Horab?"

"You borrowed them for Newmarket. If you returned them they should be in the bedroom behind the door."

"Go and have a look, John."

John found them and gave them to him. In a very business-like way Michael finished his drink, refilled his glass, then moved over to the window and scanned the reddening sky. "Yes," he said at length. "It's there, Horab."

"Oi! oi!" said Greenbloom. "We will drink to that star."

He half-filled a crystal goblet with brandy, deftly cut a thin slice of lemon and, floating it on the surface, piled it high with caster sugar from a shaker on the mantelpiece. "A Nicholashka," he said, "a delightfully virile Pomeranian drink!" Lighting a Turkish cigarette he started to limp around the room drinking and smoking at a great pace.

John drank his tea in silence and having finished his egg consumed several more slices of kosher cake. Greenbloom was very hospitable, he obviously liked to see his possessions used, and Michael, having finished a very large whisky and being already halfway through another one, would not be likely to be censorious, therefore quite openly and with pleasant self-confidence John took his glass over to the large bottle-laden table and refilled it with vodka. It seemed to be harmless stuff, he thought, almost like water save for the dry warmth it left on the tongue when once it had passed down the throat. Perhaps if he had another glass or two of it he might begin to regain his lost cheerfulness. He turned around to find Michael watching him gloomily. He had miscalculated, and afraid that he might be going to be deprived of his satisfaction, he took a generous swig of the pale spirit.

"What's that you've got in the glass?"

"Vodka."

"Oh—I wouldn't take too much of that if I were you, it's dangerous stuff."

"Do you think I ought to have a little whisky instead?"

"Good Lord no! You know Mother's feelings about whisky, she'd be frightfully upset."

"She'd never know."

"That's not the point. One mustn't base one's life on the assumption that—"

Greenbloom, in his rapid journeyings from one end of the room to the other, stopped between them.

"Oh don't worry him, Mick. Let him stretch his legs, it's what he needs. There is much to be done, we all three have to make our arrangements."

"What arrangements?" Michael paused as though suddenly reminded of something. "Look here, Horab. What's all this about London? I believe I heard you saying something about it when I was boiling the egg."

"We're meeting Rachel." He moved over to the telephone and

dialled the Exchange. "Dinner and a show. *Hello operator, give me Golders Green* 20463. Have you got a woman? *No no I was talking to my friend—*"

"How do you mean?" asked Michael uneasily.

"Well you'll have to bring someone. We could take that little shoppie of yours from Cowley but I think it would be better if we were to meet one of your London ones. They tend to be a little smarter and you know how Rachel is about clothes. *Hello, is that you Rachel? Ah Mrs. Schwartz, Guten tag. Kindly get Rachel for me at once.* Well who is it to be? Somebody with appearance, that big woman; she cannot dress but she has presence. What is her name?"

"You mean Kate?"

"Yes yes, but her surname and telephone number?"

"Frobisher 43592, but really, Horab, it's rather short notice and I very much doubt—"

"Her surname! Something to do with mistletoe."

"Holly," said Michael.

"*Hello Rachel. We are coming up to town. . . . Yes, by seven at the latest. Three things: first book for a show, a good one, five seats in the stalls. Next book a table at Claridges or the Luxor, and last ring Mick's woman, Kate Holly, Frobisher* 43592 *and tell her she's to be there. . . . All right then the Luxor for certain. . . . No, no, he doesn't need one—officially he is too young, he is Michael's brother. Did you get the trinket? . . . And you like it? . . . Good.*"

He put down the receiver and got up. "We must hurry, you will need to change."

"We can't possibly bring John."

"He is coming. That is why I am bringing him."

"What on earth do you mean?"

"I mean that we would none of us be going if I did not wish to bring your brother—it is simple enough, he must come with us because I am bringing him. Don't worry about money, everything will be paid for. You have the money the boy gave you?"

Michael was taken aback and started to fumble in his pocket.

"No no, keep it, it is yours."

"It's not *that*, Horab—you're always so generous—it's only that you don't seem to realize that John has to be back at the school by ten o'clock at the latest. He's had a good tea haven't you John? And I should think he's pretty tired and wouldn't mind getting back a little earlier than we'd arranged, would you?"

They both turned and looked at him, Greenbloom coldly, Michael with warm concern. John returned Greenbloom's motionless glance with intensity, trying to discern from the long black eyes the answer which would be most pleasing to their owner.

"Are you going in the Bentley?" he asked.

"We are."

"And then the theatre?"

"Yes, a play."

"I wish I could come."

Michael was quicker than Greenbloom, he leapt at the desire trying to beat it down while it was still rising towards the dark ceiling.

"Of course you do, old chap, one always wants to be a jump ahead of one's age-group until one has the misfortune—"

"Enough," said Greenbloom. "You may cheat yourself but John is young. He will come with us."

"And you I suppose will ring up the prebendary and the housemaster and then explain things to my people?" began Michael.

"Precisely," said Greenbloom, "but not tonight. If necessary in the morning I will personally interview them both and put through a trunk call to your mother."

"You can't do this sort of thing, Horab. This is England, not Switzerland. I know very little about Chillon, but I can assure you that if this is the sort of laxity that was permitted there—"

"In Europe one is educated," said Greenbloom, "one is taught to live, one is freed and there are *no* age-groups. I intend to include a passage on education in my Wittgenstein when I reach the fourth volume but there is no time to discuss it now. Where is your dinner jacket? If it is in pawn you had better borrow one of mine."

"I don't like it," said Michael. "Things of this sort never turn out well. I don't think you realize how young John is."

"Young? He is older than us both. It is there in the eyes, in the face and hands, in the way he stands." He broke off and then turned on Michael with sudden anger. "You have never looked at your brother! In all the years that you have known him you have failed to regard him, but I have only had to look once to know that his youth is over."

"Of course, if you're going to start dramatizing," said Michael, moving hopelessly over in the direction of the decanter.

"I never dramatize; I merely respond as we're meant to respond, but you English have only one response to everything and that is the cultivation of restraint. You are not born restrained, you do not die restrained; but in the little interval which separates the two you practise no other response, and that is why you prefer whisky to wine."

"Oh have it your own way," said Michael. "He'll be leaving at the end of the term anyway, so I don't suppose that much harm will come of it, though I don't see how you're going to be able to give a convincing explanation to the headmaster on Sunday morning."

"I have a doctor in London and I imagine that even in these barbaric gymnasia which in England you call schools, they have the beginnings of respect for Adlerian psychology."

"I very much doubt if they've ever heard of it."

"Then tomorrow will mark a great educational advance. I will get you my clothes." He hurried into the bedroom and they were left alone. Michael looked deeply into the bottom of his warm glass and John knew that he would say nothing to him because Greenbloom's vehemence had deafened them both. They waited under the reverberations of all that had been said like strangers who had suffered a clumsy introduction by an uneasy host; and then, a few moments later, Greenbloom re-emerged carrying over his arm a dinner jacket, a boiled shirt, a pair of pumps and a black tie which he slung on to the arm of his chair.

"We have just five minutes, Mick," he said. "We must not keep them waiting." He returned to the bedroom and closed the door behind him.

Michael took off his things slowly and started to put on the borrowed clothes. John finished his vodka.

"What did he mean about the doctor?" he asked Michael.

"Oh, I imagine he thinks you need taking out of yourself." Michael paused and looked at him. "*Do* you?"

"I'm not sure, but I do find I keep thinking about it all. Nothing seems real, except *that*."

"You mean the moors?"

"Yes, the whole thing: those last days, the caves, bloodhounds, the police and—finding her—" He swallowed. "She was so— I loved her."

With his braces half on Michael leaned over and patted his back. John sobbed; the whole dimness of the room shifted and changed while slow dark tears ran out of his eyes and down his cheeks.

"I'm sorry, Mick! It's just something I can't talk about to anyone."

The door opened and Greenbloom reappeared. From the quick movement of his head as he entered the room it was obvious that he had intended to interrupt them; he made no pretence of having an excuse for his intrusion, and he spoke at once.

"You see?" he said thickly. "You're mad, Mick; you're all mad. *Gentiles!*" He opened the door a little wider. "What he wants is a good time: action, change, movement. I will write to your mother. Take the keys and bring the Bentley to the front gate. We'll meet you there in five minutes." He tossed the keys to Michael, who caught them easily and then, still in process of dressing, hurried obediently out of the room. They heard him clattering down the wooden stairs.

"What are you drinking?" asked Greenbloom.

"Vodka."

"Here, have a whisky." He handed him a glass. "Drink it. Drink it fast and then weep it out of you. Wail and weep— talk if you like. Say anything that comes into your head."

"I loved her," said John. "She was what I've always wanted, and now she's dead."

"She was murdered," said Greenbloom, "strangled."

"Yes, she was—strangled."

"What you have always wanted was strangled," repeated Greenbloom. "Aren't you angry?"

John put down his full glass. "Yes, I am."

"Are you *very* angry?"

"Very!"

"No, you are not. If you were angry you would not be weeping." He came closer and lowered his voice. At this moment he was no more than a voice. He seemed to be like that voice which is insistent in the silence and darkness that precedes sleep. John heard him speaking from some place deep within his own head, and what was said between them was said between John and some other remoter part of himself. "If I were the one," the voice whispered, "the man in the cave, the man you met on the moors, if I were that man and you were alone with me in this room, what would you want to do to me?"

John looked in the direction he remembered. "Kill you," he said.

"Well, why don't you?" Greenbloom hung beside him like a dummy, his arms loose and lax at his sides. "Why don't you stop weeping and kill me when I *am* the man?"

"Because you're *not* the man, you're only a Jew friend of my brother's—and because—"

"Go on."

"Because it wouldn't do any good. She'd still be dead."

"Exactly!" said Greenbloom, standing suddenly straight. "*She* would still be dead, and *you* would still be alive?"

"Yes."

"Suppose then that I am the man, and I kill *you*. Would that be better?"

John considered it; if somebody killed *him* he would be unable to know that Victoria was dead; leaving aside all thoughts of Heaven or Hell, which did not seem very real at the moment, he would be freed of feeling for her and of wanting what he had lost.

"No," he said, "that would be worse. As long as I'm alive, she's alive too in a way, inside me; but if I am killed—"

"If you are killed," Greenbloom interrupted slowly, "what

you have always wanted will have ceased to exist, because you will not be there to want it."

Through the whisky and the vodka, through the grey indistinctness of the room, beyond the sagacious little face confronting his own, he saw it clearly: the negation of a negation, an all-encompassing emptiness in a state of appalling and vacuous equilibrium.

"Yes," he said, "yes, you're right." He nodded to himself, and suddenly shouted it out into the room. "You're right! *Greenbloom is right!*"

"Of course I am," said Greenbloom. "I am right and you are fortunate, fortunate because you have known what it was you have always wanted without having taken any direct part in its destruction. The rest of us must wait."

"Who?" asked John.

"*We,*" said Greenbloom, "the great majority who have still to know what we have always wanted." Abruptly he limped out of the room and John followed him down the stairs, leaving the door open behind him.

After a dreadful journey in the open Bentley with the hood flapping and cracking beside them like a running battle, they drew up in front of the Luxor a little over an hour later. Greenbloom gave the commissionaire a pound note, and after telling him to see to the car, led them through the glass doors at a running limp.

He looked extraordinarily dapper: a thin penguin in the black and white of his dinner jacket and boiled shirt; and the oddity and haste of his gait, the mobility of his small head swivelling from side to side without visibly affecting the remainder of his body, ensured that even in this environment he was both noticeable and noticed. But he passed through the standing people, dim figures in the softly illumined space, as though they had been only clothes hanging in a large cupboard.

Rachel and Kate Holly were seated uneasily by one of the low black tables in the farthest corner of the lounge, and in all save their patent relief at the arrival of Greenbloom and Michael, presented a sharp contrast to one another.

Rachel was small and expensive-looking with film-star teeth and finely plucked eyebrows over dark blue eyes, whereas Kate Holly was a big-boned, manly girl, curiously untidy in every detail of her person and manner. She smiled carelessly, talked and laughed generously, and had little bits of bedroom fluff and loose golden hairs clinging to the shoulders of her cherry-coloured sweater. John warmed to her at once; she was obviously common, the sort of north-country girl to whom he was accustomed, the sort of girl Michael had always liked. He did not in the least blame him for wanting to go out with her though he thought it a little unfair of him to get her into a place like the Luxor with a girl like Rachel and a man as sophisticated as Greenbloom.

Greenbloom himself did not seem in the least surprised by her appearance. The fact that she was quite differently dressed from everybody in the hotel, that she and Rachel had obviously found very little to say to one another in their twenty minutes of waiting, and that she had a broad though indefinable country accent of some sort, weighed not at all with him. He shook her hand hurriedly, gave her a deep smile and asked her what she would drink, all in a matter of seconds, and then without even glancing at Rachel fixed his impatient gaze on a passing waiter and ordered a bottle of champagne and a plate of lobster pâtés. This done he at last turned to Rachel and said, "Well, what did you book for?"

From the security of the fur coat draped over the back of her chair, Rachel smiled up at him and then at the others.

"Iss-n't he a man?" she asked softly.

"He rings up at five o'clock, tells me to collect a woman—a complete stranger—change my clothes, and then book the best seats for the bess-t show in town, all in the same evening." Beneath Kate Holly's chin she extended a wrist flashing with a tiny diamond-encrusted watch, and then continued, "Not only that, but he arrives twenty minutes late, makes no introductions of any ss-ort whatsoever, and then as arrogantly as a prince, he wants to know what I've booked for."

Greenbloom snatched at the extended hand and glanced greedily at the watch.

"Like it?" he asked.

"Oh, yes, Horab, I do! It was lovely of you. Don't *you* think it's ni-c-ce, Michael?" She lisped and prolonged the word just a fraction. "Don't you think he's sweet and that I ought to forgive him when he gives me press-ents like this?"

Holding the scented hand in his own, Michael examined the watch a little gingerly. "Beautiful, Rachel." He turned to Kate. "Beautiful, isn't it, Kate? And just right for a wrist like Rachel's. Have a look at it, John."

John stepped forward, wanting desperately to say something impressive so that he might be rewarded by one of her soft sentences.

"I've never seen anything so small and so—so dainty."

She smiled up at him. "Small and dainty—like me?"

"Yes," he said, "that's what I meant."

Her fingers tapped a little tattoo on the back of his hand, and then she withdrew the wrist, the diamonds and the fingers.

"Who is he?" she asked. "He's *very* young."

"Mick's brother," said Greenbloom, "but you are not to talk to him. He wants to be left alone." He sat down on the arm of her chair. "Well, what did you book for?"

"She's booked for the play at the Haymarket. That actor with the nose," said Kate Holly. "What's name of it, Michael?"

"You must mean Gielgud. I can't remember what he's playing in at the moment. Are you sure it was the Haymarket?"

"Of course I am."

"Good heavens, it's not *Musical Chairs*? You haven't booked seats for that surely, have you Rachel?"

"And why not, Michael dear? It's the only play worth seeing. And I know that Horab will like it."

"Is it hot?" asked Greenbloom. "Plenty of sex and luxuriance and no bedrooms?"

"Well," she confessed, "it *has* got one. But you don't see it, really you don't, Horab."

"Oh." Greenbloom refilled his glass. "Drink up, everyone! Drink up! We're going to be late. You had better order a taxi, Mick. The Bentley's difficult to park and the London police do not seem to like it."

"You know, Horab, I don't honestly think we ought to take John to see *Musical Chairs*," said Michael, "he's far too young and I *am* responsible for him."

"You're not," said Greenbloom. "I've already told you that John is my idea, my guest. Only I am responsible, and perhaps in a minor degree, Rachel too, eh Rachel?"

"Yes, Horab, I like him." She gave him another smile. "He's sweet, and he's going to be so good-looking, and he's *sso* sad."

"And you heard her? There's a *bedroom*." Greenbloom spat the word out. "Where there's a bedroom there is no sex, none at all: all serious love-making is done elsewhere. So order the taxi, Mick, and stop worrying."

Michael swallowed the remainder of his lobster pâté.

"The little lad can come with me," he said. "We must show him the ropes. Now, come on, John, I'll show you how it's done."

As soon as they were out of earshot of the others, Michael took his arm and steered him down a long discreetly lighted corridor which led off at right angles from the entrance hall of the hotel.

"I thought we were going to get a taxi," John said.

"We are. But first of all I want to talk to you, in the Gentleman's if we can find it."

They turned another corner, passed a number of closed doors and, unsuccessful in their search, were about to retrace their steps when they saw two business men emerge from the last door on the right. They looked clean and pleased with themselves.

"That must be it; they've got it written all over them." Michael smiled for the first time. "That's what I hate about Horab's taste in hotels; they're always so respectable. Myself, I like a nice little pub with the word 'Gentlemen' written up where everyone can see it."

They pushed open the door, only to find themselves in a narrow tiled passage which ended in another door in which was set a square glass panel. Through it they saw a glowing interior in which one or two black and ponderous figures glided slowly about their business like fish in an aquarium. Michael paused.

"Confound it! I believe this must be the hairdressing saloon."

John peered through the glass.

"No," he said, "I don't think so. There's a chap having his shoes cleaned."

Michael pushed open the door and there came to them the mingled odour of pine and camphor and the busy sound of running water.

"Ah!" said Michael as he hurried ahead. "We're on the track."

They crossed the outer sanctum or foyer where a shoeblack was hard at work on the feet of another business man, traversed an archway, and reached a long amber-lighted room almost completely filled with handbasins and looking-glasses. At the far end of it were two closed swing doors bright with chromium and glass. With a final gesture of impatience Michael rushed across the intervening space and dived between the doors. John followed him as he made straight for the nearest of a group of glazed white standups.

They were beautiful and it struck him that people were very dull to take them so much for granted. No one ever mentioned them in essays or poems and he supposed that nobody ever would, though Rupert Brooke had come the nearest to it when he talked about the "keen impassioned beauty of a great machine." These *were* a great machine, they seemed to stretch in all directions as though they had been designed to accommodate an army. Each was equipped with a shining copper pipe, a transparent reservoir of disinfectant and a brass nozzle which at regular intervals sprayed perfumed water down its flawless face. At the bottom was a smooth sloping gutter spanned by precise metal bridges and guarded in front by a frosted glass plate set at an angle so that it might protect the shoes of patrons from any least spot of moisture from above. The atmosphere was religious and John found himself thinking in whispers as he took up his position beside Michael.

"I must say they do these things well at the big pubs," Michael said. "I should imagine you could get anything done here from a manicure to a Turkish bath."

"That's just what I was thinking. It's got a sort of holy atmosphere like a cathedral."

Michael looked shocked. "Scarcely that, laddie, we mustn't

mix our metaphors! If anything, it's more in the pagan tradition, like the Roman vomitoria; and quite right too, when one considers that it is intended to serve a function inseparable from that of the Bacchic."

"Does that mean drinking?"

"Yes, but it was merely an observation, and there isn't time to discuss it now." Michael moved away in the direction of the chromium-plated doors. "Horab may follow us at any minute; for some reason of his own he seems bent on separating us. Look here, how much money did you say you'd brought with you?"

"I told you," said John defensively. "I haven't brought any—I've got none."

Michael extracted a ten-shilling note from his breast pocket and handed it to him.

"Here! It's a nuisance, but you'd better take this. You can pay me back in the holidays."

John took the note suspiciously. "What's it for?"

"It's to get you back to Oxford." Against the background of the glass Michael regarded him very seriously. "Don't worry about paying me back for the moment, because really this is Horab's money and he doesn't like people badgering him about debts."

"You mean about credits?"

"No! No! You've misunderstood me, but don't let's waste time. The important thing is for you to get into the first possible train and report to your housemaster."

"But I don't *want* to! I want to go to the theatre. Horab's booked for me and everything, and besides I've got a late pass—nearly three hours yet—and so far we seem to have done nothing except visit pubs and lavatories." He felt absurdly near to tears again, and as if to emphasize his mood the automatic flusher began to operate throughout the length and breadth of the room; with a short premonitory hiss like a soda syphon, water and disinfectant began to flow copiously down the glistening surfaces which surrounded them.

The sound galvanized Michael; followed by John he pushed open the doors and hurried across to a handbasin.

"Now be sensible, old chap! It's just seven-forty-five, and the earliest train you could catch from Paddington would be the *eight-fifteen*. Allowing half an hour between here and the station, and even that would be cutting it fine, you would only just reach Oxford in time to get out to Beowulf's before your pass expires."

"Yes, but—"

"But quite apart from that," his voice was as remorseless and measured as the flushing apparatus sweeping away impurities next door, "quite apart from that the whole situation is unsuitable."

"Unsuitable? You mean the play we're going to see?"

"That is the least of my worries." He was washing his hands very carefully.

"Oh dear," said John. "What else is worrying you?"

"If only you would be your age, laddie. I know that you'll probably counter with Horab's remarks about your lost youth—he's inclined to dramatize, but one ignores that and really you should be able to see that your being here this evening is as embarrassing to Rachel and Kate and probably to Horab himself as it is to me. They don't see an awful lot of each other, one can't when one's in the thick of exams and so forth, and naturally after the show they'll want to say good night to one another and enjoy a little—intimacy. In addition, as Rachel herself pointed out—"

"You mean that I'm too young," said John angrily. "Is that it?"

"Frankly, yes, but not primarily. You see, old chap, whatever Horab likes to say, you *are* my responsibility both from the point of view of the school and, more important, from the *parental* angle."

He let the water out of the basin and gazed at himself earnestly in the looking-glass as though he were appealing to a judicious and favourable friend. "I mean an evening like this wouldn't make awfully good reading at home, would it? You can't really imagine Mother and Father feeling that all is for the best in the best of all possible worlds when they hear that you've been dashing about London in the middle of the term with people like Horab and Rachel can you?"

"I suppose not, but I don't see who's going to tell them about it. And anyway what will Horab say if you shunt me off back to Oxford without saying anything to him? He seems to like me and to want me to be with him, and in a queer way I rather like *him*."

Michael tapped his shoulder affectionately. "I don't want to hurt you, Johnny—you must have had enough of that lately—but at the risk of repeating myself I must emphasize that Horab happens to be *my* friend and consequently I have a good deal more insight into his motives than you're likely to have. Horab likes to *appear* to run things, all Jews do, but the moment he's presented with a *fait accompli* he accepts it at once. He's fickle you know, capricious, and you must take it from me that it was only a flutter —a *lubie*, the sudden whim of an *enfant gaté* which made him insist on bringing you along tonight; and if you must know he only thought of it this afternoon."

"I thought you said he'd invited me yesterday."

Michael sighed. "You're forcing me to it," he said indulgently, "you seem to want me to hurt you—I never knew such a chap for arguing, you're worse than Uncle Felix. To be brutally truthful, it's the publicity that's taken Horab's fancy, he admitted it to me this evening. His rather unpleasant way of putting it was to suggest that publicity is a racial weakness with the Jews—he cited the New Testament as an example—and he made it perfectly clear that if no one had ever heard of you he'd find the whole situation as much of a bore as any other undergraduate saddled with a teen-ager in London; but as things are and through no fault of your own you've got a sort of notoriety which makes Horab think he's sorry for you."

He paused and John interrupted quickly, "He *is* sorry for me. He's much sorrier for me than you are because he's not sorry for me, he's sorry *with* me. And he's *doing* something about it! He wants to take me away somewhere—he mentioned Paris—or write about me."

Michael groaned. "Oh Lord! I suppose he's been telling you about his aeroplane, has he? Or was it the book?"

"No, he only mentioned the book once and that was when you were there, something about Wittgenstein. Who *was* Wittgenstein?"

"Who *is* Wittgenstein, you mean; he's still alive. I can't tell you anything about him except that he's one of a vast variety of people and concepts that Horab is going to touch on in a book he intends to write. Another of his obsessions is the scapegoat idea and quite obviously he looks upon you as a recent example and that's why he's making such a confounded nuisance of himself over this evening. Don't you see?"

"You mean he doesn't really sympathize with me at all? He's just using me because I fit in with some idea of his?"

"I'm afraid so, but there's something else as well; I'm quite certain that if you happened to be Jewish Horab would not be taking the least notice of you despite the tragedy."

"Why not?"

"Because I'm pretty sure he's not, in any sense, sorry for us; he's simply exulting in our humiliation as Christians. *Now* do you understand?"

"Yes, I think so," said John slowly. "But why do you let him?"

"There isn't time to explain now, but briefly I'm trying to help him. He's a man completely without faith, and it flatters his vanity to let him think for the present that I a Gentile, a Christian Gentile, am allowing him to dominate me. It's the only hope I have of influencing him and of winning him around." He broke off. "I'm afraid we can't go into it any further at the moment, John; and really you know it's nothing with which you need concern yourself, is it?"

"It's not my fault Greenbloom's taking an interest in me, and I don't see why you should have all the fun while I just go back to the beastly school when I'm supposed to be having half-term with you. And what about the doctor? Greenbloom said he was sure his doctor would be able to sort me out and get rid of this feeling I'm always having that I'm separated from everybody. *He* seems to understand."

"Look, old chap, you've only got twenty-five minutes to catch that train." With a studied, indulgent reluctance Michael put his hand into his pocket. "Here's another half-crown for you, it'll do for the taxi; take it and run."

They swung around as the doors opened and Greenbloom hurled himself towards them.

"For God's sake! We're going to miss the whole of the first

scene, what on earth have you been doing? I sent you to order that taxi ten minutes ago and you know that I object to being kept waiting."

"It's John," said Michael. "He's thought better of it. He doesn't feel he ought to come and I've decided to let him catch the eight-fifteen and get back to Beowulf's before his pass expires."

Greenbloom straightened his tie and wriggled his head a little higher over the top of his white collar.

"The taxi," he said, "it is obstructing the entrance."

Like an Old Testament prophet he drove them before him down the length of the corridors past the uniformed commissionaire and into the attendant taxi.

Once inside it there was no further discussion and Michael behaved as though there had never at any time been any conflict of views between himself and anybody else. It struck John then that Greenbloom shared with Mother a capacity for such intense self-interest that lesser people and their smaller desires simply ceased to exist when he chose to exercise his power to the full. It was not that either of them necessarily fought down opposition to their aims, it was only that they themselves were so totally engrossed in their private vision of a situation that their view ultimately prevailed over that of others to such an extent that even the memory of difference was expunged and forgotten. Michael now was bland, almost gay, and carried on a cheerful and bantering conversation with Rachel and Kate all the way to the theatre.

Their way smoothed by Greenbloom's lavish tips, in the space of what seemed to be at the most only five or ten minutes, they found themselves sitting in the stalls of the Haymarket watching the unfolding of the story of *Musical Chairs*.

From the programme it appeared that the setting was an oil-field in the Middle East staffed by two very English married men and from the outset it was obvious that the action was to be concerned primarily with the intimacies and emotional stresses engendered in their relative isolation between these two men and their sharp, discontented wives. The dialogue was very modern and seemed to John to be even smarter, shallower and more brutally insincere than that of Noël Coward who until this moment had been his idol among contemporary playwrights. The effect of the short lines and cold sentiments so neatly and carelessly expressed by these four people as they played out their tragedy in front of a single stark pylon glimpsed through a cardboard window in the backcloth was to make him feel that at last he had an object in growing-up. This, he felt, was the real world whose language it should be the object of everyone to speak wittily and with merciless precision. These people were not in confusion, they knew what they were doing and what they ought to say as they did it; they were never dull or incomplete in their sentences and though they suffered, they underwent their pain so modishly that it was impossible to feel that they felt any real discomfort so long as they found an epigram ready to their lips at the crucial moment.

Beside John, at infrequent intervals, Greenbloom uttered a harsh cry of pain which, until Rachel explained that it was his laughter and that he was enjoying himself, seriously worried him; but far more often he writhed about in his seat bending and flexing his good leg and snapping the springs of his artificial one while a spatter of angry comments and expletives enlivened the darkness about him.

At the first interval, even before the curtain had descended behind the footlights, he uncoiled himself from his seat beside the gangway and drew them out after him as he led the way to the bar where he insisted on their splitting a bottle of whisky in order, as he put it, to make some attempt to "save the play." Occupying the whole of one end of the small counter on which he leaned with his back to the two middle-aged women serving the drinks, he addressed the filling room furiously, glaring over his guests' heads at the open door through which other late arrivals were entering.

"Why doesn't something *happen?*" he demanded loudly. "Why don't they get on with it? It is quite obvious that the man with tuberculosis who plays the piano so badly is going to seduce the manager's wife and that his own wife will ultimately drown herself in the storage tank. Well, why don't they *do* it and let us get on with the *action?* We cannot continue to waste

time sitting out here between the intervals with nothing to anticipate in the way of *meaning*. Wittgenstein, had he been so foolish
as to book seats in the first place, would already by this time
have demanded his money back. The cast would be playing to
an empty theatre, and *that* is more than they deserve when they
can give us nothing more rewarding than an artifice of this sort.
Some of us came here in order to be entertained, others, and I
claim that we are among them, came here in order to be made to
think and so far no least effort has been made to satisfy either
category."

"I think you're being a little unfair, Horab," said Michael seriously, "after all a play has got to have a plot and although your
solution may prove to be the correct one I think there *are* alter-
natives."

"Of course there are! I do not deny it. The tuberculosis
fellow, Geoffrey or whatever he's called, might stop playing the
piano for a moment and go and drown *himself* when his own
wife goes to bed with the man who's always worrying about
their failure to strike sufficient oil. But what difference does it
make? Tell me that!" His eyes suddenly swivelled away from
Michael and his attention became fixed on a short man with a
bald head who was trying to order a drink.

"*You*, sir!" said Greenbloom, raising his voice even higher.
"I can see from your attitude that you are a critic. You appear
to have overheard my remarks about this farce we are suffering.
Well, tell me, am I not right? Are any of us going to leave this
theatre feeling either purged or entertained as a result of the
patience and attention we have accorded the play?"

The smaller man retreated a step and upset somebody's drink.
He looked as embarrassed as a passer-by suddenly singled out by
a Hyde Park orator to support a cause which he had always
found offensive. Hoping to escape quietly in the confusion occasioned by the spilling of the drink, he turned his back on
Greenbloom and started to apologize volubly to the lady with
the wet dress. But it was no good; proffering a large silk handkerchief, Greenbloom stepped forward and continued his remarks as though nothing had happened.

"It's ridiculous! They get us here under false pretenses, take our time and our money and then present us with a series of contrived situations which are not only entirely without point but are also predictable to the meanest intelligence from the moment the curtain goes up." He put a hand on to the shorter man's shoulder. "I haven't the advantage of knowing which paper you represent, but I am sure, sir, that as a responsible critic you must agree with me?"

"Take your hands off me at once!" said his victim, colouring up with the easy rage of the obese. "I am *not* a critic and I am, when permitted, greatly enjoying the play I have paid to see." He turned his back with finality, and taking his wife by the arm, piloted her away towards a different corner of the bar.

"Of course!" exclaimed Greenbloom, "one should expect no more from a public which will submit to drama of this sort. London is dead, England is dead, and when I have finished my book I shall refuse to allow a single edition to be distributed in the United Kingdom."

Rachel tucked her hand into his arm.

"You *ssilly* darling, that poor man has been sitting just in front of us and you do not realize what a penance it is to be near you when you are not enjoying a play."

Greenbloom refilled his glass and drank it hastily. "Well, unless there are developments in the next act, and by developments I mean action both unforseen and credible, he will shortly be able to indulge in his hoglike enjoyment of this nonsense undisturbed by myself. We will give them one more chance, five or ten minutes at the most, and if in that time they cannot succeed in portraying some human situation through which one may discern a vestige of significance, we will leave and eat, dance or drink somewhere else."

The interval bell rang and the room began to empty.

"Rachel," he asked, "what's the cabaret like at the Palm Beach this season?"

"Good, I think; but really, Horab, you mustn't be so impatient, must he? He's behaving like a spoiled child, isn't he, Michael?"

"If you ask me," Kate Holly's voice was as measured as a steam-hammer, "and don't tell me that nobody did, *I* should say that Mr. Greenbloom's afraid of missing something." She turned on him benignly. "What's up with you? Who's chasing you? Or is it just that you've got too much money?"

Greenbloom's abstraction, his air of carrying on a patter of conversation within himself to which no external response was expected, resolved slowly. Then, as his long eyes took in the broad contour of her face and his ears transmitted the sense of her challenge, he rounded on her with extraordinary vehemence.

"You're enjoying it, are you? *You* are interested in the as yet unrealized sexual designs of the man at the piano on the woman with the flat chest? The fact that somebody's tie has already been found in the bedroom of somebody else's wife excites you, does it? You find it significant that they have been drilling now for six months and will certainly not strike oil, either factually or figuratively, until towards the middle of the third act when it will be too late for anyone to raise anyone else from the dead?" He stopped and smiled at her as he might have smiled at a domestic pet.

"Well—" she began.

"These situations," he said distinctly and sibilantly, "so delicately poised on the cracked nib of the dramatist's pen, keep you on the crest of an aesthetic expectation so dizzy that you are prepared to sit and wait for a dénouement which cannot fail to plunge you into the abysm of cliché in approximately two hours' time? Yes?"

Kate Holly turned to Michael, "He's off again!"

Michael grinned. "You know our *Horab!*" he said. "It's only his way of—"

"Don't worry," she clapped Greenbloom heavily on the back, "I'm quite capable of taking care of myself with any man—in or out of bed—and if that's his way of asking me if I'm enjoying myself and finding it a smashing good play, then I'd say yes to all his questions. I *do* want to know who's going to go to bed with who and whether Geoffrey's going to jump into the oil well or die in a sanatorium; and I *do* like the way he plays the piano; and if I had the money Mr. Greenbloom's got I'd send them all up a spray of orchids at the end of it."

Greenbloom filled her glass. "In that case I am satisfied. I shall abandon my work on Wittgenstein and write three farces a

month for production in London, Berlin and Chicago, and see
that you have complimentary tickets to whichever one you care
to patronize."

"Well, in that case, you'd better send them to us all because
we're all enjoying it except you, that poor little man you frightened included. And what's more, *I* don't think you know *what*
you want. Tell us, Mr. Greenbloom, what do you want to
happen? What would satisfy *you*?"

"Yes," said John speaking for the first time. "I think this is a
wonderful evening and I'm really happy. If I'd known it was
going to be like this when I set off this morning—meeting such
wonderful people, tearing about in Bentleys and aeroplanes, I
would have—"

"Here!" said Kate Holly. "What aeroplane have you been
riding in? You didn't fly down, did you?"

"Of course he didn't," said Michael taking away John's glass.
"This is exactly what I expected. He's had too much to drink
and there's going to be the very dickens of a row when they get
to hear about it tomorrow morning."

"I haven't." John gazed around at them joyfully. "I'm just
happy like you were in the Carpenter's Arms this morning; in
fact, I'm happier! When *you* drink you only seem to get miserable, 'solemn as an owl, solemn as an owl,' just as Mother says;
but I see everything as it should be, and I want to know how
Horab would have written it. How *would* you have written it?"
he asked again of the tall, wavering figure which represented
Greenbloom.

"Differently!" said Greenbloom as the second bell rang. "*Quite*
differently!" He drained his glass and, taking Rachel with him,
limped off into the stalls leaving the others in the darkened bar.

They looked at one another with surprise. His sudden going
had instantly cast a slight chill on them, breaking the continuity
of their gaiety and filling them with an emotion which lay somewhere between guilt and embarrassment.

Kate Holly was the first to speak. She fluffed up the back of
Michael's dark red hair with a broad hand. "Cheer up, Mick!
It's just his way, he's one of the ones that was born too late!
Mind you I'm not saying anything against him; even without his

money he'd be a nice feller and he's not half as potty as he makes himself out to be; in fact he's downright clever and there's only one way to treat clever jacks and that's to jump on them now and again with both feet."

Michael laughed. "You're a good psychologist, Kate." His expression changed as he caught John's eye. "It's not Horab who's worrying me, it's John here. I did my best to get him to go back to Oxford when he was sober and if it hadn't been for Horab's intervention I think that even despite John's obstinacy I'd probably have succeeded. *Now* of course the whole situation's made doubly difficult by the fact that he's half-seas over, and how on earth we're going to get him back to school in time, I can't think."

"Does it matter? When I was at school I was always playing truant and I always seemed to get away with it."

"Of course it matters. Even under ordinary circumstances he'd probably be expelled for a thing like this; but when one remembers that he's obviously already *persona non grata* at Beowulf's as a result of that appalling case, then it's quite on the cards that when he eventually rolls up tomorrow morning with an obvious hangover they will either refuse him a reference for any other school or what's worse plead mental imbalance and start taking refuge in medical opinion."

"Rot!" said John unpleasantly, "I'm not mad. Greenbloom doesn't think I'm mad! He understands me, he knows that it's the world which is mad. All these fools in this play, all these fat scented people sitting on their bottoms watching a lot of other cardboard men and women pretending to be smart about situations which don't exist and then trooping in here to drink whisky brandy and gin-and-lime and then going back to clap something they don't understand, it's they who are mad and Greenbloom is right. He's *right!*"

Michael shrugged his shoulders and appealed hopelessly to Kate Holly.

"You see?"

"He's only a little overexcited, aren't you, Johnny?" She put both her arms over his shoulders and stood comfortably behind him swinging him backwards and forwards as though he were a child and she his mother. "He's a good lad really and given a chance he'll soon get over all this."

"That's just what he won't be given, unless we get him back to the school tonight."

"Well in that case we *will* get him back, won't we, John? And you'll be a good boy and help us as much as you can, won't you?"

With his eyes half-closed John rocked contentedly backwards and forwards, forwards and backwards, against her round, soft stomach.

"Yes, I will," he said. "It'll all come right in the end. It's like the play, it'll be a disappointment but it will all come right in the end."

"How?" asked Michael.

"Easy!" said Kate. "Tell old Greenbloom we'd like a night drive to Oxford. Tell him we think he's the best driver in England and that we'll bet him a fiver he can't make Oxford in under an hour and a half. That'll fetch him, and what's more it'll fetch his girl friend too, she's the sort that wouldn't trust him with anything under fifty on a dark night and I'd be a match for her anywhere," she minced out the words, "in Cannes, Venice, *or* Le Touquet! Come on, let's try it!"

"You mean you'll spend the night in Oxford?" Michael sounded scandalized.

"Oh no," she said, rocking John more rhythmically than ever, "I'll just spread my little wings and fly straight home like Mother told me."

Michael avoided John's eyes. "I don't really know that you ought to, Kate."

"Go on! Johnny won't tell, will you, John?" She paused. "What's up? Am I losing my looks or something? Or have you been getting too much sun?"

Michael turned abruptly. "It's not a bad idea," he said over his shoulder. "There's just a chance he'll fall for it, but for Heaven's sake don't overact about the play."

"How do you mean?" asked John.

"Well don't pretend that it's boring you or he'll at once decide to see it through. Try and give the impression that you're enjoying it as much as ever and take your cues from me—particularly *you*, John; I'm only doing this for your sake you know and if you'd taken my advice in the first place—"

"In other words," said Kate as they followed him into the theatre, "your big brother's a martyr and he's going to—"

Michael turned around angrily. "Shut up!" he said.

Half an hour later they were shuttling their way out of London at a furious pace somewhere in the suburbs of Uxbridge.

It was now apparent to John that Greenbloom had a quite unique attitude towards driving a motorcar. On the way into London he had noticed that he evidently believed the whole process to require aggression from the man at the wheel as though he were threatened by some vast and silent enemy standing between him and his destination. Now, as the experience was repeated even more forcibly in the windy darkness of the night, it occurred to him that Greenbloom must be like certain Indians from remote provinces who were so unused to mechanical travel that they viewed the trains in which they sat as stationary boxes past which successive towns and villages moved until their particular station itself arrived. In Greenbloom's case the only difference was that since he was himself the driver and in control of the speed at which the landscape passed him he was evidently quite unable to assume the purely passive rôle of his oriental counterpart.

In addition to this, his shortsightedness combined with his violent temperament tended to set him at odds not only with the landscape at large but also with any passengers he might be carrying. He waged a ceaseless battle with the road hurling itself against his front wheels while at the same time he loudly demanded information from everyone present. With amazing agility, like a person playing a one-man band, he managed to steer, change gear, brake, accelerate and simultaneously question and curse anyone whose information he considered to have been either inaccurate or tardy.

Now, as they left Uxbridge behind them and roared out into the dark countryside beyond Denham, he subjected Michael to a barrage of questions and comments: *"Steady!"*

"What do you mean, 'steady'?" Michael, although he had driven many hundreds of miles beside Greenbloom, had never become accustomed to the experience. "*You're* driving, not me!"

"Don't interrupt! Keep your attention on the road."

"I am keeping my attention on the road—*look out!*"

They described a swooping curve around a cyclist. Greenbloom turned fully on Michael. "I think I need say no more. You would have seen that fellow's light minutes ago if you hadn't been dispersing your attention by arguing with me."

"For God's sake keep your eyes on the road, Horab!"

"A lorry!" shouted John.

"Where?"

Michael and John strained unbearably backwards against the seat pressing their feet hard against the floorboards.

"Just ahead!" they shouted together.

"That of course is ridiculous," said Greenbloom as he overtook it. "It was precisely because I was concentrating on the lorry that I needed your help with the cyclist. You really mustn't be facetious when we're driving at a speed like this."

They were quite unable to reply but sat there together with dry mouths as the Bentley swept around a left bend into an ominously straight section of road.

"What's this coming up on the left, Mick? *Good God, you should have warned me minutes ago. It nearly hit us.*"

"My dear Horab! If you can see a moving lorry at a hundred yards how was I to know that you could not recognize a stationary bus at fifty?"

"Is that a crossroads or an island?"

"It's both," said John.

"You go around it and then carry straight on," interposed Michael quickly.

Greenbloom depressed the clutch in mistake for the brakes, the enormous engine in front of them screamed like a siren and in the nick of time he changed gear, grabbed the handbrake and slewed them around a concrete circle with a central signpost. They expected him to stop on the far side so that they might collect themselves and see what had happened to Rachel and Kate Holly who by this time had ceased even their earlier pathetic shrieks. Instead, they began to pick up speed, and as the needle on the dashboard floated slowly around past the eighty mark Greenbloom spoke calmly: in the dim light which illumined his chin and lips from below they saw that he was smiling with terrifying reasonableness.

"You know, you'll really have to try and give me earlier warning if you're going to continue to assist me, Mick. In daylight one can afford to relax a little around corners because the traffic slows one up; but driving at night is quite different from—" He leaned forward: "Hello, what's that house doing out there? Plumb in the middle of the—"

"*Fork right!*" Michael's voice broke into an adenoidal falsetto which threaded through the weaker cries wrung from Rachel and Kate Holly behind him. It was too late, they swept between two white gateposts with a lodge on the left of them, slid along a private drive which seemed to shorten visibly from the moment they entered it and, with Greenbloom rearing up as he stood on the brake pedal, came to rest in the middle of a rosebed outside a large country house. Greenbloom switched off the ignition and there was silence.

"Everyone must change places," he announced. "I can't possibly continue to drive with things as they are. Where's my flask, Rachel?"

Kate Holly opened her door. "I'm walkin'," she said flatly. "You're not taking me another yard, front or back."

"Don't be ridiculous! Don't you realize that but for my quickness in avoiding that building you'd all have been dead? If someone had had the wit to warn me a little sooner," he did not even glance at Michael, "there would have been no danger at all, as it is—Rachel, for God's sake find my flask!"

"But the *damage*, Horab! The damage!" she moaned.

"What damage? Did we hit something?"

Michael spoke, "Of course we did, it's under the car."

Greenbloom groaned. "Would somebody mind telling me first of all what we hit and secondly what it is that is at present lying under the car."

"I think it was a sundial or something," said John. "It may have been a birdbath."

"Thank God for my bumpers. I only had them fitted last vac and they've proved a godsend already. We will all have a drink and then we will see how they've stood up to it."

"Don't you think it would be as well to get off this flowerbed first?" suggested Michael.

"Exactly." He started the engine. "I shall need a little help, I had no time to notice if there were any obstructions behind us. Mick, you'd better get out and give me directions."

"I'm afraid that's impossible," said Michael. "Just for the moment my legs won't carry me."

"Of course they won't. I keep telling you we've all had a very narrow escape. Where's that flask? Give it to Mick."

Rachel handed it over and Mick drank and passed it on to Greenbloom.

"That's better," he said. "Can you manage it now, Mick? We don't want to be here all night and I suppose we'll have to explain to the owner. I'm going to suggest that he should have a notice put up at his gate giving motorists a clear warning of his concealed entrance."

"It's *not* a concealed entrance," said Michael wearily as he got out of the car and took up his position behind it.

Leaning out on either side Greenbloom and John watched him as he signalled to them.

"Straight back!" he called. "Straight back!"

Greenbloom fumbled at the gears and the car rumbled forward over a small rockery and slid down into the drive facing the front door.

Greenbloom got out and rang the bell. In a few moments the light went on in the hall and the door opened.

The young man confronting them wore black and smiled charmingly. "Sir?"

"Is anyone at home?"

"Sir Halcyon Summas left for the Riviera in February, sir, and is not expected to return until June when Lady Summas leaves for—" His cheeks stiffened in his attempt to counteract the increasing irreverence of his smile. "Lady Summas is in her studio, sir."

Greenbloom's head jerked up savagely. "In her *studio*? At this hour?"

"Lady Summas writes—poetry, sir," said the young man with great restraint. "She gave emphatic orders that she was not to be disturbed."

"She will *not* be!" said Greenbloom with a shudder. He straightened his shoulders.

"We have just had what might have been a very nasty accident which would never have happened if your main gate had been closed."

The young man stepped out into the drive. "I'm very sorry, sir. Was anyone hurt?"

"Fortunately no. But some of my party, the ladies, were very shaken as you can imagine and we have only one small flask between us."

From the background Mick loped up to them as they stood in the rectangle of light thrown from the hall on to the battered front of the Bentley. The others remained in the car straining their ears to catch the syllables of the conversation.

"It was an oversight about the gate, sir," said the butler, "and I know that Sir Halcyon will be very distressed by the lodge-keeper's failure to close it."

Michael interrupted. "I'm afraid we hit something in the middle of the rosebed. It is impossible to see exactly what it was."

"That would be the urn, sir, a Georgian one."

"We'll have to see about that," said Greenbloom shortly. "I will leave you my card. But first I feel the least we can do is to give the ladies a drink."

"Of course, sir. If you'd like to come in?"

"Thank you! We can't stay long though. We're on our way to Oxford."

They followed him into a large drawing room with a parquet floor and, having removed the dust sheets, sat around a pie-crust table and ate the biscuits which accompanied a decanter of brandy pronounced by Greenbloom to be "reasonably good."

Some ten minutes later they were once again on the road to Oxford.

This time Greenbloom had arranged them differently; and

to John, sitting between his taut body, the pale face peering through the window like a nighthawk, and the soft rather odorous comfort of Kate Holly, their progress assumed an inevitability that was not only restful but in some way even safe. It was as though they had passed through some barrier of danger beyond which accepted laws ceased to operate.

He had seen the illusion of such safety depicted on films where traffic corners and obstructions of all kinds miraculously vanished at the ultimate moment against all expectation and allowed pursuer or pursued to reach their journey's end in safety; but because it was simultaneously perceived by all the senses and because no one knew whether Greenbloom was the hero or the villain, the present experience was entirely different. At the cinema it was usually the hero who was safe and the villain who came to satisfying grief; but Greenbloom might equally well have been chasing something with every good intention or fleeing from it with a black heart, and they whose lives might closely depend upon his rôle had no knowledge of the plot in which they were cast.

Yet John was certainly not frightened; the danger, whatever it may have been, now lay behind them; they had long ago overtaken it with partial impunity and now they were in a new country, the Greenbloom country, where whatever happened, whether it were for an unreal best or worst, was of no importance.

The realization of this was quietly exhilarating and affected them all. Perceptibly, as they sped on through the night they began to relax, no longer troubling to follow the course of the road or to warn Greenbloom of approaching signposts or traffic. Glancing behind him, John saw that Rachel and Michael, having lighted cigarettes, were no longer sitting upright but had subsided easily into the body of the car where they were sitting far apart from each other in a dreamy silence.

For his own part, he began to enjoy Kate Holly's closeness and leaned more heavily on her full shoulder as he reviewed the events of the day with the sort of dispassionate and increasing pleasure which precedes sleep.

Greenbloom was wonderful, he decided; he was a prophet like

John the Baptist or one of the earlier ones, the Isaiahs and Jeremiahs so often quoted by the prebendary and Rudmose; a man of the desert crying out wonderful things in a voice which was itself as dry and parched as the waste he inhabited.

All prophets dwelt in deserts and Greenbloom was no exception; he carried his own desert with him and even in the most opulent surroundings could spread it about him like a brown cloak. His rooms at Balliol were just a blind to hoodwink people and make them think that he was modern and rich. Really he was poor; a gaunt person in a rough robe who despised the wealth he had been given and who dwelt in a time and country of his own beyond the common imagining.

Obviously he was waiting for something; he had said so; "The rest of us must wait," he had said, and he had meant it. He must be a prophet or he would not be waiting for something; all prophets were waiting for something and Greenbloom already had everything: jewels, girls, this Bentley, even a three-seater aeroplane if Michael were to be believed; yet he was still expecting ardently some other thing beside which all these possessions were of no importance whatever.

It was true he had admitted that he did not know exactly what he was expecting: it had apparently been something more than the stars for which he searched week by week; it had also been something more than the book he was supposed to be writing about Wittgenstein. The book, so vast, so inclusive, which weighed him down whenever it was mentioned and had seemed distasteful to him whenever Michael mentioned it. Lastly, his expectation, whatever it might be, evidently had no connection with the career he intended to follow after he went down from Oxford, because, like the book, he never referred to this except in the most vague and bewildering terms. Yet John was sure that the event for which he waited would ultimately rise clearly out of these three things, and the fact that Greenbloom was so unspecific about it only made him more truly a prophet. Prophets who were easily understandable were not prophets at all; they were just preachers or politicians, bores like Oily Albert and Mr. Baldwin.

You could laugh at Greenbloom of course and it would do no

harm either to you or to him provided that you knew the difference between a clown and a prophet. No doubt because
whatever he did he was acting not only for the present but for
the furtherance of some project which could only be concluded
in the future, giftless people with no vision would see him only
as a clown; but those who had such faith in him as John would
laugh only with a respectful reservation. After all, what did an
urn and a flowerbed matter when you were passing over them
on your way to some horizon lighted with an unearthly light?
That butler had respected him; had it been anyone else driving
up in that rude way, smashing everything that lay in his path
and then demanding apologies, the butler would have been
haughty and full of threats; but as it was, he, like John, had
recognized Greenbloom's quality and had rushed to the pantry
to get him biscuits and brandy and treated them all as though
they had been very important friends of his employer.

It was lucky that Greenbloom liked John and was interested
in him; he had been wonderfully clever in his handling of
Michael, and obviously he would not have taken all that trouble
to overrule him about the trip if he had not realized that John
knew him for what he was and appreciated his secret. He would
tell Greenbloom anything, he decided; far more than he would
ever tell Michael. Greenbloom had discerned John's own dark
secret and had entered it from the East crying of the great light
which one day would blaze upon it so that the way out of it
might easily be found. Yes! Greenbloom was his friend, he
would confide in him; he might, as a preliminary, even consider
returning the money he had stolen if Greenbloom seemed to
want it at any time, and certainly from now on he would immediately do anything he suggested. He only hoped that he would
not grow tired of him and drop him after this one wonderful
experience. If he could only find some means of continuing to
interest him then he might ask him out again, possibly without
Michael, and if *that* happened then the remainder of this last term
at Beowulf's might be just bearable.

Sitting up, he leaned forward and peered at the dashboard
clock; it showed that it was after half-past ten already and although they had reached the outskirts of Oxford some minutes

ago he realized he could not possibly be back at the school before eleven o'clock, and at the very least that would mean a beating from Rudmose in the morning. He glanced through the wind-screen. Greenbloom was driving as fast as ever; the houses and hedges were flashing past, and ahead of them, as they leapt down the gentle hill into the town, was Magdalen Bridge. He saw the tall tower of the college, the fat stone balustrades of the bridge and, standing stock-still in the centre of it like a rigid statue, the dark shape of a single policeman. A moment later they heard the faint ghost of his whistle far behind them as they flew up the slope towards Carfax, ran straight over the red lights into the High, and, finally after several more turns drew up outside Mick's rooms in a little street somewhere near the Carpenter's Arms.

Greenbloom produced his flask.

"Somebody whistled," he said. "Did you hear it, Mick?"

"Only a policeman." Michael's tone was dry.

"What policeman? Where? I saw only one—on Magdalen Bridge, and the noise I heard occurred just before Carfax."

"That, I imagine, was the one. You were doing about eighty, you know, Horab."

"Are you sure?"

"He was doing eighty-five," said Kate. "I've had my eyes glued to that speedometer ever since we started."

"Well, as long as you're sure," said Greenbloom with relief. "He couldn't possibly have got my number at that speed."

Michael put a hand on Kate Holly's shoulder and she smiled at him quickly. "No," he said yawning, "always supposing no one else heard his whistle and that five or six of them are not converging on us while you drink the last of the Scotch."

"Good old Mick!" said Greenbloom. "Here, take it and get out. We really haven't got the time to start squaring the police. I've got to get Rachel fixed up somewhere before it's too late."

Michael took the flask. "There's just one other thing, Horab, before you go. What are you going to do about John? He's already three-quarters of an hour late on his pass and somebody will have to explain to his housemaster—"

"Do not worry! But for God's sake get out and let us get

started. John is coming with *me*, and I shall deal with everything as it arises. Kate, my dear, you'd better get out and let Rachel come into the front. I have some telephone calls to make and there is much to do."

"There's only *one* thing to do," Michael spoke from the pavement, "and that is to get John back to the school. You'd better tell them about the accident."

Greenbloom leaned over and closed the door beside Rachel.

"I have been considering everything very carefully, leave John to me. We will explain in the morning."

"The morning will be far too late. You will have to explain tonight and if you are going to insist on seeing John's housemaster, though I don't advise it, for Heaven's sake don't have anything more to drink on the way."

"No! No! No!" said Greenbloom with great impatience. "You are too limited. It is not a question of explanation, one cannot go through life explaining to people—there are matters you do not understand, but fortunately for your brother they are clear to me, quite clear. One thing only I wish to know; I take it that you did say he would in any case be leaving this frightful school at the end of the term, that they have bowed before the publicity and will be asking him to go?"

"It's not *settled*. You mustn't start acting on—" Michael got on to the running board of the Bentley.

"Everything is settled." Greenbloom turned to John. "That *is* the position about your expulsion?"

"I'm sure it is," said John eagerly. "This morning, Rudmose —that's the housemaster—was telling me that I'd do much better to go to some Jewish tutor friend of his in Worthing."

Greenbloom sat very still. He became a waxen figure protesting against all circumstance by his profound immobility. "As I thought," he said quietly. "Another exile! A scapegoat to be sent out into the wilderness laden with offerings. Get off the car, Michael. We are starting!"

"You're *drunk*!" shouted Michael bitterly. "Rachel, try and make the damn fool understand that if he goes up to the school in this mood we shall all be sent down at the week end."

"Michael *deear*!" whispered Rachel. "What can *I* do? You

know what Horab is when he's like *thisss*! His tide is coming in and no one can stop it; one sss-imply has to get out of the way. Please, *sweeet* Michael, get off the car or you will end up like the urn."

"But where are you going?" implored Michael. "Horab, tell me where you are going?"

"If you will only get down from the running board he will tell you; I know he will, because tonight he is fond of me and I am very, very fond of him because he is so exciting when he's like this, aren't you, Horab?"

Greenbloom did not even nod, the engine of the Bentley began to boom softly as the great body slid forward. In a few yards Michael jumped off and began to run along the pavement beside them.

"I'm off! Now tell me where?"

"Tell him!" said Greenbloom to Rachel.

"But I do not know."

"*Tell* him!" repeated Greenbloom as the car gathered speed. Rachel leaned out of the window and kissed her hand to Michael. "He says we are going to Paris."

With beautiful timing the car sprang forward and a few minutes later they drew up outside the entrance of the Mitre Hotel.

Despite the hot coffee and the ham sandwiches they had eaten in the deserted lounge, John found the morning air chilling and uncongenial as he waited with Rachel while two rumpled mechanics wheeled the Moth out of the hangar. Across Port Meadow the mist of the rising dew lay almost level with the backs of the cows grazing and coughing in the middle distance. The poplars and willows lining the banks of the Cherwell far away to the west were invisible, but already the sun was picking out the crests and trees of the Whiteham Hills.

Rachel in her mink coat looked pale and somehow wizened in the clean slant of the light. He watched her slyly as she stood there beside him alternately glancing over towards Greenbloom and then at the little mirror which lived in the flap of her handbag. Overnight, her face had lost its distinctness: neither the eyelids, the lips, nor the curved and minute nose had the lovely precision he had noticed the previous evening; there was a blurring of edges, a loss of boundary, as though each separate feature had missed its place and character and mingled with its neighbours in the night. It must worry her, he thought, or she would not have been looking so distracted or found it necessary to make so many little dabbing movements with her lipstick, eye pencil and powder puff.

The fact that she should be so self-concerned at a time like this irritated him. He was sure that there was nothing she could do about it. She would just have to wait until the day grew older, till it got later; and then presumably if they were all still alive and in Paris her face would come right again.

She looked up suddenly and catching his frown smiled at him.

"You like watching me, John?"

"Yes." He was awkward. "At least I wasn't really watching you; I was thinking."

"And what were you thinking about? Was it *sso* distasteful?"

"I was wondering about Greenbloom—"

"You funny boy! Why do you always call him Greenbloom?"

"I don't know; it's just how I think of him, I suppose."

"And what were you wondering?"

"Oh—dozens of things."

"Things like what?"

"Well, how he manages to keep an aeroplane at Oxford and get people out of bed at this hour to service it for him; and how on earth he's ever going to find the way to Paris; and what we are all supposed to do when we get there; and what Mick and the school and my parents will say when they hear about it."

"Goodness! *What* a lot of questions!"

"Yes, I know." He smiled. "It's not that I'm really worried, of course; it's only that this morning is the first chance I've had of thinking about things. I wish you could answer some of them for me."

"Oh, but I can't I'm afraid—not all of them. Perhaps we had better start with Horab; he is very rich, you know?"

"Yes, I guessed he must be—he leaves money lying about in his rooms." He paused and looked around him swiftly at the great beauty of the morning. "As a matter of fact, a few days ago, I stole some of it." He corrected himself. "No, it was only yesterday—that's odd, it seems much longer ago. Do you think you could give it back to him before we start?"

He found and held out the notes to her. Over their crumpled edges she looked up at him, her face bright with sudden laughter.

"Oh John! You wicked *perss-son!*" Her amusement overcame her; the tiny blue-eyed face creased until its tears coursed down over her cheeks.

"Please stop it!" he said angrily.

"But—I—*can't!* To take Horab's money when you have only *jusst* met him—and then—to give it *back* to him." She dabbed at her face with a powder puff. "Oh, he'll never get over it!"

"I don't see that it's funny."

"Oh, but it *is!* *Sso* funny—I'll tell you John, you must promise me you'll give it back to him in front of me. I want to watch his face."

He ground his heel on a fat worm-cast. "No, *you* give it to him."

"*Me?* Never! I *never* give Horab *money.*" She was very serious again. "Horab gives *me,* Rachel, money; and he's lucky that I will take it."

"Why?"

"*Well!*" She drew in a deep breath and, putting away her cosmetics, looked up at the sky and then at the hangar and lastly over in the direction of the quiet cows as though she were appealing for their support.

"Oh, I know you're pretty and young," he said sulkily. "But I think you're jolly lucky to have a person like Greenbloom running you about all over the place in Bentleys and aeroplanes."

"So that's what you think is it, John?"

"Yes."

"I wonder *why.*" The word emerged from the shaping of her lips as softly as a kiss.

"Well, because anybody's lucky to be loved by someone—"

"By someone who is rich?"

"Yes, or by anyone for that matter. Anyone *alive,* I mean."

Her eyes, so interested, suddenly ceased to look into his face; their gaze shifted to his feet.

"Oh, I see," she said softly. "I see! Horab was telling me."
He said nothing.

"Poor John Blaydon! We will talk about something else—about the University Flying Club and how Horab paid the mechanics—" She laughed brightly. "*He* says he bribed them but *I* say he *paid* them; we often argue about it; he says no payments are ever made, only bribes. But never mind, it cost him five pounds each, you know, five whole pounds for each man."

"Did it?"

"Yes." She was watching him. "And then we shall talk about Paris and what we shall see when we get there, shall we?"

"If you like—I don't really mind though if love interests you more."

"Oh, but it does, Johnny, it *does*. Love and money! Money and love! I hardly ever think about anything else, and if there were a goddess of both I'd say my prayers to her every night."

"Would you?"

"But of course! There should be a golden Venus, an Aphrodite all of gold, for Rachel to pray to and light little candles for."

"Oh," he said; and then, "Rachel?"

"Yes?"

"What do you think he will say when I do tell him?"

"About the money, you mean?"

He nodded.

"He will say '*was sich in der Sprache spiegelt, kann sie nicht darstellen.*'"

She watched him closely.

"Is that German?"

"Yes, it is from Wittgenstein. He always quotes from Wittgenstein when he is cross."

"What does it mean?"

"It means, 'That which mirrors itself in language, language cannot represent.' In other words that he is so angry he will not know what to say. He says it to me very often."

"I wish I knew who Wittgenstein was," he said.

"Don't worry. Horab will tell you. I have some of his book in my case. The very end of it."

"The *end* of it? I thought he hadn't started it yet."

"Oh, but he has. He has started at the end. He says that is the only way to deal with Wittgenstein."

"How very odd."

"Not really," she said. "You were talking about love just now and you said it was lucky to love somebody who was alive, didn't you?"

"Yes."

"Horab would not agree. He says that we love most when it is too late, when it has ended. So you see that in a way everything begins at the end."

He was silent; he wished they were on their way. Over by the hangar the little plane was nearly ready. He watched the men empty the last can of petrol into the funnel protruding from the petrol tank and saw Greenbloom's head appear out of the cabin window just above the star painted on the white fuselage. Something touched his left hand as it hung by his side and he looked down to see Rachel caressing it gently, tiny stroking movements as though she were playing a stringed instrument.

He withdrew his hand. "What is it?"

"Only that I wish I could make you see that it is not at all so lucky to *be* loved as it is to *love*."

"Isn't it?"

"No. It is far luckier to love somebody whether they are alive or dead; and if *you* love somebody like that, John, you are richer than Horab and happier than Rachel."

He was trying to read the letters above the yellow star, but his shortsightedness made it difficult. He screwed up his eyes and slowly they became apparent:

SCAPEGOAT

"Do you see?" she asked again.

"No," he said flatly. "I don't. I'd rather be loved by some-one *alive*."

"One day you will be, Johnny, you *will!*" She walked away from him over towards the plane. One of the men was handing her tiny suitcase up to Greenbloom and seeing it she turned and laughed at John.

"*Sso* fortunate that whenever Horab takes me anywhere I should always have my case ready. I keep one packed now in case I have one of his telephone calls." He caught up with her.

"Once," she went on, "the first time, I was unprepared and he took me to Le Touquet. Well, I had to buy everything out of my allowance, every single little thing, and there were scarcely any francs left over and yet Horab would not give me any more. He was getting mean you know; oh sso *mean*! Really, you wouldn't believe how close he can be when he chooses— a regular old Shylock! I call him *Mazeltov* when he's like that, I tell him he's an old Shemite, the meanest of the twelve Tribes, and he gets *sso* angry."

"Does it do any good?"

"No, *that* doesn't."

"Well what does?"

"Ahh, that's a s-secret." She prolonged the word so that it sounded like a tiny snake hissing. "Rachel's s-secret, every Rachel that ever was born."

They walked on together increasing their pace a little as they saw that Greenbloom was gesticulating at them through the window of the small cabin.

"I don't see how on earth we're all going to get in," said John uneasily. "Is it meant to hold three?"

"Indeed it is! Father, Mother and one child. *I* am the child. I weight only forty kilos and you are nearly as thin as Horab though you are very tall for your age."

"And does he know the way? Can he navigate or whatever it's called?"

"I don't expect so, but it doesn't really matter. Horab always finds his way in the end, and there are plenty of little airfields in France and as long as he's satisfied with the weather report he won't change his mind even if it should mean that he'll have to come down somewhere a little short of Paris and go on by taxi."

"Is he a good pilot?"

John was beginning to feel very nervous. Although they had

nearly reached the De Havilland Moth it still looked dreadfully insubstantial; the very fact that it was constructed of paint and glass doors and windscreens, had rubber tires and aluminium struts, made it only more difficult to accept.

He had never seen an aeroplane closely before and on the ground; its resemblance to a motorcar would have been re-assuring had he not known that it was supposed to fulfil a quite different function: the seemingly impossible act of rising into the air and carrying with it not only its own engine but also their three heavy bodies higher than the lightest of clouds. The factualness of it as it stood before him immediately terrified him. Until this moment the whole sequence of events had seemed quite unreal, a dream delightful and strange in whose gentle cur-rent he had drifted utterly away from the awful world of Beowulf's, the moors and his own self-preoccupation; but now, at this moment, when his dream was found to contain the un-related solidity of an aeroplane which was to fly him into a reality of air and cloud more tenuous than any dream, he found himself numbed by reluctance.

Reveries and facts did not mix; aeroplanes should never be seen on the ground. To force people to accept them out of their element like this was to confront them with the ultimate dilemma; and he felt that rather than step into the Moth he would be dumbly prepared to forgo the whole of his enchanted escape and go back to Michael and to the school. But it was too late; Greenbloom, he realized, would never allow him to turn back now; he was a jealous god, a prophet who would not be denied, and therefore somehow he would have to make himself believe in the aeroplane and say nothing to either of them of the cold dismay which froze him as he followed Rachel's example and clambered in under the wing to take his seat beside her in the back of the cabin.

Rachel leaned forward:

"Poor John is terrified, Horab! He wants to know if you are a good pilot."

Greenbloom, who was now wearing a white helmet like a woman's bathing cap, gave a signal to one of the men and pulled dexterously at some levers on the dashboard.

"Of course I am. Why should I not be?"

"Well you're not an awfully good driver, are you?" said John.

"Certainly not! No accomplished pilot is ever a good driver. It is a difference of conception, '*Die Frage nach der Existenz eines formalen begriffes ist unsinnig. Denn kein Satz kann eine solche Frage beantworten.*'" He frowned angrily.

"Oh, I see," said John.

Rachel gave a little titter of laughter. "Of course you don't see, you charlatan! Shall I translate it for you?"

"Yes, please."

"It means, 'The question about the existence of a formal concept is senseless. For no proposition can answer such a question!' It is from the *Tractatus Logico-Philosophicus* and Horab always quotes it when he is stuck for an answer."

"I suppose it's from this Wittgenstein man?"

"You are quite right."

"Where did *you* hear about him?"

"In Vienna, they are very excited about him there and I try to keep up with him because if I did not Horab would be cross."

"Wittgenstein is essential," said Greenbloom. "Even Bertrand Russell has discovered that, although he is *not* an intelligent man." He turned around. "You had better fasten your belts. Rachel! Show him how to fasten his belt. What is the time?"

"Six o'clock."

"We are a little late, but it is nobody's fault. The ground mist was in any case a little too thick for the start I'd scheduled. Even so, we should be at *Les Deux Magots* in good time for a *Mandarin*."

He raised his hand and the man at the propeller started to twitch it viciously. The engine sneezed out some pale blue smoke, Greenbloom depressed another switch and at the fourth swing they were enclosed in a flux of sound. The metal, glass and fabric of the tiny machine thundered over them like a wave as they sat there in a wind that was filled with the rude smell of exhaust gas and benzol. Everything came to life: the seats shook, the glass vibrated, and outside John's window appeared the wind-torn head of the other mechanic. He signalled to John to open the door and then bellowed out through his hand into his ear.

He looked alarmed and urgent, and thinking that the plane was on fire or about to explode, John had a desperate impulse to leap straight out on to the newly remote and glorious grass. It was quite impossible to hear what the man was saying.

"*What?*" he shouted. "I can't hear. Say it again."

"The cëows, sir." The man made two horns out of his hands and, holding them on either side of his head, wobbled it slowly from side to side. "Tell 'em. Tell Mr. Greenbloom, to watch ëout for the cëows on his take-off!"

"Oh, the cows." He was relieved; now that they were safely in the aeroplane no cow could ever harm them. It was Greenbloom country again and the bad moment was over. A wild, thick excitement was filling him from his toes to his ears, and though someone had told him now that this was to be his last morning alive, he would have made no further effort ever to get out of the Moth.

This was the moment for which he had been born. This was the bright beginning which was to end the whole of the insane past: to fly with Rachel and Greenbloom to Paris in the early morning.

There was no need to pass on the message; Greenbloom had seen and understood the gesture. He signalled curtly to the man, put the engine through its paces, waggled a bent aluminium rod between his knees, and signalled once again. The chocks were pulled away and they began to taxi out into the thinning mist; red sunlight gushed into the cabin as they turned in strange graceful figures over the rippling grass; Greenbloom glanced at the windsock floating free in the morning wind, tested the controls again, and then pulled the throttle in the dashboard out to its farthest limit.

The Moth leapt as though it had been given an unexpected and potent injection and then began to rush forward towards the rosy streaming face of the sun which hung full ahead of them. In a moment the horizon became visible as the tail lifted and the windscreen tilted lower to reveal the spires and treetops of Oxford; the vibrations diminished, hesitated and then ceased, as the grass, the whole flat expanse, withdrew its claim upon them. The last edge of their shadow flew back behind them and

they were sustained higher and higher above the pale mist which
floated over the meadow from which they had risen.

Looking out above and below, John saw flocks of birds flying
to their feeding grounds, the buildings of the hangar performing
a slow horizontal cartwheel and the golden stones and dewy
lawns of Oxford turning smaller and smaller into neatness and
order as they rose even higher into the smokeless air. He looked
desperately for Beowulf's, for one last convincing glimpse of
the school; but he could not see it; the whole city seemed to be
hiding its particulars from the clarity of his vantage point and
he could recognize no single point or feature as, far beneath
them, the streets churches and squares receded into the swell of
the shadowed landscape.

Beside him, Greenbloom pointed at one of the black dials in
the dashboard. It was overprinted in white:

ALTITUDE IN FEET
(X 100)

and the needle was wavering around the 50 mark, which meant
that they were five thousand feet up in the air. At this height
Greenbloom pushed in the throttle a little and pulled a small
lever marked TRIM in the roof of the cabin; the Moth flattened
out and the engine noise became quieter. John turned around and
Rachel handed him a thick map case which he passed on to
Greenbloom, who ignored it.

"Tell her to pass me a drink," he shouted.

Rachel rummaged behind her in the back of the fuselage and
brought out two large leather-bound flasks with silver caps
marked WHISKY and BRANDY. John filled the cap labelled BRANDY
and handed it to Greenbloom, who, having drained it at a gulp,
ordered him to refill it and pass it on to Rachel after he had
himself had a drink from it. He shook his head. He did not want
a drink, so he passed both flasks back to Rachel who put them
in a cubbyhole behind her and started to make up her face again.

Greenbloom turned around to John and waved royally at the
open sky. "Do you like it?" he shouted.

"It's—" There were no words which could describe the glory
of it and so he contented himself in trying to smile all the in-

sufficient adjectives which came to his mind. Greenbloom nodded confidently and John studied his face in the peaked, close-fitting helmet. Against the dead whiteness of his strange covering the skin looked more luminous than ever, rosily gilded by the fall of the new sunlight on its pale surface. Only the curling Egyptian asp was needed in order to complete the resemblance to the golden death mask of a Pharaoh which had first struck him at the moment of their meeting. He saw that the black eyes were sleepy and that over them the lids, tinged with mauve, hung heavily like those of a dancer. Leaning surreptitiously a little farther forward, he saw that it was only the eye nearest to him which was lighted, the other one was in half-shadow, and this caused him to turn around with surprise and search out through his window to find the new direction of the sun. It was no longer in front of them but had apparently moved around to the right and appeared even to be slightly below the wing tip.

He was amazed by this; it seemed impossible that he should be able to look *down* on the sun and he wondered why no one had ever mentioned this before in the many books he had read about flying. There was no doubt that relatively the sun at this moment appeared to be far below them; there were even one or two flat clouds, lilac on top, rose pink below, hanging between the Moth and its blazing spherical face.

Like the rising sun, Paris of course must lie east of England and they were flying towards it; at least they had been when they started, he remembered it distinctly; but now they must be moving northeast, otherwise the sun would not be shining a little to the right of them. He searched the instrument panel for a compass but could not find one amongst the many busy black circles.

"Where are we?" he shouted to Greenbloom.

"North London any moment now: Ruislip, Eastcote, Harrow." He waved vaguely towards the propeller. "Clouding over—see all you can."

"Aren't we flying north then?"

"No, no—*south!*"

Astonishing, he thought; but of course, despite appearances, **they** couldn't possibly be above the sun, so presumably their relationships were all changed and none of the ordinary rules could be relied upon.

"Deviation," roared Greenbloom. "*Drift!*"

John nodded affirmatively and assumed a contented expression; but secretly he gazed out of his window greedily as he attempted to reconcile the surprising facts. At first he could see nothing but mosslike woods and an apparently entirely flat landscape of hedged fields traversed by a thin network of road-threads; but then, quite far ahead of them, he at last discerned a recurrent series of glints and flashes, several white cocoons of condensing steam from railway lines and the thunderous opacity of a great area of buildings and smoke heavily overshadowed by a cloud mass. He drew in a deep breath delightedly and favoured Greenbloom with an open smile; he was right, they would soon be over France.

As the cloudbank drew nearer they began to climb again into the whiter sunlight of the new day. There was now very little of the land to be seen through the window; they hung heavily over a blinding static ocean of cloud from which smooth snowy mountains rolled and wreathed with almost imperceptible secrecy. Sometimes these accumulated masses rose high above them on either side so that they flew in a cold, unseen shadow between the walls of white and blazing valleys; at others, they out-topped the highest clouds and traversed almost interminable plains and deserts of reflected light. Very occasionally there would be a lake of slate-blue depth below them, a cobalt glimpse of what might have been either land or sea far beneath the strata of the clouds; but in contrast to the radiance in which they were suspended these breaks were so dark and shadowed that it was difficult to discern any single feature contained within them. Only once in the first hour did John catch sight of the serpentine Thames beneath them; and then for a long time there was no further gap sufficiently large to help him until they were well out over the middle of what he was sure must be the English Channel.

Here, above the ocean, the clouds began to thin out and separate a little as though even they themselves moved like dissolving icebergs through a cold sea of air which was nevertheless warmer than that which flowed over the great land mass of England. Looking back he saw that England was itself shaped in the clouds, that they lay above the land in a tumbled outline of her coasts and bays casting their gloom over her landscape narrowly and exactly. Ahead, quite low on the horizon, was a less distinct mass which he guessed must be coincident with the French coast; but between this and the Moth lay the sparsely clouded space of the grey-blue channel.

He had never realized how wide the channel was; they seemed to have been flying above it for something over half an hour before the opposing coast became sufficiently clear for him to try and identify particular features. Then, when finally they were about to cross the deep fringe of frozen waves, cloud again intervened and Greenbloom, who had come down a little for the sea crossing, pulled on the stick and forced the Moth to ascend once more into the endless variations of the cloudscape.

John turned and shouted to Rachel:

"Was that the French coast?"

She nodded.

"What part?" She shook her head gaily and yawned.

"Brittany," said Greenbloom. "Off course a little—strato-cumulus!"

Rachel handed him a note: "Have we plenty of petrol?"

Greenbloom glanced at the fuel gauge. "Half an hour—land somewhere—fill up."

"On an aerodrome?" asked John.

"Give me the map!"

Rachel passed it and John leaned over and spread it across Greenbloom's knees. It was scored in red with little flags marked: Good, Bad, Indifferent, Impossible.

"What are those?" he asked as Greenbloom's long fingers slid over the green patterns.

"Forced landings—old ones."

"Forced landings?"

Rachel nudged him and shook her head quickly; in a few moments she gave him another note:

"Don't keep asking him questions," it said. "He likes to be

trusted. If he thinks you have lost faith in him—may do something reckless."

John nodded vigorously. The inside of his mouth had become glutinous and slightly bitter; he remembered something he had read somewhere about the "thick saliva of fear." Forced landings were a last resort, or at least so he had always supposed; nobody ever attempted one unless they were desperate, and yet Greenbloom seemed to have made at least a dozen of them if his map were trustworthy. Forced landings, successful ones, depended on all sorts of factors such as windspeed and direction, suitable approach, length of run and landing speeds. He found himself trying desperately to work out how long it had taken them to get off the ground at Port Meadow so that he might assess the size of field they would need in order to land in France. He decided that it would have to be quite a large field, a very large one, say twice the length of the upper playing field at Beowulf's; there would have to be no cars, buildings, telegraph poles, nor pylons.

His heart suddenly very apparent to him, each wild beat thumping up into his ears, he started searching the dashboard for the fuel gauge: the white needle was now very near the round O and he could imagine the petrol sinking perceptibly in the tank, washing backwards and forwards over the metal bottom like water in an emptying bath.

"*This cumulus!*" said Greenbloom angrily. "Have to get below it."

He pushed the short aluminium stick forward, cut down on the revolutions, and they began to sink towards the cloud floor. Nearer and nearer rose the delicate sculpture until it seemed that any moment some perceptible change must become apparent in their progress; but nothing happened. They continued to sink as easily as they had done in the untrammeled sunlight, and the fact that the great solidity of the clouds could do nothing to slow them up or hold them above the invisible ground made John for the first time fully aware of their peril. Around him the clean panes of glass had vanished; instead they were fogged over and breathed upon as though by an icy dragon; drops of water blown by the wind of the propeller jerked wildly across them and through the cleared spaces there was nothing to be seen but the enormous vacancy of the cloud in whose vapour they were wrapped and blinded as they floated ever nearer to the deadly ground.

They might be descending at a hundred miles an hour into the peak of a mountain, a church spire, a factory or an electric pylon; but they could not possibly know. They would never know. Vividly, reliving again the weeks of his own publicity, he imagined the headlines in the newspaper, the short-lived tears and talk; and then tried to banish the insistent thought of the nothingness which might await him, the nothingness he had discussed with Greenbloom only half a day ago.

His panic held him numb in his seat. He could not move or swallow; even his eyes seemed to be glazing between their unblinking lids. And then suddenly the Moth fell clear: once again there was light and colour and beneath them a flat green landscape scattered over with villages, roads and woodland.

The variety of it astonished him; even after so short a time in the filtered emptiness of the air and clouds the sudden sight of so many new colours, of such a giant activity as the land implied, shocked his senses, reminding him at once of the book of Genesis: of the land separating itself from the water after the coming of the light, and of the Spirit brooding over them on the first day of creation.

Even without people, even if all this had been a grey-green desert, it would have been prodigious; and he realized that although he had never flown before he had responded more easily to the great void of Heaven than to the material fact of the world. To meet it like this after so much whiteness and emptiness was to see it as though for the first time, to understand the first meaning of geography which, as old Rudmose had often explained, derived from γη meaning "land" and γραφειν meaning "to draw." Here beneath him was the land drawn together out of vacuity, shaped and moulded in an enormous ball of rock and ocean and put to circling the sun as though by a cunning, long-departed hand.

He was glad that on this first encounter with the reality of Creation he should have had Greenbloom with him. Identifying him as he increasingly did with the Old Testament, it was only fitting that he should have been beside him at the moment of this personal revelation; and confident now as never before, he relaxed in his seat as they continued to sink slowly down towards the fields of France.

Greenbloom was perfectly calm; his small predatory head swung quickly from side to side as he searched the landscape for a suitable run-in and swung the Moth over the tapestry of woods and fields. For a few minutes they continued this restive questing like a fish hovering over the bed of a running river, drifting in the flow of the wind and light lying between fields and clouds; then Greenbloom evidently saw what he wanted. He muttered something, banked the Moth into a steep right turn which threw them over to their sides, and headed across a low hill to a distant expanse of grass.

As they drew nearer, a tiny grandstand appeared and John was able to see the white posts and railings of an oval racecourse set neatly out ahead of them. They came up to it quickly; Greenbloom looked for chimney smoke from a nearby cottage, circled into the wind, and having adjusted the trim, cut down on the engine revolutions as they began to stream forward towards the last section of the racecourse.

Once again their shadow flew to meet them; they flashed over a hedge, over a section of the rails stretching far over to the right towards a group of trees, and then as the flickering propeller responded smoothly to the accelerator, as even the molehills became distinct as small mountains, they met the racing grass and fled over it in a perfect three-point landing.

Greenbloom applied the brakes; they were thrown forward on their seats, the posts on either side of them slowed up, the propeller spun idly, and quite swiftly they drew up in front of an empty enclosure to the left of the grandstand. Greenbloom switched off the engine and there was a full silence; it drew around them like the sucking aftermath of a wave, thick and turgid, filled with bright pebbles of sound: wind noises, the creek of plovers and somewhere far away the braying of a donkey.

Greenbloom pulled up his trouser leg and adjusted a small lever beside the metal kneecap, he flicked it from DRIVING printed in blue letters to WALKING printed in green and then leaned back in his seat.

"France!" he said loudly. "Pass over the flask. We will drink to a successful flight and a quite superlative landing."

They all drank and then Rachel said, "I really must find a little place—that coffee!"

"*Coffee!*" said Greenbloom scornfully. "*This* is the coffee country; from now on we shall drink coffee as black as an Arabian's eye, sweeter than love. Go to the grandstand, Rachel, you will find a *Dames* there somewhere."

"Never!" said Rachel. "I *detesst* them."

They opened the doors and stepped down on to the race-track. The shadows were still quite long and the air was delicately scented with the morning. John looked around him; he had never seen a French racecourse before and at first he was a little disappointed by the lack of any obvious "foreignness" in the architecture: only a solitary flag fluttering above the centre of the grandstand gave any clue to their situation. He looked at the broad vertical stripes and thought of the French Revolution. Visions of the Scarlet Pimpernel, *Le Tricoleur*, of lazy *châteaux*, even memories of Monsieur Camambert and *les oiseaux* filled his head so that he could have danced with excitement on the resilient turf.

"It is ten o'clock." In Rachel's absence Greenbloom was limping impatiently about in front of the Moth. "We must find out exactly where we are. All things considered I should imagine we must have come down somewhere between Rouen and Paris, say between *Chaumont-en-vexin* and *Chantilly*." The words slid like liquid off his tongue and he started a snatch of song:

> "*Auprès de ma blonde*
> *Qu'il fait bon, fait bon, fait bon—*"

he croaked, taking off his helmet and giving it to John.

"Put this in the plane and find me my beret," he said. "It is under the seat somewhere. I am going to get hold of a *paysan* and find out about supplies of *essence* and *les taxis*. We are late."

John found the beret and then ran after him as he made his way up the road running from the grandstand towards the group of trees they had seen. He dropped into step beside him as he put on the beret and hobbled rapidly in the direction of the smoke eddying from a hidden chimney stack.

Behind them someone shouted and they turned around; a small man had emerged from a door at the back of the grandstand. He was carrying a besom and he looked sleepy.

"*Aie!*" he shouted. "*Aie!*"

They turned and hurried over to him as he waited there, looking obsequious but a little dazed.

"*Pardon!*" said Greenbloom rapidly. "*J'espère que nous ne vous avons pas dérangé. Vous étiez en train de faire un petit somme, paraît-il!*"

The man touched his forehead and smiled; he smelt strongly of alcohol but even if his breath had been innocent they would have known by his air of broad complacency, by the sweep of his frequent gestures with the broom, that he had been drinking heavily; and then in confirmation of their suspicions he bowed and beckoned them to follow him into the room from which he had emerged. At the door he paused, bowed again, and ushered them in ahead of him.

The little room was furnished with two or three broken chairs on which sacks were spread, a large first-aid cupboard with red crosses on its doors, a jockey's weighing scale and a trestle table with a pair of binoculars on it.

Greenbloom at once sat down on one of the chairs and spread a *carte routière* across the table. He pointed at it.

"*Combien de kilomètres y a t-il d'ici à la Capitale?*" he asked.

The little man leaned over it unsteadily. "*Français,*" he said, and then rolled with laughter, his thin face assuming a festoon of creases as he rocked about in front of them.

"*Mais certainement,*" said Greenbloom. "*Vive La France!*"

At this the *concierge* stood to attention, his laughter ceased instantly and his face assumed an expression of great cunning. He fumbled in his trouser pocket, brought out a bunch of keys and moving over to the first-aid cabinet unlocked it. He did it with such familiarity that they knew at once the reason for his delay in making his appearance. Quite obviously he had been afraid that the police or his employers had found him out at last; their sudden descent into his bored and bottled morning must have filled him with terror as he sat there drinking the stimulants reserved for injured jockeys.

Watching them a little uncertainly he drew out from the cupboard three dirty glasses and a half-empty bottle of brandy.

" '*Sfine*," he muttered. "*Cognac! Triste arles. Biste.*"

"*Mon Dieu!*" said Greenbloom. "He's drunk."

"What's he saying?" asked John.

"Oh—'*Fine*,' the French for a shot of brandy. The man is so far gone that it's a little difficult to follow him."

He accepted a tot of the brandy, touched glasses with him and drained it at a gulp. "Try and get hold of the bottle," he went on. "Once they're retired these *maquignons* drink like fish."

John slid the bottle behind him on the table and Greenbloom directed the *concierge's* attention to the map once more.

"*Nous sommes descendus par avion. C'est necessaire que nous gagnons Paris sur-le-champ. Combien de kilomètres à la Capitale?*"

"Capital?" repeated the man. "*Oui.*" He looked around for the bottle.

"*Non*," shouted Greenbloom pointing at the man. "*Pas encore! Paris, mon vieux; où est Paris?*"

The effect of Greenbloom's sandpaper shout was instant; the little man froze to attention as Greenbloom got up and stood over him.

"*Ah donne nord nutte'n'at arle bût Paris*," he said rapidly, "*andide nutte ave't faire 'tesse idee ou yeux te boeuf inde donne yeux route.*"

Greenbloom's finger wavered over the map. "*Répétez çèla, lentement!*"

But the *concierge* ignored him and continued to stand before him looking apologetically first at John and then at the map.

"What *did* he say?" asked John nervously. Greenbloom was beginning to bristle with anger. "I am not sure!" He spoke slowly and ruminatively. "Had I been sure I would not have asked the fool to repeat it. I am convinced that he is talking some kind of a patois or dialect which is new to me. He must be a Basque."

He turned on the man.

"*Basque?*" he fired at him. "*Arcachon? Les Landes? Hendaye? Pau?*"

"Pôt?" the man repeated solemnly.

"*Oui-oui*," said Greenbloom. He pronounced it "wayoo-way" and the man looked bewildered for a moment and then he moved helpfully to the door.

"*Lourdaud! Imbécile! Butor! Vous n'avez rien compris à ce que je voulais dire. Il y a combien de kilomètres d'ici à Paris?*"

"*Saint—Jesu!*" said the man and stopped.

With exasperation Greenbloom seized the bottle of brandy and poured what was left of it into two glasses. "*Saint*," he said to John. "You heard him, the idiot can't even say "*cent*" correctly; it's the hideous adenoidal drawl of the Pays Basque. I can only suppose that he's trying to tell me that it is *cent kilomètres* to Paris." He drank his brandy, wiped his lips carefully and then with a patent effort at politeness handed the other glass to the *concierge*, who cheered up at once.

"*Eiffel yeux d'enscrive pour moi*," he said hesitantly. "*Ah'd mai bedouhin mise bist endevoir feu te decouver quoi'te contre yeux fromme, eh tiens—*"

"Stop!" said Greenbloom.

"*'Sieur!*"

"*Un moment! Taisez vous.*" He turned to John. "It is hopeless. We will have to find someone else. I'm beginning to think this fellow may not be French at all. He must be a foreigner of some sort. Go and get Rachel and tell her we're going to find a telephone and get hold of a taxi."

The *concierge* jumped forward eagerly.

"Taxi!" he said loudly and distinctly.

"*Oui.*" Greenbloom's smile returned. "*Taxi, toute de suite!*"

The man nodded vigorously. "*Oui*," he said, drawing out a chair and pointing to it. "*Oui, yeux b'aisseyez—ici.*"

"*Très bien—ici, taxi ici.*" Greenbloom turned to John. "In the most atrocious accent he's telling us that he wants us to sit down in his absence. One presumes that he either owns or knows of a local taxi."

They sat down obediently, waited while the caretaker locked the brandy in the cupboard, smoothed his hair in front of a section of mirror, and finally hurried off down the road in the direction of the cottage whose smoke they had seen.

As soon as he was out of sight they went out in search of Rachel and found her waiting disconsolately by the plane.

"Wherever have you been?" she asked. "I thought you must have gone off to get a taxi."

"Indirectly that is exactly what we did," said Greenbloom. "Within five or ten minutes it should be here."

"Why were you so long?"

"We met a drunken Frenchman," said John, "and Greenbloom—"

"They will have to be careful," Greenbloom interrupted, "a peasant drinking spirits at this hour! There will be a war or revolution or both. Germany will go through the Maginot like a bayonet through Gruyère."

Rachel looked at him sympathetically. "Poor Horab, didn't he give you a drink?"

"Yes, Rachel." He stepped forward quickly and catching her hand bent it backwards so that she leaned agonizingly away from him laughing and crying up into his face. "He did, *ma petite*! He *did* give Horab a drink; but that is not the point. Greenbloom is *not* a peasant—*is* he?"

"No," she said and he at once relaxed his grip. She sprang away from him and spat precisely on to his left foot.

"Pig! *Cochon! Salaud!*" She quivered with fury.

Greenbloom produced his silk handkerchief and wiped his shoe; he smiled at John. "Pretty when she spits, isn't she," he said. "Would *you* like her?"

"Er—"

"She is very clever; she has a superior intelligence; she is intuitive and *always* just one leap ahead of a blundering male."

"I think Rachel is very beautiful," said John. "Particularly in the evening."

Greenbloom grated a harsh call like a corn crake's. "Take her!"

he said. "She will do you good and together you may laugh at me; *this is France!*"

He sprang at her as she stood there small and graceful as some exotic little animal sprung from the grass in the night; he kissed her as carelessly and easily as he would have fondled such a domestic pet, picking her up tightly in his two hands, dropping her back on to the grass; then he walked away in the direction of the road.

Rachel opened her handbag and gazed into the mirror; she looked pale and withdrawn for a moment.

"Horrible man!" she said. "He treats me like an hors d'oeuvre or an oyster."

John laughed. "You like it really, don't you?"

She stamped her foot. "No I don't. I want permanence. I am a Jewess and I am tired of the desert." He watched her as she stood there ruffled and self-absorbed, fluffing at her hair with a jewelled hand. Suddenly she looked up.

"Come here, John."

He moved over to her and she looked around quickly after Greenbloom.

"Yes, what is it?"

"You know where we are?" she whispered.

"No, not exactly; Greenbloom said somewhere near a place called *Chantilly*."

Rachel tittered behind the small expert painting of the lipstick she was applying. "You mean to tell me that you have not discovered?"

"Discovered what?"

She put away her lipstick and powder, "Why! That we are perhaps a thousand miles from Paris."

"*A thousand miles?*"

"Perhaps a little less; but certainly seven hundred."

"I don't understand." He felt his mouth beginning to hang open. "What do you mean? Where are we?"

"In Ireland," she said.

"But—"

"We are in *Ireland*," she repeated. "I found a *Ladies* in the back of the grandstand and there was a large notice giving the rules of the course—dozens of notices. This is the Curragh racecourse and we are in County *Kildare*."

"But that little man, the *concierge*—the flag," he paused and pointed up at it as it fluttered above the grandstand.

"*Irish* both of them," she said. "Green, white and orange, the national flag of the Irish Free State, and as for your little man he may have been drunk but that means nothing. The Irish drink even more than the French."

"But he *spoke* French," said John.

"Are you sure? Horab did not seem to have understood it. Are you quite certain that he was not just muttering with an Irish accent and trying to put a few French words in here and there because he thought *you* were French? Did you, for instance, hear any actual French words?"

"Yes I did: words like *nord* and *devoir* and *arles*—I remember that distinctly because it made me think of Van Gogh."

Rachel laughed, "Oh well, perhaps he was in France during the Great War. He might even have *been* a Frenchman; I believe the Irish sell many of their best horses to French owners. That is just the sort of thing that happens to Horab, or rather Horab is the sort of person who happens to such *things*: he attracts events because he is a prophet."

"But then there was London," said John, "and the Thames and the channel, I saw them *all* from the plane."

"Bristol, the Severn Valley and the Irish Sea; I worked it out from the English map while I was waiting for you. Even if we had crossed the Welsh Mountains in Pembrokeshire we would not have seen them because there was too much cloud. When I realized how many terribly narrow escapes we must have had I was terrified. Some of those great clouds we saw towering above us like white mountains might easily have *been* white mountains."

John shuddered.

"We should have known," she went on, "or *I* should; all the time the sun was behind us, we were flying west instead of east. The wind was behind us too and increased our range and our air speed." She sighed. "Poor Horab! No wonder he is so cross."

"But he doesn't know."

"Of course he knows! At first I was not sure; but when he hurt me like that, when he talked about my intuition as though he would have liked to s-strangle me, then I was quite certain."

"*Were* you?"

"But *yess*! Horab is very male and he hates his women to be right. But quite apart from that this is not the first time such a thing has happened; once we went to Holland by mistake, another time to Guernsey instead of the Scilly Islands; and as you have seen he is very good at making forced landings."

"I'm glad he *is*!"

"Perhaps I should have warned you before we started; but I felt so sorry for you, you looked so s-sad, Johnny, so sad!"

He said nothing; he was trying to account for it all, to shape some coherent design into which everything would fit: the prophet, the departed sense of exhilaration, Wittgenstein, the journey to the east which had taken them west. She stroked his hand again; by this small gesture she re-entered the dizzy world of his speculation. Like everything that had happened she was difficult to know; he scarcely believed in her, she was as unreal as France and Greenbloom's stars.

"But it's been fun, John, has-sn't it? You don't really regret it, do you?"

"No," he said. How soft was her hand, as soft as Victoria's had been before it crumbled to earth in the earth.

"Do you?" she repeated.

Perhaps her hand would not yet be earth; it took a long time. Saints were supposed not to rot and Victoria had been a saint: more innocent than a bird that flies, a flower that blows, and yet more than all the flowers and birds that ever fluttered through the bright air.

"Oh you are *worried*! You are pale and ill with worry. You poor boy, you ate no breakfast and since then Horab has fed you on a diet of s-surprises. Sit down for a minute—the grass is quite dry, sit down."

He obeyed her and she sat down beside him.

"Now," she said, "I'll tell you what you must do. You live in Anglesey, don't you?"

"Yes."

"And you still have Horab's money?"

"Yes."

She opened her handbag. "Give it to me—*quickly*."

He handed the francs and the Reichsmarks to her. She counted them, reckoning on the scarlet abacus of her lacquered nails, and then gave him ten pound notes in exchange. "That is a little more than they are worth; but never mind, with all that money you will be able to find your way to Dublin as soon as we reach a town. If necessary you could spend the night in a good hotel and be, for a time, a real man of the world," she smiled at him understandingly, "and then in the morning you will be able to catch a boat from where-ever-it-is to that place in Anglesey, I forget its name."

"Holyhead?"

"Yes, that is quite near where you live, isn't it?"

"Yes, of course it is." He brightened a little. "That's a wonderful idea! I can just say that I ran away from Beowulf's—I've always wanted to run away from somewhere and I'm sure they'll understand."

"Of course they will. Even if they didn't understand, this would make them, and it will please Horab." She clapped her hands. "Yes, he will be very pleased and it will be useful to *me* when the time comes."

"And to begin with I needn't say anything about Ireland or France or Greenbloom?"

She shrugged. "Not if you don't want to."

"Oh I *do* want to, and one day I will." He was afraid he might have hurt her; he must try and remember that she was real and could be hurt. Now that it was all over, now that he was already walking down the drive beside the golden wallflowers to the cottage in Anglesey, it was difficult to hold on to her existence as a person; she would keep fading. "It's only that I know they're worried about Mick; he doesn't seem to be passing many exams. And then David—"

"Your eldest brother? Oh, yes, I have heard that he was difficult, but then they should know that all the cleverest men are difficult. That is what universities are for, so that young men may be difficult and come to no harm."

"Oxford's very expensive," he said, "and they're not so well off as they once were."

Her little chin stuck out and her lips mouthed a pout of disdain. For the smallest part of a moment he saw her as being Jewish: a tiny wrinkled woman in a shop, bargaining. "If they have not the money they should not incur the expense or the *ris-sk*; a potter does not fire flawed china."

"No," he said.

"Horab, too, is difficult; but he is gifted and after this he is going to be *terrible*. If I am to manage him at all I shall need to be alone with him."

"Because of his mistake?"

"Yes. We shall have to keep up the pretence that this is France all the time until we leave. Horab will drink nonstop until we are out of Ireland; he hates it, he calls it the Island of Taints! It upsets his whole philosophy and he won't be able to write about or even to quote Wittgenstein until we are safely out of it. I am quite sure that at this very moment he will be drinking poteen or something with that little Irish jockey. That is what is delaying him."

"How on earth will you manage?"

"Oh, I will let him drink just enough to keep him confused, and all the time until we leave I will pretend to act as his interpreter, talking to such people as we meet in patois. He will know that I'm not really, but it will save his face." She paused. "Not exactly that, you know. Horab is not afraid of being thought foolish; it *iss* simply that he has to be protected, like all great thinkers, from the unrealities of life, what Wittgenstein calls—"

John got up. "Do tell me," he said, "who *is* Wittgenstein?"

From her place on the grass she blinked up at him a little abstractedly.

"Wittgenstein is a comparatively young philosopher who was born in *Vy'enna*, educated there and at Charlottenburg and Cambridge. It was money well spent; he published his first work in 1921, and though it owes something to your Bertrand *Russ-ell* —a ssilly materialist whom Horab despises—it attracted great attention from the logical positivists."

"I'm afraid I've never heard of them. Couldn't you just tell me what Wittgenstein really believes?"

"Oh!" She stood up stiffly, swaying a little as she found her balance. "I don't think anybody really *knows* that; and Wittgenstein would not *want* them to! You see, he is a mystic who believes that mystics can express nothing that can ever really be understood by anybody. He says that his book was intended to draw a limit to the expression of thought; and at the end of it he says 'that whereof one cannot speak, one must be silent.' This excites Horab very much; it implies that by mathematics and logic the true meaning of the whole of the New Testament is beyond man's power either to *express-ss* or to understand."

"Really?"

"But yes."

"Do you mean that it isn't true?"

"Not at all. It is neither true nor false, it is simple a mistake, something that could never convince because it concerns things outside the limits of the thoughts which can be expressed."

"And is that very important?"

"To Horab it is very important, and to millions of others too, because, if Wittgenstein is right, then they are not waiting for something that has already happened. Horab does not like waiting even for things that are *going* to happen; it makes him very angry."

"Then why does he hate Bertrand Russell if he is a backer of this Wittgenstein man?"

Rachel frowned, the contraction of her eyebrows was as quick as the shuffle a bird gives its wings when it is cold. "Oh John, there is no *time*. Tell me, are you feeling better now?"

"Yes, thank you." He was for a moment a little nervous of her. "I'm sorry to go on about it all, but somehow all this France and Ireland business seems to be connected with Wittgenstein. Everything has happened so strangely since yesterday afternoon. Later on I'll have to try and sort it out and then it may not be possible to ask questions because I suppose I may never see either of you again?"

She turned her back on him and began to walk over to the road. When she spoke it was as though she were speaking to herself. "Horab, you *may* see; I know you will hear of him! But I'm afraid it is true that *we* may never meet again."

He stayed where he was and called out to her. "You sound very sure!"

"I *am* sure—very soon I shall be leaving England. I am going back to *Vy'enna*. I am going to get married."

She walked on and leaned her back against the white rail of the racecourse.

"Married?" he called out. "Who to? To Greenbloom?"

From where he stood he saw the quick secrecy of her smile as she answered, "No. Not to Greenbloom—to a friend of his."

"But—" he said.

Behind them they heard the braying of a motor horn; they turned simultaneously and faced the group of trees which received the end of the narrow white road. In a few moments a very old Citroën came rolling out of the shadows, kicking up the dust as it bounced along over the flints. When it drew nearer they saw that Greenbloom was driving and that the caretaker was sitting beside him singing happily.

John hurried over to Rachel as the car drew up.

"Ah, *merveilleux!*" said Rachel. "How lovely to ride in a Citroën again! With this we shall soon be in Paris."

From his place beside Greenbloom the caretaker favoured her with a splintering smile and then burst once more into song:

> "*Eau pray de ma blahndie,*
> *Kale Fé Bongh . . . Fé Bongh . . .*"

he sang. He stopped suddenly and, putting an arm around Greenbloom, said, "*aise tarte mi leur French. Arme chantan' French sang.*"

Greenbloom ignored him. "We are not going to Paris," he said thickly. "Get in everyone. We are going to collect petrol in the village and then we are leaving by air."

"But *mon cher!* It is so beautiful here." Rachel climbed under the rails and leaned through the window of the Citroën. "John has not seen anything yet; he has not even seen *Le Tour Eiffel.*"

"He will see it later. Tomorrow he will see the Tower of Beni Hassan in Rabat. I have decided to move on south to the

Desert. There is no time to be lost; we have telegrams to dispatch and there is much to be done before we take off." They got in silently and Greenbloom turned the car. John whispered to Rachel, "Where is Rabat?"

Greenbloom turned around, "Rabat is in French Morocco," he said curtly. "No distance at all from Paris. We shall fly south, refuel at Cannes and cross the Mediterranean this evening."

He put his foot down on the accelerator and the Citroën swept away with them into the cold shadows underlying the throng of the trees.

5. Rooker's Close

No movement but will make its havoc
In the moted air. Have you watched the stir
Of dust behind you on the stair, the hassock
Yield its quota to your prayer?

"What I can' unnerstan'," sang Cledwyn Jones in his Rhondda English, "iz why the old man iz censorin' all the letters this past faëw weeks. Humphrey takes them up to his study before breakfast an' *he* brings them down and hands them out *purs'nally*; he never ewsed to do it, well what for's he doin' it now?"

Across the table Stuart winked at John. "It's a mystery, 'Cardiff,' old boy! He's probably got on to your police record in South Wales; agree, Bowden?"

"Yes," said John, remembering his new name just in time. If only Stuart weren't so invincibly Public School with his confounded surnames. Across the top of his coffee cup Cledwyn's little Welsh face was watching him closely.

"Well, I think you may be right there, Jimmy, but I'm bettin' it's not me he's on to. I'll swear it's somethin' to do with John here."

"Why?" asked John casually, watching the waitress at the far table.

Cledwyn looked cunning and it suited him, "Something Humphrey said, that's why."

"Oh, *Humphrey!*" said Stuart. "Humphrey, the Homo Henchman, what did he say?"

"I ask him what was the idea an' he squeezed my arm—"

"Big thrill—"

" 'Ee squeezed my arm and said, 'Ask Mr. Bowden, sir; Mr. Bowden should know.' "

"Horrible hints!" Stuart drawled. "The plot thickens! Mys-

281

tery at Rooker's Close among Mr. Ikey Victor's strictly public school, strictly arseward—that is to say backward—young gentlemen." He blew out a cheekful of Turkish cigarette smoke. "Trouble with Jones is that he's always looking for intrigue an' dirty goin's on in the woodshed, isn't he, Bowden?"

"He's Welsh," said John, trying to look disinterested. He gestured at the waitress, "I wouldn't mind a date with her, would you? Haven't seen that one before, wonder where Flora is."

"The usual," said Stuart, "she suffers terrible, poor gal."

But Jones was not to be deflected; chewing his square fingers, a habit which enraged John, he continued to observe him carefully.

"Beginnin' of term," he went on, taking advantage of a corner of skin on his thumb, "there was a policeman in with the ol' man, an' ever since 'e's been censorin' our letters and what Cledwyn wants to know is why. 'E has no right to do it. He even censors Peter's from the bank, so there must be something funny goin' on."

"Rot!" said John. "It's only the special constable racket. He likes to keep in with the police, all Jews do, and with Victor it's part of his English pose like his interest in cricket and the trench fever nonsense every time he gets a stomach ache."

"Shake!" said Stuart. "Still, he must have been somewhere near the front line at some time or another or he wouldn't have got a wound stripe."

"Probably an explosion in the lats," said John. "Well behind the lines. I only ever met one Jew who would have *fought* in a war—"

"And that was *Greenbloom*!" said Stuart. "Don't tell us, we know."

John reached out for a biscuit.

"If you'd met him—" he began.

"Hey! Steady on with the biscuits, you've taken the last."

"It's O.K., I'll order some more! 'S'one way of getting introjuiced." Jones got to his feet and sidled over to the waitress. They saw the jaunty smile, the overbrilliantined hair, almost the cock of a little tail.

Stuart looked at John.

"*Not* strictly public school, Bowden," he said, "but I suppose one must learn to mix."

"He's all right," said John, "he can't help being Welsh."

"I bet they've got plenty of money."

"Must have, or he wouldn't be here. Old Nosy sticks the fees up every term. Still, he gets results."

"Does he, hell! I very much doubt if he'll ever get *me* through. I've failed the entrance exam three times already and this is my last shot. If I get ploughed this time the governor is threatening me with a job in a bank like dear little pansy Peter."

"How awful!"

Stuart's face twisted. "God! He *is* a drip."

"Poor devil!"

"There but for the Grace of God—! Bowden old boy, you've only got to lose your father, have nice blue eyes and flaxen curley-wurls and get landed into Rooker's Close at the age of twelve by your doting mummy and you're there for life with a brand new daddy!"

"Not me! I'd have walked out years ago."

"That's what you think! But suppose your dead daddy had settled money on you, bonds and bills of sale," Stuart gestured with his hands, "and supposing he'd made old Stinkbomb a trustee and that Mummy had ever such great faith in a fine converted churchman like Mr. Gilbert Victor, what then?" He looked up as Jones resumed his place. "We're talking about Peter," he said.

"Man, he's pretty! But he serves for Father Delaura Sundays and that lets you out. If it weren't for Peter you'd all be running around the altar with bells and candles every Sunday in the term."

"Personally I like my Christianity in small doses," said Stuart, "and not mixed up with bedtime kisses from the old man."

"It's a funny setup when you come to think of it," said Jones.

"Unhealthy!" said Stuart. "Worse than a public school. Mind you, I think it's only fatherly affection gone wrong; but all the same, if the old —— started trying to buss *me* every night after I'd said my prayers I'd let him have it right in the—"

They were both a little shocked by the coldness of his tone, the venom which distorted his dark-eyed face; but it was a pleasurable shock like an execution.

"What about Humphrey?" suggested John.

"God knows! He's obviously a homo: signet rings, belted overcoats, face lotions and pointed shoes, *and* he's in the old man's confidence. My governor'd bust an artery if he knew the half of it, but I don't tell him." He glanced at his watch. "Talking of which, what about this afternoon, Jones? Are you game?"

"Every time! Every time, man!" Jones patted his pocket and it jingled. " 'Ear that? That's for the petrol and there's enough over for whatever blows up at the tea dance."

Stuart turned to John. "What about you?"

"No thanks, I'm not risking it. One of these days you'll both get nabbed."

"In *Worthing*, perhaps! He's got choir boys, dog collars and church workers planted all over the town, to say nothing of dear Humphrey's Saturday afternoon off from his so-called buttling; but Brighton's as safe as houses."

"What exactly are you going to do when you get there?"

"The usual: pick up a couple of women at a tea dance, spend as little as possible on 'em and then run 'em up on to the downs. Come on, join us and share expenses!"

"Not likely! What's your excuse this time?"

"The match! Mr. Leveson-Gower's Gentlemen versus The County. All we've got to do is to buy an evening paper and memorize close-of-play scores. It's a cinch!"

John shook his head.

"Yellow! That's what 'ee iz," said Jones.

"You're dead right, I am. Victor's been watching me like a cat lately." He realized his mistake a little too late. Jones had started to chew his thumb again and the narrow eyes were on him.

"Juss what I said! *An'* it's something to do with the letters."

"Oh, for God's sake!" groaned Stuart turning his back on him. "We must get organized. What are *you* going to do, Bowden?"

"I'm going down on to the beach to bathe."

"Oh, the leg show! Time you grew up old boy; never get anywhere just *looking*."

John dissembled. "It's better than nothing; besides, I'm making progress. One of 'em smiled at me three times last Saturday."

"What's the good of that? We'll be paying for more than *smiles*, won't we, Jones?"

"You certainly will when the old man catches you," said John.

"Bull!" said Stuart. "You're the one he'll catch. Instead of drooling about on the beach with your tongue hanging out, you want to go in and win."

"There's something in that, but until I feel a little less fatherly interest radiating in my direction I'm playing safe."

"What did I tell you?" said Jones. "Bowden is yellow an' I'm bettin' it's for a good reason." They pocketed the last of the biscuits, paid the bill and sidled out into Montague Street.

A vigorous breeze was blowing from the front, and as they passed the side streets they could just see the bright blue bar of the sea over the promenade wall and the small silhouettes of walkers bath-chairs and kiosks against the skyline. "Half an hour till lunch," said Stuart. "Just time to get Mavis to put on a few records in Marks and Spencer's and then fill up the Sphinx for the afternoon's frolic."

Later, they drove back along the wind-swept front, down Grand Avenue with its exotic fir trees, and turned left into Mill Road. They parked the car in front of the yellow plate:

GILBERT VICTOR, M.A., L.C.P.
PRIVATE TUITION

and walked up the short drive to the house.

In the conservatory, its mildewed vine covered as always in the summer with bunches of minute green grapes, they met St. Clair on his way out. They neither liked St. Clair nor disliked him; he was all right, but only just. For one thing he was an R.C., and that, as Stuart put it, was "unhealthy"; in addition, and this had more to do with their attitude, he was resident in the town—a Worthingtonian.

He lived with his malarial mother in a flat somewhere between Mill Street and the Western Promenade, no one quite knew where. His father was in Malaya in the consular service and the breakdown in his mother's health had meant the end of his education at Beaumont College and his subsequent arrival at Rooker's Close during the preceding term. He was thus in two senses cut off from them, and rightly or wrongly they felt that he disapproved of them and that consequently he was not to be trusted. There was a certain smugness about him which angered them: though he never talked women or smut he never betrayed evident disapproval when they did so themselves, and though at such times his silence was not ostentatious they could not help noticing that he never troubled to laugh at their jokes. Religion was the only subject on which he could be drawn; and for this reason because he seemed to enjoy arguments about Henry the Eighth and the Inquisition, because he seemed always to be vastly amused by the fact that Mr. Victor encouraged them to serve at the altar of St. Jude's, they seldom gave him the satisfaction of discussing the pros and cons of Roman Catholicism.

But today, warm from their recent conversation about the plans for the afternoon and quick to the suspicion that for all they knew St. Clair might himself constitute one of the hidden threats to their safety, they were all disposed to challenge him. The sight of him; his pink serene face, the neat wad of books under his arm and the hint they gave of orderliness and domesticity within the ambience of the town which was at once their delight and their enemy, enraged them. Instantly, at Stuart's first words to him, they were united by a quiet antipathy.

"Going, dear boy?"

"I am; why?" St. Clair's smile was vexatiously certain.

"Are you sure you've got everything now, Patrick?"

"Quite certain thanks."

"*The Aeneid?*"

"Yes."

"Monday's maths?"

"Yes."

"Last year's papers?"

"Everything, thank you very much."

Stuart paused; St. Clair's good humour was patent.

"And St. Clair—?"

"Yes Stuart?"

"Have you been to your confession? Have you cleaned the slate, dear boy, so that you can make a fresh start on Monday with all the lovely little sins that it's such fun to commit?"

"I have."

"Good! How very convenient."

"Yes," said St. Clair, "it is. But you've no idea how I envy *you*, Stuart. You won't forget to say a little prayer for me tomorrow, will you? The old man tells me you're assisting at the seven o'clock in the morning."

"Am I? Hell! That's dear Peter's privilege."

"Oh no, Stuart! Not according to *my* information. Peter has been promoted to the little heresy that takes place at eleven o'clock with vestments and incense as laid down in the fortieth article of the New Faith and recently defined by an Archbishop of Canterbury." He smiled happily. "So you won't forget me, will you, Stuart? You'll look so beautiful at that hour and I know that you will mean well despite your invincible ignorance."

"Only lend me a rosary, St. Clair, and I'll play with my little beads all through the service." He sniffed the air. "But come, we mustn't keep you from your devotions or the Pope might feel a draught. Tell me, St. Clair, what are we being given for lunch today?"

"League of Nations pudding, I should imagine. Isn't that the usual fare on a Saturday?"

"No doubt, no doubt. Well, don't forget now, make a good confession!"

"I shall, Stuart."

He turned and they saw him mount his bicycle outside the conservatory and disappear around the red-brick wall which separated Rooker's Close from the road.

"I wonder if he was joking," said Stuart. "If he wasn't I'm going to put a stop to this somehow. Trouble is that with a dog collar in the family it's so damn difficult to approach my governor; though what on earth good he thinks all this serving nonsense is going to do me, I can't think. Haileybury made me decide to bring up my children to be free-thinkers if I'm lucky enough to have any; a few more terms in this place and I'll make damn certain they'll grow up into happy little atheists."

"Well, you should tackle the old man, isn't it?" said Jones. "Tell 'im you won't do it."

"Don't be a fool! If I were to cut up rough over this he would cancel his permission for me to run the Sphinx. I had a big enough job wangling it in the first place; practically had to pretend that I thought I might be getting a vocation."

They heard Humphrey beating the gong for lunch and hurried upstairs to the bathroom.

"Keep it light at lunch!" Stuart whispered as they made their way to the dining room. "Bags of interest in the Brighton cricket."

Humphrey opened the door for them and stood to one side as they passed him. As always at this time of the day he had on his black uniform and his servant face; he smelled faintly of silver polish.

At the far end of the table Mr. Gilbert Victor sat squarely over the dish cover; and beside him, very upright, his blue tie bearing out the blueness of his eyes, sat Peter. In some scarcely definable way he contrived to enlarge the authority of Mr. Victor; they were, the moment they saw him, made more sensible of their lateness, of their failure to conform to all that Mr. Victor expected of them.

They took up their places silently and Mr. Victor stood up.

"Oh Lord bless this food to our use and ourselves to Thy service."

Jones and Peter joined him in making the sign of the cross; so much for his Welsh Methodism, thought John as he compromised with a wave of one hand and noticed that Stuart ignored the ritual entirely.

Mr. Victor smiled automatically at Humphrey and the dish cover was removed to reveal the Saturday silverside and its surrounding suet dumplings.

Mr. Victor's bristling eyebrows drew closer together as he sharpened the carving knife and began to carve.

"Water, please!" Stuart nudged John who looked over at Peter apologetically.

"Water, please, Probitt."

Peter passed the carafe and the glasses were filled. Plates of silverside began to arrive in front of them and they helped themselves to cabbage and mashed potato. Suddenly Stuart spoke again, "Good morning at the bank, Probitt?"

Peter glanced at Mr. Victor, who did not look up, and then smiled his most open smile.

"Splendid, thanks."

Mr. Victor patted his hand.

"Peter is going to play tennis this afternoon," he announced.

They made approving noises and Mr. Victor glanced down the table sharply.

"Rooker's Close is to be represented at the club courts this afternoon. I wonder what are the plans of Haileybury, Beowulf's and Cardiff?"

"We rather thought of the cricket, sir, didn't we, Jones?" said Stuart.

"Yes, sir. Thought it would be a very good match, sir, we did," sang Jones.

"At Brighton?"

"Yes, sir."

Mr. Victor frowned. "A very long way to go surely, and a long way to return?"

"We have the Sphinx, sir." Stuart was disarming and they laughed carefully.

"I rather fancied there might be a *lady* in the case, Haileybury."

"Oh, no, sir."

"I had even supposed that you might, this Saturday as last, want my permission to accompany her on her travels?" Not looking for any reply, eating with a sudden raw gusto, they waited; but Mr. Victor ate on for a few moments leaving them in suspense as they chewed busily at the red beef and white cabbage.

At last he spoke.

"Are all three of you proposing to—watch the cricket?" he asked with a fractional hesitation.

"No, sir." John watched the expert manipulation of Mr. Victor's knife and fork.

"What then are Beowulf's intentions?"

"I thought I might have a bathe sir."

"In Brighton?" The question was very quick.

"Why no, sir."

" *'Why no, sir.'* " With a side smile at Peter, Mr. Victor mimicked his satisfaction. "Why not, sir? May I ask?"

"Because I prefer to bathe here in Worthing, sir."

"Because perhaps you do not trust the lady with the four wheels, *Bowden?*"

"No, sir, not that; but I like the Worthing beach."

"He likes the Worthing beach," said Mr. Victor in a tone which suggested malice and charity at the same time. "Very commendable! So, my dear Beowulf's, do I; and so I know does Peter, though I think *we* prefer it in the winter when it is not so crowded, don't we, Peter?"

"I think it *is* preferable, sir."

Mr. Victor wiped his lips on his table napkin and attempted to conceal a small belch as he did so.

"I am sorry that Peter will be unaccompanied on the courts this afternoon. But Saturday, after all, is Saturday, and as long as we remember that it precedes Sunday we shall come to no harm. What time are you proposing to return from Brighton, Stuart? You know our rules here?"

"Yes, sir."

What guts he had, thought John. He looked as insolently innocent as he did when in church.

"Then you will of course be back for the evening meal at eight o'clock?"

"Of course, sir, as long as the Sphinx doesn't let us down."

"That, naturally, is *enigmatical!*" punned Mr. Victor without waiting for Peter's laugh. "I shall look forward to your account of the afternoon's innings. No doubt, between you, you will regale us all with it during the meal?"

"We shall watch like hawks, sir, won't we, Jones?"

Jones of course was common; his coarse acneiform skin was giving him away. He was as red as the piece of silverside he was eating.

"Closer than 'awks!"

"It will then be unnecessary," went on Mr. Victor smoothly,

"for any of us to go to the expense of buying an evening news-paper."

Once again they turned their attention to the salty food on their plates, but their silence did not discomfort Mr. Victor; it was what he was accustomed to achieving. John thought of him as a snake who expected his rabbits to remain still.

"And after the account of the match we must retire in good time for the morning service. I rather hoped that you, Stuart, would be able to assist Father Delaura at the seven o'clock? Peter is fortunate enough to be assisting at the sung Eucharist at eleven." He repeated the little belch into the napkin and over its white folds the sweet green eyes were directed at his victim. "I take it that you will not refuse?"

There was no doubt of it, his sudden flush as he replied made Stuart look even more handsome. "No, sir."

Mr. Victor rang the bell for Humphrey and they ate their way through the League of Nations pudding to the accompaniment of slightly warmer conversation.

Afterwards, Mr. Victor stuffed his pipe with Player's No Name tobacco and stood by the mantelpiece with his short arm resting across Peter's shoulders. They swayed gently together for a few moments like passengers on a ship, and then Mr. Victor's arm dropped a little wearily to his side. He puffed out a gout of tobacco smoke and his black eyebrows drew together over the caverns which now concealed his eyes in the darker part of the room. He crooked his finger at John.

"In a few moments, Bowden, I would like to have a word with you in my study."

"Yes, sir."

"If you are sure you can spare the *time*?" He paused so that the question might not seem purely rhetorical. "I would like to see you in ten minutes—*in* the study."

"All right, sir."

With a last pat at Peter's buttocks Mr. Victor made for the door.

Humphrey, of course, was there on the other side of it wait-ing to open it for him. Leaving a trail of tobacco smoke behind

him, they heard him patter across the hall to his ground-floor
sanctum.

They looked at one another.

"What's the idea, Probitt?" asked Stuart as soon as the door
closed.

"What idea?" Peter smiled defensively. His blue eyes flicked
over to Humphrey and back as he busied himself with the crumb
tray.

"Letting me in for the seven o'clock, of course; I've done it
six times this term already."

"You'd better ask the governor, hadn't he, Humphrey? It's
not my fault if Father Delaura wants me to do the eleven."

"*Duw!* 'e's in a black mood," said Jones. " 'Oos been bitin'
him, Humphrey? *You'd* know, isn't it?"

Humphrey, whose bent back had been all attention every
nuance of their conversation, straightened himself and faced
them. "*I* don't know, Mr. Jones; if you'd been 'ere longer
you'd 'ave bin used to 'im, wouldn't 'e, Mr. Peter?"

"I've been 'ere äyeteen months, man, an' I know enough to
know there's trouble with 'im. Someone's been scandalizin', that's
what. What's 'ee been 'earing about Brighton, eh? What's he
meanin'? *Duw anwyl!* Anyone'd think as we weren't *going* to
the cricket the way he carried on all through the beef and
puddin'."

"Where else would he be expecting you to go, sir?" The
question was for Jones but the glance that accompanied it was
directed at Peter. "What else could they do in Brighton on a
Saturday, Mr. Peter?"

"Exactly," said Peter yawning pleasantly. "Stuart and Jones
should not worry so much. Anyone would think they had uneasy consciences, wouldn't they, Humphrey?"

"They might indeed, sir," said Humphrey with an exchange
of smiles. "After all, there was the regatta last Saturday, the
Concourg D'Elleganse the Saturday before that, and there's the
cricket, *this*; and they were all in Brighton. It's a long way to
go to do nothing; there must be some attraction."

"What yew meanne?" Jones's coarse little face reddened. "We
did see the regatta and we *did* see the Car Parade—"

"Oh shut up, Jones," Stuart said quickly. "They're only pulling your leg, they know damn well we saw them, and it's none of their business if we didn't."

"Mr. Bowden's goin' on the beach," said Humphrey suddenly leaning and smiling into John's face and squeezing his forearm gently.

Peter made for the door and paused.

"Don't forget the governor's request, Bowden. I think he meant it," he said.

"I don't need you to tell me that," said John.

"Trouble!" said Jones as soon as he had gone. "An' Peter knows what it's all about. Told you there was trouble this morning. It's the letters, it's all connected with the letters, that's what!"

"What letters is those, Mr. Jones?" asked Humphrey.

"No letters," Stuart intervened coldly. "If you've finished in here, Humphrey, we won't keep you."

"I've quite finished, thank you, Mr. Stuart. I've got to get finished in the pantry yet and if I'm to catch the bus in time I'll have to look slippy. I'm planning a nice quiet afternoon with my friend—" he paused to gain the maximum effect—"watchin' the cricket at Brighton."

He whisked the cloth off the table, folded it over his arm and left them alone.

"There you are!" said John. "They're on to it, all the lot of them. Cledwyn's quite right, someone's been talking; you've been seen. It may be nine-tenths guesswork on the old man's part; on the other hand it may be nine-tenths certainty and if you take my tip you'll watch the cricket this afternoon till your eyes bulge." They turned to him, searching for words; but he could not wait.

"I must go," he said over his shoulder. "I'm just wondering what the old pig's got up his sleeve for me."

"Let us take a stroll in the garden," said Mr. Victor as soon as John entered the study. "The antirrhinums are doing very well this year; so far neither rust nor moth hath corrupted them."

"No, sir."

"You remember the quotation, of course."

"No, sir—I mean yes, sir."

Mr. Victor smiled. "He who hesitates is lost, Bowden; always remember that."

He opened the French windows and they stepped out into the walled garden. They made their way in silence across the grass to the gap between the yew hedges, and in the sombre enclosed space where clumps of antirrhinums surrounded a central rose-bed they sat down on the white seat.

Mr. Victor stretched his short arm along the back of it, pulled at his pipe and subjected John to a long meditative stare.

"Though the very walls have ears," he said, "I think there is less possibility of our being overheard out here than in my study."

"Sir?"

"You may smoke if you wish, Blaydon."

"Thank you, sir."

He did not blink at the use of his own name, though after so many months of being Bowden it sounded strange to him. Gratefully he accepted a South African cigarette from the proffered case; he hated this particular brand but the gesture was conciliatory and therefore a good omen.

"About the letters, Blaydon; no doubt you realize why I have been forced to take over the delivery of all letters in recent weeks? You really must ask your intimate friends to be more careful in addressing their envelopes and to remember our circumstances here. In the past fortnight no less than three letters have arrived addressed to the pupil named *Blaydon*, and with the possibility of renewed publicity that name is still likely to be fresh in people's minds."

"Yes, sir, I'm sorry about it. The trouble is that I can never be quite sure who's going to decide to write to me and unless my father remembers to change the envelopes or include them in his own letters, there's always a chance of a slip."

"In addition, as you may or may not know a sergeant of police called on me the other day."

"*Did* he, sir?"

"You are surprised?"

"I didn't know they were still interested, sir."

"The police are always interested in an unsolved murder and in a case as tragic and brutal as that in which *you* had the misfortune to be involved, you may be sure that their interest will continue until they are sure either of the identity of the culprit or else of his death. The police never forget, Blaydon. That is a terrible thought, isn't it?"

"Yes, sir." Facing the dark yews across the brilliance of the rosebed, it *was* a terrible thought. He spoke quickly. "What did he want, sir?"

"The sergeant was anxious to refresh his memory on certain points in the record of your evidence at the inquest nearly three years ago. I told him I was not prepared to give consent to an interview until I knew the attitude of your parents."

"Thank you, sir."

"Fortunately, I was able to discover that what I had suspected from the first was true; I am not a special constable for nothing! The sergeant's interest proved to be personal rather than official; he is an ambitious young man out for further promotion, and after I had reminded him of my acquaintance with his superintendent, I found it comparatively easy to deal with him."

"Yes, sir." He wondered how long he would have to continue to sit there saying "yes, sir" and "no, sir," at regular intervals. He was longing to escape to the beach and the gay people who knew nothing of Mr. Victor, the moors or the police.

"But that is not why I wished to talk to you this afternoon, Blaydon—not directly. No less than your temporary change of name, your time at Rooker's Close was intended not only to spare you the discomfort associated with that dreadful case, but to help you resume your normal rôle in life and to strengthen your faith."

"I see, sir."

This was not Gilbert Victor, or Gilbert Stein, or whatever his real name had been before he changed it; this smooth patter was a language and a disguise which he had assumed as easily as in other circumstances he would have talked German or acted the part of a Sussex squire. As tragedians or clowns the Jews were the greatest actors humanity had ever produced, he thought, even Greenbloom.

"I have noticed of late, Blaydon, that you are tending to spend all or nearly all of your spare time by yourself?"

Mr. Victor's arm was removed from behind him, it swept past his ear and came to rest on his thigh. Through his deep-set, mournful eyes its owner gazed into his face.

"You see, John, I understand you, I see into you as I see into all my young men. I had the idea of you from the very first, even before you ever reached Rooker's Close, before you came hesitantly in your new grey flannels into my study on that first day of the Easter term." The fingers on his thigh fell with a soft emphasis. "Poor Rudmose's earlier letters had been very informative and I kept them all most carefully; he too—and I know that he rests in peace—understood you perhaps better than you know, and I think it was largely the tone of those letters of his which persuaded me to take you in the first place."

"He was very kind to me, sir."

He must remember to pray for Rudmose sometime; it was always so much more satisfactory praying for people who were quite definitely dead; one felt that it could not possibly do any harm to one's faith because if it were without effect at least one never knew it. And if anyone needed prayers it was a suicide. He thought of Rudmose waiting there on that last night for the London express to thunder over his thin neck on the railway running parallel to the canal.

"I know he was, John, but sometimes I wonder if you appreciate kindness. There are certain emotions, moods, unusual temperaments which only very few people understand. Some people appear to themselves to be doomed to loneliness from the time of their adolescence, and in their attempt to evade it they may suffer terribly. You may be just such a person, John; you *may* be! But there again who is to say how much of the Prince of Denmark's singularity was due to his father's death and how much to the heredity his mother conferred on him from the womb?" He broke off and his hand was suddenly removed to his pipe.

"All is not well with you, Blaydon, all is not well, is it?"

"I don't know what you mean, sir."

Was all well with Rudmose? he wondered. With Peter? With Mr. Victor himself or with anyone alive or dead?

Mr. Victor got up with surprising swiftness as though the garden seat had suddenly become too hot for him.

"This evening, John, I want you to go to your confession. Do you understand me?"

"I don't think I do, sir."

Mr. Victor leaned forward and took his arm.

"We will circle the roses," he said. "To move in a circle is very elemental; it is very soothing. Never forget that the universe itself was set by its Maker to travel in circles."

John got up and side by side at a gently increasing pace they began to move around the rosebed.

"Until now, I have not cared to ask you to serve at St. Jude's like many other past and present Anglo-Catholic resident-pupils. But I really think that the time has now come for you to get into the way of it again; your father told me in one of his letters that you used to serve fairly regularly between the ages of twelve and fourteen?"

"Have you heard from my father recently then, sir?"

"Naturally, or I would not have suggested this to you. First I want you to make your confession, John. We must be spiritually purged before we presume to assist at the high altar. Father Delaura, although he does not insist on preliminary confession, does, I know, prefer his servers to avail themselves of the sacrament at frequent intervals."

"My father said I needn't make my confession until I felt like it."

He was tired of the whole thing; all he wanted was to forget about everything not immediately connected with the present. Today was Saturday and a few hundred yards away was the beach.

"Even Protestants acknowledge the Ten Commandments and 'honour their fathers and mothers in the days of their youth.' *Your* father has evidently changed his mind; very possibly he has prayed for guidance in making his decision."

It was Mother of course; he couldn't very well explain that to Victor, it would take too long; and in any case being a Jew, a convert and a bachelor he could not possibly understand that a woman, and a clergyman's wife at that, could ever rule a household as she ruled theirs. Mother must have decided that a little spiritual pressure should be put on him and had probably dictated the letter which Father had written. He was more determined than ever that he would not go to his confession without making some show of resistance.

"But the doctor, sir. *He* didn't think I ought to go yet."

"That, if I remember rightly, was some time ago. You have certainly seen no doctor in the past eight weeks of the present term."

The voice, remorseless and inexorable, continued to enunciate the syllables beside him. They moved gently together from sun to shadow and then back into the sun again as they circled the inside of the standing yews. Mr. Victor's hand had now rested so long above his elbow that the heat from it was perceptible to his skin. The smell of his pipe smoke, bitter because it had reached the wet section of the tobacco, made him feel sick. It stirred the memory of the sergeant's pipe in the far-off days of punishment drill at the Abbey; it reminded him of the escape to David's wedding, and of Victoria.

"After all," his voice was high and strained even to his own ear, "*I* didn't do anything, sir. I did nothing; I want to forget it. It's two years ago and I want to be left in peace. I don't want to make my confession. *He* should make his confession; they should find *him* and make him go to his confession before they hang him. That is what they should do." He took in a deep breath. "But even though they'll never forget and though *I'll* never forget, they'll never find him, *never!*"

Mr. Victor had stopped. John saw his blurred outline in the shade cast by the tall hedge. There was silence and his pipe lay neglected in his hand.

"I am sorry, John, that it should have been necessary to upset you like this. Your response to my suggestion only makes me feel more sure than ever that it was and is a good suggestion, that your need of absolution is very great."

There was no more that John could say.

"But quite apart from that, there is your mother's point of

view, and *that* is expressed in this letter." Slowly he produced a letter from his pocket, clean and uncrumpled; he held it out and John saw the familiar, eager handwriting.

"Need I read it to you, John?"

He felt the infuriating prick of tears behind his eyelids. Mr. Victor spoke very softly.

"Peter has very kindly arranged to go with you to Father Delaura at five o'clock this afternoon and I have suggested that you might have tea together at Bobby's at four-fifteen."

"Yes, sir."

"You will not keep him waiting, will you, John? Peter is a very unselfish boy and is giving up a part of his afternoon on your behalf."

"That is very kind of him."

"Very well then, there's no more to be said. I have some writing to do in my study, so I must leave you now."

He walked away as far as the yew hedge gap where he stopped and turned.

"And Bowden?"

"Yes, sir."

"They *will* catch the criminal, you need not fear—sin never goes unpunished."

The olive-grey face turned, the hooked nose was no longer silhouetted against the dark hedge, the dumpy short-necked figure passed out of his sight and he was left alone standing in the rose garden beneath the cloudless sky.

He lay prone on the high terrace of the pebbles, his head pillowed on his folded arms. Below him he could hear the shouts of the bathers as they tumbled in the sea and all about him were the casual voices of the beach parties: the laughter or wails of young children, the clucking of mothers, and the irascible tones of fathers down for the week end. The sun was warm on his back and he dozed indulgently, enjoying the unreality of the voices, the sense of detachment which is experienced when the eyes are half-closed and the body relaxed.

It was extraordinary how easily the world receded under such circumstances; trivial remarks overheard, the most banal of conversations, assumed the immediate poignancy of an out-of-date photograph or gramophone record so that it became increasingly difficult to believe in the importance of anything, and the whole world, the entire generation of one's own time, became unreal and somehow purposeless—no more momentous or meaningful than the calls of children at play.

In the wind which blew from the direction of the bandstand he could hear the muted blare of a military concert and nearer at hand the flapping canvas of the bathing tents lined up below the promenade. By opening his eyes he could see the group of girls whom he so ardently longed to know and to whose conversation he had listened greedily nearly every week end for the past eight weeks.

He knew their names now: there was Audrey of the brown skin, always sunning herself scientifically and delighting in having someone massage sun-tan oil into her back. There was Sheila, a nearly silver blonde of exquisite fragility, who rarely bathed but always posed herself on a cushion with her knees drawn up to her chin as she sat no more than ten yards from his speculative eye. There were two or three others, not such constant beach-fans, casual droppers-in who would arrive with shrieks of greeting, stay for a time making up their faces or running down for a quick peck at the sea and then departing as gaily and suddenly as they had come. He thought of them idly as migrants like the swallows arriving at the twitter of noon, skimming the sunshine of the day and then loudly and rather churlishly going off about their small, perpetually delightful and exclusive concerns.

There were too, of course, the men, rarely the same ones for long, who made up the numbers at different times.

Together the parties provided a never-ending source of pleasure to him, a pleasure sharpened with the salt of pain in his longing to join in their remote and apparently eternal gaiety, to be one of their number: a Jack or a Bill rubbing oil into Audrey's back or twitting Sheila about her shyness of the water, cracking easy jokes and making retorts at which they would be bound to laugh; and then casually, as though it were nothing at all, making a date for the same evening or the next morning.

Profoundly, he desired to be older, different, not so serious, to be able to speak their facile language and be a master of their unself-conscious behaviour. So much did he long for this ease that his isolation and the fact that he dared never properly get to know them because of his increasing terror of Mr. Victor, were both a comfort to him, a barrier behind which he could shelter, dreaming impossible dreams which he would never have to act out.

He tried to persuade himself that one day when he *was* older, as patently mature as a Bill or a Jack, as bouncingly slick as a Kit or a Tony, he would automatically inherit the franchise so obviously enjoyed by all whose education and surveillance was finished and done with; that he would be able to assume the sureness of purpose and ease of manner which was theirs. But secretly he knew that this would never be so, that all his life he would have to guess at behaviour, walk carefully and watch as narrowly as a tramp at table.

They were quite friendly towards him nowadays, quite often smiled at him when there were no other men with them; and he was sure that sometimes they wondered about him, that they even talked about him when his back was turned, when he made his way down to the sea, or went into his tent to change before returning to Rooker's Close. They probably wondered why he was so remote, why, on the one occasion they had offered him a cup of tea from Audrey's thermos flask, he had so diffidently refused it.

But he knew they were not greatly interested in him, that unlike nearly all the other odd men of their acquaintance, he did not count; at sixteen he was too young for them. His arrival never occasioned the least change in their attitude to one another, whereas it had often amused him to see that the appearance of their own escorts invariably had its effect on their relationship.

Sometimes they would be dull, scarcely speaking to one another, their conversation monosyllabic and snippety, their self-preoccupation as intense as that of cats at a saucer; then, the moment one or two of their men had arrived, they would become gay and alert, newly fond of one another, sitting close together, enjoying shared and tantalizing jokes which no matter how hard they were pressed they would not divulge. Later, when the men had gone, their vivacity would for a time be sustained like the brightness of a blown ember and would take quite some time before it dimmed and let them relapse into their former dullness.

At other times there would be quite a contrary effect; they would be sharp with one another, glancing brightly when they spoke, collecting their things with terrible efficiency and politeness and saying good-bye elaborately when it was time for them to separate. He would be left wondering if they would ever return together again; whether, abandoning their strange friendship, they might not part finally and cease to be the nucleus of so many arrivals and greetings.

But always, in the course of the week, their differences would apparently be resolved and he could find them there together as he had found them this afternoon, unruffled, gay and secretly very busy about something which entailed doing nothing save only sitting, talking and waiting under the bright blue sky.

Lying there, his eye at the level of the smooth globes of chalk and slate which made up the beach, he could see Audrey's thin brown foot and watch the restless movements of her toes as she talked to Sheila.

He followed the course of the leg up to the rounded knee, glimpsed the bright cover of the magazine which rested upon it and the lacquered nails of the hand upon the open page; but he could not see her face, only the fuzzy halo of her hair in the bewildering sunshine. He closed his eyes against the blue-white glare and listened contentedly to the fall of their conversation.

" 'Bout thirty, p'raps twenty-seven; *you* know, mature!" Audrey's voice was desultory, pretending to disinterest. "But you'll see him when he comes, if he *does* come! He said he'd be here by three-thirty. I wasn't all that interested, he danced well of course, does a wonderful feather step in the slow waltz, and he was—well, *amusing*. So I said he could use the tent if he wanted to, sort of casual; I don't think I even said we'd be here for certain."

Sheila's yawn was ostentatious, it was breathed out briefly from beneath a damping hand.

"How long is he staying?"

"Don't know, never asked him. I shouldn't *think* he's a weekender." She turned a page of the magazine. "He said it'd depend on how he liked his hotel."

"Oh, he's at a *hotel*, is he?"

"Imperial." This time Audrey yawned. "Got quite a nice car too, one of those ones with straps on the bonnet."

"How did he—? I mean how did you—? Who introduced you?" asked Sheila.

"Can't really remember."

"Surely you didn't—"

Audrey's interruption was quick and was accompanied by the flick of another turned page.

"Oh, yes, I can. It was that boy of Bill's sister, Tony What's-his-name, the one with the little moustache. *He'd* met him in the American Bar and brought him along to our table. I knew it must be something like that, but I seem to meet so many that it's hard to remember." She hummed a snatch of song. "Surely you didn't think I let him pick me up without knowing his name or anything about him?"

"What did you have to drink last night?"

"Two gin-and-limes. Why?"

"Oh nothing." Sheila was watching a ship on the horizon. "I just wondered if you had a headache, that's all."

"Do I look as though I had a headache?"

"Not 'specially, but you sound a bit like it."

"Well, you shouldn't be so nosy. You don't find *me* going on when you've met a boy and wanting to know every least detail of when and where and how." Audrey paused and then with an obvious effort at sweetness asked, "Is Jack coming? Did he make any date for tonight?"

"He can't get this afternoon; but I said we'd be at the club as usual, that's if you haven't made any other arrangements with anyone else."

"No, not yet, but I suppose I may before tonight."

They were silent for a moment; their battles were like those of hens, he decided, a flurry of beak and claw almost instantly concluded and leaving them strolling about aimlessly and with unchanged expressions.

Sheila was now attending to her cuticles with an orange-stick while Audrey was reading her magazine.

"Listen to this," she said suddenly, " 'I am in love with a married man who is twice my age, his wife is in a mental hospital and he says the doctors hold out no hope of her recovery. He wants me to become engaged but he cannot get a divorce yet. Do you think I should allow him to anticipate our engagement until we are sure.' "

They both tittered.

"Fancy *asking* anyone," said Audrey, "and the way she puts it 'anticipate our engagement.' "

"Oh, they make them up," said Sheila, "or else people send them in for a joke. Bill had a friend once who sent in a letter asking for advice about superfluous hair; it was a scream because really he was growing a moustache."

"Silly!" said Audrey.

"You ought to write in about your new boy friend; trouble is you wouldn't get an answer in time as to whether it would be safe to let him date you so soon after meeting him. By the way, what's his name? You never told me."

"Desmond Something-or-other. I keep telling you I wasn't that interested; he's not my type, he's much more your cup of tea like those tobacco advertisements."

"Oh, go on! Mind you, you've quite piqued my curiosity. I'm really beginning to hope he will turn up soon."

"Well, if he doesn't he won't find me here," said Audrey, "it's half-past three and I've something better to do than sit about here all afternoon waiting for him."

"Shopping?"

"No, my perm, I'm going to Jeanette's at four-fifteen for a Marcel wave."

"Lucky thing! I've always wanted to have a perm."

"If you ask me your hair's your best feature."

"I'm glad you think so."

They fell silent once again and John heard the little rasp of a file as Sheila manipulated it expertly against the points of her long nails. Three-thirty, he thought. If he were to meet Peter at Bobby's in three-quarters of an hour it was time he had his bathe. He got to his feet and the two girls smiled over at him.

"Going in?" asked Audrey.

"Yes. What's it like?"

"Like it always is— lovely once you're out!"

He laughed. One of Bill's jokes or Tony's, he supposed. But how sweet they looked sitting there on the brown pebbles: butterflies on a wall flashing their colours in the sun, talking butterfly-talk. Behind them fat, red women humped along the promenade in cotton dresses and cardigans. How would these ever becomes *those*? It was natural history upside down for butterflies so light and airy to turn into such heavy red caterpillars, he thought as he made his solitary way to the edge of the water.

They would think him standoffish and queer for his lack of response, but it could not be helped. One day perhaps some similar pair, though not quite so common, would be awaiting *his* arrival with expectancy, quarrelling quietly about him and brushing their antennae together like tiny flexible rapiers. In a dull, automatic way he would probably marry one of them and down the years watch her turning slowly into a fat, red woman like those others.

His thoughts dissoived as he plunged into the water and swam out swiftly beyond the farthest of the shouting bathers. Turning around he saw that the beach had receded and enlarged. He was astonished at the extent of it and at the rapidity with which it had become at once panoramic and Lilliputian like the pictures they sold in the postcard kiosks. He was unable to distinguish the particular breakwaters between which he had been sitting. Sheila and Audrey must be one of the many tiny groups of coloured mould growing on the brown strand; but he was quite unable to know which group, and although he was no more than three hundred yards from the shore it now seemed utterly absurd to suppose that any of their concerns really mattered in the very least. Yet their conversation was as loud and clear in his mind as though he were actually still hearing it. What they had wished for, wanted or feared, the thousand implications of the things they had said were as large as they had ever been, had not diminished in the slightest degree.

He lay on his back and floated face upwards so that he saw only the sky above him bleached by the enormous light of the sun. Tonight he had to make his confession to Father Delaura and he was still dreading it.

Hitherto he had never made his confession to anyone away from home and he associated the rite more closely than anything else with his family and the parish church: Mother, dragging them all off at the end of Lent to her latest protégé—she changed her confessor even more often than she changed her doctor; the distribution of the little cards by Father the night before, little cards on which all the possible sins were neatly tabulated under their separate headings. There were consolations of course: the gaiety of the supper afterwards, the exaltation of conscious virtue in the mysterious but assured cleanliness in which it was so hard to believe. At home confession, like going to the dentist, had its cosy ritual quality; but here in Worthing with only Rooker's Close awaiting him at the end of it, how different it would be.

God, presumably, was everywhere; and though He was so far removed, higher even than the sun, upon His ears the longings and the self-accusations of the human mould upon the beach must fall intimately and urgently. He *must* care and if he did and could in some way cleanse the past, then it was a small price to pay to have to transmit one's cries through the narrow, effeminate ear of Father Delaura.

He rolled over on to his stomach in the glazed surface of the sea and swam back to the beach.

Audrey's friend had arrived, he saw, as he passed the two girls and went into the tent he had hired. He glanced at the man with some interest as he passed, but he saw only his back. He was squatting on his haunches facing them and John took in only the breadth of his shoulders beneath the close-cropped head, the full, sharply creased trouser legs and the blue suède shoes.

Inside the tent he listened eagerly, hoping to discern above the flapping of the canvas the nuances of the new conversation. He thought of the stranger obscurely as a rival, a rival in more than the ordinary sense; someone whom he might himself be when he was older, someone equipped with all the perquisites at present denied him: self-assurance, a motorcar, leisure and golden good looks.

Drawing aside the curtain a little he peered out. The man was taking a photograph; whistling softly, he was peering down into the view-finder of an expensive camera and the two girls were posed casually together just in front of him: Sheila with her hands clasped in front of her ankles and Audrey leaning back on her outstretched arms with an enormous sun hat flopping over her neck and shoulders. They were both very self-conscious, strained and determined to seem unimpressed. They were making the ironic jokes people always make when they are confronted by a camera.

The man himself was preoccupied, thoroughly enjoying himself, getting the utmost pleasure out of his advantage. John saw him stretch out a hand and grasp one of Audrey's ankles to move it a little further into the centre of his picture. He noted the flash of his blue eyes as he looked up at her and made some brief joke. The intimacy of the gesture both chilled and enraged him. Conceited fool! Why didn't he get on with it? It was only a snapshot, no need to make such a to-do over it; but of course that was just what he wanted: to hold all their attention, flatter them, and from the moment of his arrival assert his male superiority and establish an intimacy to which they must respond.

They *were* responding; the empty-headed little asses were laughing at him and with him, they were jostling each other and each of them was trying to steal the greater share of his attention.

John closed the tent flap and started to dress. If he were quick he would be in good time to meet Peter. He would have a cigarette in the sun and then make his way to Bobby's.

The stranger had spoiled the afternoon: he was just the type of man he loathed most, experienced and cocky. Everything about him—the sharp crease in his flannels, the blue shoes and the golden hair—led him to a sharper appreciation of his own inferiority. He was just the sort of man who *would* own a fast car and stay in luxury and leisure at southcoast hotels picking up girls on the beach.

Outside he heard a pause in the conversation and laughter, a pause that was filled in by the repetition of the man's whistled tune, an idle speculative trill: three notes full of a sort of self-love and contentment, three notes curiously evocative, reminding him of something, of someone. He stiffened: the wind brushing the tent, the creaking of the framework, the continuous wash of the sea and the shouts of the swimmers receded. He was in a cave; it was dark, and through the darkness he heard the clatter of feet moving through water, was sensible of the pause and the silence which precedes communication and received once again with all of his hearing the notes of the whistle, the same vain, lazy notes he had never heard repeated until this moment.

All of her death, all of his love, all of his hatred, rose up within him black and choking so that for a moment he swayed within the airy greenness of the tent and put out his hands blindly before him, seeking for some means of physical support against the dynamic of his emotion. He shook his head slowly from side to side, hearing the measure of his own breathing so remotely that he seemed no longer to be within his body but to be watching it from afar with a completely detached compassion. And the day came back to him, once again he knew where he was and what had happened: Victoria's murderer was at this moment sitting outside the tent in which he stood, only twelve paces away from him.

He knew this with a greater certainty than if he had seen the man only yesterday in the full light of the sun. One upward glance of the eyes over the camera, the upward flash of the eyes above the torchlight; the set of the head upon the shoulders in the car, the blazered back and the close-cropped golden head he had seen as he came up from the beach; these things and many other paired apprehensions too numerous to be named had now been finally sealed and signed by the notes of the tune whistled over two years ago—and today.

He stepped out of the tent on to the wide terrace of the pebbles and stood for a moment in the wind and sunshine. He did not know what he must do; he did not know what he would do; something of him lingered behind him in the tent, in the moment of realization he had experienced within it. A part of him, an aspect of his sensibility, was divorced from the present in which he moved, so that he felt himself to be ageless, living simultaneously now and in the past; and the knowledge gave him an extraordinary sense of power. Whatever he did it would be right; if he did nothing, he would give himself no offence; if he confronted the man and turned him over to the police who were still searching for him, he would be no more than the passive instrument of a terrible justice. In himself, for the first time since he had grown up, he was nothing, need do nothing, and yet could do anything and be sure of doing right.

He sat down unsteadily, his knees trembling as he bent them beneath him. With cold hands he sought for the packet of cigarettes he kept in his coat pocket and drawing one out placed it between his lips.

Beside him the stranger got up.

"I think I'll risk it," he said; and if his voice had changed it had changed only in the way that recollections become more like themselves when the need to recall them is banished by the actuality of the thing recalled.

"Are you coming in with me, Audrey?"

"No, we'll watch. Once is enough for me."

"Come on! I'll teach you the backstroke."

"Not today, please, Desmond! Just look at me, I've got gooseflesh as it is; it's this horrible wind." She blinked up at him in the bright sunlight. "I told you to come early, you've missed your chance now."

"My chance of what?" He was stooping and running his hand over her brown back.

"Swimming with me of course. What else?"

His hand lingered on the full curve of her shoulder muscle; John saw the thumb and index finger contract until their knuckles blanched.

"OW! You pinched me!"

"Did it hurt?"

Even from where he was John could see her eyes had moistened in response to the pain, that pleasure hung briefly in the laxity of her mouth.

"You don't know your own strength," she said with aggrievement. "I'll have a bruise there for the rest of the summer."

"A souvenir!"

His swimming trunks swinging from his idle hand, he moved off towards their tent. John got up and walked after him. He felt nothing; he felt as though he were floating in the strong wind which blew from the sea, as though he were being impelled weightlessly over the pebbles. In front of the door of the tent he put out a hand and touched the blue sleeve of the man's blazer and he turned around very sharply.

"Excuse me! Could you give me a light please?"

There was a flash of teeth above the brown chin.

"Certainly!" The cigarette lighter was proffered; the flame licked the top of his trembling cigarette, but he did not draw on it.

"Do you remember me?" he asked.

The little cap extinguished the flame and the lighter was abruptly withdrawn.

"No, I don't think so. Ought I to?"

John removed the unlighted cigarette from between his lips.

"Do you remember the caves?"

"*Caves?*" The smile had gone but the teeth still showed.

"Yes, the caves. Victoria! *The murder!*"

"You're crazy. *What* caves?"

"You know," said John. "You murdered her in the caves. She was a young girl. Don't you remember? You strangled a girl called Victoria Blount in the Stump Cross Caves in Yorkshire three years ago. The police are still looking for you. I'm John Blaydon and beeause I was with her just before you did it, I know it was you. You'll have to come to the police with me straight away."

The man put a hand on his shoulder.

"Look! I think *you'd* better see a doctor—you've had too much sun."

"No," said John. "I knew it was you when you whistled. Please don't make it difficult for me. Don't you *see?* I'm not making a mistake. I don't want to do this, because it's too late now, it can't do any good for anyone; but if I don't do it, the way things have happened, I shall never be sure. If I hadn't moved, if I'd let you go, I know it would have been all right; but I didn't let you go, so you will have to come with me; you'll have to give yourself up."

He moved in front of the entrance to the tent. Beyond the man's shoulder he was aware of the attention of the girls. They had turned around and were watching, trying to overhear; but he knew that they couldn't because he and the man were both talking so intimately.

"Get out of the way, son!"

"No! You'll have to come to the police with me. If I've made a mistake, if you think I've made a mistake, why don't you come? It will only take a minute or two."

"You silly little sod! Get out of my way I tell you."

A hand grasped him by the lapels and he was thrust to one side with horrible violence. The stranger disappeared inside the tent.

John stepped forward to the entrance.

"All right! I'll send the girls for the police and I'll wait here until they come. I'm sorry, but I can't let you go—not *now*."

There was no answer from inside the tent; he watched the nooses of the cords which fastened the flaps being drawn slowly tight from the inside and made his way back to the girls.

"Whatever's the matter?" asked Audrey. She turned to Sheila. "He looks queer, doesn't he?"

"He looks all right. What were you talking about to Desmond? Did you want him to light your cigarette?"

"He's stolen my wallet," said John, lying with immediate inspiration. "I saw it in his pocket and he won't give it back to me. I want one of you to go and get a policeman—there's one on duty on the promenade. If you don't mind I'll wait here while you get him so that your friend can't escape."

They looked at him with astonishment.

"Your wallet? Are you sure?" asked Sheila.

"Of course I'm sure." He was impatient. "Do you think I *want* a scene! For Heaven's sake hurry up and get a policeman—*please*. It has all my month's pocket money in it—five pounds."

"But he can't have stolen your wallet. He's never been near your tent."

"How do you know?" he asked. "You haven't been with

him all the time. He might have taken it from the back of the tent on his way to the beach. He was late getting here, wasn't he? He's a stranger—you've never met him before, have you? It would be easy to dodge down below the edge of the promenade and put a hand under the tent. And anyway, my wallet's in his pocket."

Sheila got up.

"It *could* be! You did only meet him yesterday, Aud, and there *has* been a lot of pocket picking this summer. Anyway, if one of us is going to go for the police it'd better be me because I've got my clothes on."

"Don't be silly," said Audrey. "There's three of us to one of him. We don't want our names in the *Worthington Gazette*. I'll soon see about this." She ran over to the tent and they followed her.

"Desmond!" she called and they waited. "Can you come out a minute? It's Audrey, there's been a misunderstanding—"

There was no answer, and Audrey turned to John.

"He must be very annoyed," she said, "and I don't wonder. But if you're quite sure—?"

"I am."

"Well then, you'd better go in. If he starts any trouble we can soon get help."

John undid the fastenings and pulled aside the flap of the tent. "Come out!"

They peered in: the tent was empty. The canvas at the back had been neatly divided by a sharp knife, and through the rent, vibrating coarsely in the wind, they could see the legs and feet of people passing on the promenade directly behind.

"Well, if that doesn't beat everything!"

It was Sheila who had spoken, and with a strange concerted impulse, a desire to ascertain what was already quite certain, they followed her as she stepped in to the barren rectangle.

"I told you I didn't like the look of him from the very first."

Audrey bit her lip. "It's a Corporation tent!" she said. "We'll have to pay for it."

"That's nothing! What about this boy's wallet and the five pounds? Now we *shall* be in the papers."

They stepped out into the sunshine again. They felt isolated, quite separate from everyone else on the beach, disposed to take some positive action but quite unsure of its nature. They noticed little things about one another's faces and mannerisms. They were both embarrassed and indifferent.

Sheila was the first to speak. "It just shows," she said.

"It shows what?" asked Audrey keenly.

"*My type*, indeed! I wouldn't have taken up with *him*, introductions or no introductions. He couldn't even look us in the eyes when he was talking, and I don't wonder."

Audrey opened a beach bag and, taking out a packet of cigarettes, lighted one.

"Well you made enough fuss of him when he was here taking the photographs. You even wanted him to take one of you by yourself." She hurried into the tent again as though she were seeking a hiding place where she would be safe from Sheila's reply. They heard her voice.

"I wonder if he's pinched anything else—I left my handbag in here."

"Oh, *there* you are, Bowden!" Behind them someone had spoken and John turned guiltily.

It was Peter, immaculate in white flannels, his pink face glowing with tennis and disapproval.

"There's been a theft," said Sheila.

"A theft? What of?"

"Oh nothing," said John quickly. "I'm sorry I was late—I'll explain on the way back."

Sheila was looking at Peter with interest.

"Are you a friend of his?"

"I hope so."

"Well, he's had his pocket picked. We were all lying here on the beach and a man friend of my friend Audrey's joined us; he was a stranger really—"

"He wasn't," said Audrey emerging from the tent. "I was introduced to him last night at the Imperial—"

Sheila frowned at her, smiled at Peter and went on, "All right then, he was a friend of Audrey's and he joined us about half an hour ago and somehow managed to steal your friend's wallet."

She turned to John. "You saw it in his pocket didn't you, and it had five pounds in it."

"Five *pounds.* Are you sure, Bowden?"

"Yes, just about. But look here! Oughtn't we to be going? The old man said we had to be there at five." He wanted time to think behind the lies he had been forced to tell.

"*Quite!*" This was Peter's latest expression. He had picked it up from the other cashiers at the bank. "But I don't think we ought to leave things like this. Five pounds sterling is the dickens of a lot. Mr. Victor will be very worried if we don't do something about it. Have you reported it to the police?"

"No." It was Sheila again and John was beginning to feel like a Punch and Judy operator who finds that his puppets have come to life and are involving him in terrible difficulties with the audience. "That's just what I was going to say." She paused for effect and smiled up at Peter. "Perhaps we ought to introduce ourselves? I've seen you before of course, but I don't expect you remember me. I sometimes come to the tennis club with a friend of mine for tea—my name's Sheila Miller. If you like I'll come with you to the police station."

Peter coughed. John wondered why he always made him think of *Three Men in a Boat.* He realized that thoughts so trivial, so minimally caustic, should not arise at such a time; but he had observed before that when people were subjected to stress they very frequently had recourse to trifles. He had heard of people endangering their lives by searching for collar studs on sinking liners. Peter was still apologizing.

". . . kind of you, Miss Miller, but I think I ought to discuss it with Bowden here first. You see, in a way I am his senior—little difficult to explain just now. Thank you for all you've done though—er, when did this man disappear? Did he say he was going—make some excuse or something?"

"No," said Sheila. "He only said he was going to have a bathe so we offered to lend him our tent and he went in there to change and never came out again." She twitched aside the tent flap. "You can see what he did. He just cut open the back with a razor or something and went straight out on to the promenade.

By now he'll have packed up his bags at the hotel and be off in his car somewhere else."

"The Imperial's only two minutes walk from here."

"Exactly," said John. "That's why I didn't want to waste any more time." He did not want to mention the word "confession."

"I think the best thing we can do is to keep our appointment and I'll report the whole thing to Mr. Victor when we get in."

He moved away eagerly and saw that the action had had the desired effect on Peter, who, torn between embarrassment and politeness, was standing hesitantly in front of the two girls.

"Quite! Yes, I think you're right, Bowden."

"Well, come on then!"

"Er—good-bye and thank you very much, both of you."

"Oh, that's all right," said Sheila. "If you want us you'll always find us here. We'd like to know what happens, wouldn't we, Audrey? It'll teach us to be more careful next time, and all that. He must have been a real criminal, so convincing, so quick with his lies and his razor."

"Don't be stupid," retorted Audrey. "Nothing's proved yet. I bet if people started accusing you of stealing you might do just the same as he did, supposing you had the brains to think of it."

"That's as may be! But personally I thought he was nasty from the moment he arrived." Sheila smiled at Peter again. "I always go by first impressions, don't you, Mr.—"

"Probitt," said Peter. "Er—Peter Probitt."

Good God, thought John, she's interested in him; she never asked me *my* name.

He turned around and whistled vulgarly at Peter between his teeth, accompanying the summons with a jerk of his head towards the promenade.

Peter's smooth forehead creased with vexation.

"Have some manners, Bowden," he said angrily, and then, extending his hand to Sheila, "Well, thank you, Miss Miller. I don't know what will come of all this, but if necessary I'll get in touch with you later."

As they touched hands Audrey turned away and started to gather together the beach clothes. With some element of the sorrow he was unable to feel for himself or for the murderer, John found that for a moment he was able to be sorry for Audrey. He turned away and began to climb the steps to the promenade. Peter followed him and together they made their way along it.

For some minutes they moved towards the pier without speaking. John resisted the urge to walk in step with his companion and continued to progress obstinately and in disunity by taking one and a half small steps to every pace of Peter's. Obscurely, he felt that he was handcuffed to him, that the people they passed must be aware of the guilt with which Peter would surely be clothing him; that such people must be embarrassed to see him being led so ignominiously home to Mr. Victor via Father Delaura and his confession.

He even fancied that as they approached, other persons on the promenade swerved a little to one side and looked the other way; and though with one part of his mind he knew the fancy to be absurd, with the other he continued to justify it because in a deeper sense he knew it to be true.

Peter knew that he had been lying about the five pounds, or that if unknown to Mr. Victor he had indeed possessed such a sum then it must either have been dishonestly acquired or purposely concealed. Peter must also be quite certain that he had struck up a guilty friendship with Sheila and Audrey and would now be convinced that his real purpose in visiting the beach had been to develop it. In this way, Peter, partially wrong in each of his conclusions, was nevertheless right in his assumption that John was a liar.

The lie had been forced on him by his unwillingness to account for the disappearance of the stranger, and this reluctance had in turn arisen from the terrible associations he had wished to forget; but centrally his lie had made the whole of him suspect to such an extent that he was unable to know how much or how little he was blameworthy.

In this state of mind his only comfort lay in the fact that he felt Peter himself to be involved in the consequences of the guilt which had spread outwards from the act of the murderer two years ago. Peter's smugness would lead him to further arrogance;

though some was due he would give no credit at all to John's
motive in lying; he would enjoy the power the lie gave him both
with regard to John and to the favour he would expect to find
with Mr. Victor; without ever realizing he had done so, he would
harden his already complacent heart and be for a time insensible
of the harm that had been done to him.

Walking along through the wind past the cream-painted hotels,
the green balconies and the scarlet fusillades of the Council
geraniums, this idea enchanted John. He extended it gradually
to include the people who passed them: old ladies in basket-
work chairs, humble, dazed-looking people in poorer clothes sitting on the official seats and in the bare glass shelters. He saw
them all as being unwittingly involved in what had happened;
all in greater or lesser degree guilty, and only very few of them
knowing it. He at least, he thought with a sudden jubilation, was
not ignorant of his guilt and what was more was on his way
to his confession, would shortly be approaching One who must
understand and who, though He was not given to weighing
merits, was at least as capable of it as of pardoning offences.

They turned down to St. Jude's Church and for the first time
Peter spoke, "You know, Bowden, if you really did lose five
pounds I think perhaps I ought to go straight to the police after
I have introduced you to Father Delaura."

"I'd rather you didn't."

"I'm sure you would! But frankly, I think Mr. Victor would
say it was very slack of us to have delayed so long—I suppose,
by the way, he knows you had the money? I mean there's no
chance of our concealing it from him?"

"No, he does *not* know."

"Really?"

"Why should he know everything? He's not *my* guardian.
If my people like to send me a little money, it's no business of
his."

"But then, of course, one of your girl friends might report it;
in which case—"

"They're *not* my girl friends—I'd never spoken to them before this afternoon."

"But they distinctly said that this pick-pocket fellow had

joined you when you were all lying together on the beach?"

"No, they didn't—or at least if they did they didn't mean we were lying there *together*." He waved at the people on the promenade and spoke slowly and emphatically as though he were explaining something to an imbecile. "These people, all of them who are walking on the promenade with us, are not *with* us, not really. An idiot, or someone who was deliberately trying to distort the truth might suggest that they *were* with us; but surely you can see what I mean?" His venom had the desired effect; Peter flushed. He braced himself so that he walked more uprightly and self-confidently.

"That's what they *said*, Bowden! I must say I was surprised. Mr. Victor usually gets to know of these things and quite apart from that, in view of his great interest in you, I didn't think that you were as ungrateful as—the others."

"As *what* others?"

"Stuart and Jones." He committed himself reluctantly and John seized his advantage.

"I don't know anything about Stuart and Jones, and if I did I'd keep it to myself, *really* to myself. They're not afraid of anyone, they know perfectly well what the old man's attitude is and they also know that there are plenty of people to carry tales and think the worst."

"That's a little beside the point. A thing like this could be very damaging to Rooker's Close, and lying about it isn't going to make it less so. I think you'll have to make a clean breast of it when you get back and conceal *nothing*. It's the least you can do if you are determined to prevent my telling the police."

"Oh, the police! I'm sick of the police."

"In any case," went on Peter smoothly, "I think you'll find Father Delaura will agree with me. You'll naturally have to mention it to him during your confession, won't you? After all, you did lie about the amount of money you had and I'm sure that if you asked him, Father would agree that Mr. Victor ought to be told."

"Hell! Who on earth do you think you are, Probitt? My confession's got nothing to do with you whatsoever; I'm not even sure that I shall make it."

"That's your own affair, Bowden. I was only pointing out that there's no need to make things unnecessarily difficult for *me*. I have to do what is right, and surely once you've made your confession you can't object to my telling Mr. Victor about this afternoon?"

"Oh no, not at all. Go ahead! I wouldn't spoil your party for the world. Tell him everything, enjoy yourself and be sure to mention the girls. If you like you can say you *saw* me sun-bathing with them or even patting their bottoms; I don't mind. If that's all that's worrying you, you have my full permission to trot straight back, knock on the old man's door and tell him the whole juicy story." He paused and turned as they reached the lych gate of the church. "But I think, since we're now in the Holy precincts, that I ought to tell you one thing."

Peter, cleaner and straighter than ever, tried to pass him, but John moved in front of him.

"No, listen! I'm being Christian, let me finish. I think I ought to tell you that whatever you tell him he won't punish me. Do you understand? He won't be in the least angry, not in the very least. He may love *you* more afterwards, I don't say he won't; but he won't punish *me*."

His face as he said this was bright with glee; in a few minutes he was going to be absolved from everything, old and new. He would confess even this, the "malice and uncharitableness" which he was so enjoying. Afterwards, he would be different, would even love Peter, but now it was quite in order to hurt him for his infuriating and blind interference. He danced ahead of him over the gravel into the cold stone porch and waited.

Probitt joined him.

"I don't know what's the matter with you today, Bowden, but I do think you ought to try and control yourself at a time like this."

"But I *do*. I *am*! All the time I'm controlling myself. You've no idea what thoughts I'm throttling, what words I'm strangling, what deeds I'm denying myself. Only God knows."

Probitt walked over to the door.

"Shut up!" he whispered. "Someone will hear you."

"I hope they do, I want them to; it's just why I've come."

Ignoring him, Probitt walked ahead past the table with the pamphlets and money boxes on it, past the alcove with the ornate font, to the central aisle where he paused and genuflected before the distant altar. John followed him and caught him up halfway down the nave.

"Where are you going?"

"To get Father Delaura; he will be in the sacristy."

"You mean the *vestry!*"

"Father Delaura likes it to be called the sacristy. I think you'd better wait here, Bowden; I'll be back in a few minutes."

John kneeled down in the nearest pew and placed his hands hopefully together. What he had said about wanting to be heard was now already, he realized, untrue: he was in no mood to make his confession to anyone, least of all to a clergyman like Father Delaura. The whole idea of approaching him in this alien building so far from home filled him with a sense of drawing-room shame.

It was too late to turn back, too late even to do anything further about the murderer, if it *had* been the murderer; he was here in the church and in a few minutes he would have to go creeping over to the prayer stool in the side chapel and say something. He could always confess to a few lies of course; he didn't even have to think of the particulars of these because they were as much a part of the business of living as tips for waitresses.

Above the rood screen, an enormous crucifix impended with the dead Christ hanging upon it: a neat hole in his side, a fallen head, and wounded feet and hands scrupulously devoid of blood. His eyes took in the figure carelessly, wandering from the neatly placed feet to the plaited thorns crowning the wooden hair.

They ought to have shown the thieves as well, he thought, one on either side of Him. Perhaps they ought also to have shown Barabbas passing before Him on his way to another town.

Barabbas had been a murderer and had been released. God must have known that he would be released because if he had not, Christ, who was himself God, would have been reprieved; the cup *would* have passed from him and a problem posed somewhere between Heaven and earth that would surely have proved insoluble even to God. But God took care of His own; He never made mistakes, and if this afternoon he had allowed another murderer to go free, then presumably it was only what He Himself had intended from the first.

He could not see that it was anything to do with *him* and he wondered whether or not he ought to mention it at all in his confession. Had he been cowardly? He did not know. Had he been merciful? He had not felt any real compassion for the man, only pity for himself, the secret pity he always felt deep within him when he saw someone else punished. Quite distinctly, however, he remembered that he had felt guilty. Walking along the promenade he had felt his guilt to be so pervasive that it had embraced not only everyone they passed but the whole town and the whole world as well.

He did not feel guilty now; he felt only bewildered and tired. The figure on the Cross high above his head *looked* significant, looked as though it held the secret answer to all his confusion; but he could not come at it, remained far below it, separated from it by a dimension more considerable even than time.

He rose hurriedly to his feet as the vestry door on the right of the aisle opened to admit Father Delaura and Peter to the nave. John walked over to them and Peter introduced them.

Father Delaura was shorter than he had appeared from the height of the pulpit and the perspective of the chancel. He was very pale and his grey eyes were deeply recessed beneath a lined forehead partially hidden by a black biretta. He reminded John instantly of the Inquisition and he shook the cold hand as reluctantly as he shook the hands of doctors and dentists.

Peter stood there prominently for a moment, fussing around him like a rabbit which had produced a conjurer; and then, making a series of deep genuflections to the altar, he turned and left them and made his way down the long nave.

Father Delaura told John that he would be ready quite shortly and then went across to the Lady Chapel.

For the second time John kneeled down and started to make his preparation. It was now obviously imperative that he should cease his vain speculations and make up his mind what he was going to confess. Father Delaura was patently expecting him to produce a reasonable tally of sins and unless they were forthcoming he might easily suspect him of withholding things; of making what Uncle Felix termed a "snide confession."

From the Lady Chapel he heard the creak of Father Delaura's chair and an impatient, unfettered cough. Without thinking he got up and started to walk down the aisle. He had decided that he was not there, that nothing he was experiencing was really happening at all. What moved down the aisle, what genuflected a little unsteadily to the altar and then took its place beside Father Delaura was no more than the animal puppet of his will. Once there he had no further interest in it, would let it say or do what it would, while he himself remained aloft and remote, as remote as the wooden effigy on the Cross high above the rood screen.

From his new distance which was yet a proximity to the event closer than any he could otherwise have achieved, he noted that the priest's chin was sunken on his surplice, that he smelled faintly of tobacco and that the lines on his forehead were grey-green.

Father Delaura pronounced some preliminary prayers, the muttering came to an end and then John heard his own voice beginning to stumble out the syllables of a quite unreal guilt.

"I have lied, I have sworn, I have been lazy, I have been impure. I have—"

"Go on."

"I have thought improper thoughts, I have been dishonest."

"When?"

"When I was at school."

"Recently?"

"No, Father."

"Did you steal money?"

"Yes, I think so once."

"Have you returned it?"

"No, Father—not yet."

"How much did you steal?"

"I can't remember, it was so long ago." He thought of Greenbloom and Rachel and, as the silence lengthened under the vaulted roof, waited to hear what he would say next.

"Go on."

"There are so many things: laziness—I hardly ever say my prayers—I find that I hate people, that I'm always hoping that something will happen to them. I don't seem to be able to look at girls without—"

"Without what, my son?"

"Without thinking about them in the wrong way."

"Habitually?"

"Not always, Father, not as much lately."

"How long is it since you made your last confession?"

"I can't remember, Father."

"You must remember, my son, you must try to remember. When you come to your confession you must be sensible of occasions. It is not enough to be general."

"Yes, Father."

"We must not dwell on our guilt; but in order that our contrition may be real, we must not shrink from recalling the occasions of our sins in the preparation which precedes our confession of them."

"Yes, Father."

"Very well then, my son, go on."

Again there was the pause. Far beneath him, where he hung over the spectacle of his guilt, the pews creaked and outside the church someone walked whistling under the pruned trees. The figure kneeling beside the priest eased itself fractionally on the prayer stool and the lips began to move rapidly, the words winnowing out, the voice no longer the one he had come to know, but higher and narrower as though the throat were constricted.

"It all began a long time ago, Father, because I once knew someone who wasn't like this. You didn't know her, you never saw her when you were young; but *I* did and I loved her before she was killed—"

"Wait!" The priest got up suddenly, a book falling from his lap on to the tiled floor.

"Forgive me, Father, it's all true. She *was* killed; she was murdered years and years ago, and today I saw him again, the man who murdered her in Yorkshire when we lived there together and that's why I have done everything that I ever have done."

Father Delaura sat down again; he was breathing faster and his eyes were half-closed.

"I realize that if she hadn't died there would have been some other reason—there always is; but this is *my* reason and I want you to hear it. That's why I came today, although I didn't want to. If you can understand, Father, I want to be forgiven for something I never did as well as for all the things I did do—terrible things, little things all the time, not necessarily done but always wanting to be done, and although I may not do them, they seem to be making me different just because they're there. That's why you'll have to get me forgiven, Father, why He'll have to forgive me, so that I can be different like I was before it all happened."

The white face looked up towards the foot of the high crucifix and beside it the hand of the priest turned over the pages of the book on his lap.

"I think you had better say no more at present. I am not sure that you are well, and though of course that makes no difference to the glorious forgiveness which reposes in the sacrifice of our Lord Jesus Christ, it has a bearing upon the advice I shall give you. In cases of this sort the words of absolution may be granted even in the face of an incompleted confession. I will now pronounce those words and you must have no fear of not being forgiven *fully* for everything you may or may not have done, whether you can recall it or not."

John bent his head.

"Is there anything further you would like to say?"

"No, Father."

"Are you quite sure you are well?"

"Yes, Father, I am quite well. I know what I have said and it is all true."

"Before I give you absolution I must ask you to be sure that you pay back the money you stole to the person from whom you stole it."

"Yes, I will. Father—there *is* one other thing."

"Yes?"

"Can you tell me why I feel that I ought to be forgiven for something I never did? Why do I keep thinking about it all the

time? Why have I felt different ever since it happened? Was it
wrong of me to love her? Is that why I go on and on like this?
Will I never be the same again? Happy like other people?"

Father Delaura sighed and turned another page of the book.

"These are difficult questions. I think I must ask you to confide in your guardian, Mr. Victor. The seal of confession is
absolute; but sometimes, where permission is not withheld, we
feel that we may seek advice from those who are concerned so
long as we do not divulge the particulars of the penitent's sins.
I feel sure that you can be helped to reorientate yourself if you
will allow me to suggest to your guardian that you should see
a medical man without delay. May I suggest that?"

"Yes, Father, if you must. But Mr. Victor does know about
it all."

"Nevertheless, my son, I do feel that a part of your difficulties
lies beyond the church's sphere. We try nowadays to work with
the professions, and while you must never have any fear that God
out if His infinite mercy has not completely absolved you from
your past, at the same time there is nothing to prevent you from
seeking such scientific help as is so providentially at hand in our
time. Mr. Victor no doubt will—" He broke off and then in a
different voice said, "I will now pronounce the words of absolution."

John waited for a few moments after the echo of the last
words had died away to nothingness in the dark roof. He walked
back down the swinging aisle to his own place in one of the
centre pews and kneeled down.

He could remember nothing distinctly; only the two words
"Mr. Victor," "Mr. Victor." He prayed them over to himself
and looked up again at the beautiful but remote crucifix. It
seemed immeasurably far away, a distant ornament that had no
part in the fabric of the church. At one time he had begun to
feel light as though a burden were indeed being replaced by impatient wings lifting his knees from the hassock; but they had
failed and his shoulders were now heavier than ever, he was back
to his unchanged self; he had failed Father Delaura, and Mr.
Victor would be waiting for him.

In the Lady Chapel Father Delaura had finished his prayers.

Coldly, a little sadly perhaps, without a glance in John's direction, he hurried in his black and white to the vestry door and disappeared behind it.

The church was quite empty; it contained only himself and the dead God on the Cross. In front of him something caught his eye, the yellow shine of a brass plate affixed to the back of the next pew. He read it carefully:

> THIS PEW WAS OCCUPIED BY
> H.M. KING EDWARD VII
> ON THE OCCASION OF HIS VISIT
> to
> WORTHING
> September 1905

Leaning over the grainy wood, John inspected the seat three feet beneath his eyes; it was quite unremarkable, no different from all the others.

Crossing himself for the last time he hurried out of the church.

As he clattered back along the dry pavement he ignored yet was sensible of everything; people and trees passed him with the unreality of a train-landscape at the cinema. In the shopping streets the green buses roared and groaned, flags clapped in the wind; while behind the tailors' windows, segregated in their glass boxes, well-dressed young men and women stood inviolate on their pedestals, their faces more evenly tanned than Audrey's, their clothing more sharply creased than the murderer's.

He hurried up the concrete entrance to Rooker's Close and, running through the conservatory into the hall, burst into Mr. Victor's brown study without knocking.

With an almost maidenly deprecation Peter looked around at once. He sat very upright on the arm of Mr. Victor's chair and at the sight of John rose on to the twin columns of his white trousers. Mr. Victor was slower; with chilling self-control he continued to gaze for a moment or two at the printer's proofs on his lap and then very deliberately raised and traversed his grey face until it was directed at the open doorway.

"I'm sorry, sir! I had to see you, straight away. I expect

Probitt has told you? I've just been to my confession and it was no good. Can I talk to you, sir?"

Probitt felt for the tie he was not wearing and then made for the French windows. "I'll go out this way, sir."

In the way a man ignores his dearest possessions when his title to them is threatened by violence, in the way a householder will stumble to his bedroom door on the night of a burglary, insensible of everything for which he is about to do battle, Mr. Victor ignored him; something live and threatening had walked in on his privacy and all his household gods were temporarily forgotten. As he sat there, slowly concentrating his entire attention upon the source of the disturbance, he was more terrible than a lion, less actively angry than a spider, and John shivered.

"I have been expecting you, Bowden! Father Delaura has already telephoned me." He settled back in the chair. "I might add that I was *not* expecting you quite like this. Where are your manners, Blaydon?"

"Oh, I'm sorry sir." Clumsily he started to shut the door, forgot it and, turning around, stepped farther into the study. "It's terribly important. You see, I let him go and now I've got a dreadful feeling that I should have had him arrested before it was too late."

"Really? That is most interesting."

"Yes, sir."

"I think you had better sit down." He glanced at the ceiling and then back at John. "I asked you to sit *down* and I would rather that you did not speak for a few moments; I think it would be wisest."

"But—"

"No, Blaydon! Kindly be seated on the upright chair and remain silent."

The determined immobility of the man facing him, his refusal to respond to the sense of urgency which had carried John so swiftly through the afternoon, was beginning to have its effect. Already he was experiencing a reawakening of the self-criticism which until now had lain dormant. A different view of his behaviour sought insistently to replace the one which had actuated him ever since he left the beach; he saw himself as someone

gauche, gormless and hysterical, an overdramatic adolescent mag-
nifying circumstances which were quite unremarkable, behaving
like some odious only-child in a third-rate farce. He sat down
and Mr. Victor replaced his pipe between his lips.

"I am going through the galleys of my essay on 'The Tears of
Christ,' " he said quietly. "I greatly enjoy correcting proofs and
I think—I *hope* that for some few minutes it may interest you
to help me; but I do not want you to speak, Blaydon."

"No, sir."

"Neither a yea nor a nay, Blaydon."

John took a fold of the velvety lining of his lower lip between
his teeth and bit it. A small piece was detached and he swallowed
it and then explored the gap with his tongue.

" 'What do we mean by the Tears of Christ?' " Mr. Victor
blew out a question mark of pipe smoke and read on: " 'Surely,
we mean more than tears?' A rhetorical question, Blaydon, and
though as a rule I deprecate rhetoric it still has its place in aca-
demic exegesis. 'The direct New Testament references to the
tears of Christ Jesus are not numerous.' I might remark that at
this point I have inserted an appropriate footnote. 'Though there
are indirect eschatological inferences from which we may safely
assume that Our Lord did in fact weep on many occasions:
notably in the Gospel according to St. Luke Chapter 19 Verse
41.' " He looked up. "You will no doubt recall another reference
without my repeating it, and though I could take your silence
as an affirmation I will repeat it nevertheless:

" 'Oh, Jerusalem, Jerusalem, which killest the prophets, and
stonest them that are sent unto thee; how often would I have
gathered thy children together, as a hen doth gather her brood
under her wings, and ye would not!'

A very beautiful stanza and one that should remind us that quite
apart from everything else, Our Blessed Lord had inherited from
His human forebears the gift of supreme poetry for which the
Jews have always been remarkable. But I will read on: 'We may,
I think, consider the tears of Christ—Lacrima Christi—under three
discrete headings: first, the physiological.' " He ejected another
little gout of smoke, "This, Bowden, as you doubtless realize, will

permit of my disposing of some of the grosser excesses of Modernism! 'Second, emotional.' That paragraph needs considerable revision and so on the present occasion we must forgo it. 'Thirdly, we may examine the philosophical implications of these Holy Tears.' " He patted his galley proofs together with all the affection of a poker player who has been dealt a royal flush. "Now this section, I must confess, originally gave me so much cause for thought that I had even considered abandoning it altogether as a matter proper only for discussion by the mystical theologians. Apart from everything else, to deal adequately with this profound mystery, it would have been necessary to reprint large sections of pre-Reformation commentaries which are already on the syllabus of the theological students for whom my own little work is intended." He looked up. "You follow me, I hope?" Meeting the half-smile with his own eyes, John said nothing.

Mr. Victor's sunken gaze glinted as he replaced the proofs on his desk and crossed one short calf over the opposing knee. He smiled threateningly and glanced at his watch.

"You may now, if you are sure you are more collected, break your silence, Blaydon. You were talking, I believe, of having let someone go; and you mentioned in passing that your recent confession to my respected and dear friend Father Delaura was 'no good.' Perhaps you would now comment on these statements, *in order.*"

"Yes, sir." John filled his chest. "I expect Probitt told you about the beach, but he didn't understand. I *had* to tell him a lie, the man hadn't picked my pocket at all. The reason I wanted to have him arrested was because I had recognized him—he was the murderer."

He noticed that there was no tremor of the thin, scrupulously clean fingers as Mr. Victor's hands came together over his waistcoat.

"Just so."

"He was the *murderer!*" John repeated.

Because Mr. Victor's face was in shadow he could not see whether or not it had changed colour. "So you said."

"He was the man who murdered Victoria three years ago in Yorkshire, and when I accused him he ran away."

"He ran away."

The placidity of the interruption, as expressionless as an echo, unnerved him still further. He exerted himself once more.

"He pretended he thought I was ill and then shoved me out of his way and escaped through the back of the tent."

Mr. Victor had been leaning in his chair until this moment; but now, despite the fact he had made no perceptible movement, he appeared to be crouching. "What tent, Blaydon?"

"The tent belonging to the—a tent on the beach, sir."

"Belonging to the what? The *who*?"

"Some girls." It sounded lewd. "Some women." This sounded Biblical and even more suggestive. "Ladies, sir, Audrey and— Sheila, Miss Miller. But that's not important." It *wasn't* important, he wasn't going to have it made to seem important. He was being hypnotized. It was becoming increasingly difficult to believe in his own attitude; the still power of the man in the chair was having a paralyzing effect on his conviction. "The point is, sir, that the man escaped; he'll have gone off in his car to another town and unless we—"

"A moment, Blaydon! These ladies with whom we are on such familiar terms—you say that this stranger made his escape through their tent? He was not with *you*?"

"No, he was—"

"I take it, then, that you were with the owners of the tent?"

"No, sir, I wasn't. I explained that to Probitt."

"I know you did."

"I was lying near them but I wasn't talking to them, *really* sir! He came along later and—"

"But you know their *Christian* names, Blaydon? Or are those too an invention on your part?"

"Those *are* their names; I heard them talking to each other, that's how I know their names."

"Ah, yes! Your remarkable powers of memory outside working hours. Did you report the loss of this imaginary wallet to the ladies concerned?"

"Yes, sir, as I've already explained, I *had* to."

"And did they believe you?"

"I think so."

"A little surprising surely? That two strangers should believe that a third party had been robbed of a wallet by yet another person who had had no access to his clothing?"

"What, sir?"

Over the pale hook of the nose the fierce eyebrows drew slowly together and Mr. Victor spoke very slowly. "Unless of course the stolen wallet had been in the tent used by the alleged thief, the tent belonging to the ladies.

John separated his tongue from his palate. "I'm sorry, sir, I don't understand. I seem to be muddled."

In his chair Mr. Victor executed a tiny wriggle, a little massage of the buttocks against the soft cushion.

"So I see! But I think I can help you. I am suggesting, Blaydon, that in defiance of our rules you have struck up a friendship with two of the town girls on the beach. That in addition to being on such intimate terms with them that you habitually use their first names, you are in the habit of sharing their tent with them."

He stood up, a black bald-headed figure against the drowsing garden. John saw that his hands were quite still, that his pace to the fireplace was measured, and his turn in front of the crested tobacco jar on the mantelpiece unhurried and precise.

Somewhere in the depths of his mind he had ceased to mourn his lost impetus; somewhere behind the bricking up of the light he knew a clear despair that hung against a back wall whitely; he was scarcely concerned with it.

Mr. Victor looked at him with contempt. The shortened upper lip revealed the young dentures, the old eyelids drooped in their shadows and the nostrils dilated on hairy depths.

"This—this gutter-cunning, this adolescent prurience would have been enough." The narrow torrent of his words filled the room. "For *you*, Bowden, apparently it was not enough; not content with threatening the good name of this . . . you add to your tally by running hot foot to the church and attempting to involve Father Delaura." Mr. Victor's pale yellow hands disappeared from his sides to meet and embrace somewhere behind his buttocks. "Clever of you, Blaydon, remarkably clever! *That* is what has alarmed me. He felt that he might have failed in his function as a priest, but I was able to reassure him. I told him as I had earlier told you that I had recently myself had cause for concern . . . regretted my haste in having sent you to him without a little further reflection. Doing myself something of an injustice perhaps, because this afternoon I did my best to gain your confidence, to dissuade you from any evil you might even then have been contemplating and to— Made unhappy, Blaydon, to think what must have been the state of your mind after your rejection of me—of my help in the rose garden four hours ago. It is one thing to commit an offence blindly; it is quite another when what is done is premeditated."

John sat up. "*Premeditated.*" The word, so fresh in his mind, reached through to him.

"I don't understand," he said.

Mr. Victor took a pace towards him; he seemed to suck himself forward and hover a few feet over the seaweed-brown carpet, pale and bulbous like a giant squid wreathed in its ejected ink.

"You don't know what you're saying; you don't know what you're thinking. It sounds as though you're reading out of a book again and it's making me muddled."

Mr. Victor retreated and John stood up. The change of posture helped him; it was symbolic of the return of his belief in himself. With one of those lightning strokes of insight which illuminate people in their darkest situations, he saw that he had inherited from his mother the ability to gain an instant power from the emotion of anger. At such times he was, like her, possessed of a dynamic, an arrogant and intuitive coherence which few people could withstand for long.

Mr. Victor, he knew, had already sensed the change in him; the short retreat he had made towards the mantelpiece was in itself conciliatory.

"Sit down, Bowden, please sit down." A hand reached forward and rested on John's shoulder. "Though I may have been a little vehement in my remarks it was only because I was trying to help you to see the truth about yourself. Confusion is a terrible thing, but however painful the process may prove, one must not cling to it when one finds it being dispersed—*destroyed*!"

"No, sir."

"Then sit down."

"If you don't mind I'd rather stand."

Mr. Victor frowned, a movement as quick as a lizard's and as wary.

"Very well then," he sighed. "Let us resume. Perhaps you had better tell me, con*fess* to me, if I may put it like that, the *full* extent of your relationship with these girls on the beach."

"There was no relationship—nothing at all."

"I fear that I know *something* about young men—more obviously than you give me credit for."

"Yes, sir."

"In the most exact sense of the word, I have a *rudimentary* knowledge of which I am rather tired. So let us make an end of these lies."

"They're not lies, sir."

"But Blaydon! You have already admitted that you lied to Peter—to Probitt, that you lied to the stranger you met on the beach, and that you lied to these women."

John said nothing.

"If you are frightened, Bowden, and it is usually fear that makes young men lie, I can assure you that at my hands you have no cause for fear." He was regaining his own self-confidence. "That is, of course, unless you continue to lie."

John muttered.

"It is ugly to mutter, Blaydon! I do not like young men to mutter. Hatred is an unpleasant and destructive emotion and I am quite aware that at this moment you are filled with hatred for me, are you not?"

They found one another's eyes with horrible ease.

"I am, sir."

Mr. Victor smiled. "We must not digress, pleasant as it may be to do so. I must repeat that if you continue to lie I shall have to take steps to punish you. I cannot afford to have pupils who set their wills against my own; both my livelihood and my reputation depend upon my being the master in my own house."

He said, "Yes, sir." The moment of his advantage seemed to have side-slipped, but he awaited the repetition of it with confidence.

"Very well then! Perhaps you will now admit to me the truth I might have suspected some weeks ago when your visits to the beach, your new-found pleasure in bathing in those unclean waters, first became apparent."

"I like the sea, sir, that's all." From somewhere he smiled, re-membering Anglesey in that last idle summer following the trip with Greenbloom, the white waves heaving against the washed rocks.

"It is *not* all. You are prevaricating and your guile seems to cause you some amusement. For a moment I thought that my use of the word 'premeditation' had upset you in some way; I was prepared to be lenient to you. I see now that my first impression was correct. You take a pleasure in your cunning, you enjoy it. I have no more time to spare, Bowden or Blaydon, whichever you prefer to be called, admit your guilt, confess to your lies, assure me of your premeditation and—"

"Don't use that word! Don't use it." He moved forward and looked through the interval of the air which separated them.

He could feel the blood draining from his face, leaving it as paper-white as the newspapers he had read at the time. The man had planned it all in the morning, had returned to have tea with them, even while drinking from her cup in the cave he had been working out in his mind ways of getting her to himself, of killing her. He had talked and smiled, been friendly with his lips and eyes, while behind them he had been thinking of what he might do and how he might do it.

Mr. Victor stood his ground. John could still discern his out-line and he knew that this time the moment would not be lost to him.

"Go back, Blaydon. Sit down. Take your chair."

"*You* are the liar and you don't even know that you are lying. I told you the truth but you can't hear it. Everything I said was true; if you suggest that I thought of the girls in the way you often think of Probitt, *that* doesn't matter; it doesn't mean any-thing. I never did more than think of them and I did not encour-age the thoughts, and *I* knew what I was thinking. But you don't; you have no idea what you are thinking. You don't know what you are thinking about me and you don't know what you are thinking about Probitt; but *we* do, all of us, from Humphrey to Jones. We are not like Probitt; we are different and if you weren't blind you would be able to see it."

"You are ill, Blaydon, you are ill." He stretched out a hand as though to draw a curtain across the French window and then, just as John had forgotten the door, he forgot the window.

"It *was* the murderer. I saw him. Nothing else matters, not what I was thinking nor what you were thinking nor Probitt nor the priest. It is the truth that matters and you can't hide it. Although I had done nothing except know him like you have known me and Probitt, he frightened me and that is why I ran to my confession. I wanted to find out the truth before I did anything—"

"The door, Bowden, the door is ajar—a moment."

John addressed himself to the looking glass over the mantelpiece. He saw Mr. Victor hurry behind him, diminished, smaller than the brown tobacco jar behind which he passed in his run to the far corner of the study.

"But I shall never go again. Never. The church was empty and the priest was empty—only Christ, dead on the Cross, not even bleeding, and King Edward the Seventh, the place where he sat; and then back here to you breathing lies at me, accusing me and frightening me because you are guilty about something yourself. I know what it is and it doesn't really matter—I suppose it's Probitt, something to do with him anyway. But why should I be blamed for what you are thinking and what you have done? I've got enough to be wrong about and so have you. We should help one another, we should—"

"*Bowden!*" Mr. Victor shouted at him; his hands caught him around the waist and he swivelled him away from the mirror. John wrenched himself free and stepped backwards into the light streaming in through the French windows.

"Don't touch me! I don't like to be touched by men and I'm not ill. It's just that nobody knows what they are thinking. Father Delaura is lying; he doesn't mean to, but he would never have rung you up if he had been sure of himself. The murderer is lying, and *you* are lying; that's why you talk so much. If someone found the truth they wouldn't talk at all; unless they were saints they would be silent. But nobody since the saints has found it and that's why everybody is talking. I shall go to the police; they'll understand. They are specialists in lying; I'll tell them and they'll believe me because they know which lies to believe."

He was silent and satisfied; he could look at Mr. Victor quite calmly, see him become a face and body again as he stood against the arm of his chair, his pipe shaking slightly in his hand, a fine gleam of sweat on his grey forehead.

"I want you to have a cup of tea with me, Bowden. Kindly press the bell."

"Yes, sir."

John moved over to the white china switch with flowers painted on it and pressed the central stud.

"Humphrey is out," said Mr. Victor suddenly sitting down on the hide-covered chair. "Mrs. Foley no doubt—"

John sat down on the edge of the chair.

"I see I have done you an injustice, Bowden. There is very much more in all this—I want if I can—"

The door opened and Mrs. Foley came in. She was wearing her usual white kitchen coat like a laundress; she gave Mr. Victor her sheetlike smile.

"A pot of tea if you please, Mrs. Foley."

"Toast, sir?"

"No, thank you. Would you like toast, Blayd—Bowden?"

"No, thank you, sir."

"Just the tea then, Mrs. Foley."

The door closed behind her. Mr. Victor got out his handkerchief and passed it swiftly across his forehead.

"It is a little close in here. I wonder if you would mind opening the French windows. The wind appears to have dropped.

"Thank you, Bowden. As I was saying, I want if possible to persuade you to reconsider your decision about going to the police. Don't think that I am in any way trying to interfere with your conscience, Bowden, or with the course of justice; that is very far from my intention; but I rather hope that when we have examined the facts calmly, you might yourself see that it's quite possible that no good may come of such an action."

"That would be their affair, sir."

"Quite! But not entirely; *you* would be involved and so too, though this is not really important, would Rooker's Close." He smiled slowly, "You see how frank I am being. You have forced me to it; we are none of us, unfortunately, saints and therefore for the time being we have need of the words you so greatly distrust."

"I exaggerated a little, sir, but at the time I saw it all so clearly."

"Yes, yes! But let us keep to the matter in hand. I am, as I say, being frank with you, John. I don't want if it can be avoided—honestly avoided—to have the Blaydon case reopened under these circumstances and at this time."

"No, sir."

"And I know that you have not lied to me; that is quite certain. I also *know* that you are mistaken—listen to me very carefully, if you please."

"Yes, sir."

"You are not unwell. But quite obviously you are a highly imaginative boy and something happened this afternoon which unleashed that imagination: a variety of circumstances, a strange moment in time, a complex of events connected with your confession which clouded your judgement. Would you mind telling me exactly what it was which made you so certain that the stranger you met on the beach was in fact the murderer whom you had only previously seen three years ago for the space of half an hour in the darkness of a cave?"

"It was his whistle. He whistled the same tune, the same tune he whistled in the—the same three notes that were whistled—"

"And what was your reaction? What did you do immediately afterwards, more important, what did you *feel*?"

"The wind in the tent. It was green in there, I heard the wind and then it went. I was back in the cave and he was there splashing towards us, striking matches. I felt—"

"Yes, yes. Go on."

"I felt as though nothing had ever happened since. I felt like the darkness, quite empty, waiting for something to happen in it. I was what I *had* been, changed back again. I couldn't move at all for a moment; it was very strange, very horrible, like a person dying twice."

"I think that will do." He got up and opened the door in response to the knock which John had not heard.

He returned with the tea-cosied tray and put it on the desk as Mrs. Foley closed the door. He poured out the tea meticulously, running it into the milk at the bottom of the cups, and then handed one to John.

"Drink this!" he said, "and relax. Afterwards, when we have cleared up matters a little further, we must discuss your future. After *that* I think it would be a good thing for you to take a brisk walk before supper."

"I think I would rather lie down or read a book, sir."

He sipped his tea and wondered what did it all matter. It had seemed certain and important, but if it was not certain, it was not important. Nothing was important because nothing was true. He thought of Father Delaura ringing up like that, so quickly.

Mr. Victor replaced his cup on his saucer. "Let us start by examining in order the points of evidence you will have to offer to the police in order to convince them of the necessity for action; let us put ourselves in the *place* of the police. After that, let us consider the possible effects of their action, *if any*, on the immediate future—on *your* future, John."

"Yes, sir."

"I am beginning to think that Rooker's Close may not after all be quite the most suitable place for you. . . ."

In the garden he saw the stand of the yew hedges surrounding the rosebed and guessed at the scent of them. To talk in circles, to move in circles, as Mr. Victor had said, was very soothing.

He closed his eyes.

6. Island Summer

Give them ear! and let the dead,
Interred no deeper than Antigone's lost tears
For Polyneices, rise again and choose
To travel with you further than the ears hear
Or the heart can lose.

He put Father's bicycle away in the garage, unstrapped his satchel from the little grid at the back, and swinging it carelessly, walked slowly down the drive to the cottage.

The others of course would all have passed the exam, they always did; and even if one or two of them *had* failed it would not greatly matter. *He* was eighteen, but their average age could not be much more than fifteen, and another year at the County School would not affect them in the least; their parents would scrape the fees together somehow and the news would spread through Benllwch, Bodorgan or Pengross that John Hughes "Chemist," Nellie "Chips" or Owen "Pie Bron" had "failed school certificate, look you!" There would be shakings of heads for a Saturday or two and then it would all be forgotten.

But if *he* had failed this time after all the money spent on him at the Abbey, Beowulf's, Rooker's Close and a year's ignominiously hard work under the seedy conditions of the County School at Llanabbas, it would be the end of him; either the Point or Father's sixteen bore.

He couldn't face even another term at the County School, let alone the prospect of a second year—even supposing he were given the chance of it. As it was, his age and his background had been as much an embarrassment to the school staff as they had been to the family and to himself; but neither the school nor the family could possibly know what it had been like for him to have to catch the school train every morning at ten past seven, to sit wearing the school cap in the carriage listening to the stream of colloquial Welsh while trying to appear inconspicuous, though one was English, older than anyone else and, once, a public school boy.

If one used the gun there would be the difficulty of pulling the triggers; people usually managed it by rigging up strings or wires, but when that was done it couldn't possibly be made to look like an accident, and he was damned if people were going to be allowed to despise his *death*.

It would have to be the Point then; just after the turn of the tide when the race was at its fullest. For the hundredth time he visualized it: the casual wave to people by the springboard, the perfect knifelike dive and the half-mile swim out to the lighthouse. He would swim very beautifully so that they would remember it: the clear cold passage alongside the rocks out to the *Pwll Glas*, the Blue Pool, where he had so often fished for bream with Father in the earliest Anglesey days, and then on farther into the forbidden waters beyond the lighthouse. Once he had reached these it would be unnecessary to do anything more; the current would take over. How many times he had sat above it on the rocks throwing the heads of sea pinks into the smooth water, watching them hesitate, turning slowly around and around before they began to slide out, gently at first, and then faster and faster, as the millions of gallons of the bay's sea water emptied itself into the frenzy of the race.

In the past ten years two people had drowned in the race, and at least three or four been rescued from it when *in extremis*. He of course was terrified of it: the whirlpools with their turning mouths, ample enough to suck down an elephant, the great smooth eiderdown hills, the sheets of green glass surrounded by hissing wavetops, and the continuous roar which on still days could be heard even from the top of the "mountain."

It would be clean though and probably fairly quick, particularly if he put up no real resistance but drank in the thick water eagerly. He would just have to be brave during the first part as the current took hold of him; after that, he could give a few shouts and signals for the look of the thing and then abandon himself to the strength of it, somersaulting his body into its green and white folds like a child on the counterpane of its mother's bed.

Terrible that he wasn't really interested any longer in what people might say or anxious that they should care; *that* meant that the idea was becoming real and truly personal, a private matter between himself—and *himself*.

Halfway down the drive he stopped. How could a decision rest between himself and himself? He must really be mad, a split personality, if he were beginning to think of himself as two people. Suicide was a single act between one person and—who else? God, of course; that's what *they* would say. But either there *was* no God or else there were a hundred gods all cancelling one another out: Mother's god, Rudmose's god, Victor's god, Greenbloom's god, Mrs. Blount's god, Father's god, his brother David's god; in fact, a million gods, as many gods as there were people; a lunacy of gods, a revolting, magnified concatenation of super-humanity clustered on the summit of some Olympus a little higher than the world. And who made Olympus? he asked himself. Men made it and peopled it with gods in their own image. Well, his god had better watch out or he would soon find himself without a worshipper just as old Rudmose's had done.

He stooped and picked a red wallflower from beside the drive —very beautiful, so beautiful that the scent of it hurt him as he pushed it through the hole in his lapel. It was good camouflage, would make him look as though he thought he might have been quietly successful in the exam, would discomfort Mary, who did not like him to look pleased with himself, clean and spruce; who preferred him when he was hangdog, in a black and dangerous mood under whose influence he might do or say some unpre-meditated thing which would arouse Mother to a white fury and precipitate one of the rows that were so essential to them all. Yes, the wallflower was a good idea; like incense it could cover the aura of his thoughts so that no one would discern them; and it was appropriate too for the party at Porth Newydd in the eve-ning, would make them think that all was well and that he was looking forward to his week end.

He pushed open the front door and hung his satchel in the cloakroom. Good! Greenbloom *had* arrived and presumably his poet friend as well. There were two white suitcases, marked with the initials H. G., standing beneath the coats together with a very battered one fastened with a leather strap and covered with French labels. He looked at the name:

MR. JANE BOSCAWEN-JONES
C/O THE GOAT HOTEL
LLANGOLLEN

Extraordinary name for a man, but then of course poets were different. How, he wondered, had Boscawen-Jones managed to persuade his parents to christen him Jane so that when he grew up he could become a poet. What would he look like? Shelley? Rupert Brooke? Keats? Would he be Welsh or English-Welsh? Mick knew very little about him, only that he was Greenbloom's newest discovery and that shortly the private press which Greenbloom had recently started would be publishing a book of his poetry.

In fact, they were supposed to be staying at Plas David, paying Mary ten guineas a week each while Boscawen-Jones completed some of the verse "in this beautiful country house only one mile from the little bay of St. David where home cooking and unhotel-like comfort, combined with every care for your well-being in every way, are the marks of our unique hospitality"—he remembered the glowing wording of Mother's brochure the year Mary had gone into the guest-house business.

At another time the prospect of two such wild guests would have excited John; but now, with the results of the exam looming ahead, and the knowledge of his impaired prestige with the family, he felt only awkward and detached, unanxious to try and impress either of them with any facet of his character, too steeply involved in his own recurrent despair to want to "show off" even by silence.

He walked through the raftered dining room into the long drawing room which jutted backward from the front of the cottage to the dog field and the vegetable garden. The left-hand windows were open and boxes of sunlight streamed across the room on to the tired covers of the armchairs, on to the baby grand and the little Dresden mirror with its crisp confection of flowers and cupids on the opposite wall.

Like the wallflower glowing in his lapel these things filled him with a pain that was at once dear and almost intolerable, reminding him of the reality of a happiness which he wished had never existed so that he might not now know the full extent of his present misery. Under the impact of it, he realized that if, in fact, he did make the swim to the race in a few weeks' time, then these inanimate things would be the real though indirect instruments of his death: a wallflower, a Dresden mirror and the rosewood curve of a Bechstein piano. Such things should never have been allowed the constancy denied such people as himself, but should themselves have changed as he had changed, slowly and completely, since first he had seen them as a child in the grey and silver drawing room of the Beddington vicarage fifteen years ago.

Inclining his head to sniff once more the scent of the wallflower, a line of poetry he had once read somewhere spoke clearly in his mind:

"And now that my disease is made most manifest to me,
I fear the throwers by the wall—
Remembering dead flowers and fires."

From the piazza outside the windows he heard the rattle of a teacup and the clipped syllables of Mary's words:

"Well if they're all going over to Porth Newydd surely they won't want dinner at the Plas first? In any case it's very unfair on the staff, Michael taking them off into Benllwch like that the moment they arrived. I didn't even know that they *had* arrived until I came over and saw their cases in the cloakroom. What did they want in Benllwch, Mother?"

"Yes, it was very naughty of them." Mother was indulgently full of China tea. "But I couldn't stop them; apparently this awful friend of his had run out of typing paper—"

"Surely, you didn't believe *that*! They've gone to the Rhosybol Arms and they'll come back demanding dinner at the last minute just as we're starting on the washing-up of all the other guests."

"I told them *distinctly* that they'd have to be back by seven if they wanted a meal before they went over to Porth Newydd. Horab wants John and Michael to have dinner with them and that will save Nanny."

"No, I can't do with any extras, there's not enough tongue. I'm budgeting very carefully this quarter, Mother. If we had a licence I could afford to be lavish with the food, but as it is—"

"Don't be shortsighted, dear, you can charge an extra guinea each for a dinner like yours, and Michael and John can make up with the ends; serve it up in the kitchen and see that Betty gives the right helpings to the right people."

"But I don't want *them* over there. I have no say in the last-minute guests as a rule, but as far as my own brothers are concerned—you really don't understand the extra work it entails. I want to have everything finished before George arrives at eight-thirty—we're going to go down to the bay and put out the lobster pots at low tide."

"Well! You'll have to look slippy," Father's voice broke in plaintively. "Low tide's at eight-fifteen tonight."

"Shut up, Teddy!" said Mother.

"I was only telling her that if she wants to get the pots out this evening she'll have to catch the ebb— What about bait? They like a bit of rotten herring; have you ordered bait from—"

"Oh, be quiet!" said Mary. "Why must you always interrupt— What was I saying?" She paused. "John's not invited over to Lady Geraldine's, is he?"

"Yes, she particularly wants all the men she can lay her hands on; six of The Wycombe Abbey girls arrived for the summer holidays last week end and she's at her wit's end to entertain them, the poor darling."

"But you're not letting him go, surely?"

"Yes dear! Why, did you want him for anything?"

"No, but I don't think he *ought* to go. He spends far too much time loafing about over there in the holidays and in any case I want him to help with the washing-up."

"I think it might be good for him, he's been looking very pale lately."

"Hmph!" Mary's ejaculation came through the window like a rifle crack. "You know why *that* is."

"The lad's very exercised over his exam results," said Father. "As long as they're not too late getting back—I wanted John to serve at the nine o'clock and I have an awful job to get him out of his bed in the morning."

"Of course you do!" Mary picked up speed and enthusiasm. "He's been adolescent far too long, and going over to Lady Gerry's with the place full of young girls will only make him worse. I think we should wait and see whether he's *passed* this exam before we allow him to run all around the island with Michael's friends. And in any case, after the Ireland business two years ago, I thought it had been agreed that he wasn't going to be allowed to come under the influence of Horab again."

"Well, we'll see," said Mother. "I think that this term he really has worked very hard and I'm still quite sure that one of these days he will surprise us all."

"Yes, by ending up in prison or in an asylum. What John wants is an honest job of work that'll take him out of himself—he can't go on brooding over the Yorkshire affair for ever. Just look what he's cost you—he must have cost you and Daddy at least twice as much as me and Melanie put together, and what good has it done him? He's eighteen and he hasn't even got his school certificate yet. If he doesn't hurry up George says that they won't take him at any medical school let alone at Dublin where they—"

"Oh please, *Mary*, don't! I can't stand it and you know how it hurts me. I think it's most inconsiderate of you to bring it all up like this. *You* haven't got any sons, you can't know what it's like—how I worry at night. I've begged you not to mention it time and again—it's all over now and I'm quite sure he's getting over it. We must love him—mustn't we, Teddy?—and have faith that one day his great gifts—"

"*What* great gifts? He hasn't got any gifts. That's just what annoys me, *worries* me, Mother darling. You will keep putting your head into the sand and imagining John's going to be a great man of some sort. I don't want to hurt you, honestly I don't, but I do feel that if you'd only face up to it and realize that John is just a rather ordinary problem boy, that he hasn't shown any signs of any talents whatsoever, except for getting himself expelled from every school he's ever been sent to—"

From his position by the window John could hear the angry little puffs she inflicted on her cigarette. "George is not against him, he's very fond of him and *he's* just finished his fourth year course in psychology and he says that John is quite definitely—"

He heard the sound of Mother's sobs, Mary's voice faltering, and could anticipate her sudden dismay at the fatal signal of Mother's tears, the swift retrenchment she would make in order to avert the storm which would surely follow. He had heard it all before, *over*heard it all before a dozen times; it no longer even hurt him; it merely bored him; it had not one-tenth of the power to pierce and wound the secret boundaries of his sensibility possessed by the inanimate things which surrounded him.

He knew how it would end: in Father seizing the opportunity of allying himself with Mother for a few uncomfortable minutes, in some talk of urgent prayers over at the little church, and in Mary striding off jaggedly down the drive to Plas David to retail the whole story first to Melanie and Betty *Cae Ficer*, the maid, later to George arriving in his sports car for yet another week end of his exhausting courtship.

Leaving the drawing room on tiptoe, opening and closing the door very quietly, he went through to the bathroom and washed thoroughly in front of the open window through which the sun and the scent of the wallflowers flooded like a golden waterfall. He parted his hair carefully, borrowed some of Father's cheap solid brilliantine—"Perfumed with lavender," as it said on the tin—and then, lighting a cigarette, strolled out through the front door down the drive to the garage.

He waited there for about five minutes halfway between the two houses: Plas David, rose-pink beneath its pine trees, the signboard swinging gently in the wind, and Llanasaph, his home, a whitewashed agglomeration of cubes and rectangles like a multiple cottage built by some mad Welsh architect.

He pretended to himself that he had only just arrived, that he had not yet walked down the drive nor entered the house. He went on to suppose that he had done well in the exam in

Bangor, had quite definitely passed it, and that next term he would be starting medicine in Ireland. In the meantime, he told himself, life was very pleasurable and exciting. Greenbloom and a poet had arrived in Greenbloom's new Hispano Suiza; and shortly, he, John, would be having dinner with them and Michael at Plas David, his sister's superior guest house, after which they would all run over to Lady Geraldine Bodorgan's house and meet at least half a dozen beautiful young girls from one of England's most exclusive schools who would be paying guests with the family's aristocratic friends for at least eight weeks.

He went over all this in his mind twice, stiffening it by the addition of desirable little details in the second recitation until he was quite convinced of its truth; and then as he heard Mary's footsteps crunching over the brown gravel he opened and closed the garage door with a bang, turned the corner and walked towards her comfortably, letting the smoke from his Woodbine trail behind him opulently as he patted the wallflower in his buttonhole. He was enjoying it so much that of course he didn't notice her until they were abreast of one another. She stopped and he looked at her.

Her eyelids were a little swollen at the roots of the lashes, and between them the dark brown eyes, so like his own, smouldered behind their recent tears.

"You're very late. How did you get on?"

"Splendidly!"

"What was it today?"

"Maths."

"I thought that was your weak subject?"

"Yes, but I was lucky; I made hay of it."

"*That* sounds cheering for us all."

"*I* mean in the good sense."

"Oh."

"Has Greenbloom arrived?"

"Yes."

"Oh good! Are they in the house?"

"No, they've gone into Benllwch with Michael."

"Oh, what time's dinner?"

"You're having it over at the Plas and it will be at seven

o'clock. Afterwards Mother wants you to help me with the washing-up, if there's time; so don't be late."

"How do you mean, if there's time?" he asked.

"Oh, Geraldine's invited you all over to Porth Newydd; but
you're not to use the car. Greenbloom will be taking you."

"What fun—I say, what's his friend like?"

"I haven't seen him, but I should imagine that he'll be long-
haired, unhealthy and dirty."

"Why?"

"Because he writes poetry and is permanently out of work.
He sponges on Greenbloom—in the way Michael once did."

"Ah!" He spoke with careful urbanity. "You think he'll come
to a bad end, do you?"

"What do you mean? I never said so; you can't come to a
bad end if you haven't made a good beginning—and I bet he
hasn't!"

"Oh, nothing! I only meant either *prison or an asylum!*"

Mary turned away, frowning to herself.

"You're mad! You'd better get washed and come over right
away. You can lay the table."

"Too adolescent, that's my trouble—pale in the mornings."
He smiled and began to walk down towards the house, leaving
her where she was; but before he had taken three paces, she had
caught up with him.

"Have you just got back?"

"Yes, I think so."

"Where are your books then?"

"In the house." It was a fatal slip. "I mean in the garage."

"They're not—you're lying."

"Why should I?"

"Because you've been listening—eavesdropping. You've already
been into the house and—"

"And what?"

"You went into the drawing room and listened to our conversation through the window, didn't you?"

"Your guess is as good as mine."

She drew on her cigarette, eyeing him with cold distaste
through the smoke.

"Why don't you admit it?"

"I do; but it wasn't conversation, you see, not where *you* were concerned anyway. It was horrible! It made me feel ill; it made me feel I'd like to go and drown myself—in the race."

"Sometimes I think it would be best for everyone if you did."

"Oh good!" He seized and shook her hand before she could snatch it away. "I'm so glad you agree with me. One day, I promise I'll do it and I'll wait for you there."

She wiped her hand on her dress and then threw her cigarette into the wallflowers beside the drive.

"When George comes I'm going to get him to speak seriously to Mother and Father about you."

"Good old George!" He turned once again. "All the dirty work; now and for the rest of his life."

He began to run; he ran past the well, up the three steps between the hydrangeas, around the corner of the house, past the trough garden and on to the terrace where Mother and Father were sitting in front of the blinding white wall on either side of the discarded tea tray.

"Hello, pet!" He kissed Mother quickly; her short arm came around his shoulders for a moment. "What a late tea you're having!"

"Take the tray in to Nanny," she said. "How did you get on, John?"

"Not too bad! I did reasonably well in the geometry, I think, a good three quarters of the algebra, and a bit dubiously in the mechanics." He felt warm towards her because she had stood to his defence more loyally than he would ever have supposed. Usually he found it difficult to be physically demonstrative to Mother; but now he was able to override the boundaries of his distaste and to embrace her eagerly, kissing her soft and always cold cheek. "It's your fault, you know, Mother darling; we get it from you, we're all absolutely hopeless when it comes to figures."

"At Uppingham," said Father somnolently, "I topped the sixth in maths and classics, didn't I, Kitty?"

"How should I know? I didn't meet you till you'd left Oxford. Don't be daft, Teddy!"

"Squashed again!"

"Well, it's so stupid! As if what you did at Uppingham in the last century was going to be of any help to anyone fifty years later. It's John we're worried about." She uncrossed her small legs irritably on her little chaise longue. "Hurry up and take that tray in," she said to John, "Mary wants you to go and give them a hand at the Plas before dinner."

"I know." He picked up the tray and went in through the garden door of the drawing room.

Nanny was in the tiny kitchen basting the chicken. He kissed her, noticing the prick of the little hairs on her upper lip.

"Oh, you're back." Pleasure illumined her tiredness. "I was just wonderin' about you. Did you get on all right today, dear?"

"Yes, I'm sure I did—if I didn't I'm going to go and drown myself, Poo," he replied, using her pet name.

"You mustn't say things like that, that's very wicked, pet. Yer mother and father—"

"I'm not telling *them*," he said. "It's our secret. *You'd* miss me, wouldn't you, Poo?"

"It's very wrong to think of such things; don't say it to yer mother even as a joke. She'd be very upset. Yer mother is very fond of you."

"Yes, when Mary and Melanie aren't about."

"You're having dinner over there with this Mr. Greenbloom and his friend. That'll be nice, won't it? I said you'd like that, and Lady Bodorgan was on the telephone to yer mother, so you'll all be going over there after yer dinner. She's got some pretty girls there for you, so just remember and don't go thinking wicked things any more and upsetting yer mother."

"You're sweet! If I have passed I'll buy you a huge present: a hat or a pair of shoes for your collection."

"Yer mother and father have been over to the church twice praying for you, so go back to them now like a good boy."

"All right." He moved closer to her and whispered. "Don't say anything will you, pet? I was quite serious and I felt it might help if I told someone jokingly—it sometimes does. I can't explain, but sometimes I feel so terribly unhappy that it seems the only thing to do. I don't believe in anything these days; can you understand what it's like?"

She dribbled quick spoonfuls of fat over the chicken.

"It's very wicked to think such things! Go on now, dear! She'll wonder what's keeping you."

"But *you* know me, Poo, don't you? You've looked after me ever since I was born. You don't think I'm a fool, do you, or that I'm a bit mad? I'm not, am I? Just tell me that I'm not and then I'll feel better."

She looked very worried, worried and sweaty. It was like questioning a pillow or expecting sympathy and understanding from a cushion. It was worse, because pillows and cushions could not sweat or feel; they could not really be loved. He patted her back and lied. "Don't worry, Poo, I was only joking. I'm feeling very happy really and it was sweet of you to put in a word about the dinner party."

"That Mr. Churchill who's always making trouble in Parliament, and a lot of other great men weren't good at school, dear; they were backward, very backward, and look where they've got to. I know you're very clever and so does yer mother; you're just a—" she searched for the comfortable word—"late developer like Mr. Geoffrey, that's all; and one of these days we'll all be proud of you."

"Do you really believe that? Honestly?"

"We all do, yer Uncle Felix always said you was the cleverest of them all. Now please go out to them. Yer mother'll be upset if she thinks you're talking to me. Go and tell her how well you've done."

"Good-bye, Poo." He left her stooping over the oven in the bright heat of the kitchen fire and walked out on to the terrace.

"Poo says we've definitely been invited over to Lady Geraldine's."

"Yes, but you're not to be late back, Daddy wants you to serve at the nine o'clock in the morning and there's to be no pub-crawling with Greenbloom and his friend."

"That's all right. There can't be, not for Horab—it's Shabbath." He stopped. "Good heavens! He won't be able to come, he's not allowed to do anything until the evening star appears on Saturdays."

"Oh that's all over. His family don't know, but he's lapsed, hasn't he, Teddy?"

"He's no longer Orthodox," said Father, "he was telling us about it within five minutes of his arrival. Good thing too—they can't eat pork, you know, John."

Mother looked at him and then at John.

"As if *that* mattered! I can see that it's all going to be left to me. How are we going to get anything out of him for the new rood screen if that's all *you* can say—" She mimicked Father's slow, rather portentous voice. " 'They can't eat pork, you know!' I really think you must be going senile, Teddy. What's the good of all these Uppingham prizes you're always swanking about and your First at Oxford and all the years of experience you've had if you only talk like that? This is our great chance; I told the old vicar only yesterday that he should have the money for his rood screen in a fortnight at the latest."

Father winked at John. "Well, how was I to know? I thought *you* were going to convert him! You never told me that I was to be 'in on it' as the current phrase has it, an Americanism, I believe."

"Oh, you make me tired." Her vehemence was inexhaustible. "You know that I know nothing about doctrine and exo—ex—"

"She means exegesis," interrupted Father.

"Well, exegesis or whatever it's called. *I* can only get him to the church, arouse his interest, and perhaps before he knows where he is get him on to his knees. Of *course*, I was relying on you to coach him on the theological side."

She sighed. "If only old Pall were still alive, between us we'd soon have won him around—enough money for the crypt, the church hall, *and* the rood screen."

"Oh, *Herbert!*" said Father scornfully. "A Durham man!"

Mother got up. "Well let's see if you can do better; at least my father knew that it wasn't just a question of pork!"

"I shall have to do a bit of reading if you're really relying on me." Father was pleased. "But you'll have to give me a few days' grace, pet. First of all I shall have to find my books; they were all turned out of the study in the last great spring cleaning. Little Melanie said she thought they were in the loft at Plas David—*in the loft!*"

Following Mother's example he too got up and stood in the yellowing sunlight a little uncertainly just behind her. He was watching anxiously to try and determine in which direction she would move next; he did not want to be left there alone.

Mother moved off around to the dog field and they followed her. She turned around impatiently.

"You'd better go and feed the hens. They'll be back any minute and I want them to have a glass of sherry before they go over to dinner—that is if they haven't filled themselves up to the neck in the Rhosybol Arms! And don't forget to wash your hands, Teddy. I don't want you coming in covered in bran and with hen dirt all over your shoes. John, go and ask Nanny for the sherry and get a tray ready and after that come and help me with the dogs; I want to know how you got on in the exam today."

Obediently they turned away and a little dejectedly walked down the steps on to the drive.

"That's done it!" said Father with satisfaction. "I'm in her black books again now. We shan't hear the last of this for weeks."

"Oh, I don't know, Father."

"Did *you* know she was expecting me to coach this fellow in Christianity?" He was still savouring the aftermath of his pleasure in the very definite commission he had exacted from her. "I thought he was a follower of Nietzsche—I had a curate once who steeped himself in it. He started preaching the most abominable sermons, poor fellow!"

"Why 'poor fellow'?" asked John.

"Interruptions at the end! I had to get in touch with my Bishop about it. Got no sympathy from *that* quarter; he'd once been rather keen on Nietzsche himself and told me that I must be tolerant—that Pinch was only cutting his theological teeth!" He sniggered. "*Theological teeth!* Did you ever hear such rubbish?"

"What happened to him?"

"Who, the Bishop?"

"*No*, this curate fellow—Pinch?"

"Oh, *him*? Your Mother got rid of him and he went to Birmingham—right place too; the Bishop there was a *Modernist* and that was too much for him—for Pinch I mean—he took a holiday at Saltburn and swam out too far and got himself drowned."

"Did he really?"

Father looked at him blackly. Beneath the high white forehead his small eyes were as dark as a rook's. "Of course he did. I don't tell lies. Pinch was a coward. He was eaten up with himself and took to reading Nietzsche instead of the New Testament."

There was silence for a moment and John suppressed a shiver. "It might have been an accident," he said hesitantly.

Father was very dry.

"It might have been, but it wasn't. There were notices all over the place warning bathers about the current and he chose one of the worst possible days. It was suicide and everyone knew it."

"Oh."

They stood there for a moment longer. The sun had begun to fall behind the "mountain" and the blue shadows were thickening over the fields and the whitewashed cottages which studded the green slope high above them. The little road from Pen-y-sarn dropped like a cobalt girdle to the hem of the narrow coastal plain.

"Do you ever pray for him, Father?"

"Of course I do. The war had poisoned his mind, poor fellow."

He broke off and pointed at the mountain road. Father always broke off when he was questioned overclosely on matters of faith, perhaps as a reaction to Mother's volubility; for their religions, despite nearly forty years of marriage, were a little different.

"We'd better hurry, John! There's Greenbloom's car. They'll be here in a few moments and I've got to get water and corn for those hens."

"Yes, Father. I say, what's this other fellow like? This Boscawen-Jones man?"

"Oh, he's a gentleman I should say. I didn't get much chance to talk to him with Kitty and Mick there; you know what she is, I never seem to be able to get a word in edgeways when she's talking. He looks all right, John—bit pale and seedy. I'm told he writes."

"Was he clean? I mean is he one of these long-haired, slovenly chaps that one reads about, sandals and corduroy trousers and so on?"

"What's that? Didn't notice; he looks tired. Look here, I'm sorry, John, I'll have to get a move on if I'm to get a glass of sherry with you. You might go and get that bottle opened, I'm looking forward to it."

He moved off stiffly in the direction of the water butt and John went into the house.

Later, Mother sat in all her gardening dirt on the little chair known as her "nursing chair" because she always said that one after the other she had breast-fed the family in it from the turn of the century. From the vantage point of this situation she talked intensively to Greenbloom while Mick, Father and Jane Boscawen-Jones, who had been introduced as Jane B-J for convenience, sat around her and listened, lazily alert.

Greenbloom, after two years of living in Paris, had developed his French self. There was a feminine quality about his clothes: a shirt sprigged with tiny flowers, very flat suède sandals and smoothly tailored trousers. He wore his hair a trifle longer and his harsh voice had absorbed both the French gutturals and sentence-rhythm, and he used his hands and shoulders more freely as he talked. He was, too, a trifle fuller in the face, more plump in his pauses as though the rich food and wine had conferred a certain judiciousness and deliberation upon him. Beside him, Boscawen-Jones looked frail; a hunched young man with old lines on his forehead, hollow cheeks and fine hair of the sort which thins quickly in the thirties; very difficult and given to twitching his narrow foot as he listened to the conversation. This foot-twitching gave him away in John's eyes; its writhings registered his reaction to every nuance of the conversation, as he sat there perched on the arm of Greenbloom's chair watching Mother exercising herself against the tolerant scepticism of his patron. Clearly, he was not liking what he saw.

As a writer, and therefore presumably as an observant person, even ten minutes with Mother when she was like this should have been sufficient to convince him that her capacity for the sort of honesty which deceives, would be dangerous even to the dull. Greenbloom was not dull, he was an enthusiast; and Mother, when she was sufficiently interested, could carry away even the most discreet of people by loving their enthusiasms just a little less than she loved them, which was utterly and with the most beautifying discernment.

Boscawen-Jones, if he were to profit from the encounter which he was watching so closely, would certainly have to be alert, John decided, as he circled around and filled up the sherry glasses.

It occurred to him then that they seemed like a school of gamblers as they sat there—with Mother as the banker—all with a private stake on the hazard of the conversation as they awaited the advent of their own particular advantage.

Father, wanting only Mother's attention and approval, was putting small stakes on a variety of different numbers, while Michael, having drunk too much in Benllwch, was plunging dumbly and more heavily on fewer fancies: the chance of returning with Greenbloom for a few weeks to the flat in Paris for example, or even of abandoning his Articles in London and accepting Greenbloom's offer of some unspecified position in the family vineyard near Tours. The outcome of course depended entirely upon Mother's reaction to Greenbloom; if she succeeded in liking him afresh now that his affair with Rachel was over and felt that his lapse from Judaism might imply a readier sympathy for Christianity; or if she were able to exact a promise of money from him for the rood screen, then all would be well for Michael and Father; if, on the other hand, they struck sparks between them as they had done in the past over his affair with Rachel, or if Greenbloom laughed at the wrong moment, then the whole family and the entire visit would suffer her displeasure and only Boscawen-Jones would profit from the disaster.

Hostility was apparent in every particular of his behaviour: his careful silences, his refusal to smile, or worse, the swift effacement of any smile ultimately wrung from him by a direct appeal. He alone, John decided, must have something real to lose, or must fancy that he had; and he wondered what it could be.

It could not be money, as according to Michael, Greenbloom had already spent far too much on his publishing venture to back out of it without any warning, and it was in any case far too soon for such a volte-face because Greenbloom had a certain loyalty to himself and rarely thought to abandon his past completely, holding that it was undignified to sever connections finally with any thing for which one had once entertained affection or respect.

Perhaps Boscawen-Jones was in love with Greenbloom; that would explain everything. He might easily be in love with his exoticism, his fiery enthusiasms, his impatience and the sudden despair to which he was still subject when he would sit as he had sat four years ago, green and greyly impassive, while John shaved him in his rooms at Oxford. Perhaps, too, his great wealth did play its part in Boscawen-Jones's attitude to him. There was something about a man as wealthy as Greenbloom; there was something about wealth itself; to have so much money taking an interest in one. Girls were right to let it count, John thought, to let it sway them; even to let it seduce them as once Danaë had been seduced by Zeus descending in a shower of gold.

Certainly Boscawen-Jones was behaving like a lover, like a jealous woman who, knowing that her hold is insecure or fancying that it is so, is soured and alerted by enthusiasm or interest displayed in any direction but her own, even though they be accorded only to a picture a child or a poodle. His foot-twisting, his spoiled, delicate, anxious face smoothed out to hide his concern, he was watching Mother hungrily, intent on missing no opportunity of distaste as she sat there working on Greenbloom with her grubby hands gesticulating and her eyes shining out beneath her freshly hennaed hair.

"And what about this horrible Wittgenstein man, Horab? Are

you still backing him, publishing things about his anti-Christian
books?"

Greenbloom fell back in the big chair screeching with laughter.

"No, no, no, Mrs. Blaydon. Wittgenstein has served his purpose very well; but he is a little démodé—an old flirtation. You
are out of date, isn't she, Jane?"

Boscawen-Jones smiled briefly.

"A little, I think."

Mother caught his tone and cocked her head at him quickly,
but she was too late. He had concealed his gaze by looking
down at his hands, watching them as he wrapped his thin fingers
carefully one over the other, and she switched her attention back
to Greenbloom.

"Tell her about Jean-Paul," commanded Greenbloom. "My
latest discovery."

"If you don't mind, Horab," he spoke pettishly, more like
a spoiled child than ever. "Not just now—"

"Very well." Greenbloom smiled indulgently and looked
around the room at the others. "Jane is what I call a very sick
poet! He is not strong, he suffers from a condition which it
would be indelicate to name, and sometimes we must humour
him. Jane does not like to talk about certain things at certain
times so *I* will have to tell you about my friend Sartre."

"And who is *he*?" fired Mother, releasing Boscawen-Jones from
her scrutiny. "Another nasty atheist who's going to start flooding England with black pamphlets like Bernard Shaw?"

"Listen to her, listen to her!" shouted Greenbloom. "You
should be taking notes Jane. I told you to bring a notebook
with you."

Mother ignored him. "Teddy! What was that book I made
you burn last week?" Father sat up and seized his opportunity
with fatal clumsiness.

"What book? You've burned so many." He looked around
in his clandestine way at Michael and John. He wanted to please
her; but as always when he had the chance of it, he automatically
forfeited it, preferring to take comfort in the reality of her
vexation rather than in the uncertainty of her affection.

"Always burning my books," he went on. "Only yesterday

little Melanie was telling me that she saw a whole lot of 'em in the loft over at Plas David!"

Mother flashed him an angry, mock-angry smile: she was stalking more important game. "Oh, never mind. Michael! *You* brought it home, you remember the one I mean?"

"Oh, the Blag—" Michael corrected himself, "The Black Girl," he said with beery care.

"That's right." She frowned. "But wasn't there something about God in it?"

"She means *The Adventures of the Black Girl in her Search for God*," said Father. "You didn't make me burn that, you snatched it out of my hand before I'd got beyond the first page."

"Of course I did! The old fool's going senile."

"I'm *not*!" said Father.

"Not *you*! Bernard Shaw. Oh Teddy, don't be so tiresome."

"You burned it?" Greenbloom gazed proudly at Boscawen-Jones in the manner of an owner whose dog's reputation for fierceness has not let him down. "You hear, Jane, she 'as burned a first edition of the best thing Shaw is ever likely to write. This little woman has burned it unread."

"Extraordinary!" said Boscawen-Jones with great boredom.

"I didn't need to read it. I could see by Teddy's expression that it was evil, couldn't I, Teddy?" Without waiting for an answer she glared briefly at Boscawen-Jones as she retasted the flavour of his comment.

"What do you mean, 'extraordinary'?"

"Nothing!" Boscawen-Jones yawned. "Only perhaps that your action was a little—*outré*, Mrs. Blaydon."

"*Please!*" said Greenbloom peremptorily.

Mother ignored him. "*Outré*—did you say '*outré*'?" she asked Boscawen-Jones.

Still careless of his peril, not realizing that until now she had scarcely noticed him, that he had been set aside for quick scrutiny at a later time, Boscawen-Jones aped Greenbloom's tired wave of the hand.

"The wrong word perhaps," he said, "but one does not like the flavour of philistinism—it is *vieux jeu*. Certainly though I should say that to have burned the book unread was a trifle odd."

Trembling finely like a terrier at a rat hunt, Mother leaned forward at him over the intervening space of the carpet. John knew that at last she had smelt out his latent hostility and that in a moment she would set her small jaws unerringly into the centre of his weakness and close them tightly together.

Greenbloom's violent nudge was lost on Boscawen-Jones as he recoiled a little by pushing his hunched spine against the back of the armchair. Around him, with small movements the others closed in, watching sharply to see where she would strike.

"So you think it 'a trifle odd.' " Extravagantly and with odious affectation she waved her hand in a burlesque of his gesture. "Well, *I* think your opinions are a trifle odd. I suppose they might be borrowed ones; young men are always borrowing from each other; but it's a pity that they never seem to borrow anything of any value—only shoddy little mannerisms and undergraduate glibness. I've had to watch my sons doing it for years; I've learnt a lot from dealing with them. *I breast-fed them all in this chair*, some of them before the Great War—long before *you* were born."

Boscawen-Jones cleared his throat. Mother's threatening aspect coupled with the awful association of the nursing chair seemed to have a paralyzing effect on him. His hands ceased shaking and he sucked in his thin cheeks nervously like a fish so that his face looked more fragile than ever.

"And I think I ought to warn you, Mr. Boscawen-Jones, that if any more books like that come into my house *that's* where they'll go—into the fire. There's enough blasphemy in the world without people putting it between the covers of books. Oh, I know the young men think you can afford to be clever! That's the Devil! *He* always likes people to think that they're clever, that's how he catches them. He keeps on *telling* them that they're clever; he whispers it to them at night just as they're going to sleep and he's there waiting for them in the morning to whisper it again when they first wake up. After a time they begin to believe him; they get a superior expression, they use French words where an English one would do and they begin to imagine that they're great actors or painters or—poets. But then I'm quite sure that *you* don't believe in the Devil; you're too young, you know too much; it's only the old who believe in the Devil, isn't it, Mr. Boscawen-Jones?"

Boscawen-Jones uncrossed his legs carefully. The length of her speech had given him time to erect some sort of a defence. To give himself further time he coughed into his handkerchief.

"I've never given the Devil very much thought, I'm afraid," he said with an effort at loftiness.

"Well, it's time you did," she fired back at him. "It's quite time you did, because I'm perfectly sure that he's been thinking about *you* quite a lot." She paused, "I'm only hoping that you haven't come up here to write *his* sort of poetry, because if you have you will find that you won't be able to write a line, not a single line. Other people have tried their hand at Black Art at Plas David. An evil woman last year, she took drugs and tried to paint the Copper Mines to look like Hell—and they *did!*— and she very soon left. So you see you're by no means the first person to be attracted by the beauty of our island—we're quite used to people coming here and setting themselves against it and we're not frightened of them in the very least."

Putting a hand to his forehead Boscawen-Jones got up suddenly.

"I'm afraid I do not feel very well. This sort of thing—" His voice fell away as he looked quickly at Greenbloom. "If you don't mind, Horab, I think I'll go and lie down for a few minutes." .

Greenbloom, like a person who has enjoyed the first turn in a good cabaret, waved at him lazily. "By all means, *mon cher*, go to your bed. Rest! Relax for a little while. But do not say that Greenbloom was not right, that I was wrong to bring you here. I told you that it would be an experience to meet Mrs. Blaydon. Tomorrow, despite all she says," and he smiled at Mother genially, "you will write better than you have written for a very long time."

Behind him Michael got up with alacrity. "It is rather close in here," he said. "The Gulf Stream you know. If you like I'll take you over to the other house and show you to your room."

"If you must," said Greenbloom. "But I shouldn't bother, Mick; Jane is enjoying himself immensely, he has crossed swords with your mother and now, as I warned him, he must suffer. But he is happy."

He shook Mother's hand as Boscawen-Jones, accompanied by Michael, made stiffly for the door.

"I congratulate you, Mrs. Blaydon. You were splendid."

She snatched her hand away with a swift smile, "Don't be ridiculous!"

"I am not! You *were* splendid. Your *contempt*—quite beautiful! It disarmed poor Jane, he had no weapon, nothing at all save his naked pride. Magnificent! I can only thank God that I did not have the misfortune to be born one of your four sons."

"If you had, you would have been very different."

He spread his hands. "But I don't doubt it."

"And then perhaps," she went on with a resumption of some of her previous intensity, "you would not always have been trying to steal my sons; they would have been your brothers."

"*Steal your sons!* Come, come, Mrs. Blaydon!"

"Oh, *I* know, Horab. You can't fool me. First of all Michael at Oxford, and look what happened to him—a pass degree—and then John, and *he's* not got his school certificate yet, and now John and Michael together. That's why you've come, isn't it?"

"But you forget Jane! I have not yet finished devouring Jane; why then should I want to start on your sons?"

"Oh," she said, "that little man, if he is a man; *Jane!*"

"It's short for Janus," said Father, who had now finished digesting the scene of a few minutes before and was avid for a further display of her anger. "It is not a *Christian* name, it means the two-headed man, the deceiver."

But she was not with him, "That little creature couldn't deceive a flea," she said. "No wonder you had to come up *here* with him. I know why."

"Tell me," said Greenbloom. "Please, Mrs. Blaydon! *Dear* Mrs. Blaydon! Tell Greenbloom why he has come up here."

"Because you are looking for our religion," she said. "That's what you're after. For all your talk of these half-baked philosophers you're always turning up; that's what really attracts you, that's why you can't leave my sons alone; it's their faith."

He considered it; his small face still trying to resist the pleasure of the smile he desired but dared not wear, Greenbloom nodded contentedly.

"And that is why I am not your enemy?"

"Not so far," she said.

"Not as long as I give them—your sons—back to you?"

"Unharmed," she said. "So long as you give them back to me unharmed, Horab."

"I see! I will confess that in a way you may be right. I do find your sons interesting, though not so interesting as yourself and for reasons other than those you suppose, and you may be sure that I shall always see that they are returned to you unharmed even if, as with John some time ago, I may not myself accompany them." He sipped at his sherry and then looked up at her again smiling. "Tell me, do you want nothing in return for my interest? If I were to take Michael back with me to Paris during this vacation, for example, you would demand nothing from me?"

"Oh yes I would. That's just where you're wrong. You don't imagine I'd let you have my sons for nothing, do you?"

"Not for a moment, I assure you. I suppose you may be banking on my conversion, yes?"

"No," she said. "That can wait. What I want is some money."

"Money?"

"Yes." She leaned forward with her legs wide apart and her hands on her knees. "A nice fat check."

"How fat?"

"That depends," she said. "It depends on how your friend Jane behaves and the sort of poetry he writes and how *you* behave and how Michael and John behave while you are here. Say a hundred pounds, that would do very nicely for the rood screen."

"*Kitty dear!*" Father from the midst of his second glass of sherry leaned forward incredulously.

"Oh, be quiet," she said, and turning caught sight of John. "And that's not all." Her voice hardened. "John! Go over to Plas David and tell Mary that Horab will be over in a few minutes and that she can serve the dinner. There's something else, something I'm worried about." She lowered her voice again. "I'm worried about John."

He heard the words as he closed the door behind him.

How had she known? Mary had not been over again and Nanny would not have said a word. Father, of course, had seemed strange about the curate drowning himself, but not definite or sure enough to have mentioned his suspicions to Mother. So how had she known?

He walked down the drive slowly. The curious thing was that none of it made any difference to his intention; although he had watched and listened to them all in there, no single thing that had been said had touched the hard centre of his intention at all. In some way it had even strengthened it; the fact that he had been able to see what moved them all, that nothing of what should have proved surprising in their behavior had surprised him in the very least, had only confirmed him in his sense of isolation. None of them knew anything; neither Michael, who was vaguely sozzled by the Benllwch beer, nor Father, who suffered Mother, nor Mother, who suffered her love of them all, nor Greenbloom and Boscawen-Jones, who were as remote as the Eiffel Tower. They knew nothing; they were all searching and seeking, chopping and changing, and he was tired of whatever it was they represented—if it were anything at all. They at least originally must have had a sense of purpose, had grown into their uncertainty by slow and relatively painless stages; but *he*—he permitted himself to think of Victoria for a moment as he turned into the Plas David drive. At the far end of it Mary was awaiting him coldly.

At Porth Newydd, Lady Geraldine Bodorgan greeted them in the hall. In her green county hat she came up to them with great composure, smiling adorably beneath the dead-eyed stags hanging on the walls. She had the sweetest voice and at fifty-two was still a flirt in the way a child is a flirt. She flirted with life and everything in it; furniture, flowers, animals and people, even with her clothes. Her grey eyes, aristocratically exophthalmic, or seeming to be so by their size and pallor, were like those of Edward the Seventh or George the Fifth and they welcomed

everything and everyone as they conveyed the secret and graceful rapture of her life's perpetual encounters. Such eyes would
smile even behind closed lids, in sleep, or in death; and in all the
years the Blaydons had known Lady Geraldine they had never
seen them show grief, anger or dismay despite the fact that she
should have been most unhappily married to her angry little
husband, the admiral.

"My dears," she said to Michael, "how dear of you to come!"
And she seemed to include them all in her delight. "You must
come upstairs and meet the girls, they've been so looking forward to seeing you."

Introductions seemed hardly necessary. They felt that she
had not only met both Greenbloom and Boscawen-Jones before
but even that she had long ago accepted them intimately and
confided in them the untamed secrets of her heart.

Michael and John kissed her pale saffron-coloured cheek and
Michael then presented Greenbloom and Jane. She touched their
hands affectionately.

"And so we have a poet in Anglesey at last," she said to Jane.
"Did you know that poor Dickens once stayed at Llanallgo
Rectory? We must take you over to see it—we'll have a picnic
there. I don't think he liked it much—there are so many trees
around the church."

Still talking quietly she led them across the hall and through
a door to a staircase with Greenbloom and Michael on either side
of her. In some way she managed to make each of them feel
that she was alone with him and that everything she said was
especially for his ears. John knew this because he experienced
a touch of resentment at being relegated to the back of the
procession with Boscawen-Jones and realized suddenly that he
liked always when at Porth Newydd to be beside Lady Geraldine.
But he followed with a good grace up the wide staircase.

"Don't you adore this house?" she said. "I'm so very fond of
it. Clive is always threatening to leave it and move into one
of the farms at Wern, but I don't think I could bear that; I'd
really rather starve and freeze in Porth Newydd than try and
live away from all this. These are my cobras! Don't you think
they're sweet?"

They all stopped by one of the wooden cobras which with extended hoods coiled around and crowned the pedestals at the beginning of each flight of stairs.

"Victorian Gothic! Charming examples," said Jane, "and a little unusual too."

"I'm so glad you think so. Oh how *sweet* of you to think so when you're so young. You see I *am* Victorian. Imagine, I was born in 1878 and I can't get away from it; I don't *want* to: it is home. Don't you think it's home, Mr. Greenbloom? One leaves home, I know, at twenty wherever one is or whatever one does, and ever since this century began *I've* been trying to return to the last one. That's really, I suppose, why I married Clive."

"For his century!" asked Greenbloom. "You married a man for his century? Magnificent! Lady Geraldine I congratulate you."

"Thank you," she said with a dewy lower lip. "It's so amusing. When I was a young gel I used to think the choice of a husband was so important that I very nearly left it too late. But now I'm fifty I realize that it makes very little difference; they were all so sweet and so much *men* that I'd have been quite as happy with any one of them. After all, they were all Victorians though none of them was quite so Victorian as Clive, poor dear—and then as I say there was the house. You must see all of it. Wander around anywhere you like: the library, the aviary, the gun room, the gardens, the lake, oh you must see the lake and the swimming pool, Mr. Boscawen, it is charming. John will tell you all about it."

Crossing the landing, with its marquetry cabinets and rubbed floral carpets, she turned and smiled at them hazily.

"Clive's a little eccentric about the sea, and though of course being on an island we're quite surrounded by it, he never goes near it if he can help it but insists on keeping his lake as a sort of Admiralty preserve."

There was a thistledown of grievance in her pause and Greenbloom was quick to recognize it.

"Ah! An obsession, Lady Geraldine? That is good. One likes a man to have an obsession."

"Then you would adore Clive," she said without rancour. "Fortunately he doesn't often use his lake in the evening so I think it would be quite safe for you to—" she was gently emphatic—"but please don't touch his barge, he's very funny about it."

"He has a *barge*?" Greenbloom's little head jerked up with delighted astonishment.

She laughed prettily; a cascade of sound fell from her lips as perfectly modulated as a garden waterfall.

"Oh dear," she said. "Forgive me! We have this with everyone and I suppose I should have become accustomed to it—but I never have. It's not a real barge, Mr. Greenbloom, it's a punt; but Clive insists that it *is* his barge—I'm afraid he's never got over having had one in his last years in the Navy and one simply daren't mention the other word. I've trained myself always to say barge and never—" she whispered it—"*punt*. But John will show you the lake, he knows all about it."

"I think," said Greenbloom seriously, "I would rather be shown the admiral; he sounds a most interesting man. Your description of him revives my faith in England. I shall come and live here again."

"Oh no, Mr. Greenbloom, I'm afraid that's the one thing I can't arrange. Clive never meets people nowadays. He's most unsociable, and of course he's not really English, he's very Welsh."

"Of *course*! That explains it. It is always the same: the Welsh, the Irish, the Scots—English history is founded on them."

"Oh, don't say that. There was always darling Nelson." She moved over to the drawing-room door. "Now please come in and rescue poor Sambo for me. He *will* be pleased to see you. He's been trying to entertain the girls ever since they arrived. Clive of course is more absent than ever when what he calls the 'closed season' starts—he means my P.G.'s—I often wonder where he hides. It's very unkind of him to leave it all to Sambo because as you know the darling can't talk about anything very much but rugby football and the girls never seem to be very interested in that."

They did know about Sambo, all that there was to be known:

that he was about forty-eight, drank and had once played for the Army at Twickenham.

Michael opened the door and they followed her into the enormous room which on two sides overlooked the lawns and terraces. The parquet floor stretched ahead of them like a still, buff-coloured lake on which sofas, chairs, a grand piano, china, cabinets and vast cradles of flowers floated on their reflections.

"This," went on Lady Geraldine, "is my favourite room. Don't you think it would be *your* favourite room?" She invited them to agreement with one of her loveliest smiles and then without awaiting an answer slid gently forward over the shining surface as though impelled by a soft and scented breeze of her own. They smelt her perfume floating back to them as she moved between flowers and furniture up the pale horizon of the floor in the direction of the marble fireplace.

They realized then that someone had been playing the piano in the far distance. The middle chords of *The Rustle of Spring* died on the air as a girl rose from behind the keyboard, and simultaneously, they became sensible of the presence of other people disposed and dispersed amongst the great spaces and solids of the room.

A middle-aged couple, distressingly well-groomed, detached themselves from a window seat at the far end.

"The Merryweathers." Lady Geraldine's voice floated back to them as though she had whispered. "They make safes and refrigerators in Birmingham—*so* interesting! You'll love them."

John smiled to himself remembering how once he had overheard his own description from her lips, "John Blaydon, so sweet; such a *simple* boy. You will find him charming."

In different parts of the room they saw that there were girls in summer frocks scarcely distinguishable from the covered chairs and sofas on which they were posed. One was writing a letter on her knee, two others were playing chess; but Lady Geraldine drew them after her towards Sambo, who was standing stiffly before the empty fireplace, his black hair, thinning at the crown, reflected in the great rectangle of the glass above the chimney piece.

His scarlet face, pinker than a huntsman's jacket, looked almost indecent against the diffuse pastels and pallors of the room. He had been talking to a platter-faced girl of about seventeen who for some reason was wearing jodhpurs. She looked bored in an uneasy way, as though she had no right to be bored, and kept glancing for approval in the direction of the Merryweathers. John thought at once that she must be their daughter and that she had been brought there to stay because of the title and at the same time equipped with very little else save jodhpurs and the necessity for fresh gratitude to her parents.

When Lady Geraldine spoke and confirmed all of his surmise, a summary so rapid that until she spoke he did not realize that he had thought it, he knew the first moment of satisfaction he had been granted that day. It always pleased him when he proved to be right about things which he could not possibly have known.

"Now Sambo!" she said. "Here they are at last! I want you to introduce everyone to everyone while I go and see Wild-brown about the coffee and drinks in the dining room. Oh, and this, Ursula dear, is John Blaydon and his brother Michael and Mr. Greenbloom and Mr. Boscawen. Ursula's staying here with her parents, the Merryweathers." She waved over to them intimately and they both smiled with pleasure. "Ursula adores houses and horses and I'm arranging for her to finish near Paris at Boufflémont, aren't I, Ursula dear?"

"Yes, Lady Geraldine."

"And now I really must go. Poor Wildbrown is such a tyrant that I can never think of getting rid of her. Sambo! Perhaps you could organize ping-pong in the billiard room unless they'd rather dance to the gramophone or just talk. It's too dark for croquet but everyone is to do just what they want." She turned to Michael. "If only your little mother would come over more often! She's so wonderful at organizing things, she'd have everyone acting in a play within ten minutes of her arrival; I know she would. But it's sweet of her to spare you, especially in the summer when she has so many things to do. Now you'll find things to eat and drink downstairs and don't forget to go anywhere you like but please remember about the *barge*."

With a last radiant, intimate smile for them all no less than

for Sambo she turned and left them gracefully with the same
perfect composure with which she had greeted them; and at
her going, the lights seemed perceptibly to dim, the room to
grow a trifle smaller and Sambo a little older, all the girls a little
younger.

The Rustle of Spring winnowed out into the air again carrying with it the ineffable tedium of a school music room, the
two girls on the sofa resumed their chess, the Merryweathers
their *Tatler* and Sambo his stiff, upright redness in front of the
looking glass.

Beside John, Greenbloom murmured, "*Mon Dieu!*" and said
to Sambo, "I believe you are interested in football?"

Sambo touched his moustache and without moving his lips,
eyebrows or any part of his scarlet face said, "Ruggah."

There was silence between them, only saved from proving unpleasant by the activity of the girl at the piano. Under the safe
cover of the music John turned and inspected Ursula. Obviously
she was the reason for *his* invitation. Her parents would live
contentedly on the title and the address for a full fortnight; but
for her, this would be poor consolation. There were, he knew,
no horses at Porth Newydd and this girl was quite obviously
horse-mad. He wondered briefly why it was that girls who were
fond of horses were always so brightly and separately put together, so hostile. Other girls, the horseless variety, had a softness about their features, one saw them as a whole; but girls like
this were always lacking in homogeneity. They had fierce blue
eyes, aggressively red cheeks, and harsh golden hair; they grew
up to be women like Kay, Toad's wife at the Abbey. He wondered dully and with increasing depression if she were still alive.

"You live in Birmingham?"

"No. Outside it."

"Have you just arrived?"

"We've been here three days."

"It's a beautiful place, isn't it?"

"It's very cut off."

"Yes, I suppose it is." What did she mean, he wondered.

"What from? I mean what's it cut off from?"

Out of her square, post-adolescent face she looked at him with hostility tinged with scorn.

"It's cut off, that's all."

"Oh."

"If you don't mind, I think my parents want me."

"Not at all."

He did not look over to them as she left him. He was not interested in knowing whether she were lying or not; she was the sort of girl he loathed and he felt suddenly furiously angry with Lady Geraldine for tricking him into his earlier excitement. What an appalling evening it was going to be. To eat, of course, there would be Miss Wildbrown's cucumber sandwiches; to drink, her watered cider-cup with the cucumber peel floating on the top.

The thought of this cheered him up. Greenbloom and Mick would be expecting a share of the whisky reserved for Sambo and the admiral, but they would not get it. At the correct moment Sambo, who was the only one in old Clive's confidence, sharing not only his board but, if the Welsh rumour were correct, his wife's most secret affections as well, would disappear into a concealed sanctum in the east wing and leave them to the girls and their fate. There they would sit muttering in a study with scarlet wallpaper, furnished with naval bric-a-brac, drinking heavily, silently and with the precious hostility which in fifteen years had become essential to their relationship.

But Mick, Greenbloom and Boscawen-Jones would be depending on the prospect of potent refreshment to lift the evening out of the chasm into which it had fallen. They had been so very sure of it that they had only stopped for a very "short one" at the Rhosybol Arms on the drive over, and John, who alone had known of the increasing severity of Miss Wildbrown's reign at Porth Newydd, had not bothered to warn them of the austerity they must expect. When they did make the discovery they would leave promptly, he knew that; because the pubs in Wales closed at ten and already it must be nearly nine-thirty. So it would be a very short evening, and tomorrow, he remembered, was Sunday.

He began to attend to the conversation in front of the fire-place.

The Merryweathers less Ursula, who was now standing by the piano, had reintroduced themselves and moved in, while Greenbloom, who was showing signs of being worn down by Sambo's capacity for silence, was addressing them on the subject of Jane's poetry.

"Impeccably middle-class, my dear Mr. Merryweather," he was saying. "That is why I am publishing him. Whether we like it or not we are moving away from the private revolution of Yeats, Eliot and Pound into the era of middle-class art. We are moving back into all that this house stands for, Victorian revivalism, *Manchesterism*—"

"What about Birm-ing-ham?" asked Mr. Merryweather truculently, pronouncing each syllable separately.

"That too," said Greenbloom airily. "But Birminghamism with a difference. Birmingham today wants to feel that it has one foot in Windsor. It is no longer content, as it was in the days of Queen Victoria, to flaunt its own standards of wealth and aestheticism in the face of the aristocracy and be laughed at for its pains. Birmingham wants its own poetry, its own art forms, and it wants them to be both *chic* and smart. *I* am going to see that it gets them—through people like Jane here. He is the perfect type—as I said before, impeccably middle-class." He paused. "Where were you at school, Jane? I forget, Beowulf's or Epsom?"

"Ardingly," said Boscawen-Jones.

"Exactly!" said Greenbloom. "You see? He was at Ardingly. That is important. Whats-his-name was at Ardingly, that novelist fellow, but far from stopping him it has equipped him for the necessary social theft. Everything he writes is in the aristocratic tradition. In his biography he talks about his private school and his tutor as though he had been at Eton. *Eton*, my friends! When everything about him is middle-class, from his books and his antecedents to his outlook. Yet, that is why they sell; in prose he gives Birmingham the authentic Windsorism which Jane will give it in poetry. Fifteen years from now the middle class will have created an artistic revolution in England. It will have become the arbiter of taste; the mandarins will disappear and titled men of letters be reduced to writing books of biography and travel."

"What's all this got to do with poetry?" asked Mr. Merryweather.

Greenbloom yawned. "Oh nothing, my dear fellow, nothing at all. I was merely talking. One must make a noise sometimes."

Sambo spoke, "Rhk-ah! Come for a drink? There's something downstairs, I believe."

Without waiting for a reply he moved off in the direction of the stairs and with great readiness Michael, Greenbloom and Boscawen-Jones together with the Merryweathers followed him. John heard their consternation when they reached the landing and found that Sambo had disappeared; he heard them move off, talking desultorily as they went slowly down the wide staircase.

In a few moments Ursula and the other girls also got up and followed them out of the room, and John was left alone with the girl at the piano.

"Aren't you coming down?" he asked.

She stopped playing.

"No, I'm waiting for someone."

"Oh, I see."

"Can you tell me the time please?"

He glanced over at the stopped clock on the chimney piece. "I'm not sure, I think it must be about twenty to ten."

"Heavens! Is it really?"

He walked over to her. "Who are you waiting for?"

"Uprichard."

"Who is he?"

She smiled.

"It's not a 'he,' it's a 'she.' She only arrived this evening and I think she must be unpacking."

"Is she from the school too—from Wycombe Abbey?"

"Yes." She turned over a page of the music. "We broke up early because of an epidemic."

"That was lucky. What was it, measles or chicken pox or something?"

"Good gracious, no. We've all had that years ago. It was—"
she looked embarrassed—"gastric-something-or-other."

"Oh." He changed the subject.

"How do you spell Eweprichard?"

"Up-Richard, it's Irish."

She was very reserved he thought. He tried the question direct.

"Are *you* Irish?"

"Yes."

"I see, and this Uprichard girl is your special friend, is she?"
She looked irritated by his persistence. Her eyebrows contracted
briefly behind her spectacles.

"Yes," she said shortly, "but not because we're Irish. As a
matter of fact *she's* a Protestant."

"Aren't you?"

"No. I'm a Catholic."

"A *Roman* Catholic?"

"Yes. In Ireland everyone's either a Protestant or a Catholic."

"Really! Why's that?"

"Because it's a Catholic country," she said.

He laughed. "That sounds awfully clever."

"It's not—it's just true."

She started to play again. He thought at first it was a gambit,
something she might have picked up from the films, to sprinkle
a conversation with music while swaying slightly on a piano
stool. But after a few moments during which he cast around
for something else to say or for some sign of her continuing
interest in him, he noticed that she had become absorbed in the
music and realized that her slight frown as she stared at the open
sheet was directed against him and the persistence of his presence.

Deciding that he did not like Irish Catholics he stepped away
from the piano and followed the others down the stairs. At the
bottom he turned along the corridor leading to the aviary and
the orangery and went out through the glass doors into the
garden.

A warm moon, newly risen, illumined the pale slope of the
lawn falling gently to the shrubs surrounding the lake. He
walked slowly towards them through the heavy dew, hearing
the wet grass slip against his shoes as he drew nearer to the

blocks of shadow underlying the bulk of the rhododendrons and azaleas.

By this light the flowers with which they were solidly crowned gave back strange flames to the moon: they were indigo without blueness, scarlet with no vestige of red, whitenesses containing purple and black depths; and they leaped and burned without heat, seeming to vibrate against the darkness of their foliage so rapidly that no movement was apparent, yet so actively that he fancied they made the air immediately above their petals cold with the silent wind of their motion. He imagined that they were being kept there in the moonlight like dragonflies, sustained hovering on wings beating so fast that they were scarcely visible. Their beauty, so remote, unrelated to anything but themselves, scentless, motionless and all but unapparent when compared with their daylight selves, chilled him as he stood there watching them. He found then that he wanted to discover some means of declaring his presence, to affect them in a way which would force them to acknowledge him.

In the house he had been rebuffed twice by his equals, by humans; and because of this he had come out here for companionship, seeking the inanimate intimacy of the night which in childhood had never eluded him; but now he found that he was shut out of this world too as completely as though he had had no existence. It went on in his presence as carelessly and uncaringly as it must have done in his absence, held together in darkness as in daylight by a force which took no account of his existence at all.

He sniffed once again at the limp wallflower in his buttonhole. Either because he had been smoking or else because the air was saturated with dew he could smell no least trace of its earlier warm scent, and throwing it away, he reached up and started to wrench violently at one of the rhododendrons just above his head.

Behind him, as he twisted at the stubborn stem from which a crown of petals rose, he heard a door open and close and the sound of footsteps crossing the gravel to the grass; but he did not hesitate. With a last twist he severed the blossom, tearing its bark back down to the main branch so that its bast was exposed whitely to the moon, and then stepped further into the shadows about him and looked back at the house.

Greenbloom was limping across the grass towards him, making for the same gap in the shrubs which he himself had observed a few moments earlier. In a great hurry, apparently quite unaffected by the leisureliness of the moon, he moved through the darkness of the grounds as impatiently and purposefully as he went through his days, his attention fixed on some immediate or anticipated act which was quite unsusceptible either to his humour or his environment.

John stood quite still as he passed, not consciously hiding, but unable for the moment to declare himself unmistakably. He hoped that any initiative would come from Greenbloom, that he might stop and ask him what he was doing or confide in him the reason for his own sortie into the garden; but as it was, his state of half-hiding was not broken and Greenbloom, his small face pale as a wax mask, his feet making no sound on the trodden loam of the path, passed him as he went on towards the gleam of the water in the admiral's lake.

John saw his body briefly silhouetted between the dark wings of the bushes before he turned to the left along the flagstones and disappeared in the direction of the boathouse. He wondered what he could be doing and how he had managed to evade Michael and Boscawen-Jones.

Greenbloom described himself as being hyper-aesthetic and was openly scornful of purely natural beauty. John remembered a story of Michael's about a fortnight he had spent with him in Northern Italy and Rome. "Never again," Greenbloom had said on their return to his flat in Paris. "*All that beauty!* So exhausting; and Rome, with peasants making their way on all fours up Somebody's Steps and arriving at the top with Holy Water on the Knee; in future I shall confine my holidays to England and the delights of ribbon development!"

Assuredly then it could not be the moonlight which had brought him out like this, though it might possibly have been a whiff of curiosity as a result of Lady Geraldine's remarks about the lake; probably he had wanted either to have a private drink or else to evade the boredom of supper with the Merryweathers.

John listened intently but could hear no sound from the direction of the pool, and so after a few minutes he began to steal quietly down the short path. At the far end he hesitated and then leaned out into the slow light of the moon.

Greenbloom was sitting facing him on the innermost of the three long balustrades which at intervals of five or six feet encircled the oval lake.

Behind him, the moon laid down a cold ladder of light on the surface of the water against which his head and shoulders were drawn black as a daguerreotype as he drank from the cap of the long flask he wore in his hip pocket.

He wiped his lips carefully, stood the empty cap beside the flask on top of the balustrade, and without turning his head spoke aloud.

"What have you done with it?"

John stood galvanically upright in the shadows holding his breath, grateful for the fresh descent of the darkness on his eyes and face. Feeling absurdly frightened by his state of indecision, he began to count secretly to himself, preferring to believe that he had imagined the words or else that Greenbloom was drunk rather than be reduced to acknowledging the fact that he had been observed spying and prying on someone else's private moment. As he reached an unspoken count of seven in his mind, Greenbloom's voice grated out once again:

"If you have it still I would like to see it. If not, it would be interesting to know why you picked it?"

John stepped out on to the terrace.

"I didn't know anyone had seen me." He heard himself laugh uneasily.

"It is not pleasant to be observed," said Greenbloom. "I do not like it myself and that is why I made no comment when I passed *you*."

"Oh."

"It is very *un*pleasant to be watched."

"I'm sorry, I didn't mean to watch you, Greenbloom. As a matter of fact I was bored and—"

"*Only* bored?"

"Yes, I think so."

"I would not have said that you would ever be bored. I would have suggested, had I cared to make any suggestion to myself, that John Blaydon could never suffer from mere boredom after the reality of his earlier experiences." He spoke heavily with accentuated gutturals, and John felt that he was seeing Greenbloom's French self, the "foreigner" who lived with Gallic disillusionment in the night streets of Paris. His left foot, crossed over his right knee and flexed closely at the end of his good leg, swung impatiently to and fro over the squares of the flagstones; it reminded John of the twisting tail of some predatory animal: a wolf or a lynx. The patent vexation of his questioner coming so soon after his rebuffs by the two girls in the drawing room roused him in his turn, so that when he spoke it was with a vehemence which surprised him.

"Why shouldn't I be bored? *You* were bored, weren't you? Or you wouldn't have come out here? You're getting to be as bad as everyone else. You don't seem to know why you do things any more than old Mick does."

Pursuing his argument with all the remorselessness of a person who has heard but rejected an interruption, Greenbloom spoke reflectively.

"One does not tear down flowers when one is bored. One drinks or has intercourse. Possibly one travels."

"I didn't *tear it down*, I just picked it; the branch was tough."

"Lying is not morally wrong, but on occasions it can be tiring. *You* are lying; the flower is immaterial, you know that because you are intelligent. I am intelligent too and we both know that what *should* be discussed is the fact of your despair."

"My despair?"

"Yes, you have come to despair have you not? Boredom eludes you; one whom suffering has convinced of his own existence cannot be bored to *death* if you understand me; but he may well come to what we call despair, and despair, being an activity of the imagination, is reprehensible."

Their silence was emphasized by the gurgle of the flask as Greenbloom refilled the cap.

"Sartre, of course, would not agree with me." He drank briefly. "You must meet him. For him the imagination, not the style, is the man; hence he elevates despair as a priest elevates the Host, but with this difference, that *he* sacrifices a negation to a negation and prefers to be unobserved while he does so. For Jean-Paul, as *I* understand him, boredom is the equivalent of what the mystics call ecstasy: the apprehension of a vacant truth by a vacant imagination. Do you follow me?"

"Not really."

"No, I thought not; but it is unimportant. *Everything* is unimportant—even your despair." He held out the full cap of brandy, "Drink this before we are interrupted by further observers."

"Thank you."

John took the silver cap and drained it. He sat down a few feet away from Greenbloom, who waved at the pool, the encircling balustrades, the dark olive-coloured enclosure of shrubs and the silvery bulk of the admiral's boathouse at the far end.

"A madman constructed this," he said. "What did he imagine his intention was?"

"The admiral," said John tangentially, "Lady Geraldine calls him her *red* admiral, has been working on this place ever since he retired. She didn't really tell you about it at all. You ought to see it by daylight, dozens of statues and urns, bits of carved stone, pottery from the Holy Land, chimney stacks and cannons mounted in concrete with flowers and bushes growing out of them, ships' bells, flagstaffs, coloured figureheads from Nelson's navy, even a live torpedo behind the boathouse—at least *he* says it's alive: he uses it as a threat and—"

"And I suppose," interrupted Greenbloom, "he keeps his barge in the boathouse?"

"Yes. No one but John Hughes is allowed near it."

"Who is John Hughes?"

"Well actually he's the gardener, but he was in the Navy with the admiral at some time or another and the admiral always refers to him as his cox'n. As far as I understand it, an admiral always has a coxswain in the Navy who's in charge of his barge and I believe that when the admiral 'puts out,' as he calls it, John Hughes is always made to act the part. He has to run up the flags and use the punt pole and so on." John laughed unconvincingly.

"A moment if you please!" Greenbloom cut him short irritably. "I would give very much to see the spectacle of the admiral and his cox'n putting out in the barge. It would be of considerable interest to my friends in Paris. Do you think it might be arranged if we were to speak to Lady Geraldine?"

This time John's laughter was spontaneous. "Good Lord, no!" he said. "She'd be frightfully upset by the mere suggestion. The admiral never allows anybody to see him when he brings out the barge; he's even been known to threaten people with revolvers if he suspected that they were trying to watch him. As a matter of fact I believe he very seldom goes out in it nowadays. He spends most of his time adding disused equipment to the lakeside, stuff he buys from Admiralty sales and so on."

Greenbloom looked around gloomily, peering intently through long narrowed eyes at the yellowing clutter of objects standing on the banks beneath the leafy horizon of the shrubbery.

"Interesting!" he said at length. "A private madness almost as publicly expressed as Trafalgar Square."

With a sudden change of voice and manner he looked around at John sharply.

"Why did your sister Mary refer three times to your impending suicide during dinner at Plas David?"

"Did she? I—didn't notice."

"Have another drink and cease lying to me!" He waved angrily at the flask. "Fill it yourself."

"When I'm with you," said John, reaching for the flask, "I always seem to drink. Do you remember Ireland?"

"I remember the *flight to Chantilly* very well," said Greenbloom distinctly. "It was foolish of you to leave us like that without seeing anything of the *pays* or the people."

John coughed and replaced the flask.

"What happened to Rachel?" he asked. "I've often wondered. Where is she now?"

"She is in Heidelburg. Her name is now Grossblutte—Frau Rachel Grossblutte—it serves her right," said Greenbloom simply. "She married a professor of philosophy at the University there."

The duration of his pause was indeterminate and feeling that his frown was a consequence of his own subterfuge in having changed the subject, John was loath to interrupt him afresh.

"Shortly," went on Greenbloom, "both she and her husband will be refugees."

"Refugees?"

"Grossblutte is an unintelligent thinker, but I do not believe that even he is sufficiently muddle-headed to visualize any future for himself in the new National-Socialist Germany."

"Oh, you mean this Hitler man?"

"I mean the little Austrian who, until he makes the mistake of dining on the Pope and winning on the Jews, is likely to make Europe very noisy and tiring for some time to come." He broke off and then in the same tone of voice but with another full glance at John, said, "*What method had you in mind?*"

"Drowning," said John, "the Point. Beautiful! Very strong and clean. You would go under fighting, with clouds and waves and sun surrounding your head—or stars. I might do it at night, I hadn't thought of that."

"No audience then," said Greenbloom heavily. "No observer. Yes, that is good. You sound as though you may be serious." With one of his new judicious pauses he looked over at the low moon. "We will go together. Delightful!"

"You mean—you want to watch me?"

Greenbloom's laugh disturbed something sleeping in the hedge; there was a clatter of branches and wings and a drowsing bird rose in the moonlight and flew silently away between two of the flagpoles.

"Watch you? Certainly not, I will help you. It will be a case of '*encourager les autres*.' At the last moment as you take up your position on the wet rocks, you may find that you shrink from the ultimate committal. Believe me, small things at such times can wield a disproportionate influence on one's powers of action; a cold wind, for instance, a moment of emotion, even the renaissance of some false sentiment. I will be there to see that this does not happen to *you*. Quite simply, at the *moment critique*, when you have made your final dispositions of course and not before, I will *push* you. Greenbloom will precipitate the void into the Void, and then return home silently the way he has come, taking one more secret with him."

He seemed entirely serious and for a moment John was quite nonplussed. He reached out for the flask again, but Greenbloom removed it to his other side with solemn emphasis.

"No," he said, "not for *you* at a moment like this. You must think clearly if you are to appreciate the beauty of what I have offered to do for you."

"But I don't think—" John sought for the words, "somehow that doesn't seem—"

"Of course not." Greenbloom's smile was slow and coldly studied; it spread over his waxen face like a face-pack in the hands of a masseur. "One must become accustomed to these things. Tomorrow, when I have submitted to your mother's blackmail about her church, we will discuss our final arrangements together; but before that there are a few questions I should like to ask you. Your death has become important to me—I feel involved in it—a sense almost of responsibility."

"But it's got nothing to do with you, I mean you only asked me about it and eventually I told you. At first I didn't want to tell you, I didn't want to tell *anyone* seriously, but you were so insistent that you gave me no choice."

"Enough! You are still prevaricating. Let us drink to it, I think there is enough cognac left and after their betrayal of me to this *galère* of schoolgirls and materialists I have no intention of saving any for the others." He filled the cap again. "I will drink first and you second. If I may quote, we will 'seal this bargain to engrossing death.' "

"No," said John. "I won't drink! You don't understand. You see I was waiting for the exam results first."

"Nonsense, that is another prevarication. It is precisely because you envisaged such things that you took the very wise step of confiding in me. Believe me I shall not fail you, John. *Drink!*" He stood up with the full cap in his hand but John remained seated.

"What questions did you want to ask me?"

"Oh, they were quite unimportant. They will do tomorrow *after* we have discussed the more urgent arrangements for your suicide. Sunday, by the way, is an appropriate night, very appropriate, and you may count on me. Now drink! I will give you the toast."

John remained obstinately seated. The rapidity with which Greenbloom had dissipated the secrecy of his intention and assumed the initiative was even more discomforting than his matter-of-fact acquiescence and his impatience to conclude something which was really no concern of his at all.

"I won't drink," he said. "At least not until you've asked me the questions."

"Very well!" Greenbloom sighed. "I can see that I am going to have difficulties with you tomorrow night. It is not going to be so satisfactory as I had imagined. One might almost say that the quality of your despair is unworthy of us both. If you must know, I was interested only in minor details of the earlier tragedy."

"You mean the murder?"

"Yes, yes, the murder. I think it is only fitting that someone should be in possession of all the facts, and as the single surviving repository of your secret I feel that in order for the circle, the vacant circle, to be completed—as complete as these stone circles of the red admiral's, as you call him—that person should be myself. After all I have known you for some years now and I feel that I have not been without influence upon your thinking."

"Oh, all right. What do you want to know?"

"A few things. What for instance has happened to the girl's mother?"

"She's in Canada."

"Married?"

"Yes."

"To whom?"

"To Mr. Harkess." John breathed out impatiently. "If you really want to know, they married about twelve months later. *She* always sends me a Christmas card."

Greenbloom nodded. "Interesting," he said, "in a sense almost Hamletesque—Shakespearean. Now that *would* have been a play! I mean for the mother to have married the *Prince's* murderer."

"But he *wasn't* her murderer. Mr. Harkess had nothing—"

"In the narrower sense, no; in the broader sense, yes. Remotely we are all involved; he, this Mr. Harkess, was very closely involved." A yawn escaped him. "Forgive me! It is not that I am uninterested in the circumstances, the precedents of your approaching death; I can understand that to you it must seem of unique importance, but tonight I am a little tired. Tomorrow night it will be different. I have no doubt that then I shall be feeling more alert. Now what was I saying? Ah yes! This man Harkess—that was his name was it not?"

"Yes."

"It was inevitable that she should have married him; a woman would never be able to forgive a man for a thing like that."

"But I keep on telling you. He had nothing to do with it."

"Nothing?"

"No, nothing, except that he was in love with—with Victoria's mother."

Greenbloom spoke very slowly. In the light of the moon, which as it rose above the surface mists of the island grew whiter and whiter, his eyelids drew down on their pale sclera leaving only the two irises, wet and black, to gaze out upon John through their nearly occluded margins.

"And the night that your Victoria was strangled," he was precise, "where were *they*?"

"At the races—no, in bed—they were in bed." John swallowed. "You read it didn't you? It was all in the papers."

"*All?*"

Greenbloom smiled and John stood up. "No, not all. Not that bit. I never told anyone that bit. I thought it was important then but now I know it isn't. They wanted me to keep it secret, it was important to *them*."

"*Very,*" said Greenbloom. "Lyricism! The lyricism of the dispossessed!"

"I don't know what you mean, I don't want to know what you mean," said John, "I'm tired of meanings."

Still Greenbloom stood there smiling arrogantly with cold sagacity; his forehead white and unmarked in the untarnished light.

"There *are* no meanings. No meanings that we can apprehend. Ludwig Wittgenstein was right when he said that."

"Oh *Wittgenstein*! If you think that you understand it all why do you ask *me*? Why do you keep following me? Why go on about it? *I* never think about it; it was—*something*, that's all." John's voice fell away as he tried to explain. "It was—*sensible*; in a way I'm glad it happened. I know now *why I am*. Nothing else irremediable, nothing that makes sense has ever happened to me since and never can. That's what's the matter with me. I can see through everything all the time. I think I'm waiting for something like it—something as important I mean—to happen again. It should never have happened *once* to anyone; it should go on happening always: losing things to find them, love being killed while it was alive so that you could have it. I wouldn't love her now if she were here, not like I *do* love her now that she's gone. As it is, I do love her *because* she's dead and that's where I live—it's where I lived and now I can't stop it."

"Do not try to stop it. You have left it too late."

In the aftermath of his sudden warmth John shivered.

"How do you mean, 'too late'?" he asked.

"Four years—five? It is too late! You should have killed yourself within three months; as it is you have delayed too long; you have left yourself with a most powerful *raison d'être* and I begin to think that it looks as though my services may not be required tomorrow night."

"You mean you think I'll want to go on living *because* I am so unhappy?"

"Of course."

"You don't think I *will* commit suicide?"

"*Never!* You have no disinterest. Very early in life you have suffered by attachment, by a supreme attachment, that *de*tachment which it is the object of all developed men to achieve." He looked up and smiled briefly. "You must meet my friend Sartre. You might conceivably interest him and *he* would most certainly interest you. More than that, he would help you I am sure."

"But he lives in Paris doesn't he?"

"All writers if they are good live imaginatively in Paris. Sartre lives there physically as well. One day you may live there your-self. It occurs to me that perhaps in five or ten years when you start to write the story of your Victoria and how she was strangled you *will* live there."

"Do you think I'm going to be a writer then?"

"I do."

"Oh. Do you really?"

"*Mais, certainement!*"

"Why?"

"If one thinks enough, sooner or later one *must* write. Already you have been made by your life to think more than enough, more profoundly perhaps than the majority of your contempo-raries; and as I told you before, you are fortunate."

Silently Greenbloom handed him the cap of his brandy flask and John drank from it.

"It is a pity that your great little mother can never be told about this," said Greenbloom. "This afternoon I gave her an undertaking—"

They both turned as someone emerged from behind the boat-house. They saw her standing there hesitant, looking over to-wards them, marked with the white lacunae of the moonlight as it fell through the freckling leaves and branches of the taller trees behind her.

"My God!" Greenbloom quickly screwed on the cap and pocketed his flask. "Another of them, and at a moment like this! The Irish girl, presumably the one who fainted on the train. I am afraid I shall have to go."

"But wait a minute! Please don't go for a minute. Please just tell me one thing—*Greenbloom*."

"Well?"

His smile this time was natural. John saw the white flash of his teeth, the rise of the puffy lids beneath the long eyes.

"You don't think I'm mad, do you? You obviously don't, do you? You don't think I'm a fool or backward or anything like that?"

"Your sisters are—banal. Your mother, as I said before, has greatness, your brother Michael—constant possibilities; your father I do not know very well because he is the sort of man who does not want to be known very well, but he seems to me to be a good man. Certainly he has sat out your mother for many years and he is not a fool. As for yourself I can assure you that I shall continue to interest myself in your life for many years to come. Very possibly I shall be one of the first, if not *the* first, to publish you when you come to fruition."

He held out his hand and John shook it automatically. From the tail of his eye he saw that the girl, tall, paler than the statues surrounding the pool, was approaching them quickly.

"Tomorrow," went on Greenbloom, "we must discuss this again. But now I really must go. I do not like schoolgirls, I detest Irish schoolgirls and I abominate in particular the sort of girl who faints on railways trains."

"Did she? How do you know?"

"Some unpleasant people from Birmingham mentioned it over the—*cucumber sandwiches.*" He made the words sound like blasphemies.

"Oh, the Merryweathers."

John laughed; surprisingly he heard the sound fall out of him into the strange circle of the lake and its concentric balustrades.

"Yes," said Greenbloom wearily. "The Merryweathers. Forgive me, there is not a moment to be lost."

He turned and with great dexterity bobbed across the flagstones to the southern entrance just as the girl reached the top flight of the steps beneath which they had been standing.

John looked up at her. Her white dress hung limply from the thin shoulders, her hair, parted like his own on the left, bobbed and short, curled smokily about her ears and around her young forehead as she stood there listlessly, one hand on the balustrade, watching Greenbloom, following him with shadowed eyes as he hurried away beside his silent reflection in the lake.

John spoke.

"Hello!"

She turned. "Hello!"

Her smile was very quick, quite artless. He noticed that at the right-hand corner of her mouth just beside the cheek she had one mole, a tiny spidery naevus clinging just outside the cheekline.

"Who was that? The man you were talking to?"

"Greenbloom."

"What a strange name."

"No stranger than Uprichard," he said.

She started. "Who told you my name?"

"One of the girls in the house—an Irish one who plays the piano."

"Oh, Brigid! Was she looking for me?"

"I don't think so. She was just waiting."

The girl sat down on the balustrade and he walked quickly up the steps.

"Do you smoke?"

"Only for fun."

He held out his packet of Woodbines.

"I'm afraid they're only small ones," he said. "I'm economizing."

She took one and he lighted it for her; she held it badly and seeing his face in the extra light of the match she laughed, a breathy sound with very little voice in it.

"We're not allowed to really, but it's part of the holidays to have one or two."

"Yes."

They said nothing for a moment and he noticed that she shivered.

"Are you cold?"

"Bit."

"A bit?"

"Yes."

He took off his coat and before she could move draped it around her shoulders as she sat there a little hunched, concentrating on her cigarette.

"Thank you." She looked up suddenly and he saw the display of her wide-apart childish teeth between lips that were magenta-coloured in the moonlight.

"What were you talking about just now to that man?"

"To Greenbloom?"

"Yes."

"Oh—" He hesitated; from somewhere small clouds were collecting, slowly thickening, gleaming like the insides of mussel shells against the dark blue of the night sky.

"It sounded awfully odd," she went on filling in his pause. He sensed that she was not attempting to justify herself in face of what might have been an intrusion but that she really was interested. "He's got a very queer voice hasn't he? Like—"

"Rusty," he said, "like old iron."

"Yes. I could hear *him* but I couldn't hear you. It sounded most strange—like a one-way telephone conversation."

"Where were you then?"

"Behind the boathouse. There's a seat thing there."

"That's not a seat! It's a torpedo!"

"Is *that* what it is?" She laughed. "I thought it might be. Anyway it makes a jolly good seat—like a rocking horse."

He was astonished by her lack of surprise. Women never seemed to have any respect for machines.

"Did you really sit on it?" he asked.

"Of course I did." She sounded a little bored. "But you haven't told me what you were talking about to that writer person."

"Just things," he said, "or rather a thing, something that happened once."

"Oh—" She sucked at her cigarette inexpertly. "*Is* he a writer?"

"Not exactly. He's a publisher."

"Are *you* going to be a writer?"

"Yes." His affirmation surprised him; it was out before he could stop it and with sudden self-confidence he expanded it. "At least I'm going to be a doctor really but I think I'll probably go in for psychology and write books too."

"Which one are you then?"

"How do you mean, 'Which one am I?'"

"Well, Lady Geraldine told us that there were four of you coming tonight. Someone who writes, and then two brothers— she didn't say what they did—and a Frenchman as well."

"Greenbloom isn't French. He lives in Paris nowadays but he's Jewish."

"He sounded like a Frenchman."

"Oh yes, that's just because he's very suggestible. He's always changing. When I first met him in Oxford four years ago he was the most English of people with an absolutely flawless accent —very Mayfair. But since he went to live in Paris he's become awfully French in every way."

"How sweet! I think I rather like suggestible people." She fluttered away from it and he wondered if perhaps she were insincere.

"Which one *are* you? One of the brothers?"

"Which one would you like me to be?"

She looked surprised, caught his smile and suddenly laughed again, long enough this time for him to be sure that she laughed almost entirely with her breath, using her voice hardly at all.

"I don't know! I hadn't thought." Her expression changed. "As a matter of fact I wasn't particularly interested—that's why I came out here, at least it's partly why."

"Partly? Ah, I remember. *You* fainted on the train today, didn't you?"

"No, I didn't faint—I felt ill." She got up suddenly. "Something happened. It was a silly thing I suppose but it was horrible. It upset me dreadfully. Do you mind if we walk around the lake?"

"No. I'd like to."

He fell into step beside her. She took long steps like his own and with unanalyzed pleasure he noticed that they were the same height.

"What happened?" he prompted.

"It was the sort of thing you read about. A man on a train. *You* know!"

"Yes?"

"He got into my carriage—I didn't arrive till today, the others got here yesterday. I had to go to my doctor in London about— something. This man got in at Chester." She stood still as though arrested by the vividness of the memory. "After the first few stations—I was reading magazines and things—I began to feel uncomfortable. At first I didn't know why and then I found that he was looking at me all the time, *watching* me: everything I did, my hands, my feet, my legs." She coughed over her cigarette.

"Silly really, but he seemed to be almost *touching* me with his eyes."

"Horrible!" he said. "How *horrible!*"

She looked up at him quickly, her eyebrows, slender as charcoal, drawn together in surprise at his vehemence.

"It *was* horrible," she said. "I tried to explain to Brigid when I got back but she thought I'd added to it. I'm moody you see, and sometimes I get worked up and—frighten myself. But this time I wasn't. I didn't imagine or add anything to it. It was quite real. He started trying to get into conversation with me."

"What did he say?"

She moved on and he followed her and caught up with her.

"He asked me if I was feeling all right. I suppose I looked a bit pale because I hate trains and in any case I always feel ill when I've been to a doctor."

She shivered again and he glanced at her. His coat hung heavily from her shoulders and above it the centres of her white cheeks were smudged with shadow.

"Let's sit in the boathouse," he said. "It will be warm in there. It's got a thatched roof and that's always warm."

With the easy acquiescence she had shown from the moment of their meeting, she followed him in through the door at the back and took her place beside him on a swing seat with a canopy which was stored by a side wall. It was thickly piled with old punt cushions. They sat down in opposite corners.

"What did *you* say?"

"Nothing! I froze. Do you know what I mean? I felt all my muscles go stiff. For a moment I couldn't even turn a page of the magazine I was supposed to be reading. I think I was praying for the train to stop, wondering if I dared to pull the communication cord and trying to look as though I hadn't heard anything."

"Go on."

"He laughed then and said that he was a doctor and that I must forgive him for interfering but that I didn't look well. I still said nothing and after a moment he laughed again and said, 'You don't believe me, do you?' "

She threw away her cigarette and it fell with a splutter into the water beside the long shape of the admiral's punt.

"That was the awful part," she went on, "the fact that I didn't answer him or look at him or show in any way that I knew he was there didn't seem to matter to him in the least. It was as though he were talking to himself, inventing something as he went along, making it up and using me in it just because I was there and happened to be alone with him. I began to feel as though I'd got into his life or his head, that he had more control over me than I had over myself." She drew breath, "I suppose you think it's stupid, don't you?"

"No," he said, "not stupid."

"Or neurotic! I'm rather interested in psychology, it's all the rage at the Abbey just now. Have you read Freud's *Psychopathology of Everyday Life*?"

"What did he say after you'd said that you didn't believe him?"

"That's what I was coming to. He said it again, 'You don't believe me, do you?' and when I wouldn't reply, he went on, 'You're quite right, I'm not a doctor but nobody can say I'm not trying, can they? How else is a man to get to know the sort of girl a man wants to get to know if she won't admit she wants him to get to know her?' He went on like that for quite a long time, about me reminding him of some one he'd once known and —lost. The awful thing was that after a time I began to get interested. I knew it couldn't be long before we stopped at a station as there was a map of the coast with all the stations marked, on the opposite side of the carriage, and it was a slow train. I was sure I would be safe then; but as he went on talking, watching me all the time with his head back against the cushions, I found myself hoping that the train *wouldn't* stop before he'd come to the end of whatever it was he was trying to say, the story he was making up. I felt that everything depended on him reaching the end of it, that he might go mad if he didn't and that in some way it would be my fault. I don't think he meant me any harm just then; or if he did, he hadn't quite decided about it, he was just using me to help him in trying to solve something very—secret or private, what the psychology magazines call a fantasy."

John sat very still, and by pressing her feet against the floor she began to rock the seat gently backwards and forwards, ruminatively, re-creating the motion of the railway carriage, swinging the two of them evenly to and fro in the half-darkness of the boathouse. John forced his back against the cushions and stopped it, drawing them to a standstill rudely.

"What did he look like?" he asked.

"Oh, rather good-looking at first sight. Brown-skinned and blue-eyed, short hair, very curly. I found I didn't like to look at him, not only because he was what he was, but because he had *rude* eyes as though he despised everyone. That's what spoilt him, I think, and he was *just* common, not in his voice except very occasionally, but in the way he moved his mouth and refused to be quiet. Some people always have to be very much *there*. He was like that, he wanted to be noticed."

"Did he smoke?"

"No, he ate sweets, peppermints I think they were."

John sat very still on his corner of the stationary seat.

"Did he whistle?"

"Not out loud but he had a way of putting his lips together as though he were whistling to himself. He did it in between sentences." She paused. "Why are you so interested?"

"Er—" He tried to look less tense. "I can't tell you *now*. It's just that it may have had something to do with what we were talking about before you came out."

"Who? You and that Greenbloom person?"

"Yes."

With a little effort at concentration, she frowned. "Something to do with what you were talking about?"

"I said it *may* have had something to do with it. I'm not sure, that's the trouble—I never am."

"How funny! I wonder whatever it could have been!"

"Perhaps one day I'll be able to tell you. I don't know though for certain. The thing I'm interested in doesn't seem immediately important any longer; it did once but it doesn't now. I'm getting tired of it. You can't go on for ever trying to solve things, can you? They get left behind."

"Yes, I suppose they do."

She started to swing the seat again and this time he didn't stop her.

"Will you just tell me one more thing?" he asked, "and then we won't talk about it any more."

"Yes, if I can, but it's not easy. It was strange, I find it hard to think of somehow."

"What was the story he told you?"

"It was about this girl he'd known. He kept on about her, around and around in a circle—no not a circle, that was the odd thing. He'd get so far with it and then stop and start again. 'She was very like you,' he would say, 'like you liking me and you were just what she might have been if she had been old enough to be like you. And fancy, if I'd met her today as I've met you, then it would all have started again and she would have been a match for me at your age just as you are a match for me at my age, sitting there not wanting to know me, *not much*, and pretending, like *she* would have pretended—'" She broke off, "That was something like it. Can you understand how horrible it was and yet how it made you want to go on listening? Each time he took it a bit further but never to the end."

"Never to the end?"

"No, the train stopped at Penmaenmawr and before I could get up he opened the door. He leaned right forward over me and said, 'This is where I get out, this is journey's end, but it doesn't end in lovers' meeting, does it?' I said, 'I wish you would go,' and he said, 'I know you do, but thank you for listening just the same.'"

"Did he say anything else?"

"Yes, he said, 'Tell them all if they want to know; tell them all but don't tell *me*,' and he laughed."

"Was he mad?"

"Yes, I'm sure he was. He seemed to be several different people all putting on an act. He didn't behave like one person; he didn't seem to know who he was. After the train left the station I began to feel terrible. The fright he had given me began to come back and I began to loathe myself for having listened to him and for not having helped him. Yet at the same time I was quite sure that if I had given in to him in any way, if I'd spoken a single word or let him see that I was frightened and interested, he might have—it made me sick; after he had gone I really *was* sick—out of the window."

She was silent and they continued to swing backwards and forwards in the half-darkness. The fact that she kept so still, that she had ceased to do her share towards keeping up the rocking motion of the seat, made him sense her discomfort loudly, but he refused to make any comment. Instead he returned to the thoughts which her story had set on their dark procession through his mind.

It could have been the same man of course; but what did it matter? Quite soon, in fifty or sixty years, everyone would be dead, everyone of his own generation; and what had once been a crime would survive only as a curiosity. The reality of it was dead already, buried in his own heart deeper than Victoria; and Greenbloom had been right when he had said that everything was unimportant unless it made you suffer.

That seemed to be Greenbloom's new message, to welcome suffering and keep it greedily to yourself so that you would know you were alive, to let no one distract you from it by telling him about it: to drink, as some men drank, alone; to celebrate, love, hate, suffer and die as you were born, alone. He remembered some lines from a poem about Jack and Jill which he had once memorized:

> "Her lady-smock all stainèd with his blood
> She'll dry away the cold tears and the mud,
> She'll staunch his trickling scalp with vinegar
> And tell no soul her sorrows—"

It was not a comforting doctrine but at least it was much more sensible than Mother's and Father's which seemed only to have provided them with blunt weapons. No one could ever effectively love or hate anyone else no matter how much they knew, no matter how great their love or their hatred might be, simply because everyone was fundamentally alone, what Aldous Huxley had called "a solitude."

If his solitude, his own desert, had been planted with the solitary evergreen of Victoria's death, then according to Greenbloom he should have been grateful, not to any person, not to any god, not even to Victoria herself, but to the sensibility which allowed him to be aware of it as it stood there for ever vivid and vital in the vast and silent landscape of his mind.

So it did not matter, on these terms, whether or not it *had* been the same man. There were thousands of such people in the world, quite apart from the millions of men who had killed with honour in the Great War. There were multitudes of murderers and eccentrics at large whose crimes and follies were only noticed if they happened to be unfashionable. In an educated society, one that had absorbed a valid philosophy like Greenbloom's, there would be no fashions and therefore no need for police, judges or priests, because its members would realize that responsibility did not exist; that the acts of everyone were as remote as the emanations of the night stars, which, though they appeared to make up constellations and be involved one with another, were in reality separated by distances so vast that they failed to share even the same time.

And, if time was an illusion, then so were responsibility and guilt and Greenbloom was right.

Beside him the girl stirred. She withdrew her left arm from the back of the seat and, folding it across her lap, said, "I suppose I shouldn't have told you that."

"I'm sorry—what did you say?"

"I said I wished I hadn't told you that."

The repetition of the sense of her first remark recalled to him the actual words she had used and it was to these that he replied from the midst of his preoccupation.

"Of course you should have told me. I *wanted* you to tell me."

"No, I meant about being sick. A thing like that puts people off, doesn't it?"

He sat up. "Good Heavens no! I'd forgotten all about that. You *must* think me unsympathetic. I was trying to work something out, you see, and it was very difficult."

"About my man on the train?"

"Yes, partly. It was like something that happened to me once and I was wondering whether to tell you about it and then I decided I wouldn't."

"Was that what this Greenbloom man was talking about to you?"

"Yes."

"And did *he* tell you not to talk about it?"

"I suppose he did in a way."

"Well, I think that's jolly unfair," she said. "He lets you tell *him* all about it and then advises you to tell no one else, not even *me*, when I've just confided something in you that I wouldn't have dreamed of telling to anyone except perhaps Brigid."

He stared through the brackish darkness at her. Something about her spontaneity, the ingenuous schoolgirl indignation of her outburst, reminded him of Victoria. The very tone of her sentences, quick and unwatched, the little shake of her head disturbing the dark outline of her hair, brought back to him the clear remembrance of Victoria's presence as sharply as did the scent of heather or the bars of Mendelssohn's Wedding March.

With total recollection and an excitement so powerful that he was momentarily unable to speak or to move, he was once again at the lakeside in Northumberland, hearing the vanished sounds of the forest, seeing the dead and living face of Victoria as she stood before him with her eyes closed while he breathed in afresh the scent of still water, mud and growing trees.

She was not, this girl was not, never could be, the same. No one could rise from the grave and wear the liveries of the dead or carry again the particular loveliness which had flowered once and once only in one person. But she was like, she was wonderfully like. She was tall, pale, delicate and generous in the way Victoria had been generous: ready to quarrel with warmth, to sit, walk or stand with you at your suggestion and to say what she thought the moment she thought it.

She was no more afraid of unhappiness than Victoria had been, drooped in the same way when she felt depressed, thought and felt alone if she must, yet did not want to go on with it afterwards and rebuff you from behind a closed door like all those others he half-remembered. But more than all this, with all her differences—eyes that were darker, a less immediate gaiety and a lighter voice—she was alive; a person and not an idea, someone who could be seen with the eyes, quarrelled with and crossed, touched and loved with the lips, hands and the whole shivering conjunction of the mind and body.

"I'm sorry," he said, "I'm awfully sorry."

"Oh, that's all right! I'm just a fool, I always blurt things out to people and then regret it afterwards. If you really want to know I'd have told you in any case. It's no good pretending that I'm reserved. I was only doing that to try and embarrass you and make you feel mean."

"I know you were," he said. "That's why I'm sorry that I can't tell you. But perhaps one day I'll be able to."

"When?"

"Next year in Ireland," he said.

"In *Ireland*?"

"Yes. You live there, don't you? Well next year at the very latest I'll be going there. I'm going to start medicine in Trinity College, Dublin; at least I am provided I've passed an exam I've just been taking."

"Are you really?"

"Yes."

"How odd."

"Why?"

"Because I'm going there myself next year. I'm going to read modern languages—my Mother was at T.C.D. and we only live a few miles outside Dublin."

"What's your name?"

"Dymphna. What's yours?"

"John—Blaydon." She did not question it; it meant nothing to her and gratitude illumined him.

"If I'd known I was going to see you again I don't think I would have told you all that," she said. "Seriously."

"But it's wonderful!" He talked wildly, mixing the tumble of his metaphors in his sudden exhilaration. "The very best sort of introduction, something very private and generous like real hospitality, where you give something to a person, not just a name or a look at your house, but part of you—part of yourself. Things that happen to you *are* you in a way."

"Yes, but then you've given me nothing in return."

"Yes, I have. Like a good guest I've taken everything you offered and enjoyed it and been interested."

"You're very quick, aren't you?" She smiled at him through the shadows. "Are you Irish too?"

"Only a little. I've got some rather splendid cousins who live in Ireland."

"That'll be useful."

"Will it?"

"Very! It's the snobbiest country in the world. My parents nearly crippled themselves sending me to Wycombe Abbey just for the snob-value of it. Isn't it absurd?"

"No, I don't think so. I *love* splendour and flunkeys myself, and I'm always wishing we were richer or had a title in the family."

"Oh, that's different. What I meant was that it's ridiculous to behave as though you were rich when you're not. For instance, do you know why it is that I'm having to P.G. here for the next few weeks instead of going home to Kildare?"

"No."

"Because *my* parents have the house full of P.G.s themselves and there's no room for the rest of the family until some of them leave. Naturally they weren't expecting me to break up so soon. Now, you must admit *that's* stupid?"

He laughed happily. "Yes, that really is."

"And they, I know, will be saying in their most far-back voices, 'Darling Dymphna, our eldest, is staying with Admiral and the Lady Geraldine Bodorgan in Anglesey you know,' and having to stick a little bit extra on the bills of their own P.G.s in order to pay for it." She broke off. "Good Gracious! What on earth's that!"

They listened; on the lawn behind the shrubbery someone was shouting. In syllables shortened by rage yet thick and fat with the vigour behind their pronunciation, they heard the word "cox'n!" sounding out beneath the moonlight, repeated each time louder and with more fearful emphasis.

"Cox'n! *COX'N!* Call away the barge."

"Good God," said John. "It's the admiral and he's coming here."

"Whatever for?"

John got up. "You'll see," he said. "Quick! We'd better get out. No, wait! We'd better stay here or he'll see us. He may only be drunk."

"What fun! I adore drunken people, there are hundreds of them in Ireland."

"You won't adore *him*: he's frightfully dangerous when he's drunk, almost as dangerous as when he's sober. He got chucked off the Magistrate's Bench here the other day for assaulting the local doctor because he disagreed with him over a careless driving case."

"But why's he coming here?"

"That's just what I don't know." He pointed to the punt. "You see this thing—this punt?"

"Is it a punt? It doesn't look like one."

"I know it doesn't, but that's because he's put a roof and brass dolphins and things all over it to make it look like an admiral's barge—and unless he's drunk or even if he is drunk, it sounds very much as though he's going to go out in it tonight."

"*Now?*"

"It sounds like it," he whispered. "Keep quiet for a minute, he's just coming down the path."

Standing together in the open mouth of the boathouse concealed by its shadows from the moonlight shining down on the wooden staging which projected over the water, they watched the entrance at the farther end of the lake.

They saw Sambo enter first: the luminous V of his shirt, his normally scarlet face now changed by anger and the moonlight to a leaden-white colour. He walked stiffly with all the reluctance of a military prisoner and was closely followed by the burly silver-haired figure of the admiral. Even at this distance they could see the admiral's eyes, whiter than a minstrel's, gleaming out of the dark convexities of his face. Both were carrying things—Sambo with embarrassment, the admiral carelessly—and at the first of the balustrades they halted and laid them down on the stone where some minutes earlier Greenbloom had stood his flask.

The admiral, who was wearing dark slacks and an open-necked shirt, wiped his neck and forehead on a silk handkerchief and then, turning his back on Sambo, bellowed out once again across the lawn.

"*Cox'n! COX'N!* Call away the barge!"

Somewhere a dog barked; they heard its hysterical response leap frog out from the kennels around by the stables and then there was silence.

Sambo spoke. "Really, Bodorgan," he said coldly, "I think this is taking things a little far. I feel that one is entitled to an opinion without being called upon to—"

"Opinion be damned!" replied the admiral swivelling around to face him. "An insult is not an opinion. You insulted me in me own house and what is more you insulted the Navy and I intend to vindicate the Senior Service here and now." He glared around once again at the pathway.

"If that feller doesn't come soon—"

"Since it is Saturday night," said Sambo haughtily, "and Hughes is almost certainly in Beaumaris I think that if you're going to insist on this demonstration it would be as well if we postponed it until tomorrow." He stepped towards the entrance and, beside John, Dymphna shivered. He saw that in her anxiety she was biting her lower lip and that her eyes were wide.

"Are they really serious?" she whispered.

"Of course they are, they hate each other like poison—over Lady G—and they've obviously emptied the better part of a bottle of whisky between them."

"But they can't be—even in Ireland—"

The admiral spoke again. "I think I ought to warn you, Stretton, that if you are intending to return to the house I shall have no hesitation in shooting you—in the back. I have my father's revolver here and it is fully loaded."

Sambo halted at once and turned around.

"Either you are drunk, Bodorgan, or else you are mad," he said distinctly.

The admiral smiled dangerously and they saw the shine of his large false teeth as he looked across at his adversary over the shaking barrel of an old-fashioned revolver which he carried in his right hand.

"I am posting you as my cox'n with effect as from—pass me my chronometer."

In the pause, after a momentary hesitation, Sambo picked up a round object like a clock and handed it to him.

"With effect as from 22:30 hours today, G.M.T.," went on the admiral, "and keep your distance."

"If you took my remark about the Admiralty as a reflection on your own seamanship, Bodorgan—" began Sambo.

"You will address me as 'sir,' " said the admiral, "and you will bring aboard my chronometer, compass, my night-glasses, sextant and barometer."

"I am perfectly prepared to withdraw my remarks unconditionally—sir," said Sambo distinctly.

"You will then propel my barge according to instructions," went on the Admiral remorselessly, "while I prove to you that His Majesty's sea lords are *not* incapable of navigating 'anything but a desk through a sea of paper.' Those were your words I believe?"

"I repeat, sir, that I am perfectly ready to withdraw them. I think we might return to the house before Gerry—" they saw Sambo's hand go to his moustache as he corrected himself—"before Lady Geraldine—"

"My wife, whatever her other failings may be," interrupted the admiral swiftly, "knows better than to interfere with my *professional* dispositions, and as for the withdrawal of your remarks about the Service, it's too damned easy to recant when the damage is done, when a good name and a reputation have been smirched." He paused and then spoke more quietly and with heavy emphasis. "You may, if you care to, look upon myself and my colleagues of equivalent rank as a group of impotent bureaucrats incapable of dealing with the realities of situations—either private or public. If that is your opinion you are entitled to it provided, Stretton, you do not express it in my presence. When you do that it ceases to be an opinion, as I said before, and becomes an *insult*, one which it is my duty to redress without delay." He drew himself to attention and waved his revolver at the equipment on the balustrade. "You will now give me that opportunity."

With what was almost a shrug, a quick shake of his shoulders, Sambo picked up the things and, followed by the admiral, marched briskly towards the boathouse.

"What shall we do?" whispered Dymphna.

"Out, quickly!"

Together they moved silently out through the open door and around to the shadowed side of the structure pressing close against the timbered wall.

From the inside they heard the admiral bawling out his further instructions.

"You will light both lamps, port and starboard, and show a light at the masthead. It will be your duty to stream the log in order that I may make the necessary calculations, and in due time you will keep her steady fore and aft while I bring down the moon to the horizon and read my charts."

Under cover of the noise, the clatter of things being loaded into the punt, the indignant throat-clearances of Sambo, the admiral's rounded roars, they slipped away together along the upper flagged terrace past the figureheads leaning out of the shadows, the tall flagstaffs and the chimney stacks belching their still tufts of heather and geraniums.

At the far end, safely under cover of the rhododendrons concealing the pathway, they paused and looked back.

The punt was sliding out into the centre of the lake, riding through the bright lattice of the moonlight with the admiral, portly and erect as one of his own statues, standing in the bows with his sextant raised to the stars; and behind him, between the gleam of the brass dolphins whose curling tails flanked the little cabin, Sambo, punting with slow, rhythmical strokes.

Standing there, side by side, they continued to watch, hearing the thrust of the water against the punt, the succession of falling drops from the pole, the sounds of their own breathing.

John spoke:

"I *thought*—" he said.

"What?"

But he did not reply. He had not intended to speak: a great grief weighed down upon him out of Heaven.

"Tell me—" she whispered as once, long ago, Victoria might have whispered, wanting to know, wanting to share, not quite serene in the eagerness of her generosity. "What did you think?"

"All *that*—" he said loudly pointing to them—to old Clive and Sambo.

"They're pathetic, aren't they?" she suggested.

"I don't know," he said. "They hate each other. They're doing nothing, they don't see anything, they don't know anything. They can think about nothing but their hatred, although they're so old. Lady Geraldine, who's beautiful really, I suppose, but *alive*! If she were dead—"

"Yes?"

"If she were dead, what would it solve?"

"I don't know what you mean. What *do* you mean?"

"Well," he said, "once there were two people who loved the same person; and she died. I was one of them and I'd always thought that if only I could find someone like her, someone who seemed exactly like her in the way she affected *me*, I mean, that it would stop my hatred, all *that* sort of thing: those two out there under the moon." He swallowed. "Lunatics, respectable lunatics, fools, apes, old bodies and malice, men who should be wise because they've finished growing; wise enough to say, to know, to see; but they can't even *say*. They're liars both of them, blind to their own lies. They're no better than I was when once I thought I was mad, blamed it on someone else who probably *is* mad, *un*respectably mad, if you understand me. But now I'm frightened, terrified to think that I may never have been mad, that there may be no sanity anywhere for any of us whether we love or hate, find or lose, live or die."

They were silent. The punt had nearly reached the middle of the lake, Sambo had ceased to pole because the water was too deep for him, and under the high night there was no single sound to be heard.

"I know what you mean," she said, "but I think you're wrong."

"Where?"

"Well, in a way you're sorry for them, aren't you? That's what makes you so angry, your sorrow."

"Perhaps," he said, not touching her. "Let's go and find Greenbloom; he wanted to see this. I think if we could get him alone, by himself, he might be able to—say."

"Listen!" she said.

The admiral spoke. His voice rich with the satisfaction of someone perfectly in command of a situation he has long anticipated, they heard his command roll out across the disturbed surface of the water—"Half-speed ahead and steady the barge, Cox'n—" before they turned and ran hand in hand across the lawn to the drive, the lights and the moving group of small figures gathered together in front of Greenbloom's car.

Maidstone, 1953-1955.